JOURN-E

THE JOURNAL OF IMAGINATIVE LITERATURE

VOLUME 1, NUMBER 1
WHOLE NUMBER 1
VERNAL EQUINOX 2022

20 MARCH

Published by
Mind's Eye Publications™
985 Deborah Avenue
Elgin, IL 60123-1918
mindseye.pub
mindseye.us.com

Cover Art by Paul "Mutartis" Boswell
Cover Lettering by Frank Coffman
Edited by Frank Coffman

MIND'S EYE

PUBLICATIONS

ISBN: 978-1-7367114-5-3 // Trade Paperback
$20.00 US Print

JOURN-E

THE JOURNAL OF IMAGINATIVE LITERATURE

VOLUME 1, NUMBER 1
VERNAL EQUINOX 2022

20 MARCH

EDITED BY
FRANK COFFMAN

Dedication

For all *Fellow Authors, Poets, and Illustrators of The Speculative* across its Several Genres—whose many inspirations and creations have greatly enriched and which continue to explore and magnify Wonders of the High Imagination.

Table of Contents

Introduction to JOURN-E

Welcome to the first issue of JOURN-E: THE JOURNAL OF IMAGINATIVE LITERATURE. This journal will be published semi-annually on the Vernal and Autumnal Equinoxes. Calls for Submission will be posted on these same dates for the forthcoming issue.

It has been a dream and a vision of mine to create a single magazine covering the genres of the high imagination: Adventure, Detection & Mystery, Fantasy, Horror & the Supernatural, and Science Fiction. Some might say that this "dilutes" the notion of a journal, as all of these forms won't appeal to all - perhaps not even to many. Reader's have their particular "cups of tea" they will say.

But it is my belief that many readers who love the stuff of the old "Pulps" from the previous century and the dime novels that preceeded those and the rich oral traditions of myth, legend, and folklore that preceeded those will be devotees of more than one of these five types - if not all.

It is also the position of JOURN-E that a compendium of short fiction; poetry; non-fiction articles, essays, and reviews; illustrations; and "classics" directly relevant to these genres will be of interest to the lover's of these forms of imaginative, romantic [in the old sense, i.e. *not* realism], and highly creative types - as Rider Haggard insists "coeval with the existence of humanity."

This journal will be available both in print and online. The print version will be published as a perfect-bound book (indeed, this first issue is far more a book than a magazine, featuring over 250 pages) and will be available from lulu.com and from major booksellers such as Amazon, Barnes & Noble, etc. The cost will vary as the number of pages in any given issue will change.

IMPORTANT NOTE: *A FREE SAMPLER EDITION* of every issue will be available online. These samplers will show the full cover, the TOC to show the contributors represented and the types of content offered and, as the name implies, a SAMPLE of the full contents with excerpts from each of the five sections of this pentapartite journal.

The PDF version of issues will be available by subscription or purchase ($10.00 American for any current issue and the next forthcoming issue; $5.00 American for any individual issue. Each issue will also be available at issuu.com as a page-turner, flipbook - also for $5.00 American for the single issue. These online issue options will feature all color interior illustrations, while the print version will have any color illustrations converted to greyscale.

While, there are no "Letters to the Editor" - this being Issue 1 - they are most welcome and the section THE JOURN-ALL will accommodate.

Again, welcome to all. Send suggestions, constructive criticisms, comments.

Frank Coffman, Editor JOURN-E & Publisher, Mind's Eye Publications
Elgin, Illinois 18 March 2022

ADVENTURE

Being Section One
of the JOURN-E

Adventure's Call

(an Acrostic Italian Sonnet)
Frank Coffman

Adventure calls us from the everyday,
Does magic in its promise of things new.
Vistas of strange, lost worlds come into view,
Ensorcelling us as questers on the way,
Nearing our goal. Its task is to convey
Those thrills of travel and travail that few,
Under this dome of sky could say they knew.
Restless, our heroes always "seize the day."
E'specially when life's frequent tedium
Stifles our spirits, yearning to break free,
Confines us with seeming endless ho and hum,
And makes us crave to see what we might see
Lying beyond the vast horizon's edge -
Lure of Adventure makes us turn the page.

(originally appeared in
The Coven's Hornbook & Other Poems
Bold Venture Press, 2019: 168)

THE SUB-GENRE OF THE HIGH IMAGINATION known as "Adventure" is the most difficult to define of the genres included in this journal. This is due to the fact that the essential ingredients of Adventure are most often also found to some degree and in some mixture in the other genres of: Detection & Mystery, Fantasy, Horror & the Supernatural, and Science Fiction.

The Sherlock Holmes stories are called "Adventures." It would be difficult to argue that the Fantasy tales of Tolkien (High/Epic/Heroic) or Robert E. Howard (Sword & Sorcery) are not filled with "adventure." Is "adventure" not a major element in the many and various incarnations of *Star Trek* or *Star Wars?* Is there no element of "adventure" - thrills, vicarious reaction to threats of danger or death, hightened suspense in re-watching the old Universal films: *Frankenstein, The Wolfman, Dracula,* or *The Mummey,* etc. - or the "Physical Fear" tale (as Lovecraft termed it) of a rabid dog, or pscychopathic fan of a series of romance novels, or a serial murderer story such as we see exemplified by *Silence of the Lambs?*

Or the reading of folk or legendary tomes containing similar tales?

The key elements of *Pure Adventure*, seen as a separate genre are, I contend, as follows: 1) a setting that is to be understood as the "real world" we live in (either Past or Present; the Future would, of necessity, bring in Science Fiction as a melded genre), this "real world" must be accepted by the reader as *ours* - no matter how fantastic and amazing the story or characters related may seem; 2) heroes, or at least characters who rise to heroic action, thus being ennobled; 3) the persistent threat of danger or death; 4) villainous adversaries, but decidedly "worthy" ones, offering obstacles that often seem insurmountable, always, it seems, on the verge of winning the essential conflict; 5) quite often involving traveling or questing, sometimes over vast distances; 6) and very often carrying the reader to exotic places, adding to the appeal and flavor of the vicarious experience.

What this journal *will be seeking* regarding *Adventure*, and what, I believe is, in many ways, containted in this issue are tales and poems and scholarly articles and notes directly exhibiting and decidedly relevant to *any* of the following sub-genres of Adventure:

***The Lost World Adventure** (Doyle's *The Lost World*, Rider-Haggard's *She* and *King Solomon's Mines*, Cutcliffe-Hyne's *The Lost Continent*, etc.)

***The Quest** (the epics of Homer, the *Argonautica* of Apollonius of Rhodes, Virgil's *Aeneid*. *Around the World in 80 Days*, other epic and legendary tales. A long and arduous journey with a sought-after goal)

***The Traveler's Tale** (different from the Quest in that it simply recounts adventures along the travels and travails of the main characters. *The Adventure of Baron Munchausen*, *The Adventures of Marco Polo*, *Lost Horizon*, etc.)

***The Sea Story** (*Mutiny on the Bounty*, *Captains Courageous*, *Moby Dick*, *Two Years Before the Mast*, "Billy Budd," etc.)

***The Pirate Story** (actually a sub-sub-genre of the Sea Story, but with the special inclusion of pirates and piracy: Stevenson, Sabatini, etc.)

***The Oriental Adventure** (meaning both Near and Far East - tales set in the exotic places away from "the Occident." Victorian age conquests, battles, and losses, in N. Africa, the Middle East in general, India, and so on. Kipling's "The Man Who Would Be King" has the setting right, but also qualifies as a Quest. Tales set in the Mysterious Far Orient...)

***The Historical Adventure** (broadly and in general - any epoch or locality)

*The War Story (Homer's *Iliad*, of course, but clearly tales of any war bring along the danger and the threat of death, likely much travel, and genuine life and death excitement. Again - "real world" setting, not *Star Wars*)

*The Sports Story (like the War Story, but sublimated. Human conflict, but on the "battlefield" of the sports field, the pitch, the court, the course, etc. Robert E. Howard's boxing stories, even sports like golf: *The Greatest Game Every Played*, *Bobby Jones: Stroke of Genius* - although those two based on historic events, etc.)

*The Western (America's own special adventure tales. Zane Grey, Louis L'Amour, and the list goes on and on.)

*The Northern [at least that's what I'll call it] - the Klondike Gold Rush tales of Jack London, the poetry of Robert W. Service, the struggle for life and riches in the frozen North.

*The Thriller (Webster defines it as: "a work of fiction or drama designed to hold the interest by the use of a high degree of intrigue, adventure, or suspense" - we can go along with that sort of "catch-all" definition.

*The Romance Adventure (with the "modern" definition of Romance thrown into the mix. Most stories in the pure "Romance" genre of today have elements of adventure, but the more specific type sought for possible inclusion in this journal would be tales such as seen in the film *Romancing the Stone* and its sequel. I guess *Cassablanca* would qualify as well.)

Welcome to the first section of the first issue of *Journ-E: The Journal of Imaginative Literature!*

While there will be no "Letters to the Editor" in this vol. 1, no. 1 of Journ-E, This issue will end on a one page preview of **"The Journ-All,"** which will become the official email (and snail mail also, I guess) Letters to the Editor section for forthcoming issues.

Cheers! and Onward!
Frank Coffman, Editor

The Ruby of Rampur

DJ Tyrer

THE TREE TRUNK just a little way above his head exploded as a musket ball smashed into it. A dozen dacoits might not be worth one jacksepoy, but give them each a musket or bow and a scrubby hillside beneath the cruel Indian sun, perfectly placed for an ambush, and even the best soldier had a good chance of being taken down by a lucky shot.

Not that Randolph Halley regarded himself as the best of soldiers. He'd joined the East India Company army to avoid being shoved off into the church and decided to absent himself from its ranks with his faithful ressalder or cavalry officer ally, Rav, once the discipline grew too tedious to bear.

Which life of reckless adventure had brought him here to this dusty trail where, it seemed, he was due to die.

He and Rav had been forced to abandon their billet in the last town when his dalliance with an ayah led to the upset of her master and threats involving a horsewhip. Leaving in a hurry, they'd no opportunity to affiliate themselves with the merchant cafila that was due to depart within the next couple of days. Their haste had proven a disaster: even if the guards hadn't been up to much, the numbers comprising the cafila would probably have made the band of dacoits think twice. But, two lonely wanderers?

The first shots startled their mounts and the skittish tattoo ponies bolted. Randolph was tossed from his saddle and Rav leapt from his mount to run back towards him. Had their roles been reversed, Randolph was certain he wouldn't have turned back.

He scrambled across the track to a gnarled old tree, while Rav ran for the cover of some rocks. Keeping his head down, Randolph unslung his musket and loaded a shot. Warily, he looked around the trunk and picked out one of their ambushers. Carefully taking aim, he pulled the trigger and there was a crack! and the man slumped dead.

Another musket ball smashed into the tree and Randolph swore as a splinter sliced into his cheek. He could feel blood running down his face and neck.

As he methodically worked through the reloading of his gun, an arrow buried itself deeply into the trunk and another sailed past a moment later. He took aim and fired again, but couldn't tell if his shot had struck the dacoit or not.

Rav had produced his cavalry pistol and was adding to the exchange of gunfire, although his shots were largely unaimed. It was clear that the shooting wasn't going to resolve the standoff any time soon, if everyone stayed put, unless a dacoit succeeded with a lucky shot.

Their attackers began to slip their way down the hillside towards them, slinking from rock to rock, and Randolph knew they were preparing to rush them and end the ambush with steel.

Randolph leant his loaded musket against the tree and paused to load both his pistols, the large cavalry one and the tiny pocket pistol that served as a backup. He also drew his sabre and laid it across his knees: when the charge came, every moment wasted would be an extra yard for the dacoits to advance unmolested.

Then, they came: Nine men exploded from cover and ran towards where Randolph and his ally sheltered. Rav fired off two pistol shots: wild, again. One of the dacoits stumbled and fell, wounded in his leg. Randolph raised his musket and fired, hitting one man square in the chest.

Standing, sabre in his offhand, Randolph fired his cavalry pistol. The shot tore the jaw off the lead figure in a shower of blood. Then, he swapped it for his smaller pocket pistol, raised it and fired, hitting the next man in the shoulder. The dacoit stumbled, but kept coming.

Battle was joined. Four ran at Rav and two at Randolph, each armed with a curving tulwaur or scimitar. Rav had a scimitar of his own, while Randolph carried a heavy cavalry sabre best suited to slashing down from horseback, but still deadly on foot.

Randolph lunged forward with a wide swing. He might not be the greatest of warriors, but he'd long ago learnt that victory favoured the bold. The dacoit stumbled back and fell onto his backside. With him momentarily out of the fight, Randolph turned to the second dacoit, parrying the blow from his blade as it sliced towards him.

Slamming his fist forward, he smashed the hand-guard of the sabre into the man's face, shattering his nose in an explosion of blood. As the man reeled, Randolph swung his weapon again, lopping the man's head from his shoulders.

Turning back to the first dacoit, who was rising to his feet, Randolph lunged and ran the blade of his sabre through the man's guts. Not a killing wound, not till blood loss or infection took hold, at least, but sufficient to take him out of the fight. Randolph kicked the man away and ran to help his friend, Rav, who was hard pressed by his foes.

Rav had managed to cut down one of the bandits, but had suffered a deep cut to his arm and was beginning to flag.

With a roar, Randolph ran forward and engaged the nearest dacoit. The man turned and their blades clanged. A series of parries and ripostes more suited to fencing than fighting followed as they danced back and forth in a furious clash, each seeking an opening.

But, Randolph was a brawler with no notions of chivalry or fair play. Picking his moment, he dropped to the ground as if he'd lost his footing. The ragged-bearded dacoit gave a misshapen grin and raised his tulwaur. Randolph sent his foot straight up into the man's groin, then threw a handful of dirt into the man's pained face.

Even as he rolled into a crouch, Randolph brought up his sabre, bringing it down to bury the blade in the man's head, killing him.

Then, having pulled the blade free, he was lunging towards the other two, his movements almost drunk thanks to fatigue and the speed of his leap.

The blade of his sabre buried deep into the side of one, but, as the dacoit fell, the motion pulled the sabre from Randolph's hand. He was weaponless!

The remaining dacoit paused. He might have taken them both, but the loss of his fellows had clearly broken his nerve. He turned and ran.

Randolph ran after him and launched himself into him, knocking him to the ground in a billow of dust. After a brief struggle, Randolph got a grip on him and, with a quick, practised move, he snapped the man's neck.

Never leave an enemy alive, the drunken old sergeant had told him. The dead can never launch another attack on you.

Exhausted, Randolph stood.

"Huzzah, eh?" he called, dusting himself off.

Rav swore in reply. "They cut me up bad, sahib."

Randolph wiped the blood from his cheek. "Let me see if I can find those ponies, then we'll head to the next village and get some help."

He paused to bandage his friend, then set off down the track in search of the two tattoo ponies.

"I only found the one," he called a few minutes later as he headed back. "God alone knows where the other one went - maybe it grew wings and flew away - but, this'll do for you."

Randolph helped Rav onto the back of the pony and they set off down the trail, Randolph resting a loaded musket across his shoulders, just in case.

***

That evening, they had taken shelter in the home of a villager willing to offer a bed and a few chuppatties in return for a rupee. A local pundit had come to their aid, cleaning Randolph's cut, which was barely more than superficial, then turned to stitching Rav's wound.

"He will need to rest a week, sahib," the pundit said.

"Fine, fine." He could throw a little cash at the man and ensure his friend was cared for. He had something else on his mind.

"So," Randolph said, "tell me about this ruby…"

As he'd worked, the pundit had engaged in small talk. Although his grasp of English was less adept than his rudimentary medical skills, Randolph understood enough of their language to follow along and had had his attention caught by the mention of a precious stone.

"The rajah, at his palace of Rampur Sar, it is said, has a great ruby, the size of a human heart. It is the most glorious thing, sahib."

"This sounds like the real chiz," Randolph said to Rav as soon as the pundit had left.

Rav rolled his eyes.

"Whilst you're recovering, I'll go for it."

"Very well, sahib."

***

The palace at Rampur Sar was about two-day's ride away, a journey Randolph made on their remaining tattoo pony without incident.

The creamy-walled palace sat beside the deep-blue waters of a lake. There was a heady scent of jasmine in the air. Although it shared a name with the city of Rampur, the palace was idyllic in its natural surroundings.

He halted at the gate in the exterior war. Dusty from the trail, he felt he would face a challenge getting in. It was all about presentation.

The spear-armed guards at the gate in their shiny mail eyed him dubiously as he approached.

"My name is Captain Randolph Halley. I bring greetings from the Company." He gestured to himself. "I must beg your indulgence, but I was ambushed by dacoits on the trail and my companions killed."

That caught their attention and a sirdar was summoned and, having divested Randolph of his weapons, he ushered Randolph through into an audience with the wuzeer who served the rajah.

Randolph was grateful to be shown into a silk-draped room in which a punkah flapped back and forth, the palmyra-leaf fan wafting cooling air over him and easing the prickling rash of red-dog that gnawed at him.

The wuzeer, a fat man in rich, red robes, paused in sucking on his hubble-bubble and looked at Randolph.

Randolph thought he heard the wuzeer mutter, "Dikk," trouble, but, then, he smiled and asked Randolph to explain himself.

Dressed in mufty, Randolph knew he didn't present the most convincing of sights, but experience had taught him what these people wished to hear: no petty potentate, especially one who seemed little more than a glorified poligar, no matter the ostentation of his abode, wished to earn the disfavour of the East India Company. The right words would cause the wuzeer to err on the side of caution - and, one night's hospitality was all Randolph required.

The wuzeer nodded. "The rajah would be pleased to receive you. After your ordeal on the road here, we would be glad to offer you a chance to wash and change your clothes, and a bed for the night. You will be summoned for dinner. Tiffin will be served in your room."

A servant in pale-blue robes led Randolph away. A guarded door near the heart of the palace caught his attention. The servant led him upstairs to a small but well-appointed bedchamber, beside which was a room with a shallow pool that served as a bath. The servant led him over to it and took hold of his jacket and began to pull it from his shoulders.

Randolph would have preferred to be undressed and bathed by a couple of dusky beauties, but settled for allowing the man to assist him in disrobing, before washing himself, soothing away the red-dog's sting with the cool water.

When he climbed out of the pool, the servant handed him a towel with which to dry himself off, then directed him to the almyra, or wardrobe, in which Randolph found a loose-fitting cameeze shirt and a pair of baggy shalwar trousers. The garments were no dungaree cloth, but a finely-woven cotton that felt as soft as silk against his trail-roughened skin.

"Tiffin," said the servant, gesturing to the light luncheon waiting for him. The man, then, retreated outside to allow Randolph the privacy to sleep through the heat of the afternoon, till it was time for dinner with the rajah.

* * *

"Welcome to my palace, sahib," said the rajah as Randolph seated himself upon a large silk cushion to the man's left-hand side. The wuzeer was to the rajah's right. The table was set upon the veranda of the palace beside the gently-lapping waters of the lake.

Tall and thin, the rajah had the air of an ascetic about him, or, perhaps, a professional and dedicated warrior. Randolph suspected he'd been right in his assessment of him as a poligar rather than a genteel monarch. He was quite the opposite of his wuzeer.

"I am told you bring us felicitations from the East India Company," the rajah of Rampur said in perfect English. The words were so precise, Randolph couldn't tell if he was doubtful of his veracity of not: a dangerous man to play cards with or with whom to bet your life.

"Indeed. As you know, the Company is always keen to maintain contact with and knowledge of the princes of India."

"Indeed," the rajah echoed.

A sumptuous, if occasionally alarming, meal was served: the rajah didn't eschew flesh and plentiful meat was provided upon plates of gold, ranging from that of wild pigs to flying foxes stuffed with fruit, all washed down with wine and spirits of novel sorts. Randolph was careful not to drink too much, despite the temptation: he would require a clear head later.

The veranda was cut in half by a purdah, behind which screen Randolph could hear the soft and sensual sounds of women: the wives and concubines of the rajah and his officials. If the Indians had a flaw, it was this insistence upon separating the sexes and denying Randolph the opportunity to enjoy their beauty; clandestine encounters were all very well, but did nothing to relieve the tedium of observing the wuzeer's flabby form. Had he not had his mind set firmly upon the ruby, he might have allowed the temptation of the feminine to guide him upon another nocturnal adventure.

Which thoughts brought to his attention that no mention had been made of the ruby. In his experience, Indian princelings were inveterate boasters, delighting in ostentatious displays of their wealth. Given that the ruby was known outside the palace walls, it seemed peculiar for it to go unmentioned. Did the rajah doubt his veracity? For a moment, Randolph felt insulted, then admitted to himself that, if the rajah did, indeed, have his doubts, they were fully justified.

Well, he wouldn't disappoint.

* * *

Despite the austere, soldierly front he presented as he ate his meal, it seemed that the rajah inclined more towards the debauched end of the spectrum typified by his wuzeer, staying up late into the night to the accompaniment of music, even after Randolph pleaded tiredness and returned to his bed. This was an inconvenience when planning a theft under cover of darkness and, eventually, Randolph decided to take a risk rather than waste the entire night in waiting.

The guard at the gate had confiscated all Randolph's weapons save his pocket pistol, which he had kept hidden up his sleeve, and the jack knife he kept in his boot, which meant he would need to recover them. Not that Randolph intended to do any fighting, but, once he left the confines of the palace, he'd need them to stay safe on the road. He would retrieve them from the guardhouse by the gate when it was time to leave.

He slipped the knife back into his boot and the pistol into the waistband of his shalwar - as far as he was concerned, if he were going to steal the jewel, he might as well take the better-quality clothing with him.

The problem, of course, with the rajah having proven unwilling to show the ruby to him, was that he'd no idea where it was hidden, and, with the rajah still up-and-about, searching for it was a risky proposition. Still, he did at least know where it wasn't and could make an educated guess as to where it might be.

Unless he missed his guess, it would be beyond the guarded door he'd seen upon his arrival. Even if it were the rajah's personal chambers that the door concealed, the odds were good the strong-room containing the ruby was there as well.

Not that he could go in through the door. But, maybe there was a way in from the roof.

He took the sheets from his bed, guessing they would come in useful.

Randolph stepped out onto the balcony outside his room, breathing deeply of the fragrant night air. Below him, the waters of the lake reflected the delicate light of the ivory moon. There was a narrow ledge along the edge of the wall. If he were careful….

He climbed over the low balcony wall and onto the ledge. Slowly, he crept along it until he reached a trellis to climb up onto the roof. There it was, like a low tower at the palace heart. There were no convenient balconies there, but it did have windows. He carefully picked his way across the roof tiles, until he reached the tower-like rise.

Randolph took out his knife and dug it into the plaster. With a little effort he gouged out a handhold, then another further up. Slowly, he pulled himself up using the makeshift holds until he grasped the sill.

He pulled himself up onto the sill. The thin wooden fretwork that filled the window was easy enough for him to break free of its frame. He piled the pieces in one corner of the window and, then, pulled himself up.

Randolph crouched in the window and looked down into the room below. These upper windows were for ventilation: over twenty feet below was a small dais upon which a red jewel glinted with an inner light. It put him in mind of a human heart. Before the dais lay an empty bath or pool, beside which stood the rajah, his wuzeer, a couple of guards and a woman in a diaphanous saree.

An unexpected complication.

As he crouched there, the rajah's words drifted up to him: "He will be asleep by now; the sleeping draught will have taken effect. Bring him here and we shall cut out his heart to honour the Heart of Shiva."

Very definitely, a complication.

Randolph felt a sense of outrage rise within him at the idea they planned to kill him as a sacrifice to some heathen god. A betrayal of hospitality far worse than that which he'd intended. He also felt a twinge of annoyance that his plans had gone awry.

He watched as the two guards left the chamber. That left the two men and the woman with the jewel. Either he went for it now or he abandoned his plans: the problem was that, within a few minutes, the guards would find he was gone and raise the alarm...

"Damned if I'm losing out," he muttered.

Randolph took the sheets he'd taken from his room and tied them together and attached the resulting rope to a jagged remnant of the fretwork. The thin wood was hardly a sturdy anchor, but only had to hold for a few seconds for him to get down.

He dropped the makeshift rope down into the room and began to climb down. The gaze of the three inhabitants of the room was fixed adoringly upon the ruby: should any of them look up, he'd be caught.

Suddenly, a knot slipped and he winced, thinking it would unravel. But, it held.

Deciding he was close enough to the floor, he let go and dropped lightly down.

The noise caused the rajah to look around and he uttered some oath in his own tongue that Randolph couldn't understand, although he felt the force of it.

The rajah seized up a long, curved knife, but Randolph produced his pistol and fired.

With surprising alacrity, the wuzeer moved to interpose himself between them and the bullet struck his fleshy chest. A look of shock crossed his heavy features, then they fell slack and he collapsed back into his master's arms with a liquid gasp.

The woman screamed and ran towards the doors clearly intending to alert the guards outside. The wuzeer's face grew sallow and his breathing juddered to a halt. The rajah gave a cry of anger or loss and looked up at Randolph with hatred in his eyes.

Randolph ran towards the rajah and his jewel. A quick shove sent the rajah sprawling to the floor beneath the corpulent corpse of the wuzeer.

The woman lunged for the blade, but Randolph kicked it away into the empty pool.

"That'll hold you," Randolph spat at the rajah, who was still struggling beneath the wuzeer's corpse, as he seized the ruby. It felt strangely slick beneath his fingers. Quickly, Randolph stuffed it inside his cameeze, and ran back towards his rope of sheets.

Behind him, the doors opened and the guards ran in: He had only moments. He just had to pray the knots held.

They did. Reaching the window, he untied his rope so the guards couldn't attempt to follow him up. Then, he scrambled down onto the roof tiles once more.

From within the palace, a clamour of shouts and cries rose. He was now hunted: He would have to abandon the plan he'd had in mind; escape was now his priority.

Randolph scrambled across the roof and threw himself off into the lake below, hoping the rajah didn't keep it stocked with the amphibious beasts known as alligators.

Although his swimming style was crude, it was sufficient to get him to the far shore. Pulling himself out, he ran into the jungle beyond.

Randolph guessed he had till dawn: The rajah would rouse his guards in pursuit, but he doubted they would risk entering the jungle tangle before the sun rose. He needed to put as much distance between him and them as possible. Which was a simpler proposition than it was to put into practice as his feet snagged on vines and caught on gnarled roots.

* * *

The first intimation of dawn came as the flying foxes returned to their roosts in the trees above him with a cacophony of wings and shrieks.

Somewhere behind him, far closer than he would've wished, he heard the blast of horns: the hunt was on.

Randolph had no option to stand and fight; his only weapon - his powder now sodden after his swim - was his jack knife, while his pursuers would be armed with bows and muskets and, he guessed, the rajah, at least, would be riding upon the back of an elephant. He wished he were more adept at craft skills: it would be useful to be able to build a trap or two to surprise them with.

But, all he could do was run.

Before he did, he patted the bulge in his cameeze, glad that it was still there. The ruby had better be the real chiz, if he were going to die for it.

Something slithered across his path and he halted. It, too, stopped, then rose with a hiss. Randolph recoiled: it was a hooded cobra. Slowly, he backed away from it, all the time keeping his eyes upon it. The snake watched until it was satisfied he was no threat, then disappeared into the dank shadows of the jungle undergrowth.

Taking a different path, Randolph continued to push on as fast as he could through the lush plant-life.

There was the sudden crack of a musket shot and leaves exploded apart as the musket ball tore through them.

Randolph glanced over his shoulder in alarm to see an elephant's head looming over the greenery, behind which was a howdah in which stood the rajah, hunting musket in his hands. He passed it to the man behind him and received another in return.

Randolph swore and dived in amongst the plants, weaving to avoid the musket ball that shot after him. He could hear the beaters thrashing the dense growth close behind him.

Suddenly, something reddish and black leapt down before him: a tiger! It drew back its lips in a snarl that chilled his blood and made him feel faint.

But, just then, a beater blundered onto the track beside him, stick in hand. Upon seeing the tiger, the man let out a cry of terror and raised his stick to strike it.

The tiger roared and lashed out, shredding the man's flesh. Then, with a fluid lunge, it clamped its jaws upon the fallen man's skull and crushed it, silencing his shrieks.

Swallowing back bile, Randolph ran past the beast as the elephant reached them. The elephant bellowed in alarm and the tiger roared in response, then the rajah's musket cracked.

While they battled, Randolph ran on.

The pursuit continued for over an hour, until he stumbled out of the jungle and onto a steep ravine above a fast-flowing river. If he recalled correctly, fast waters meant there were unlikely to be any of the alligator beasts in there; not that diving into such white-froth waters was a sane proposition.

Randolph dived in, regardless. He found himself being tossed about and fighting to keep his head above the raging waters, but soon lost the battle. Gulping down lungfuls of water, he felt himself sinking down, not just into the waters, but into an all-consuming blackness.

* * *

Randolph woke to a tugging sensation: Something was pulling at the sleeve of his cameeze. His hand went automatically to the bulge of the red stone. Then, he swatted at the mangy yellow dog, before coughing up vile river water.

He was lying on a mud-bank on the edge of a wide, sluggish river. He guessed he had to be many, many miles from Rampur Sar and the rajah's palace. If he could just reach more civilised lands, he would be a very wealthy man...

On the nearby bank, an Indian peasant looked at him with a quizzical expression.

"Greetings," he gasped. "My name is Captain Randolph Halley, late of the East India Company Army. Can you tell me where I am?"

A Forest Encounter

Frank Coffman

At the far southern tip of Illinois
The Shawnee Forest spreads across the land
From the Ohio to the Mississippi.
Sprawling, thick woods and many a tributary
Creek or river, and rolling hills have spanned
That country centuries before, when, as a boy,
I roamed that region, careless in my youth,
Ranging near Ripple Hollow, east of McClure.
I loved those hills, those broad creeks, and those trees.
    But one day, straying late, I learned the truth!
Call me crazy if you want to, but I'm sure
I saw *the' Thing*. First a stench upon the breeze,
And then...a panther, blacker than any night -
But fully ten feet long! That *Thing* ain't right!
Of course, I ran - but not at first. I froze
When I looked into those red and glowing eyes.
    The *Thing* had killed a white-tail and it fed
Upon the gory carcass of the deer.
I can't describe the sight, the utter fear
That overcame me or the horror of those
Huge, long fangs that ripped. "I'm dead,"
I thought.
            It's only a thing that flies
Could flee - from that glance my way that meant,
"You're next" - faster than I through that wild wood.
I ran and stumbled through thickets 'till I was spent.
But something kept me moving. Then I stood
In a clearing, but could still hear distant growls.
I tell you *the' Black Cat's there' - and it still prowls!*

The Old Man
of the Mountain

Vicki Weisfeld

HIGH ABOVE A NARROW VALLEY in the Carpathian mountains, Anton and Daniela scrambled toward a secret destination. Leading the way, he squeezed behind dense shrubbery and fallen rocks to reach the mouth of an abandoned construction. She hesitated upon seeing the awkward clamber required, but he laughed and pulled her up behind him. The early evening light disappeared quickly once the teenagers took a few steps inside. Daniela reached for Anton's hand, and their flashlights waved like demented fireflies.

"Keep up!" he urged.

A dripping, calciferous liquid had sculpted grotesque stalactites overhead and left yellowish pustules on the floor. They might be trampling the acne-pocked face of a giant. Perhaps that oozing accounted for the slightly rotten, slightly medicinal odor that filled the entry. Ailment and remedy commingled. Daniela shone her flashlight to the ceiling, and they saw a fringe of plant roots exploiting every tiny crack in the overhead vault - tentacles searching for food and drink and finding empty air. Her beam settled on a lightbulb, its white wire cage scarred with rust. Farther along, another.

"Lights?" she asked. "Anton, why do I whisper?"

"Yes, lights. But none of us in the Romanian Youth Adventurers Club know how to turn them on." Anton spoke quietly too.

"Is your club hunting for treasures here?" She sounded dubious.

He laughed. "We are simply weekend explorers. The Romanian soldiers and their Nazi bosses emptied this passageway when they fled the Russians." He splayed the torchlight over the graffiti-marked walls. "Now people leave this behind."

"What is - was - this place?"

"It always was a cave. The fascists lengthened it, leveled the floor, built rooms farther back, and ran electricity. When they left, they sealed it with the pile of rocks we climbed. Last year, the mountain trembled, and a rockslide partly exposed the opening."

"Why bother exploring it? If it is empty?"

"Maybe it isn't."

They meandered deeper into the side of the mountain. Only occasional drips of water and the scuffling of their feet broke the silence, until from deep in the earth an eerie groaning vibrated the air around them, punctuated by sharp pops.

"What is that?" Daniela clung more tightly to Anton's arm.

"We have heard it before. To me it sounds like an old man turning over in his sleep, resettling his aching joints, straining the ropes of his bed."

"The old man of the mountain," she said, making him laugh again. "Maybe he is the husband of Muma Pădurii, and the old witch buried him in here! Behind the groans you can almost hear the thumping of his heart. Are you not scared?" She shivered beside him.

"Of that old wives' tale? Never. Are you?" he asked.

"Since a child I am afraid of the dark. So I am clutching your arm now. Really, I am not so scared when I am with you." She laughed thinly.

Thoughts of darkness tainted the early memories of many village children, going back a decade to wartime in their region. The long black night wasn't what terrified them, but the knowledge of what came after. She asked, "Why did the soldiers build this?"

"To store supplies? Or weapons? A secret bunker? They moved much stone and brought tons of concrete to create the floor. A big job. Surely it was worth doing." His flashlight played along the high walls and ceiling. The graffiti dwindled to a few stray scribbles, suggesting a failure of artistic inventiveness or of nerve, and even those scattered marks stopped before they walked much farther..

"How did they keep all this work a secret?"

"The entrance is not visible from the village. And our families had bigger worries." She couldn't see his frown, recalling the night the Germans came. Earlier that evening, Anton's mother had been twisting a dish towel in her hands as she asked, "Why are we important to them? This is a tiny village high in the mountains, not a center of religious thought. Why do the beliefs of our ancestors matter?" "Don't be naïve," his father replied. "Now that is all that matters."

If he could have read Daniela's mind, he would have known she too was remembering how the village parents sent their children deep into the forest or hid them in barns and cellars as the growling of trucks in the valley below grew ever nearer. The next morning, when the shouts and screams had stopped, when the echoes of gunfire had faded, when the roaring tanks and trucks were gone, eighteen children crept home - Anton alone, Daniela flanked by her older brothers. They found village streets littered with corpses and empty of parents, uncles and aunts, shopkeepers, the postman, their teacher.

Shivering in the blackness of the tunnel, Daniela said, "It is very big. Where does it lead?"

Anton loosened the vise of memory. "Who knows? Eventually fallen stones block the way, so I am told. But what is on the other side? Is it the lair of your 'old man of the mountain'?"

She playfully punched his arm. "Remember when we listened to that boring Doctor Krausz? On the radio? Describing rats in a maze?" They were following one of the tunnel's gently curving walls. "This reminds me of that. We rats - apologies, research subjects - go as far as we dare because of the possibility of reward. Treasure to find, curiosity to satisfy."

"Only one treasure is in here now." He shone the flashlight on her face, leaned in, and kissed her. This is why he had brought her here. For this kiss and, he hoped, many more.

She laughed and pushed him away, blinking. "Be careful with that light. Now I cannot see anything! What if," she persisted, "some other being - the old man of the mountain, if you will - is watching us right now, just as Doctor Krausz described? The rats did not know their every move was recorded. What if we are the same?"

She gasped as if to take the words back. It was a disturbing notion from a girl who avoided frightening ideas and the doors of memory they might crack open. But she and Anton could not erase her words. They hung in the air, thickening the darkness.

"Impossible!" He grabbed her in his arms and twirled her around a few times to erase the somber mood. Every bit as dizzying was the next kiss they shared. They swayed a bit, and the mountain grumbled louder - a cacophony of squealing cries that coalesced into a groan.

"I've never been this deep in before," he said. "We should go back." Despite the tingle he felt with her so near, the dark was too oppressive. He focused his flashlight on the tunnel before them.

"But," she said, "which way is back?"

"This way." He spoke with confidence and squeezed her shoulders.

"No, this way." She flashed her beam over the nearly featureless walls behind them to illuminate a rusty stain. "We just passed this, no?"

"Do you mean this?" He focused his light on a similar patch in the other direction.

"Where are our footprints?" They ran the flashlight beams in a circle around them. Unaccountably, no marks indicated which way they'd come.

"So, which way is it?" An unwanted note of anxiety crept into his voice.

"I do not know, Anton! But I think we go this way. Did you bring a compass?"

"They do not work down here. The magnetic...something of the Earth." In truth, he hadn't thought to bring a compass. He was too intent on stealing her away from her watchful brothers, on slipping off to be alone with her. His scalp prickled.

He moved forward. She followed close behind, tearily arguing. The dark was a muffling velvet curtain that withdrew when they reached out a hand, then closed in on them when they withdrew it. His breaths became shallow. He slowed, and she stumbled over his foot. She grabbed his arm to stop herself from falling.

"My ankle!"

"I am sorry!" he said over her yelps and put his arm around her waist. "Let me see it."

He helped her to the floor and sat down in front of her, the flashlights between them. He gently rotated her foot, and at one angle, she cried out. "A little sprain, maybe, but not broken."

"I feel so stupid."

"Let me rub it." He gently massaged her ankle and asked her to shine the light in first one direction, then the other, as he studied the unrevealing passageway walls. He emitted a frustrated snort.

"You do not know after all which direction the entrance is," she said, lower lip trembling.

"I am almost certain. Yet I am respecting your doubts."

She pulled her foot away and stood, but her leg buckled when she tried to put weight on the injured foot. She hopped in place. "This is awful. I hate this." Although he feared her next sentence might be "I hate you," she did not say it. "What if we never get out of here?"

He put an arm around her, but she squirmed away.

"I'll sit right here," she said, collapsing to the floor. She began to cry. "Go your way and, if you find the entrance, come back for me. If you do not find it, when you come back, we will go my way together."

"We should stay together, Daniela. Come." His tone was gentle, but insistent.

"I cannot go in a direction I think is wrong. I cannot do so much useless walking."

"Well, then, we will go in your direction."

"I am not positive! How could I be?"

"And so?" he asked.

"I wait here until you make certain."

He thought long enough for the griping mountain to provide a guttural commentary on the predicament. "Yes. Stay while I figure it out. You will be my landmark." He tried to sound cheerful.

Just then, the lights in the passageway blinked on. Far apart though the bulbs were and with some of them no longer working, they were infinitely more illuminating than the flashlights.

"There, you see!" he said, as if he'd engineered some sort of triumph. "Now I can find the entrance much faster. "Turn off your flashlight. Save the batteries." She did. "I will go your way first. When you see me again, we will know the way for sure."

"Anton," she said, pulling her sweater close around her. "Who turned the lights on?"

"I am happy only that they did," he said, jogging away with great energy. When he glanced behind, she curled her fingers in a tiny wave, like a baby's.

He'd jogged, he guessed, about ten minutes when he noticed roots fingering down from the ceiling, and the strange graffiti appearing on the passageway walls. Soon he smelled the pine forest that surrounded the tunnel entrance, felt fresher air. Around another slight bend, he saw the tunnel opening, the stalactites. He glimpsed the night sky outside.

"Slavă Domnuliu!" he shouted, although God had nothing to do with it. He took a few more long strides to be sure. "Yes!"

He turned to run back to Daniela. As suddenly as the overhead lights had come on, they went out. Ahead of him was utter blackness. More than the absence of light, the dark was a living, suffocating presence, soft against his face. His heart pumped wildly.

He walked forward a score of steps until he once more passed the modest bend, which hid the gray sliver of starlight behind him. He steadied himself against the gritty wall. The flashlight's dim cone of light seemed smaller than before. In truth, he wanted nothing more than to turn and flee, to exit the tunnel, to breathe the cool night air deep into his lungs.

"I cannot do this," he muttered, contemplating the solidity of the blackness in front of him. After a struggle with his conscience - he had gotten Daniela into this, after all - he willed himself into motion, saying, "You must." The mountain grumbled, followed by a lingering susurrus of sound, a thousand urgent whispers. He trembled with guilt to think how desperately he wanted to escape. But why should he escape? The people of his village hadn't. Some were killed, and some disappeared, never returning, though the children stood in the streets every day, keeping watch.

For what seemed like a considerable time, he pushed himself to walk forward, but still no sign of her. He called her name, hoping she'd hear him and hobble forward, cutting the distance he'd have to cover in this accursed place. Her last question haunted him. Who did turn the lights on?

Equally, who turned them off? Was it a who? Or merely a random electrical impulse, energy yearning for connection and briefly achieving it?

"A fault. They call it a fault. Don't they?" he muttered, meaning the lights, though if there were a fault in this expedition, he knew it was of another kind and his own. He shook his torch, and it brightened for a few steps only.

His feet and legs grew heavy. He'd never given the act of breathing any thought, but in the viscous blackness, moving air in and out of his lungs had become hard work.

Conflicting ideas muddled his mind. The entrance was not so very far away. Trying to reach her might not be the best plan. Truthfully, he might not be able to get her out. Not with his dying flashlight. Not if he had to carry her, even half-carry her. Maybe it would be better to abandon the tunnel and go for help. Not to her overprotective brothers. They would kill him. He would find someone. Someone else.

At that moment, as if she knew he contemplated abandoning her, the screams started. Over and over, Daniela's terror rang through the tunnel. Though thinned with distance, her cries tore at him.

Why was she screaming? He should be screaming - screaming with rage at himself. Was something terrible happening to her? Did a wild animal lurk deep among the fallen rocks? Did gypsies hide a camp back there? The old man of the mountain was their joke, but someone had turned on those lights. Foolishness, he thought. She's just frightened. All the more reason to return to her quickly.

The screaming grew desperate. Short bursts, punctuated with gasping, choking sounds. He clapped his palms to his ears, holding the flashlight with curled fingers and wagging his head in torment. Where her lips had touched him, his face felt on fire.

It was too much. He turned away from Daniela and ran back toward the entrance. He ran and ran, his heart racing him, not keeping pace. Still he could hear her. When the screaming abruptly stopped, the silence was awful. At last he saw a faint light ahead. But it was not the star-strewn sky. A pale glow illuminated a patch by the tunnel floor. He blinked to clear his vision.

As he approached the spot, he saw Daniela lying on her side. Again, he thanked God. He ran the last few meters, stopping short. At the bottom of the wall was a hole barely wide enough to crawl through. It had been covered by a rusting grate they had not noticed that now lay nearby. Daniela must have pulled it away. Her flashlight had fallen into a shallow pit inside.

"Daniela, amoreză! I found it! What upset you so?"

She didn't answer. But wait. She shouldn't be here. He had been on his way out. He must have mixed up the direction again. But how? Was it because of the slight curves in the tunnel walls? Was he running in circles? He had found the entrance, hadn't he?

"Here," he said, kneeling beside her to take her in his arms and filling his voice with false confidence. "I found the exit. It's back this way. I'll help you." She lay so still. His flashlight's wan beam illuminated a face yellow with fear, its unblinking eyes, black and bottomless as death itself, and a mouth frozen open in horror.

"Daniela! No!" She couldn't be dead. His mouth went dry; he felt faint. He grasped her hand, dry and cold, like the air pouring out of the hole in the wall. Her nails were broken, and her fingertips had bled, cut by the sharp edges of the grate. What was inside that gently illuminated hole? He had to know.

The mountain rumbled as he used his elbows to pull himself into the opening and shone his light on the far wall. A ladder clung there, only five meters away. The ladder disappeared into blackness, but high above was the faint outline of a door. Salvation!

He need only crawl through, drop a few feet into the pit below, and cross to the ladder. He would be free. He could carry Daniela with him. In the fresh air, surely she would revive. He ran his beam over the pit floor.

Covering it were emaciated bodies laid in precise rows. Though they were dressed in rags and shrunken to almost nothing, he recognized the people of his village. His parents and Daniela's, their whole community was there, crumbling to dust.

He glanced at the tantalizing ladder once more. He could not walk across these beloved dead. Nor could he abandon them. He crawled back from the opening and lay down next to Daniela, cradling her in his arms. The mountain roared again. Now he could separate the strands of sound. The pulsing rhythm of marching men, terrified whispers and barefoot shuffling, moans, tools striking rock, overladen wheelbarrows squeaking, the crack and pop of gunfire.

He thought of his friends in the Adventurers Club. How surprised Constantin and Vasile would be to find him and Daniela, clinging together. They had solved the village's terrible mystery, only to find that the truth was inescapable. He put his left arm around his love and stretched his right to point at the pit's opening. "Here," he whispered and surrendered himself to the mountain.

Swamp Gold

Robb T. White

THE WEIRD THING ABOUT IT, Curtis thought, was that not more than twenty minutes ago they were about to get into a fight. The only two guys in the place and they were almost at the point of swinging on each other. Now we're buying rounds, talkin' about goin' hunting in the Glades....

Curtis was already buzzed when the stranger sat down on the stool beside him and ordered a whisky, beer chaser. Didn't know why the guy had to take the seat next to him when the whole damn bar was empty. Shift change at the sugar mill wasn't for another hour and the heat outside was intense, even by South Florida standards. Curtis' shirt was still glued to his back and he wanted nothing more than to pound a few beers down, go home, shower, and sleep a couple of hours until the single women started to show up. He was still raw over Dora-Lynne leaving him.

The guy said his name was Carnell, first name Elton - "like that fat piano player, wears them goofy glasses."

"Ain't seen you in here before," Curtis replied.

"That's cuz I ain't been in here before. . . . Hey bartender," he swiveled on the stool and shouted down the bar to Red. "You got a air-conditioner in this place, I seen it dripping on the sidewalk outside so how's about you turnin' it on?"

Red looked up from his paper, ignored the jibe, and went back to his skin magazine. Red kept a stack of them behind the bar when the place was empty or when there were no women around.

Guy looked normal - greasy red John Deere hat over hair slicked back like an otter's, a black-tee with a Harley Hog and a woman showing lots of cleavage behind the bearded rider, and a pair of camo Irish Setter boots. Curtis had a pair back in his trailer - good for hunting in marshes. Snake-proof, too; a cottonmouth buried its fangs in his right heel but didn't penetrate. Curtis remembered slamming his rifle butt on the snake's head. He watched it do several figure-eights before whipping off into the sawgrass to die.

That hat nearly caused the fight. Curtis commented on the guy's helmet of black hair when Elton took it off to smooth his hair back.

"You sayin' I had my hair done at a beauty shop?"

The sly smile he offered Curtis wasn't friendly. The man's stillness gave him a bad vibe like that snake before it struck. Too got-damn hot to get into it....

"Didn't mean nothin' by it," Curtis muttered, his eyes on the man's face but aware of the position of the man's hands all the time.

"What's your name, friend?"

Gold teeth in the grin now.

That was three shots-and-beers ago. Now he was hammered and dreading the walk outside in the gravel lot to his pickup. Home to - what? A shitty trailer park and no woman.

"Hey, Curt, got you another round here, amigo. My turn to buy."

"Aw, hell, man, I'm done," Curtis declared. "The heat is gonna murder me outside."

"Then stay here and have you another drink," Carnell said.

Curtis wasn't aware of nodding in resignation, but Red must have noticed it above the bifocals because he was in motion behind the bar.

"Goddamned hotter than the surface of the sun out there," Curtis complained.

"You know what they say, 'It ain't the heat, it's the humidity,'" Elton said.

The booze, the heat, his irritation at being fired for the third time in six months - whatever, but something in the trite saying hit him exactly right and he belched a laugh. Then Elton followed it with a barking laugh. In seconds, they were giggling like schoolgirls.

Curtis drank, felt the familiar heat of whiskey in his belly, and relive the midday argument with his former boss, owner of a small landscaping firm, and wondered why he couldn't let things go. The man gave him a hard time about the peat moss Curtis was spreading over the raised flower bed when Curtis tossed his shovel at him, whacking him across the knees, and said, "Do it yourself, asshole," and walked off the job. Then the ride from a Lyft to Red's Roadhouse and, by God, here he was again, spending his last few bucks drinking with a stranger

* * *

Something Carnell was saying penetrated the reverie. "What was that?"

"Treasure," Elton said with a wide grin that showed his gold incisors.

"Ain't no treasure in that cabin," Curtis said. "That place has been torn to hell and back. If there was anything in it, somebody'd have found it by now."

Every kid growing up in Belle Glade knew that tale as well as the Baby Jesus story. Old Man Carmichael had made a fortune off the Seminoles in some crooked government deal back in the nineteen-forties and stole away into the Everglades to hoard his money. Some said it was paper money stored in Mason jars and buried in the cabin walls. Some said it was gold doubloons from long-lost Spanish explorers he'd found in the swamps out by the Miccosukee Indian Reservation. Others said the treasure was buried in Big Cypress. One thing they all agreed on: Old Man Carmichael got himself killed out there by Pig Man. Now Pig Man owns the gold and protects it from any fool coming out there looking to steal it from him.

Man, he'd heard a hundred stories about Pig Man and the gold and all the fortune hunters he'd killed and eaten - only the dumbest believed them to be true. The one real thing was the cabin. Still there - a blackened ruin, what the vandals hadn't burned down over the years.

"That old hermit, yep, he died with a shitload of money."

"You're crazy," Curtis said. "Ain't nothing but stupid rumors - "

The sound of the gold coin ringing on the bar top cut off the rest of Curtis' sentence.

Carnell gave it a flick with an index finger so it spun between them, the dim bar light giving it a strobe-like effect.

Curtis snapped out a hand in mid-twirl. He held the coin up to the dim lighting.

"I see it got your attention, huh?"

Curtis tried to read the inscription. "Who's the dude got his name on it? . . . Hey, Red, put that fur book down, c'mere a sec."

"What is it this time, Curt? You want to com plain about the a/c too?"

"Read this here coin." Curtis handed it to him. "Saint Gardens. That some kind of place?"

Carnell laughed. "It ain't no saint, man. It's the devil hisself's gold."

"Hang on," Red replied. He fished his cell phone out of his back pocket.

"Well, come on, Red. God-damn Almighty . . . I didn't come in here to watch you read the whole friggin' online dictionary - "

Red dropped the coin on the bar with a loud smack as if he were swatting a fly. "It's not a place. It's a man's name. Saint Gaw-dens, says here. He designed the coin according to Wikipedia - "

"All right, all right, thanks, Professor. Now go back to your jerkoff magazines."

Curtis used two fingers to shove the coin toward Carnell. It reminded him of touching the planchette of an Ouija board. Dora-Lynne was into witchcraft and made him play when they got high.

"It ain't who designed it what matters most," Carnell whispered, one eye on the bartender's progress.

"OK, what's it about then?"

"It's about where the rest of them are," Carnell said.

"Rest of - who?"

"This bad boy's brothers and sisters."

He placed the coin over one eye like an eyepiece and grinned, exposing those gold fangs, before letting it drop into his open palm. "Mister Saint Gardens didn't come alone into this cruel world. They's dozens more of them." He tapped the coin against Curtis' empty tumbler for emphasis.

"Don't it make such a sweet sound?"

"Yeah," Curtis replied. "Real nice. Lucky you, Carnell."

"It ain't the sound, boy. It's what it's worth."

"And what's it worth?"

"About fourteen, maybe fifteen."

"Big deal."

"Hundred."

"Say what?"

"Fourteen hundred. That's a lowball figure, too."

"You're shitting me."

"I ain't shittin' you."

"I got to go. I need me some sleep. Got me a busy night ahead. S'nice meetin' you, Elvis Carnell - I mean, Elton. Get you one more on me."

Curtis dropped a five on the bar for Red and placed his last five on the pile of ones in front of Carnell.

He was a couple steps from the bar stool when Carnell said, "Hey, you ain't asked me where I got it."

He tapped the edge of the coin three times, hard, against the chrome rail of the stool so that it rang like a bell.

Curtis turned around. "Ain't none of my business."

He was about to push open the door when he heard more words in that same guttural whisper.

"It come from that old man's cabin out there in the swamp."

One more step and he'd be all the way out the door standing in the gravel parking lot of this bar where he'd bought more drinks than he could count and where friends had bought him as many, a place where he'd had fights, won and lost some, won more than he lost. Where he'd picked up girls, including Dora-Lynne, who cleaned out their apartment and even took off with Buck, his bluetick hound.

The booze in his brain said, "Turn around!"

"Thought that might could bring you back," Carnell said.

"Dude, I want to know what you just said, and I want you to say it real slow, like, because I've got my beer goggles on and I ain't thinkin' too clear," Curtis said.

"Three of 'em, all like this one. Found with a metal detector out to Carmichael's old cabin 'bout three years ago," Carnell said. "Two got me that Silverado out there melting in the parking lot. Bought some primo camping equipment, too - "

"Whoa, there! You said 'three years ago'? And you ain't found no more gold coins."

"Never had a chance to go back," Carnell said. "Night I found them three under the muck, this guy, he tried to steal them from me."

"This guy - who?"

"Just some guy I was traveling with to split costs."

"What happened?"

"What happened? Shee-yit, I'll tell you what happened. We got into it right there in the motel. He denied it, but I found them stuck in a rubber inside his duffel bag."

"What did he say?"

"Not a whole lot with my knife sticking in his throat. I got five at Raiford, did three with good time."

"I s'spected you had a shitbird look about you," Curtis said.

"Takes one to know one. What was you in for?"

"Stolen property. Did two years. Worked the dog races in Hialeah. Then some ex-con at the track said he could fix me up with a guy who ran a chop shop out to Lauderdale. He put the word in for me and the place got raided a week later."

"You could have cut a deal, walked," Carnell said. "The new guy, no idea what was up."

"They wanted me to talk."

"That's good to hear," Carnell said and gave him a hearty slap between the shoulder blades. "I knew you was a standup guy."

Curtis thought Carnell's praise rang hollow. He'd heard it before. Guys always said they admired you for holding your shit, not pussying out, but what you had to give up was a price too high. Those cement walls and that wafer-thin mattress on a wire frame were pure misery. The sweat-stink, the non-stop jabber and clanging steel, the starchy food, gray boredom punctuated by heart-pounding bouts of fear. So many gang tightropes to walk among the Aryan Brotherhood, Chico Boy, and the Bloods. Up in Gulf Correctional near Pensacola where they sent him, corrupt guards smuggled in tobacco, cell phones, and drugs for the Auburn Park boys. Two years of dealing with snitches, "daddies" and their punks, sickos, maniacs, child-molesters, rapists - all the scum of society - and after those two years of hell on earth, he didn't want more. He just couldn't get his act together out here. Before she lit out for greener pastures, Dora-Lynne told him prison had messed with his head, made him cold and mean.

"Money could put you right, boy," Carnell said, as if he were reading Curtis' mind at that precise moment.

"People go out there all the time. Every inch of the ground around the cabin has been searched. Cops, treasure hunters with metal detectors, Boy Scouts, Girl Scouts, for all I know - "

"But ain't no one looked in the right places," Carnell said. He took a folded piece of paper from his pocket, smoothed it out on the bar top, and motioned for Curtis to move closer. "Have a look here."

Curtis leaned over Carnell's shoulder. He saw spiky red lines like you'd see on a hospital monitor - the ruined cabin - some more squiggly arrows, and a big black X.

"X marks the spot, huh?"

"Don't laugh at me, boy. I ain't no ninny-hammered halfwit like you think. I went out there one time and happened to dig around where nobody's been before. I got lucky . . . Then I got unlucky when my cellie tried to rip me off."

"Thought you said he was some guy you was traveling with."

"We shared a cell at Raiford. So what? He's the one who told me about the Carmichael cabin."

"He tell you about Pig Man, too?"

"Boy, them swamps is full of wild pigs. That's all they is. No such thing as Pig Man."

Curtis stared at the stained treasure map flattened on the bar top. It looked as if it had been folded a hundred times.

"Let's cut through the bullshit here," he said. "Why ain't you out there right now digging up all that gold instead of killing time with me in a shitkicker bar? You on parole, right, so just being caught in here can get you violated."

They mocked guys in prisons who talked too much, called them "monkey mouths."

"I seen you got that look in your eye." Carnell flashed his dog-toothed smile.

"What look?"

"I want you and me partners, see, because I got me a little problem at the moment, not any big deal but see, I got limits on my movement . . ."

He showed Curtis "the little problem" by drawing up his right pantleg over the black ankle monitor.

"Hell's-bells," Curtis exclaimed; "you're on parole, drinking in a bar wearing an ankle monitor. Are you crazy?"

"I reckon that old geezer at the end of the bar heard you but you mind not informing everybody out in the street? I'd appreciate it."

"You ain't worried?"

"You watch too much TV," Carnell said. "This thing's only a GPS tracker. By the time they download this damned thing on my leg, I'll be long gone."

"So you want me to be your shovel man, that it?"

"You told me when we met you was a landscaper."

"Former landscaper. I got fired."

"With the money lying in that marsh, fifty-fifty split, you won't have to worry about gettin' Chickenfeed wages. And any problems findin' women will be long gone.

"I get it, I get it."

"Women cost money. They didn't tell you that in kindergarten?"

Curtis did know that. He suspected Dora-Lynne was less happy about the money he brought in than the fact he'd turned cold like a lizard - her word. Coming into a fortune would be sweet revenge.

Wait! Was he crazy? His inner voice was piping up again: You ain't seriously thinking of -

"I'm in," Curtis said.

"Atta boy. Let's toast our new partnership."

"Here's to Pig Man."

* * *

Seventeen-foot pythons big enough to swallow a deer, spiders as big as your fist, black flies that bite every time they land and they land on every inch of exposed flesh everywhere. Bull gators in the Glades the size of refrigerators, which the chamber of commerce promotes in glossy brochures now that airboat rides for pasty-faced snowbirds are coming under fire for their environmental damage. The welcoming sign says "Belle Glade: Her Soil Is Her Fortune" and considers the alligator its prime specimen, although if one of these two-thousand-pound behemoths ever locked its jaws on your leg, you'll know in a big damn hurry what it is to be considered a prize specimen.

Curtis left his 30-ought-six deer rifle in his trunk alongside the AR-15 with the illegal bump stock. His .45 Colt with ACP load was heavier than the Walther, but he wanted stopping power if he needed it. Every poacher in the mangrove swamps was strapped. He kept a Ka-Bar USMC fighting knife on his belt and a fixed-blade commando dagger on the inside of his left boot. His "last resort" knife, he called it. His backpack was filled with bottled water, a package of Slim Jims, flashlight, snake-bite antivenom, and bug repellant. Carnell's flimsy map was in a baggie. He'd dusted out the marijuana seeds and placed it inside his shirt pocket. He carried a digging spade in his hand. Good for defense on the way.

Carnell's directions were hardly better than the map.

"You a hunter," he said. "I don't got to tell you how much a landscape can change in three years. You might need to do a whole lot more digging than I first did."

It wasn't the landscape that worried him. It was Carnell's memory. How much did he remember lying on his bunk dreaming of gold coins? How much was accurate?

He drove fourteen miles south on Highway 27. He didn't need directions to the cabin. The trek was three miles off the highway. He'd been there as a teenager with a bunch of guys from school. He remembers spraying graffiti on a wall back then: "Rick DeMaris likes cock." Rick was all-state that year, meaner than a pygmy rattlesnake. Curtis hated him because he'd taken his girlfriend at the time. Had a chipped front tooth from Rickie's class ring from a schoolyard fight he didn't get fixed. He called it his "badge of courage" after some dumb novel his English teacher made them read.

Halfway there, slapping mosquitoes all the way, Curtis almost turned back. "This is a goddamned snipe hunt," he muttered. "Somebody at Red's musta set me up."

He tried to think of who would do this to him but couldn't come up with a name. Still, he didn't turn back. That shimmering, dancing coin on the bar top was burned into his neocortex.

Egrets and squirrels set up a din at his advance, animals and birds calling out Beware! an intruder was in their midst. Curtis knew the Pig Man legend was all hooey - but still, out here in the wilds, tramping through muck, and swatting bugs, everywhere he looked was a reminder that he was just one creature. The fact he wasn't the creature occupying the top post on the food chain wasn't lost on him.

He'd sweated through his clothes by the time he reached the cabin. It was different, smaller than he remembered. The walls were mostly gone and creeper vines had reached inside. The roof had buckled and the shingling was all feathered, mossy. He didn't see his graffiti; it had been burned away along with most of the place. Hard to imagine any human being living out here alone, even a crazy old miser. A creature like Pig Man, however, was easy to conjure - maybe too easy; a half-man, half-pig monster with boar tusks out there watching him made him give a reassuring slap to the Ka-Bar strapped to his belt.

Curtis slugged down another bottled water and took his bearings. Carnell said to follow directly behind the back cabin window fifteen yards and dig between two rotted tree stumps.

"There ain't no damned window anymore, Carnell," he fumed. There wasn't a tree stump either. Nothing but chest-high climbing ferns draped around a bent Cypress.

Off to the left, partially hidden from view, was a dense patch of sawgrass where orchids sprouted. Wary of snakes, Curtis walked over to inspect them and tripped on a root - except that it wasn't a root. It was all that was left of an old stump.

"I came this far. I might as well do some digging."

Sweat poured from him in rivulets. He could barely see from the salt-sting in his eyes but digging wasn't rocket science. He kept plunging the spade into the foul muck and tossing it over his shoulder splattering the gorgeous orchids with filth. Two hours passed. No gold coins, nada. He didn't want to be out here in the dark so he gave himself one more hour before quitting. Forty minutes later, the clang of his shovel blade didn't sound the same as hitting a rock or a buried root.

Curtis got down on his hands and knees and began to feel with his hands. Definitely something down there. He poured a bottle of water on the lumpy fragments he felt with his hand and realized they were corroded metal, two at opposite ends of what could be the remains of a large steamer trunk. Curtis stabbed his shovel blade into the black rot with both hands, pile-driving the blade deeper, releasing ancient smells from the steaming earth.

Cursing, half-crazed with black flies and mosquitoes drawn to his sweat, he plunged the shovel in harder until it banged against a solid, unyielding mass; his hands slid down the handle and gathered a mass of painful splinters. "Gawd damn and Holy Jesus!"

A caterwaul of wetlands life responded: egrets, herons, swamp birds all cried out with shrieks and whistles. The palms of his hands were blistered with splinters but his heart soared despite the pain.

Curtis figured he'd slammed his shovel into the remnants of an old well, something the hermit had built and nature had taken back over time. He knew how wrong he was when he lifted a bar of gold out. Two more hours of digging and scraping muck free showed him twelve ingots lying side by side on the rim of the hole as neatly as they had been when they were placed inside the trunk down there. No coins, just filthy gold bars.

It was growing dark and the heavy humidity was about to give way to a storm. Bolts of lightning streaked the massive clouds boiling up from the Gulf. Time to book it to the truck. He'd figure out how to transport the gold in daylight.

Thunder boomed all around after a mile of hoofing it at a fast trot, his flashlight bouncing ahead in the pitch-black dark stabbing the tops of trees, picking up the fluorescence of nocturnal creatures' eyes watching him from a distance.

By the end of the second mile, his path through the marshes was illuminated more by the flashes of lightning than his own light beam. He dodged from side to side trying to avoid proximity to the taller trees, slipping on wet ground. One bolt ripped the limb from a Cypress he'd just passed under. The air sizzled all around him. He made good progress all the same, one leg then the other. Time and all thought disappeared. He was reduced to a marching machine, nothing more.

Lightning showed him his truck ahead where he'd left it.

Then something happened: lightning crashed behind him.

When Curtis came to, a red sun was just climbing through the mangrove. He had a throbbing pain in his head behind his ear. His vision, watery at best, told him he was sitting in the passenger side of his truck. Carnell was in the driver's seat facing him, one arm over the seat back. Curtis figured there'd be a gun in his hand though he couldn't see it. In his left hand, Carnell held a dark, heavy-looking, oblong object.

"You need to lose weight, boy. Took me pritnear a half-hour to get your dumb peckerwood ass inside this truck."

"I apologize."

"I like that," Carnell said. "A sense of humor under dire circumstances."

"Is that what you call this?"

"Sure, I bushwhacked you. I ain't gonna deny it . . . ya'll see this?"

"Why don't you shove that thing up your ass."

Curtis had a dizzy spell where he thought he might heave. He reached out a hand to steady himself but the nylon zip tie binding both his hands at the wrist prevented him.

"Careful there, now. No sudden moves or you'll get another taste of this beavertail sap. It's a family heirloom. Got it from my daddy. He died in Alabama in the big yellow chair they call Yellow Mama."

"I'm not interested in your family history."

"OK, rest time's over. Time to get to work. See that?"

"See what?"

"That ATV out there behind my truck. I brought it all the way out here just to help you load up my gold."

Curtis looked where Carnell gestured with the sap.

A mud-spattered, two-person, side-by-side with a towing wagon. It looked old and Japanese-made. Curtis hoped so. He grew up with ATVs and four-wheelers in the countryside. Had to be peeled off them to come in for supper. One glance told him the potential problems: front load capacity about a hundred pounds. Maybe twice that in back. That meant the wagon would have to carry the remaining load over the twisting, slurry of the path. The off-road tires were designed for rough terrain but swampland was a whole other thing. Curtis was amazed how fast his brain recovered from the shock of the blow. Nothing like sudden death for sharpening the mind . . . 'load up my gold'. . . Carnell wasn't bothering to disguise his intentions.

Think, boy, think -

"All right, moron, quit screwin' the dog and get out."

Curtis raised his bound hands.

"Yeah, I'm gonna cut that tie. But you be real careful what you do next, old son."

With the gun out from hiding and pointing at Curtis' stomach, Carnell drew Curtis' own commando dagger from his boot. With a whipping motion, he cut the nylon.

"Now get out. Every move you make from here on out is gonna be what I tell you to do. Got it? Do one thing I ain't told you to do, you know what'll happen, right?"

Carnell brushed Curtis' ear lobe with the barrel tip.

"Loud and clear."

"Good boy. You're driving. I done wasted enough time out here slapping at deer flies and waiting for you to come round."

Several things dawned on Curtis at once. Carnell knew exactly where the gold bars were because he buried them out there after finding them - and he had to be in a hurry when he did it. Carnell's traveling buddy didn't betray him; it was the other way around.

Curtis drove slower than necessary so he could draw out Carnell, find a weakness in the man who intended to kill him.

"You ever drive one of these?"

"I might be a redneck, but I ain't a dumb, all-out hillbilly like you. You have sex with your momma, too?"

"I just wondered, Carnell. You see, these things can be tricky on slopes and marshland and we got some tough ground ahead. This model's got a torque-bearing limited-slip front differential, which is good. That means it's got the force of a locking differential."

"Partner, you should keep quiet and save your breath for the heavy lifting you're gonna do for me."

"You're the boss. But don't panic if we take a rough corner or two and you shoot me with that gun in your lap. What I'm sayin' is that reduces steering effort and kickback - "

"Je-sus, you say one more mumbo-jumbo thing about this quad bike and it's gonna be your last."

Carnell stuck the barrel under Curtis' jaw and twisted it, leaving a small gash.

"Careful," Curtis said, "we don't want to have an accident, do we?"

"If I'd known you was such a talky bitch, I'd have got me another partner."

"You mean, like your last one? I found a femur out there while I was diggin' around the cabin. That wouldn't belong to your ex-cellie, by any chance?"

"I'll give you one thing," Carnell replied. "You are a clever sonofabitch. I guess it wouldn't hurt to satisfy your curiosity. Yeah, that's him. What's left that the animals didn't chew up. Crazy bastard spent half his life out on these Glades. Even claimed he saw your famous Pig Man once. He just chose the wrong person to help him get it out."

"I did wonder about that."

"Don't wonder too much. It ain't good for your health."

Curtis debated how to ask the next question without infuriating Carnell. The deeper into the Glades, the cockier he became. Curtis sensed a relaxing of tension in Carnell's gestures. He smells the money comin' to him, all right.

"You mind I ask one more question?"

"Ask away, friend Curtis."

"How come you couldn't move the gold yourself when you - "

" - killed him? You might say my luck changed sudden-like. That tether on my ankle back in those days was the real McCoy. It tripped an alarm the second I left the perimeter. Not enough time. This jungle was crawling with deputies, guns out, hollerin' 'Come out with your hands up!'"

"You messed up."

"Wait, I remember. You was just a dumbass patsy, took a fall, and did time. A crummy car thief."

Carnell laughed at his own cheap wit.

"You never did time in Raiford," Curtis said quietly. "Raiford's federal. What was it? Kiddie porn?"

"You ain't gonna get my goat that way, Curtis. Let's say I was making a withdrawal I wasn't entitled to."

"Bank robber."

"Got it on one."

"So you got it all timed out."

"To the minute."

"I see your charm bracelet's missing."

"My parole officer won't get the call I'm off the chain until quittin' time tonight. Trackin' system's different today. Now shut your pie hole before I give you another one in your stupid face."

The ground turned soggier, the brush thicker, and it was harder to see around curves. He deliberately maneuvered the vehicle to slew and sashay in and out of deep ruts. A couple times he throttled back, let the quad fishtail before the tires bit solid ground. A cattail whipped across Carnell's face. He jammed the barrel hard into Curtis' ribs.

"Happens again, I'll do you right there."

"Sorry."

"'Sorry' is a sorry word, my momma used to say."

The cabin came into view around the last stretch of open ground. The flies and mosquitoes settled on their heads and shoulders the moment Curtis took his foot off the gas. Columns of flying bugs twisted in filmy columns of light pouring down from the canopy of trees above them.

"Stop right here. Now get them bars loaded up."

An hour of sweat work. The biting of the flies and mosquitoes was intense. Carnell watched from the shade, drinking bottled water, as Curtis loaded up the wagon.

"That wagon's too heavy, it'll tip," he told Curtis. "Put a couple on the racks in front and back."

They started back.

"You go easy on the throttle, boy."

"You kill me, you sure you can drive this thing?"

"I'll manage."

"Never was any gold coins, was there?"

"Nope. I used the last of my stash to buy that gold coin from a pawn shop in Mobile."

Up ahead, the last curve where the ground was steepest.

"You thinkin' about it, but you better not try it."

Carnell set the barrel against Curtis' temple.

Hellfire. Now I'm gonna die for sure -

"You done good, bro. Now get us back and you just might live to tell the tale. Hell, I might even give you one of my bars for taxi service."

Curtis knew he was down to minutes. The knowledge was a block of ice in his belly. He was dehydrated, the profuse sweating had ceased as though his body turned off a spigot. Now his skin was hot, dry to the touch. His muscles were cramping up and he was having trouble focusing his vision.

The two trucks came in view as they drove through a last hardwood hammock, tall pines producing a light-dappled glade.

A Burmese python lay in their path sunning itself. A big one - at least seventeen feet.

"Goddamn snake in the way," Carnell cursed. "Clear it. Mind you, there's a gun on you every second and I can shoot a jackrabbit's nuts off at thirty yards."

"Shoot it."

"I ain't taking this gun off you. Think I'm a fool? Get out!"

Curtis got out and looked around for a branch or twig to hit the snake with.

"Quit stumbling around like a drunk!"

Curtis was thinking of taking his chances, bolting straight into the foliage when a piercing, familiar odor flooded his nostrils. Not the decomposing, steamy rot of swamp vegetation but a feral scent of a big animal.

Then he saw it. Or rather him. Pig Man.

About seven feet tall, half-hidden, a bristly face with a pair of menacing, stained tusks for incisors. Coal-black eyes staring at him.

Curtis leapt backwards, never heard the shot Carnell fired at him, but felt the slug sizzle the air past his head. A herd of wild pigs burst out of the path behind him and swarmed the quad, grunting and snorting. Carnell swung the wheel hard and gunned it, upending the quad and wagon. Gold bars spilled out. Curtis tried to get up but he couldn't move; his foot was pinned.

Carnell saw him when he came around the vehicle, gun in hand. The gold-tipped smile broader.

"I told you about them damn hogs out here."

Curtis turned his head, waited for the bullet. An eternity passed . . . but the shot didn't arrive.

Sounds of struggle, a muffled scream. Curtis craned his neck to see Pig Man lifting Carnell off the ground; then he passed out.

He came to, caught the glittering pattern of scales out of the corner of his eye.

The python wrapped itself into coils around the struggling Carnell. The snake around his neck, Carnell's gun hand was pinned and he was unable to shoot. Curtis saw terror in the man's eyes as he fought to keep the massive snake from winding more of its body around him. Then Carnell fell over with the writhing python and Curtis looked straight into Carnell's eyes. The snake bunched its muscles, elongated, and squeezed.

Carnell's face suffused with blood, his eyeballs almost popped from the pressure. A loud crack from Carnell's dislocated jaw sounded like a pistol shot. His body was covered in the snake's irregular green and yellow pattern.

Curtis rolled over and vomited. Time stopped. He heard bird cries overhead as the massive snake dragged Carnell's body from his view.

He knew he'd fainted twice; he wasn't sure. He was dying of thirst, which he thought was a better way to go than Carnell's. His last thought before passing out was that gators had a keen sense of smell for spilled blood . . .

* * *

"Am I under arrest?"

Curtis' arms were strapped down to the bed with restraints.

The doctors decided to amputate his leg at the knee. He'd been out there in the Glades too long - sunburned, dehydrated, devoured by insects, delirious from heat stroke, Curtis remained in the hospital recovering for six weeks. When the doctors released him, and the prosecutor decided not to indict, he moved out of his trailer and into an efficiency apartment in Belle Glade.

He stayed inside for two months until the incessant rain pounding the tile roof drove him half-crazy and he called an Uber for a ride.

"Haven't seen you in a while," Red said.

He pushed a glass in front of Curtis, filled it with rye, and drew a draft which he also set that in front of Curtis and stood there.

"I been busy," Curtis said without looking up.

"Yeah, I heard."

Curtis told the cops about Pig Man. The papers quoted the cops. He became a town joke. People wanted to buy him drinks just to hear the story. Red didn't move.

"Why don't ya'll go wait on those other two hundred customers you got in here and leave me the hell alone."

There was no one else in the place.

Without another word, the bartender headed back down to the end of the bar. Red put his bifocals on and picked up his newspaper.

Curtis took out his map. He'd drawn it from memory, lying in his hospital bed doped to the gills. The gold and Elton Carnell's body had not been recovered. Curtis knew if he could recover the missing ingots, he'd be rich.

The question was whether Pig Man would let him dig it up again from the hermit's cabin.

Curtis figured his problem was simple enough to solve - he needed a partner.

About Fiction

Sir Henry Rider Haggard

THE LOVE OF ROMANCE is probably coeval with the existence of humanity. So far as we can follow the history of the world we find traces of it and its effects among every people, and those who are acquainted with the habits and ways of thought of savage races will know that it flourishes as strongly in the barbarian as in the cultured breast. In short, it is like the passions, an innate quality of mankind.

In modern England this love is not by any means dying out, as must be clear, even to that class of our fellow-countrymen who, we are told, are interested in nothing but politics and religion. A writer in the Saturday Review computed not long ago that the yearly output of novels in this country is about eight hundred; and probably he was within the mark.

It is to be presumed that all this enormous mass of fiction finds a market of some sort, or it would not be produced. Of course a large quantity of it is brought into the world at the expense of the writer, who guarantees or deposits his thirty or sixty pounds, which in the former case he is certainly called upon to pay, and in the latter he never sees again. But this deducted, a large residue remains, out of which a profit must be made by the publisher, or he would not publish it.

Now, most of this crude mass of fiction is worthless. If three-fourths of it were never put into print the world would scarcely lose a single valuable idea, aspiration, or amusement. Many people are of opinion in their secret hearts that they could, if they thought it worth while to try, write a novel that would be very good indeed, and a large number of people carry this opinion into practice without scruple or remorse. But as a matter of fact, with the exception of perfect sculpture, really good romance writing is perhaps the most difficult art practised by the sons of men.

It might even be maintained that none but a great man or woman can produce a really great work of fiction.

But great men are rare, and great works are rarer still, because all great men do not write. If, however, a person is intellectually a head and shoulders above his or her fellows, that person is prima facie fit and able to write a good work. Even then he or she may not succeed, because in additional intellectual pre-eminence, a certain literary quality is necessary to the perfect flowering of the brain in books.

Perhaps, therefore, the argument would stand better conversely. The writer who can produce a noble and lasting work of art is of necessity a great man, and one who, had fortune opened to him any of the doors that lead to material grandeur and to the busy pomp of power, would have shown that the imagination, the quick sympathy, the insight, the depth of mind, and the sense of order and proportion which went to constitute the writer would have equally constituted the statesman or the general.

It is not, of course, argued that only great writers should produce books, because if this was so publishing as a trade would come to an end, and Mudie would be obliged to put up his shutters.

Also there exists a large class of people who like to read, and to whom great books would scarcely appeal. Let us imagine the consternation of the ladies of England if they were suddenly forced to an exclusive fare of George Eliot and Thackeray!

But it is argued that a large proportion of the fictional matter poured from the press into the market is superfluous, and serves no good purpose. On the contrary, it serves several distinctly bad ones. It lowers and vitiates the public taste, and it obscures the true ends of fiction. Also it brings the high and honourable profession of authorship into contempt and disrepute, for the general public, owing perhaps to the comparative poverty of literary men, has never yet quite made up its mind as to the status of their profession. Lastly, this over-production stops the sale of better work without profiting those who are responsible for it.

The publication of inferior fiction can, in short, be of no advantage to any one, except perhaps the proprietors of circulating libraries. To the author himself it must indeed be a source of nothing but misery, bitterness, and disappointment, for only those who have written one can know the amount of labour involved in the production of even a bad book. Still, the very fact that people can be found to write and publishers to publish to such an unlimited extent, shows clearly enough the enormous appetite of readers, who are prepared, like a diseased ostrich, to swallow stones, and even carrion, rather than not get their fill of novelties.

More and more, as what we call culture spreads, do men and women crave to be taken out of themselves. More and more do they long to be brought face to face with Beauty, and stretch out their arms towards that vision of the Perfect, which we only see in books and dreams. The fact that we, in these latter days, have as it were macadamized all the roads of life does not make the world softer to the feet of those who travel through it. There are now royal roads to everything, lined with staring placards, whereon he who runs may learn the sweet uses of advertisement; but it is dusty work to follow them, and some may think that our ancestors on the whole found their voyaging a shadier and fresher business. However this may be, a weary public calls continually for books, new books to make them forget, to refresh them, to occupy minds jaded with the toil and emptiness and vexation of our competitive existence.

In some ways this demand is no doubt a healthy sign. The intellect of the world must be awakening when it thus cries aloud to be satisfied. Perhaps it is not a good thing to read nothing but three-volumed novels of an inferior order, but it, at any rate, shows the possession of a certain degree of intelligence.

For there still exists among us a class of educated people, or rather of people who have had a certain sum of money spent upon their education, who are absolutely incapable of reading anything, and who never do read anything, except, perhaps, the reports of famous divorce cases and the spiciest paragraphs in Society papers. It is not their fault; they are very often good people enough in their way; and as they go to church on Sundays, and pay their rates and taxes, the world has no right to complain of them. They are born without intellects, and with undeveloped souls, that is all, and on the whole they find themselves very comfortable in that condition.

But this class is getting smaller, and all writers have cause to congratulate themselves on the fact, for the dead wall of its crass stupidity is a dreadful thing to face. Those, too, who begin by reading novels may end by reading Milton and Shakespeare. Day by day the mental area open to the operations of the English-speaking writer grows larger.

At home the Board schools pour out their thousands every year, many of whom have acquired a taste for reading, which, when once it has been born, will, we may be sure, grow apace.

Abroad the colonies are filling up with English-speaking people, who, as they grow refined and find leisure to read, will make a considerable call upon the literature of their day. But by far the largest demand for books in the English tongue comes from America, with its reading population of some forty millions. Most of the books patronized by this enormous population are stolen from English authors, who, according to American law, are outcasts, unentitled to that protection to the work of their brains and the labour of their hands which is one of the foundations of common morality. Putting aside this copyright question, however (and, indeed, it is best left undiscussed), there may be noted in passing two curious results which are being brought about in America by this wholesale perusal of English books.

The first of these is that the Americans are destroying their own lit-
erature, that cannot live in the face of the unfair competition to which it
is subjected. It will be noticed that since piracy, to use the politer word,
set in with its present severity, America has scarcely produced a writer of
the first class-no one, for instance, who can be compared to Poe, or Haw-
thorne, or Longfellow. It is not, perhaps, too rash a 'prophecy to say that,
if piracy continues, American literature proper will shortly'be chiefly rep-
resented by the columns of a very enterprising daily press. The second
result of the present state of affairs is that the whole of the of the Ameri-
can population, especially the younger portion of it, must be in course of
thouroughimpregnation with; English ideas and modes of thought as set
forth by English Writers.

We all know the extraordinary effect books read in youth have upon
the fresh and imaginative mind. It is not too much to say that many a
man's whole life is influenced by some book read in his teens, the very
title of which he may have forgotten. Consequently, it would be difficult
to overrate the effect that must be from year to year produced upon the
national character of America by the constant perusal of books born in
England. For it must be remembered that for every reader that a writer of
merit finds in England, he will find three in America.

In the face of this constant and ever-growing demand at home and
abroad writers of romance must often find themselves questioning their
inner consciousness as to what style of art it is best for them to adopt,
not only with the view of pleasing their readers, but in the interests of art
itself.

There are several schools from which they may choose. For instance,
there is that followed by the American novelists. These gentlemen, as
we know, declare that there are no stories left to be told, and certain-
ly, if it may be said without disrespect to a clever and laborious body of
writers, their works go far towards supporting the statement. They have
developed a new style of romance. Their heroines are things of silk and
cambric, who soliloquize and dissect their petty feelings, and elaborately
review the feeble promptings which serve them for passions. Their men
- well, they are emasculated specimens of an overwrought age, and, with
culture on their lips, and emptiness in their hearts, they dangle round the
heroines till their three - volumed fate is accomplished. About their work
is an atmosphere like that of the boudoir of a luxurious woman, faint and
delicate, and suggesting the essence of white rose. How different is all this
to the swiftness, and strength, and directness of the great English writers
of the past.

Why, "The surge and thunder of the Odyssey" is not more widely separated from the tinkling of modern society verses, than the laboured nothingness of this new American school of fiction from the giant life and vigour of Swift and Fielding, and Thackeray and Hawthorne. Perhaps, however, it is the art of the future, in which case we may hazard a shrewd guess that the literature of past ages will be more largely studied in days to come than it is at present.

Then to go from Pole to Pole, there is the Naturalistic school, of which Zola is the high priest. Here things are all the other way. Here the chosen function of the writer is to "Paint the mortal shame of nature with the living hues of art." Here are no silks and satins to impede our vision of the flesh and blood beneath, and here the scent is patchouli. Lewd, and bold, and bare, living for lust and lusting kor this life and its good things, and naught beyond, the heroines of realism dance, with Bacchanalian revellings, across the astonished stage of literature. Whatever there is brutal in humanity-and God knows that there is plenty-whatever there is that is carnal and filthy, is here brought into prominence, and thrust before the reader's eyes. But what becomes of the things that are pure and high - of the great aspirations and the lofty hopes and longings, which do, after all, play their part in our human economy, and which it is surely the duty of a writer to call attention to and nourish according to his gifts?

Certainty it is to be hoped that this naturalistic school of writing will never take firm root in England, for it is an accursed thing. It is impossible to help wondering if its followers ever reflect upon the mischief that they must do, and, reflecting, do not shrink from the responsibility.

To look at the matter from one point of view only, Society has made a rule that for the benefit of the whole community individuals must keep their passions within certain fixed limits, and our social system is so arranged that any transgression of this rule produces mischief of one sort or another, if not actual ruin, to the transgressor. Especially is this so if she be a woman. Now, as it is, human nature is continually fretting against these artificial bounds, and especially among young people it requires considerable fortitude and self- restraint to keep the feet from wandering. We all know, too, how much this sort of indulgence depends upon the imagination, and we all know how easy it is for a powerful writer to excite it in that direction.

Indeed, there could be nothing more easy to a writer of any strength and vision, especially if he spoke with an air of evil knowledge and intimate   authority. There are probably several men in England at this moment who, if they turned their talents to this bad end, could equal, if not outdo, Zola himself, with results that would shortly show themselves in various ways among the population. Sexual passion is the most powerful lever with which to stir the mind of man, for it lies at the root of all things human; and it is impossible to over-estimate the damage that could be worked by a single English or American writer of genius, if he grasped it with a will. "But," say these writers, "our aim is most moral; from Nana and her kith and kin may be gathered many a virtuous lesson and example." Possibly this is so, though as I write the words there rises in my mind a recollection of one or two French books where - but most people have seen such books.

Besides, it is not so much a question of the object of the school as of the fact that it continually, and in full and luscious detail, calls attention to erotic matters. Once start the average mind upon this subject, and it will go down the slope of itself. It is useless afterwards to turn round and say that, although you cut loose the cords of decent reticence which bound the fancy, you intended that it should run uphill to the white heights of virtue. If the seed of eroticism is sown broadcast its fruit will be according to the nature of the soil it falls on, but fruit it must and will. And however virtuous may be the aims with which they are produced, the publications of the French Naturalistic school are such seed as was sown by that enemy who came in the night season.

In England, to come to the third great school of fiction, we have as yet little or nothing of all this. Here, on the other hand, we are at the mercy of the Young Person, and a dreadful nuisance most of us find her. The present writer is bound to admit that, speaking personally and with humility, he thinks it a little hard that all fiction should be judged by the test as to whether or no it is suitable reading for a girl of sixteen. There are plenty of people who write books for little girls in the schoolroom; let the little girls read them, and leave the works written for men and women to their elders. It may strike the reader as inconsistent, after the remarks made above, that a plea should now be advanced for greater freedom in English literary art. But French naturalism is one thing, and the unreal, namby-pamby nonsense with which the market is flooded here is quite another. Surely there is a middle path! Why do men hardly ever read a novel? Because, in ninety-nine cases out of a hundred, it is utterly false as a picture of life; and, failing in that, it certainly does not take ground as a work of high imagination. The ordinary popular English novel represents life as it is considered desirable that schoolgirls should suppose it to be.

Consequently it is for the most part rubbish, without a spark of vitality about it, for no novel written on those false lines will live. Also, the system is futile as a means of protection, for the young lady, weaned with the account of how the good girl who jilted the man who loved her when she was told to, married the noble lord, and lived in idleness and luxury for ever after, has only to turn to the evening paper to see another picture of existence. Of course, no humble producer of fiction, meant to interest through the exercise of the intelligence rather than through the senses, can hope to compete with the enthralling details of such cases as that of Lord Cohn Campbell and Sir Charles Duke.

That is the naturalism of this country, and, like all filth, its popularity is enormous, as will be shown by the fact that the circulation of one evening paper alone was, I believe, increased during the hearing of a recent case by 60,000 copies nightly. Nor would any respectable author wish to compete with this. But he ought, subject to proper reservations and restraints, to be allowed to picture life as life is, and men and women as they are. At present, if he attempts to do this, he is denounced as immoral; and perchance the circulating library, which is curiously enough a great power in English literature, suppresses the book in its fear of losing subscriptions.

The press, too - the same press that is so active in printing "full and special" reports - is very vigilant in this matter, having the Young Person continually before its eyes. Some time ago one of the London dailies reviewed a batch of eight or nine books. Of these reviews nearly every one was in the main an inquiry into the moral character of the work, judged from the standpoint of the unknown reviewer. Of their literary merits little or nothing was said.

Now, the question that naturally arose in the mind of the reader of these notices was - "Is the novelist bound to inculcate any particular set of doctrines that may at the moment be favoured by authority?" If that is the aim and end of his art, then why is he not paid by the State like any other official? And why should not the principle be carried further? Each religion and every sect of each religion might retain their novelist. So might the Blue Ribbonites, and the Positivists, and the Purity people, and the Social Democrats, and others without end. The results would be most enlivening to the general public. Then, at any rate, the writer would be sure of the approbation of his own masters; as it is, he is at the mercy of every unknown reviewer, some of whom seem to have peculiar views- though, not to make too much of the matter, it must be remembered that the ultimate verdict is with the public.

Surely, what is wanted in English fiction is a higher ideal and more freedom to work it out. It is impossible, or, if not impossible, it requires the very highest genius, such as, perhaps, no writers possess to-day, to build up a really first-class work without the necessary materials in their due proportion. As it is, in this country, while crime may be used to any extent, passion in its fiercer and deeper forms is scarcely available, unless it is made to receive some conventional sanction. For instance, the right of dealing with bigamy is by custom conceded to the writer of romance, because in cases of bigamy vice has received the conventional sanction of marriage. True, the marriage is a mock one, but such as it is, it provides the necessary cloak But let him beware how he deals with the same subject when the sinner of the piece has not added a sham or a bigamous marriage to his evil doings, for the book will in this case be certainly called immoral. English life is surrounded by conventionalism, and English fiction has come to reflect the conventionalism, not the life, and has in consequence, with some notable exceptions, got into a very poor way, both as regards art and interest.

If this moderate and proper freedom is denied to imaginative literature alone among the arts (for, though Mr. Horsley does not approve of it, sculptors may still model from the naked), it seems probable that the usual results will follow. There will be a great reaction, the Young Person will vanish into space and be no more seen, and Naturalism in all its horror will take its root among us.

At present it is only in the French tongue that people read about the inner mysteries of life in brothels, or follow the interesting study of the passions of senile and worn-out debauchees. By-and-by, if liberty is denied, they will read them in the English. Art in the purity of its idealized truth should resemble some perfect Grecian statue It should be cold but naked, and looking thereon men should be led to think of naught but beauty. Here, however, we attire Art in every sort of dress, some of them suggestive enough in their own way, but for the most part in a pinafore.

The difference between literary Art, as the present writer submits it ought to be, and the Naturalistic Art of France is the difference between the Venus of Milo and an obscene photograph taken from the life. It seems probable that the English-speaking people will in course of time have to choose between the two.

But however this is - and the writer only submits an opinion - one thing remains clear, fiction a l'Anglaise becomes, from the author's point of view, day by day more difficult to deal with satisfactorily under its present conditions. This age is not a romantic age. Doubtless under the surface human nature is the same to-day as it was in the time of Rameses. Probably, too, the respective volumes of vice and virtue are, taking the altered circumstances into consideration, much as they were then or at any other time. But neither our good nor our evil doing is of an heroic nature, and it is things heroic and their kin and not petty things that best lend themselves to the purposes of the novelist, for by their aid he produces his strongest effects. Besides, if by chance there is a good thing on the market it is snapped up by a hundred eager newspapers, who tell the story, whatever it may be, and turn it inside out, and draw morals from it till the public loathes its sight and sound. Genius, of course, can always find materials wherewith to weave its glowing web. But these remarks, it is scarcely necessary to explain, are not made from that point of view, for only genius can talk of genius with authority, but rather from the humbler standing-ground of the ordinary conscientious labourer in the field of letters, who, loving his art for her own sake, yet earns living by following her, and is anxious to continue to do so with credit to himself.

Let genius, if genius there be, come forward and speak on its own behalf! But if the reader is inclined to doubt the proposition that novel writing is becoming every day more difficult and less interesting, let him consult his own mind, and see how many novels proper among the hundreds that have been published within the last five years, and which deal in any way with every day contemporary life, have excited his profound interest. The present writer can at the moment recall but two - one was called "My Trivial Life and Misfortunes," by an unknown author, and the other, "The Story of a South African Farm," by Ralph Iron. But then neither of these books if examined into would be found to be a novel such as the ordinary writer produces once or twice a year. Both of them are written from within, and not from without; both convey the impression of being the outward and visible result of inward personal suffering on the part of the writer, for in each the key-note is a note of pain. Differing widely from the ordinary run of manufactured books, they owe their chief interest to a certain atmosphere of spiritual intensity, which could not in all probability be even approximately reproduced. Another recent work of the same powerful class, though of more painful detail, is called "Mrs. Keith's Crime." It is, however, almost impossible to conceive their respective authors producing a second "Trivial Life and Misfortunes" or a further edition of the crimes of Mrs. Keith. These books were written from the heart. Next time their authors write it will probably be from the head and not from the heart, and they must then come down to the use of the dusty materials which are common to us all.

There is indeed a refuge for the less ambitious among us, and it lies in the paths and calm retreats of pure imagination. Here we may weave our humble tale, and point our harmless moral without being mercilessly bound down to the prose of a somewhat dreary age. Here we may even - if we feel that our wings are strong enough to bear us in that thin air - cross the bounds of the known, and, hanging between earth and heaven, gaze with curious eyes into the great profound beyond. There are still subjects that may be handled there if the man can be found bold enough to handle them. And, although some there be who consider this a lower walk in the realms of fiction, and who would probably scorn to become a "mere writer of romances," it may be urged in defence of the school that many of the most lasting triumphs of literary art belong to the producers of purely romantic fiction, witness the "Arabian Nights," "Gulliver's Travels," "The Pilgrim's Progress," "Robinson Crusoe," and other immortal works.

If the present writer may be allowed to hazard an opinion, it is that, when Naturalism has had its day, when Mr. Howells ceases to charm, and the Society novel is utterly played out, the kindly race of men in their latter as in their earlier developments will still take pleasure in those works of fancy which appeal, not to a class, or a nation, or even to an age, but to all time and humanity at large.

1887

NOTE: Haggard later regretted having written this essay - chiefly because of the negative criticism of his own work by critics who were believers in the new Realism/Naturalism. Nonetheless, his assertions that the love of Romance [in the old sense, as opposed to "Realism"/"Naturalism"] is both innate and ubiquitous - as well as being the proper mode for fiction - are important points.

"In the winter of 1886, as I remember very much against my own will, I was worried into writing an article about "Fiction" for the Contemporary Review.

It is almost needless for me to say that for a young writer who had suddenly come into some kind of fame to spring a dissertation of this kind upon the literary world over his own name was very little short of madness. Such views must necessarily make him enemies, secret or declared, by the hundred. There are two bits of advice which I will offer to the youthful author of the future. Never preach about your trade, and, above all, never criticise other practitioners of that trade, however profoundly you may disagree with them. Heaven knows there are critics enough without your taking a hand in the business. Do your work as well as you can and leave other people to do theirs, and the public to judge between them. Secondly, unless you are absolutely driven to it, as of course may happen sometimes, never enter into a controversy with a newspaper.

To return: this unfortunate article about "Fiction" made me plenty of enemies, and the mere fact of my remarkable success made me plenty more. Through no fault of mine, also, these foes found a very able leader in the person of Mr. Stead, who at that time was the editor of the *Pall Mall Gazette*. I should say, however, that of late years Mr. Stead has quite changed his attitude towards me and has indeed become very complimentary, both with reference to my literary and to my public work. For my part, too, I have long ago forgiven his onslaughts, as I can honestly say I have forgiven everybody else for every harm that they have done, or tried to do me."

Haggard - "On 'About Fiction'" from
The Days of My Life, vol 1 (1926)

Detection & Mystery

Being Section Two
of the Journ-E

SOME MODERN CRITICAL THEORISTS have [I believe correctly] asserted that *ALL* stories are Detective or Mystery stories of sorts. The tale is a "Case" presented for the Reader to "Solve." It is a search for the answer to: "What happen(ed)(s)?" The Author or Narrative Poet has laid out a trail of "clues," likely some background information to be discovered, and, quite possibly, some "Red Herrings" along the way.

And isn't it the case that we - as Readers; or the Audience of a told story or radio play or modern podcast; or the "Vidience" of a televised story or a motion picture or drama on a stage - are busy at work deciding how very sure we are about what the outcome is to be? Of course, we're elated when we find we've figured it out, *we're right!* and can tell our fellows, "See. I told you so," or we accept "defeat" by saying, "I didn't see that coming." Yes we are the detectives, drawn into the mystery (if it's well-wrought), loving the suspense and the mental, emotional, and vicarious activity on our quest for answers - our need for a "closure" of sorts and the "solution."

The genre of Detection & Mystery is quite broad and complex due to its many sub-genres. First of all, it must be divided by some distinction between Detection and Mystery. For the purposes of this journal, at least, we will distinguish the "detective story" and "detection" as any tale involving a central charater who truly takes on the role of detection - most often of a crime - either as a professional or an amateur.

A Mystery, on the other hand, is something a bit more broadly defined. Mystery narratives involve any hidden secret, which over the course of the text are revealed or discovered. A Mystery need not be focused upon a crime, merely some as yet undiscovered solution to a puzzle or secret or - literally anything that is as yet unsolved or unproven or undiscovered. The existence of Bigfoot is a mystery.

According to John Cawelti's study of the Detective genre, "The classical detective story requires four main roles: (a) the victim; (b) the criminal; (c) the detective; and (d) those threatened by the crime but incapable of solving it" (*Adventure, Mystery, and Romance: Formula Stories as Art and Popular Culture.* Chicago: U of Chicago Press, 1976:91).

Of course, there are several sub-genres of the story of detection that have evolved - either as reactions to the "classic" (what we may call the Poe-Doyle original variety of the detective story), or as attempts to expand that genre with fresh "MOs."

There follows a listing of the sub-sub genres of Detection that *JOURN-E* will be seeking:

1) **The Classic Detective Story:** invented by Poe with his seminal characters of Dupin and sidekick (usually sidekick narrator), formulaic plotting elements; perfected by Doyle with his Sherlock Holmes (the epitome) and practiced by many others, including Agatha Christie (with Poirot).

2) The Harboiled Detective: the more "realistic," "street-wise," imperfect (i.e. closer to "human") detective championed by Raymond Chandler, Dashiel Hammett, and Mickey Spillane and, more recetly, Sara Paretsky. The detective walking "the Mean Streets," most often a P.I.

3) The Police Procedural: as the name implies, the workings of the official police, the FBI, or any other governmentally sanctioned and supported law enforcement entity.

4) The Armchair Detective: Rex Stout's Nero Wolfe being the best example, remaining in his penthouse, hybridizing orchids, and letting his several helpers do the digging for clues and suspects. Then he applies his "Thinking Machine" capabilities to the solution of the crime.

5) The Amateur Detective: not a professional investigator or one who has chosen a career of detection, but one who, for whatever reason, becomes interested in a case.

6) The Accidental Detective: As we see in Buchan's *The 39 Steps* or in any story in which a person or persons become involved against their own will - usually becoming suspects themselves, finding it necessary to prove their own innocence by solving the crime by finding the real culprits.

7) The Closet Mystery/Detective Story: in which the crime, almost always murder, is committed in some secluded or contained space. Agatha Christie was a champion of this mode with *Murder on the Orient Express*, *Death on the Nile*, and others. **"The English Country House Mystery"** is a sub-sub-genre - the game of *CLUE*, or "Someone in this house is a murderer!" type of plot.

8) The Cozy: Christie with her Miss Marple is the primary exemplum of this sub-genre. Often, the distinguishing features are a small town or country village setting, an **"Unlikely Detective"** (itself, perhaps, a sub-sub genre like the "Locked Room Mystery," the absolute lack of any gratuitous sex or violence put right before the reader, it is an intellectual puzzle to be solved, ideally a "fun" or "comfortable" read.

9) The Occult Detective: investigators who specialize in cases of the supernatural or "abnatural" as Thomas Carnacki would term it. Dr. Hesselius through Seabury Quinn, Manley Wade Wellman, and many more.

10) The Spy Story and the Thriller: are close enough to these genres to be included. The latter, like the general "Mystery," is nebulous enough in definition (or lack thereof) to be a sort of "catch-all." The best definition we've found (from an online guide to Literary Terms) is - " *induces strong feelings of excitement, anxiety, tension, suspense, fear, and other similar emotions in its readers or viewers - in other words, media that* **thrills** *the audience*." << literaryterms.net >>

JACK'S BACK

by Marge Simon

ᛒLOODHOUND

Christopher Preston

$\mathfrak{A}$MONGST THE OVERGROWN PARKING LOT of a long-forgotten sugar refinery sat an ultramodern tractor-trailer, all black and baking in the sun. The trailer section was deployed, with its generator humming, satellite dish erect, stabilizers down, and bump-outs activated. The mobile command vehicle provided a stark contrast from the sea of concrete and weeds.

Inside the MCV, Agent John Tanner took a long drag of his cigarette while gazing out the office window.

In the distance, a cloud of dust signalled the approach of Tanner's target. A rust bucket sedan pulled off the road and crept toward the MCV. The car parked with their rear end facing him, Tanner figured for a possible quick getaway. It squealed until the driver killed their engine. Duct tape held a 'For Sale' sign on the car's rear window, obscuring whoever was inside.

"All right Sophie," Tanner said, turning to his European Consultant, who was sitting in one of the two guest seats. "Game time."

"Yah, I'm ready," she replied in an East-Low German accent while throwing back her blonde hair. "Not too long, though. My branch never involves the public. This type of exposure is risky for our operation. After this, no more detours."

"Only a few minutes for some clarifications about his story. I'll get the boy to bring him in."

Tanner extinguished his cigarette then turned around and opened a shelving unit's frosted glass doors. He pushed aside a picture of his son to pull free a baseball cap, it was embroidered with a New York Yankees logo. Nothing could conceal his bulldog-like features, but the hat covered most of the deep scar from an incident with El Chupacabra. His old wound was a distraction when he needed to appear friendly.

Sophie stood and pulled her seat forward to let Tanner and his gut squeeze out the office's door. Compared to Tanner, Agent Sophie Lehmann's demeanor was much more welcoming. Only her height was intimidating, resembling a seven-foot-tall porcelain doll.

Tanner entered the narrow hallway and marched past the MCV's crew bunks, kitchenette, washroom, and situation room to find one of his associates in the forward seating area. "Go grab our guest, and bring him to my office, please."

"Yes, sir," the young man replied while leaping to his feet and then disappearing out the man door to their right.

When Tanner re-entered his office, he sat down behind the dark-stained mahogany desk.

"Scheisse," Sophie said while searching around her feet, clutching a notepad in one hand. "My pen is gone. May I borrow one, please?"

He tsked, opened a drawer, and tossed her one, taking another out for himself. "You Europeans, always so unprepared."

Murmurs could be heard from the hallway. Tanner forced a smile as their associate opened the door, leading in a frail fellow. The man's suede biker jacket was much too big for him, and his jeans were thread-bare at the knees.

"Richard Bowman, I presume?" Tanner said.

He reached out and shook Richard's hand, pulling away after just a second. It took immense willpower to not cringe after touching the man's clammy palm.

"Yeah, that's me." Richard's bloodshot eyes darted around. "I'm feeling a little duped. Someone called me about my car. But you guys don't want my old wreck, that much is obvious with this slick RV you got here. You're all so fancy, too, suits and all. Except for that damn Yankees hat."

Tanner let out a small laugh. "These wheels aren't our most inconspicuous mode of transportation, but we're too busy to stay still these days. I'm John, and this here is Sophie."

Sophie remained seated but gave Richard a nod and a grin.

"We're just an interested party. Fans," Tanner said while leaning back in his chair. "And no, you aren't in trouble. Take your jacket off and make yourself comfortable. You must be a local, wearing that thing. We have some great air conditioning in here, but that Arizona sun is beating on us pretty good."

Their associate helped the man remove his tattered jacket, and then exited the room. Richard sat down with caution on the empty wooden chair. Looking across the desk at Tanner, he asked, "Do I need a lawyer?"

"As I said, we mean no trouble. Me and my friend here were just captivated by your story and wanted to know more," Tanner replied.

Richard rubbed his skull through a receding hairline. "Is this about the podcast? Because those conspiracy nuts forced me to say those things. And you still owe me the five-hundred dollars promised for my car, and I'm not giving you the keys."

"Of course, we'll pay."

He placed cash on the table, sliding it toward Richard. The man snatched it up, counted, then pocketed his pay.

Tanner continued, "it is about your interview, yes, so just indulge me. You'd be surprised what we believe. Did you really encounter him? The Pied Piper?"

Richard shifted in his seat, like his skin was crawling. "Yeah. Nobody believes me, but that's the honest truth."

"On the podcast, you mentioned meeting him as a child. Why only talk about it now?"

"I'd forgotten about it. The encounter. Or maybe I'd blocked it out. It was a long time ago, but, uh, memories have been coming back to me lately. Getting unlocked and taking over my every waking minute. Maybe the last five, six months."

Sophie shot Tanner a quick look.

Tanner pushed on. "And what happened back then? What can you recall?"

Richard looked around, seeming to land his gaze on artifacts behind the cabinet's frosted glass, then scratched his forearms. "Not gonna think I'm crazy?"

"Crazy is what we love most, Mister Bowman." Sophie's accent seemed to distract Richard from his itching.

"What you love… as just fans? That's all?"

"Exactly."

"Well, Ma'am, my family had planned a trip shortly after the Berlin wall fell with my grandpa, a veteran, to do some sightseeing. I was young, seven years old. While we were in a street market one morning, I heard a tune. Soothing, enchanting even." He raised a skeletal index finger and let it dance in front of his face while humming a soft tune. "Other kids heard it, too, and some scampered off to find the source. I joined them because I couldn't think about doing anything other than that. Some of them darted into an alleyway, so I did too. There were screams of parents, like mine and some others, from behind me. That's when I spotted him."

Tanner paused his notetaking. "The Pied Piper?"

"He's tall, taller than you." Richard pointed to Sophie. "Colorful, old-timey clothing. Sunken eyes that were a type of yellow or gold, and a gray beard. That flute in hand. His foot held up a sewer grate that all the other kids were jumping down into. I didn't want them to leave without me." Richard reached out with a hand to something invisible in front of him.

Tanner watched in mild amusement, letting the man find himself once more.

"Then I was struck by a car. A Volkswagen Beetle was crossing the alley. The flute man never came to get me, to take me with him and the others. I was left there to die. When I was found, they stabilized me and was sent back here with my family for years of rehab."

"One hell of a story. We've never once come across a single living victim of the Piper. For someone nearly a millennium old, he's continued to be very efficient. And on the podcast, you said he calls you, even now? And you still want to join him?"

"Yes… I mean, I understand the myths surrounding him from doing some reading. About the rats and so on. But whenever I think of him, I feel comfort. He's still in here, you know." Richard tapped his forehead with a thumb. "These thoughts are so powerful. Begging me to just start walking in some direction to find him. Maybe East? My wife doesn't get it, my kids neither."

Richard once again hummed some nonsensical tune. Perhaps, Tanner figured, the man was hearing something entirely different in his mind.

"You realize those children all died, and you would have, too… if he had gotten you. The Piper uses their youth to extend his life. From what we've witnessed, debt is still part of his schtick. Do you know of the debt your parents must have created with him?" Tanner leaned forward. "How did your folks come to afford such a trip in the first place?"

Richard itched his neck stubble while peering into Tanner's eyes. "Time to tell me who y'all really are."

"Just an interested party," Sophie reiterated.

Standing up from behind his desk, Tanner cracked his back and walked over to the trailer window. While staring out into the blinding midday sun, he replied, "We are part of an organization that doesn't exist. Hence, the lack of badges and branding. We're kept in the shadows, where the monsters also live, to keep people safe. More myths than you care to know are real. Some aren't as literal as the Piper, but sometimes they are. In fact, it's because of him that I signed on to this organization. He took my son almost eight years ago. My boy would've been studying for his driver's license by now."

When Tanner looked back, he caught a glimpse of Sophie's raised eyebrow.

"Oh, I'm sorry," Richard mumbled.

"The Piper moves around over the years when locals catch on to him. Always off to greener pastures. Well, he's here now. In America. We brought Sophie in as an expert from our European branch to assist in the hunt. Satellite footage, security cameras, any digital footprints all mean shit when trying to track him. That wizard has more than one trick up his sleeve."

"But, how do you know it's really him?"

"We have some of the best data analysts around. They were the ones who correlated stories of child abductions, and by the findings of young remains left in sewers. And now, by your memories being activated again. Frankly, I'm amazed how long-lasting and far-reaching his enchantments are. No wonder we've never come across someone like you."

The man's hands went up to either gaunt cheek. "Is he close? Where do you think he is?"

Sophie shook her head slight enough for only Tanner to notice.

He trudged on anyway. "Durham, North Carolina. Somewhere near Durham Bulls Athletic Park."

"John! That wasn't part of the - "

Tanner raised his hand toward the consultant, deferring her ire until after their guest left. She settled herself with a huff, crossing her arms.

Richard asked, "Why there, ya think?"

"Why not? We Americans love our baseball. There must be hundreds of prayers every night at that field. He hears those, you know. The prayers. The Bulls have been having a stellar season, shattering their slump."

"Are you going there, to North Carolina? Take me with you!"

"Okay, that's it." Sophie stood, and pulled Richard up off his seat. "We got what we needed. Your life is worth more than the call of that flute, Mister Bowman. Do not travel to Durham. Promise me."

"I… I have to go." He weaselled free and pushed the door open.

"Don't forget your jacket, Richard!" Tanner shouted.

Their associate handed off Richard's jacket as he exited. Tanner watched on from his window as Richard threw his jacket on while scampered down the command vehicle's entrance steps.

"You should not have told him anything. That was stupid. He's going to go to Durham, Tanner. You put him in harm's way," Sophie scolded.

"Is that so?"

She leaned forward. "He has a family."

"I did, too."

* * *

Miles from anywhere important in Georgia, the mobile command vehicle pulled into a private airplane hangar during the early hours before dawn. Several associates scrambled to close the hanger door, concealing their state-of-the-art equipment from the few hobbyists and employees scattered about the airfield.

The mud-caked vehicle came to a rest on the concrete. Its airbrakes emitting an exhaustive hiss.

Tanner and Sophie descended as a dozen staff buzzed around. He lit up a cigarette while walking, much to Sophie's noticeable dismay. Smoke trails escaped his nostrils on each exhale. They continued along the expansive floor to a projected monitor, which several technicians huddled around with laptops. A signal pinged over Memphis, Tennessee. It had a red trail that stretched back to Arizona. He watched as Sophie took in what was displayed, putting the pieces of his plan together.

She turned to him and asked, "is that Richard? You told me no funny games, Tanner."

"Our guidance systems don't mean a thing against the Piper. Now, we've got a good ol' fashioned bloodhound."

"You mean bait."

Tanner winked.

She turned to several others who were disembarking from the MCV. "Which one of you cowboys bugged the poor man's jacket?"

None responded.

He continued to explain, "Richard hasn't slept since leaving his home last night. Almost outpacing us. Once enchanted by the flute, that man became hopelessly and forever addicted. What he did with the information I provided is what he would've eventually figured out anyway. After all, no addict can truly be cured." He took a long drag of his cigarette, glanced at it once more, then flicked the butt away. "One man's struggle is another's opportunity."

"Opportunity for what? We already know where the Piper is operating."

He signaled for Sophie to follow him around to the other side of the monitoring station. There was something the size of several cars pushed together under a grey tarp. Tanner pulled the tarp off to reveal a drone. White and armed to the teeth with all manner of surveillance systems, and a row of red-tipped missiles. A predator.

"I just need him close enough for this to do its job," Tanner muttered.

"What? The Piper's case has been approved for extermination but that doesn't mean we can't try containment first."

Tanner scoffed. "Is this where I need to hear your branch's pitch on prevention awareness again? Just post a public sign. Sharks in shallow water. Turtles crossing. That sort 'a thing?"

"If people simply knew to stop asking for more than their lot in life, he would starve and die."

Tanner crossed his arms and leaned against the drone. "Or he'd just drop the pretense of granting wishes and go right to child-eating."

"Ah. So, don't even try then?" She appeared to start walking away, only to turn back. "And a drone? you said it yourself. Technology has no effect on him."

"But fire and brimstone from a height of twenty-five thousand feet will. These rockets are simple chemistry, no onboard guidance. Even the oldest monsters are susceptible. Once our bloodhound, Richard, sniffs out the target, I'm raining hell on him."

Sophie's eyes peered into Tanner's, looking for what he figured was conviction. "I was wrong, then, in calling Richard bait. A sacrificial lamb is more accurate. In the middle of a city, no less! Any collateral damage will go in front of the Internal Review Committee. They'll look at this through our charter's morality clause. I know, I've served on the IRC before. We banished the South-Asian branch's top agent for less. The Chief himself signed off on that one."

"This isn't my first rodeo, Sophie. I'm looking to save lives of thousands in the future. Richard's fate may be foreseeable but, as an addict, not preventable. Besides, you aren't putting enough faith in my accuracy. The evil being is my only target. I may yet surprise you."

"Giftzwerg," she said while rubbing her eyes.

Tanner laughed, patted her shoulder, and walked back to the monitoring station. He swiped a cold coffee from an empty table, sipped it back, and watched on as the dot crept toward North Carolina.

"It doesn't have to be like this, Tanner," she muttered, joining him again at his side. "There will be another way. His family doesn't need to lose their father. And when we do neutralize the Piper on our own terms, his spell will be broken. Prove to me that you aren't motivated simply by revenge."

To this, Tanner considered not responding at all. After a moment, he simply said, "Debts must always be repaid."

* * *

After half a day of preparation, paperwork, and debriefing of upper management, the agents loaded back into their MCV. Tanner's predator drone took to the skies. They accelerated back onto the main road to close in on Durham. Richard was somewhere ahead, having passed their position half an hour prior.

Tanner managed to get some sleep in the crew bunks. In a dream, he saw his son down in the sewers of Dublin. Donned in a little league outfit that sported a Yankees logo on its crest, the boy's favourite team.

His white pants were stained brown by sewage. An elongated hand took him by the neck, silencing a scream. Tanner tried to run forward but was stuck. The hand yanked his son backward, down the old sewer pipe until disappearing into shadows.

After jolting awake, Tanner tore the bunk curtain open to let in some light. He found his baseball hat beside him and gripped it between both hands. The closer they were to the Piper, the less Tanner could hold back images of what had been taken from him, and of what he wanted back more than anything. He bit his lip to quell a tremble.

Stumbling down the slim hallway as the truck bounced and swayed, Tanner slipped his hat back on and stopped at the kitchenette to run a single-serve coffee machine. Its brew was much warmer than the last, but bitter like tar.

The situation room was crammed when Tanner entered. Sophie and two technicians had their laptops out around an oval table. She was still in her suit, though it looked in need of a cleaning. Each of them with their backs touching walls that, whenever the MCV was deployed, would be expanded. The wall monitor hung on the inside wall, opposite two tinted windows. It showed their drone feed. Their predator was flying with its camera pointing straight down, buzzing by blocks of houses and buildings covered in shadows as dusk set in.

Sophie waited for him to get comfortable and log on to his computer before saying, "Guten tag, Tanner."

With a tip of his hat, he replied in a butchered accent, "Guten tag, fraulein. What's the latest?"

"First, you watch this." She turned her screen toward him. The video was queued up on the image of a frowning woman with frizzy, brown hair. A logo of Scottsdale News hung in the bottom right corner.

He leaned over and hit play.

The woman being interviewed identified herself as Donna Bowman, Richard's wife. After months of him acting reclusive, she was distraught about his sudden disappearance. Donna also mentioned the possibility of a malevolent force possessing him.

A reporter asked, "If your husband is listening, what would you want to tell him?"

"Please come home, Richard. The kids are worried about you. We'll just forget about all the fights. Just, come home."

The video switched over to an ad as Tanner leaned back. "Is this supposed to sway me?"

She studied him, as if looking for a crack in the foundation. "I wish you would just admit this is about revenge. Why did he take your son? What were you in need of that required making a deal with the Piper?"

"You said earlier that folks shouldn't ask for more than they're owed, right? Well, when is someone able to know exactly how much is truly owed to them?"

Sophie just stayed quiet, waiting for Tanner to elaborate.

"You might struggle to believe this one, Sophie, but I haven't always been the best at knowing the answer to that. I wasn't born to wealth. Just to survive, I learned to take." Saying this roused a smile from his cracked lips. "During a family vacation, I swiped a necklace for my wife from some jeweller in Dublin. She was elated, and I was happy to know that having a family hadn't made me soft. That I was still streetwise. Turns out, that whole district had employed the Piper's services to stop thieves in exchange for safe passage. And a full belly."

"Oh god," Sophie whispered. "Our branch had lost track of him in the UK a decade ago."

Tanner continued, "the Chief introduced himself to me one particularly rough night months later. He provided an opportunity for employment, and to maybe save others."

Feeling flush, he looked toward the two technicians who had stopped what they were doing to listen. They both swerved away from eye contact to bury themselves once again in data.

Sophie, however, stared right back, reminding him how stubborn Germans were.

She cut their silent pause short to say, "Richard is nearing the baseball field. I've activated an East coast fire team. The three of them are armed and undercover. They have linked up and will be able to intercept in two minutes."

"You what?" Tanner struggled to not scream. "Call them off. If they interfere, we'll lose the Piper's trail all over again."

"You let them get the visual, and we extract Richard before it's too late. Then, if they confirm no nearby civilians, you drop the ordnance."

"Extraction…" He sipped his coffee to calm pulsing nerves. "I'm not letting the Piper slip away. Not this time. And that fire team activation is coming from your branch's budget."

She nodded, then listened in on her earpiece. "I'm getting Richard through the audio bug loud and clear. He's hearing something. Something that isn't coming through with his voice."

After a few keystrokes from Sophie, the room's audio lit up with a ding. They all listened to Richard saying, "I can hear you calling. Please, let me join you."

The drone descended for a better view. One technician zoomed in and placed a red square around Richard for the monitor, highlighting that he had stopped at the baseball stadium's front steps. Richard's car had blocked part of the road, and frustrated drivers honked their horns while navigating their way around.

"How far out are we?" asked Tanner.

"Twenty, maybe twenty-five minutes," Sophie replied.

A new voice chimed in over the speakers, "Overwatch, this is Alpha One. We have eyes on the target. Do we move in to extract? Over."

One of the technicians placed a green square over a black SUV. They had pulled up just in front of a restaurant across the street.

Sophie tapped a comms key on her monitor. "Negative, Alpha One. Not until visual confirmation of Jackpot. Due to enchantment, they will not show on the drone feed. Your eyeballs are all that count. Over."

Richard's voice came back. "You were here... but not anymore. Close, but not here..."

The red square stayed on him as he got back in the driver's seat, pushing his dying car into the flow of traffic once more.

Their fire team's SUV pursued.

"Happy for our bloodhound yet? He'd already be gone, Sophie. The Piper always knows when we're closing in."

She said nothing, seeming to distract herself from another argument while bringing up all manner of maps and images. Minutes dragged by while watching the green and red boxes chase each other along the Durham Freeway. The last bit of sun disappeared, activating their drone's night vision.

Richard exited toward Duke University, winding his way through the campus streets with little regard for street signs or pedestrian walkways.

The mobile command vehicle swerved through busy traffic, closing in on Richard's position.

Tanner's empty coffee cup hit the ground and rolled between their feet while he remained fixated on the screen. "This is good. He's staying away from the dorms."

He hoped for an open staging area, like the gardens or Maplewood Cemetery that Tanner could see on their maps. The rusted Toyota continued forward, black smoke billowing out of the back as it slowed in front of the Duke University Golf Club. A public course, with sand traps and water features, like Sandy Creek. Heavily wooded.

"It's closed for the day," Sophie mentioned. "I cannot see any movement from groundskeepers or stragglers either."

"I can hear you calling me!" Richard shouted through the speakers in a glorious tone as he exited his vehicle. Richard hadn't seemed to take much notice of the SUV screeching to a halt fifty feet back, its occupants exiting.

"Overwatch, our line of sight has gone to hell. There's also something… a sound, like a screech. Switching to night vision for visual confirmation. Over."

Sophie hit her microphone once again. "Negative, Alpha One. This audio feed is not picking up any screech. Jackpot's enchantment will conceal him through night vision or infrared. You need to get in closer. Over."

The drone's feed continued to track Richard as he walked over a fairway. Tanner noticed a distortion of their high-definition picture start in the treeline that lay ahead of Richard's path. Faint at first, like ripples in a pond. It grew to bend and contort the trees, threatening to overtake Richard's red square as well. "He's there. Somewhere."

One of the technicians zoomed out the feed and highlighted a moving blue square. It was the MCV, barreling down US-501 alongside Sandy Creek.

"We're just on the other side of them." Tanner hit a nearby comms button on the wall. "Driver! Pull over and deploy."

The occupants all clung onto the bolted-down table and laptops, while the vehicle jutted right and slammed to a stop. Stabilizers dropped, leveling them off. The room expanded, giving Tanner a more comfortable distance from his consultant. Outside the starboard window, he hoped to see more, but could only make out gigantic pine and maple trees in the evening sky. They were as blind as their fire team.

"Alpha One, why aren't you catching up? Over." Sophie asked.

"We, we can't! It's our ears! Ah… piercing!"

"Sophie, they're done. Listen closely, we can also hear it now too." Tanner pointed toward the window. "Not through the speakers but outside. It must be the flute. Like an audible headache, keeping away unwanted guests. Richard's childhood enchantment must be allowing him to only hear the right tune."

"But how do we get him out now? Please, Tanner, work with me on this."

"We don't," Tanner conjured a softer tone. "His sacrifice now will either be just another victim, or instrumental in stopping that evil being."

"You did this! His blood is on your hands! I'll file the IRC complaint myself when we're through here. Why even tell him about your son? To just manipulate the poor man further?"

"No, Sophie. He was always going to self-destruct. I just felt he deserved to know what he was dying for."

"Well," Sophie winced and wiped the smallest tear of frustration from her left eye. "Maybe we aren't defeating evil at all. Maybe we're only transferring it. Absorbing it to ourselves, becoming like the things we share the shadows with. You steered him into destruction, no matter the noble cause. There were other ways."

"Overwatch, there's a kid! Some girl. She's running past us! Over."

Sophie looked back to her monitor. "Intercept, Alpha One. Get her out of there!"

On the monitor, one of the fire team members grabbed hold of the girl. Her screams to be freed could be heard over the audio feed.

"They won't be able to hold that child for long, much less any others that come. I'm already losing Richard's location in that distortion. We must fire now. There's a good two hundred yards between our men and the Piper. That's good enough." Tanner pulled up the drone weapon controls.

"And if he already has children with him?"

Tanner just continued staring.

"God," she uttered, putting her head in both hands.

Richard came through once more, though shrouded in static. "Yes, yes, it is you! I've waited so long."

Looking up, Sophie said, "that's... how can we still hear him?"

Tanner replied, "Tibetan monks blessed the pieces he's wearing for protection from sorcery. Sounds like it worked..." He paused, as did everyone else in the room when a new voice came over the speakers.

A growl.

"Nien...alt...lassen..."

"That's him!" Sophie shouted.

Richard could be heard sobbing as the Piper expressed guttural displeasure. After a few more seconds, the feed became almost inaudible with the sound of rustling.

"They've made contact." Tanner traced a target symbol in the middle of the distortion, where he could still barely make out the red box. "Sophie, tell the fire team to evacuate. Bombs away."

"No, John! The Piper is rejecting him. He's trying to turn Richard away! Maybe, if we just give him a bit more time, maybe they'll separate and then - "

"Firing!"

The German consultant shouted into her earpiece for Alpha One's team to evacuate as Tanner pressed the 'fire' key, holding back just enough years of anger to not send the keyboard through the table. Streaks of air-to-surface missiles filled his screen. He leapt from his seat, through the situation room's door, and burst open the MCV's outer entrance.

The first missile struck. Its explosion chucked out a concussive boom that shook Tanner's suit jacket. Followed by another, then another. Fireballs blossomed and reached upward, high above the treeline. Cars going in either direction on the US-501 screeched to a halt and slammed into one another.

Five missiles in all, levelling acres of land. The heat they generated made Tanner involuntarily scowl. Or possibly smile. And when the fire was gone, so, too, was the headache-inducing sound.

* * *

The sun was rising when Tanner entered the MCV once again. Running point on onlookers and first responders while his team cleaned up in privacy was always tiresome. Made worse by his dashed hopes to have been surveying the site himself. An associate helped him remove his jacket with the words 'Fire Department' stitched onto its back. He opened his office door. Empty. Tanner turned back to his associate. "Where's Agent Lehmann?"

The young man answered, "Oh, she left with the fire team, sir. Maybe two hours ago now. Also, the sewer gas explosion news reports you asked Danica in Media to procure will be pushed out for major outlets in thirty minutes."

"Thanks," he replied.

He closed the door and slunk into his leather chair, hardly believing what was in front of him. Atop his desk lay three objects that weren't there earlier.

The first object was a flute. Split open, with the upper half missing. Aged by hundreds of years and encrusted with black ash.

Tanner picked it up with care and studied its details. After a moment, it seemed to weigh heavier, gaining unseen mass. A thought came and went of him crushing it with his hands. Instead, he opened the enclosed shelving behind him and placed it inside, between a leprechaun belt buckle and the picture of his son.

Upon closing the cabinet's frosted glass doors, Tanner jumped at the stranger who stared back at him in the reflection. A man, but sickly white.

Golden eyes within deep-set sockets. Grey hair and beard. Rotten teeth that were visible in their snarl.

As quick as the image had appeared, it dissipated, revealing only himself. He spun around to find nobody else there. With his heart beating wildly, Tanner managed to mumble, "I hate magic."

After letting out a long exhale to steady himself, he returned his attention to the desk. Two items remained - a pen, the same one he let Sophie borrow days ago, and a folded note. He slid the pen into his drawer, scooted his chair in, and flipped the note open.

John Tanner,
Congratulations on purging the world of one more rat.
We recovered this artifact, and I could not think of a more fitting person to possess it. Other than that, the forensic team came across no other evidence of the Piper or, thankfully, any children. Only of Richard, may he rest in peace. Hopefully, your bombs were worth the cost.
I trust that this concludes your need for my services, and that I may be released from my contract to return home.
Kind Regards,
Sophie Lehmann - Consulting Agent of Foreign Affairs
PS - I have returned your pen so that no debt is owed.

A Defence of Detective Stories

G. K. Chesterton

On the detective story as a legitimate form of art.

IN ATTEMPTING TO REACH the genuine psychological reason for the popularity of detective stories, it is necessary to rid ourselves of many mere phrases. It is not true, for example, that the populace prefer bad literature to good, and accept detective stories because they are bad literature. The mere absence of artistic subtlety does not make a book popular. Bradshaw's Railway Guide contains few gleams of psychological comedy, yet it is not read aloud uproariously on winter evenings. If detective stories are read with more exuberance than railway guides, it is certainly because they are more artistic. Many good books have fortunately been popular; many bad books, still more fortunately, have been unpopular. A good detective story would probably be even more popular than a bad one. The trouble in this matter is that many people do not realize that there is such a thing as a good detective story; it is to them like speaking of a good devil. To write a story about a burglary is, in their eyes, a sort of spiritual manner of committing it. To persons of somewhat weak sensibility this is natural enough; it must be confessed that many detective stories are as full of sensational crime as one of Shakespeare's plays.

There is, however, between a good detective story and a bad detective story as much, or, rather more, difference than there is between a good epic and a bad one. Not only is a detective story a perfectly legitimate form of art, but it has certain definite and real advantages as an agent of the public weal.

The first essential value of the detective story lies in this, that it is the earliest and only form of popular literature in which is expressed some sense of the poetry of modern life. Men lived among mighty mountains and eternal forests for ages before they realized that they were poetical; it may reasonably be inferred that some of our descendants may see the chimney-pots as rich a purple as the mountain-peaks, and find the lamp-posts as old and natural as the trees. Of this realization of a great city itself as something wild and obvious the detective story is certainly the 'Iliad.' No one can have failed to notice that in these stories the hero or the investigator crosses London with something of the loneliness and liberty of a prince in a tale of elfland, that in the course of that incalculable journey the casual omnibus assumes the primal colours of a fairy ship. The lights of the city begin to glow like innumerable goblin eyes, since they are the guardians of some secret, however crude, which the writer knows and the reader does not. Every twist of the road is like a finger pointing to it; every fantastic skyline of chimney-pots seems wildly and derisively signalling the meaning of the mystery.

This realization of the poetry of London is not a small thing. A city is, properly speaking, more poetic even than a countryside, for while Nature is a chaos of unconscious forces, a city is a chaos of conscious ones. The crest of the flower or the pattern of the lichen may or may not be significant symbols. But there is no stone in the street and no brick in the wall that is not actually a deliberate symbol - a message from some man, as much as if it were a telegram or a post-card. The narrowest street possesses, in every crook and twist of its intention, the soul of the man who built it, perhaps long in his grave. Every brick has as human a hieroglyph as if it were a graven brick of Babylon; every late on the roof is as educational a document as if it were a slate covered with addition and subtraction sums.

Anything which tends, even under the fantastic form of the minutiae of Sherlock Holmes, to assert this romance of detail in civilization, to emphasize this unfathomably human character in flints and tiles, is a good thing. It is good that the average man should fall into the habit of looking imaginatively at ten men in the street even if it is only on the chance that the eleventh might be a notorious thief. We may dream, perhaps, that it might be possible to have another and higher romance of London, that men's souls have stranger adventures than their bodies, and that it would be harder and more exciting to hunt their virtues than to hunt their crimes. But since our great authors (with the admirable exception of Stevenson) decline to write of that thrilling mood and moment when the eyes of the great city, like the eyes of a cat, begin to flame in the dark, we must give fair credit to the popular literature which, amid a babble of pedantry and preciosity, declines to regard the present as prosaic or the common as commonplace. Popular art in all ages has been interested in contemporary manners and costume; it dressed the groups around the Crucifixion in the garb of Florentine gentlefolk or Flemish burghers. In the last century it was the custom for distinguished actors to present Macbeth in a powdered wig and ruffles.

How far we are ourselves in this age from such conviction of the poetry of our own life and manners may easily be conceived by anyone who chooses to imagine a picture of Alfred the Great toasting the cakes dressed in tourist's knickerbockers, or a performance of 'Hamlet' in which the Prince appeared in a frock-coat, with a crepe band round his hat. But this instinct of the age to look back, like Lot's wife, could not go on for ever. A rude, popular literature of the romantic possibilities of the modern city was bound to arise. It has arisen in the popular detective stories, as rough and refreshing as the ballads of Robin Hood.

There is, however, another good work that is done by detective stories. While it is the constant tendency of the Old Adam to rebel against so universal and automatic a thing as civilization, to preach departure and rebellion, the romance of police activity keeps in some sense before the mind the fact that civilization itself is the most sensational of departures and the most romantic of rebellions. By dealing with the unsleeping sentinels who guard the outposts of society, it tends to remind us that we live in an armed camp, making war with a chaotic world, and that the criminals, the children of chaos, are nothing but the traitors within our gates. When the detective in a police romance stands alone, and somewhat fatuously fearless amid the knives and fists of a thieves' kitchen, it does certainly serve to make us remember that it is the agent of social justice who is the original and poetic figure; while the burglars and footpads are merely placid old cosmic conservatives, happy in the immemorial respectability of apes and wolves. The romance of the police force is thus the whole romance of man. It is based on the fact that morality is the most dark and daring of conspiracies. It reminds us that the whole noiseless and unnoticeable police management by which we are ruled and protected is only a successful knight-errantry.

The Defendant (1901) is a collection of essays by G. K. Chesterton The essays originally appeared in *The Speaker* but were edited and revised.

Disinfected

John C. Mannone

Sky is still dark with cracks of light
when we arrive at the river. Fog
from after-rain mists the brackish
gray water and the amorphous shape
floating between the harbor pylons

just as the informant said.
The charred remains sloshes, waves
slap concrete; crabs latched to torso
clawing remnants of breast - someone's
lover, someone's daughter.

We grapple her body, drag it
to shore and into a plastic bag:
her nose, mouth, tinted with blood,
her insides exploded from flames.
Probably tortured before her body

was cast into swift water.
The ride to the morgue, silent, except
for the swish of puddled rain entrained
by tire treads - a static hush, perhaps
a lament for this young woman.

Body bag crinkles when it's unzipped..
Under fluorescent lights, the conflagration
didn't leave much that pallor. Mouth
gaped open, but taciturn. Only screams
of horror socket her eyes. I hear it

as if it were my own child's voice.
That night, in my bed, I lie still
unable to sleep, the stench
of bleach in my nostrils, my hands
shriveled from scrubbing, scrubbing

clean the blood that seeped out.
My own heart sutured by duty, my eyes
still burning from what they've seen
and from the horror they haven't.

All's Fair

Brandon Barrows

TAMARA LAY IN A CHAISE, slim, golden legs stretched before her. Her body gleamed in the sunlight streaming from the wide open sky and her white bikini startling against the tanned darkness of her skin. Beads of sweat covered her forehead, a trace of lipstick showed on full lips, and heavy sunglasses hid her eyes. Even with the sunglasses, it was a wonder she could stand to be out here on deck. The way she and Finlay drank the night before, I was surprised she could handle any light at all.

I clicked my tongue and turned to the railing. I didn't like it, but Tamara's overdrinking was a small price to pay for the things her money could buy. The ocean was not on that list, but her ship, a sixty-foot cruiser called the Texas Gal, was and I loved it. I loved being on the water, feeling the ship slicing through the blue-green water of the Gulf as easily as a hot knife through butter, and just as smoothly. The Texas Gal wasn't the largest ship around, but it was one of the most expensive and luxurious to call Galveston's Pelican Rest Marina home. Tamara took great pride in that fact, even though she didn't know a damned thing about the ship besides its price-tag. Still, I couldn't blame her; the Texas Gal was hers and it was her money that bought it. When money is really all you have, why not be proud?

Sea breeze played with my hair. Spray speckled my face. I closed my eyes, enjoying the moment, trying to push away the thoughts hounding me. Thoughts of Tamara…

"How much farther, Tammy?"

…and thoughts of murder.

Over the noise of the ship's engines and the sounds of the Gulf, Finlay's voice broke into my moment of peace. The hate and the rage roared back to the forefront of my mind. I turned from the railing and saw him standing on the other side of Tamara's chaise. His long, black hair blew in the breeze and still managed to catch the sun and send back sparkling highlights. His features were delicate, almost girlish, except for the perpetual five o'clock shadow he somehow maintained. He was barefoot and shirtless, wearing only a pair of white yachting slacks to show off abs that a steroid freak would envy.

I tried not to compare myself to him but it was difficult; Tamara liked her men muscular and young. I kept myself trim and fit, but Finlay was twenty-three and my last birthday was my twenty-ninth. Tamara's friends and household staff murmured and wondered at how long she kept me around. Her men's tenure was usually measured in months, but I'd been her "companion" for almost two years now, winning out over several competitors. Finlay was only the most recent.

Tamara ignored Finlay and shifted in the chaise. I looked her over again, trying not to be obvious. She admitted to being thirty-eight, which meant she was probably at least forty-five. She didn't look it. She could pass for thirty-five easily - maybe thirty in low light. Either way, I was quite a bit younger than her, but I knew it wouldn't matter if she decided that it was time for me to go. She was very wealthy and her attitude towards sex was more in line with the old playboy cliché than anything else. She never married and I doubted she ever would, just as long as her money could attract younger playmates. It made me a little ashamed to think of myself that way, but I had no illusions about what I was - or that my days were numbered. All I could do was hold on for as long as possible.

"Tammy?" Finlay whined. I hated hearing him call her that. I don't know why she tolerated it. I knew she liked the way Finlay looked, among other of his attributes, but what else could he offer? He couldn't hold a conversation that wasn't about sports or his work-out routine, and he pouted at the drop of a hat. None of it stopped her from adding him to her string. At least she hadn't moved him into the house yet, though, thank God. That meant I still had a chance, as long as I didn't hesitate.

Without turning to him, Tamara finally answered. "Soon, Fin, darling. Just be patient. I promise you, it'll be worth it."

She lowered her sunglasses and shifted, glancing up towards the pilothouse where Hanson, the captain she hired for the summer season, stood at the helm. Hanson noticed and waved, but she didn't return the gesture.

Tamara turned to me. "Jim, would you fix me a mojito? It's getting a little warm and we must still have an hour or so before we reach the site."

That's right; this wasn't just a cruise. We were headed towards the wreck of a Spanish ship discovered several years ago. It was long ago picked clean of anything valuable, but the wreck itself remained and made an interesting destination for divers. Tamara took me there last summer, showed me the wreck herself, and when it came up in casual conversation a few days ago, I could just see the jealously on Finlay's face. It gave me a warm glow inside, knowing Tamara and I did something together that he couldn't experience. It cooled when she suggested the three of us go back. As much as I hated it, I couldn't refuse or bow out. And then, last night, I got the idea... the perfect way to keep Finlay from Tamara and keep myself in the clover a while longer.

"If you're going down, Jimmy," - I winced when Finlay called me that - "I'd like a beer. Uh, a light beer." He glanced at Tamara, but she paid him no attention.

"Sure," I said, smiling and actually meaning it. Enjoy it, you little shit, I thought. You'll never have another. "One mojito and one beer, coming up."

I went below to the galley. I was almost finished with Tamara's drink when Finlay came into the tiny kitchen, walking on the balls of his feet like a fighter, unconsciously aggressive.

He slid past me and opened the refrigerator, found himself a beer - not a light one - pulled the tab, and then turned to me, raising the can in mock salute. "Down the hatch." He chugged, then wiped his mouth on the back of his hand, and belched.

"Couldn't wait?" I asked, not really caring.

"Nah. Wanted to make sure you didn't do anything to it." His smile turned derisive, then shifted into a sneer. "Why don't you just give it up, man? She's done with you, she just doesn't know it yet."

I finished Tamara's drink, put it aside, and poured myself an ounce of rum before answering. "We'll see," was all I said.

Finlay lifted his hand, palm open as if to shove me maybe, then thought better and lowered it. We were both fit and strong and twenty-nine isn't as old as he probably wanted to think. Instead, he sipped from his beer, slowly this time, keeping his eyes on me. He said, "You've had your time with Tammy. Longer than anyone else, I heard."

"So?"

"So give someone else a chance to live the high life, will you? Don't be greedy."

I laughed. I couldn't help it. Did he really think he could just talk me out of my relationship with Tamara, even such as it was? I didn't love her and I know she didn't love me - I wasn't that naïve - but I'd lived with her for a long time now. We enjoyed each other's company and I enjoyed her money. Plenty of relationships were built on a lot less and for much worse reasons.

Finlay's face scrunched up and turned red, like a kid about to throw a tantrum. He thought I was laughing at him instead of the absurdity of what he said. He crumpled the empty can and tossed it into the sink, then pushed past me. Before he left the galley, though, he turned. I waited, but he didn't say anything, just glared. Then he disappeared, headed back to the deck. I smiled and downed my drink, then picked up Tamara's mojito, and followed.

* * *

Between the bright, warm sun and the cool, blue sea I stood on the edge of the forward deck, enjoying the sensations of my body, not thinking, just feeling, and trying to keep my head clear. All the irritation of the last few weeks, since Tamara discovered Finlay, faded to background noise. I felt good, knowing it was almost over.

A light touch on my bicep broke the spell. It was Tamara. She smiled, the same tiny, smoldering smile she showed me when we first met. The same smoldering smile she gave Finlay these days. My pleasure of the last few minutes evaporated in the heat of the white-hot hatred exploding inside of me, picturing her smiling at him and what he said in the galley. Maybe, when it came to Tamara, I wasn't quite as detached as I believed.

"Enjoying yourself, Jim?" she asked.

I tamped the rage down and forced myself to smile back. "Always, as long as I'm near you."

"You're sweet," she said, flatly, as if it didn't matter one way or another.

The sound of the cruiser's two big engines changed, throttling down, becoming a soft put-put-put, then sighing and falling silent. The Texas Gal glided to a stop and began to rise and fall with the gentle motion of the Gulf.

"This is it, Miss Walter!" Hanson called.

Suddenly, Finlay was beside us, grasping the railing with both hands, excited. "This is it?" he asked, like an idiot.

"Yes, darling," Tamara said.

I looked down at the clear, blue-green water. The shadow of the wreck shimmered beneath us, hulking in its nest of sand and sargassum. This was a shelf area and the water was shallow, no more than thirty feet. When Tamara and I explored the ship, we used masks and flippers, but no scuba gear. She could swim like a fish and hold her breath like a pearl-diver. I kept up with her, but it was a struggle. I didn't know how strong a swimmer Finlay was, but we brought scuba gear for this dive, so my plan was risky. Everything would need to be timed perfectly. My heart twisted in my chest with anticipation and fear.

"Woooow," Finlay said, drawing the word out for several beats. He looked to Tamara. "We can just, like, go down there? Nobody owns it or nothing? Or anything," he corrected himself.

"Yes, darling. Free and clear to explore." Tamara smiled indulgently and tugged at the fabric of the swim-trunks he'd changed into. Finlay was like a child - and that was what Tamara wanted. Someone to rely on her, look up to her, give her all the power. I gritted my teeth.

"Jim will take you down," she said, surprising both me and Finlay.

My eyes met Finlay's for an instant before he broke it off. He began to whine, "But Tammy - "

"No, darling." Tamara put a hand on his chest. "I saw it once. That's enough for me. This trip is for your sake. I saw how jealous you were," - she glanced my way - "when you heard about it."

"I just thought - "

"Don't." Tamara put her finger to Finlay's lips. "It's not your strong suit."

She walked back across the deck, her hips swaying rhythmically, working with the motion of the ship rather than against it, and opened one of the on-deck storage compartments. I joined her and selected flippers and a mask, hoisted a tank and harness, then gestured to Finlay. "Come on. Get your gear." He hesitated, still pouting a little, then relented, his excitement at seeing the wreck overcoming his disappointment and jealousy.

A few minutes later, all geared up, we stood side by side on the deck, taking slow, deep breaths, oxygenating our blood, making muscles ripple and dance across our bodies. Tamara sat in her chaise again, watching us, approval plain on her face as we put on our little show for her. Take a good last look at him, I thought, fighting to keep the smile from my face.

I lowered my mask. "Ready?" Finlay glanced at Tamara, then nodded to me, and dove over the side. I clamped my mouth around the rebreather, counted to five, and followed.

The water enveloped me, closing over my head like a warm blanket. It felt good after the morning's sun. I oriented myself in the crystal waters and saw Finlay already on his way to the floor and the wreck. I kicked after him, sinking ten, fifteen, twenty feet, feeling pressure on my inner ear and little tingles inside my skull, while admiring the underwater world. Finlay was focused only on the wreck, making a beeline for it. I couldn't blame him. Even on its side, half-buried, covered in seaweed and black, yawning holes, it was impressive. For an instant, I imagined what it must have looked like, proudly sailing the Gulf in the days when Texas was just a dream no one even had yet.

I kicked harder and my flippers drove me forward faster until I was abreast of Finlay. He threw me a thumb's up, our rivalry temporarily forgotten in his excitement.

We reached the wreck. Finlay went one way, heading towards where the prow once was - now hidden in the sand or perhaps snapped off entirely - while I went around the stern. I lost sight of him and let myself simply drift for a moment before turning and moving up and over the broken deck of the ship. A colorful Dorado fish popped out of a hole in the rotting wood, surprising us both before darting away again.

There was time to kill. The tanks held about thirty minutes' air. I swam here and there, keeping close to the wreck, making sure I always knew where Finlay was. After a while, I felt the slight pressure in my lungs that told me my tank was running low, providing less oxygen. Finlay's would be, as well. I checked the pressure gauge; maybe five minutes of air left. I could hold my breath another five or so minutes if I had to, but I would still have to be fast if this was going to work.

I kicked gently, keeping tight against the wreck, and slipped across to the opposite side. It was only a few seconds before I spotted Finlay, engrossed in something that caught his eye through a hole to what must have been the captain's quarters. I hesitated, unsure if he was aware of me or not, and then the heavy heat inside my lungs reminded me that there was no time for uncertainty.

I kicked forward hard, throwing myself against Finlay's back, clamping an elbow around his neck and my legs around his, pinning both of us in place. With my free hand, I tore the rebreather from his mouth. Immediately he began to thrash and a stream of bubbles flew upwards as he tried, by instinct, to yell out or scream. That was good; it would make this all the easier.

For a moment, Finlay froze and I thought he was giving up. Then his body exploded into frantic motion, thrashing wildly, twisting in my grip like a harpoon-spitted tarpon desperately fighting for life while unaware that it was already dead. Finlay was dead because that was just the way it had to be. I wouldn't get a second chance if I failed here.

The younger man was fit, but I was learning that his muscles were mostly just bulk - for show rather than use. I don't know which of us would have won a fistfight, but in this kind of battle, he had no chance. All I needed to do was keep my elbows and ankles locked and wait.

And that's what I did, for long agonizing minutes, feeling the pressure in my own chest building, becoming more intolerable, even as Finlay's struggles grew weaker and weaker before finally ending altogether. Finlay stopped moving. For an instant, I thought it was over, then he made one last, feeble attempt to break my hold. It was no use. He was already too far gone and now we simply floated together, his long, sleek hair a black cloud engulfing both of our heads. I was no longer holding a man, though, only a waterlogged wreck.

I won, but time was almost gone. My tank was empty. There was ringing in my ears and I was lightheaded. If I didn't move soon, I'd be dead, too - but still I couldn't surface. Not yet.

I disengaged my legs from Finlay's, but kept my grip around his neck, and kicked my flippers, pushing the both of us to the side of the broken ship. While waiting out the tanks, I spotted what I wanted and now I wedged one of Finlay's flippered feet into a small, jagged hole near where a hatch to the forecastle once was. I released my grip; he floated upwards several inches then snagged, his ankle trapping him in a way that looked natural to me.

Tightlipped, I smiled and turned, kicking as hard as I could towards the surface. Blood boiled inside my brain and my chest felt like the weight of the entire ocean pressed against it. Suddenly, something inside me broke. Hard, driving spikes shot through me; my guts twisted and cramped. My vision grew dim and everything seemed far away. I panicked. I wanted a breath more than I ever wanted anything else in my entire life. I almost opened my mouth to take one, forgetting the empty tank, but part of my brain shrieked a different note than the scream for oxygen.

Tamara. One single word came to mind, along with a torrent of images from the two years we shared: things we did together, places we went, and my actions over the last few minutes to keep all those other moments from slipping away. In a way, this was all for her.

My head cleared. I righted myself, pointing my feet towards the Gulf's floor and my head towards the sunlight dancing on the waves above. It seemed miles away, but it was there and it was real and I was going to make it. There was no choice, just as there was none with Finlay. It couldn't all go to waste.

Finally, I broke the surface. Air streamed into my lungs. It was so sudden that it hurt as badly as the lack of air did. It was a good kind of hurt, though, the kind that lets you know you're still alive. I closed my eyes, breathing deeply, ignoring the pain and the weariness, just letting myself float.

When I regained enough strength, I swam to the ladder affixed to the side of the Texas Gal and hoisted myself up. I took a colossal risk to protect the lifestyle I was accustomed to, but I won. I was always a good gambler. Now, I just needed to break the news to Tamara about Finlay's "accident" and things would go back to the way they were - for a while at least. Even Tamara wouldn't dare look for a new boy-toy until after a suitable period of public mourning.

I heaved myself over the railing and onto the deck, exhausted and grateful for something solid under my feet again. I expected Tamara to greet me, but her chaise was empty. It took me a moment to spot her, up in the pilothouse - with Hanson. Their arms were around each other, reminiscent of how I dealt with Finlay, but their lips were locked together as well and Hanson's big, rough hands were roaming over Tamara's nearly-nude body.

A star went nova behind my eyes, red and fiery and as painful as my near-drowning. With everything I went through to rid myself of one rival, it never even occurred to me that I actually had two. Part of me wanted to rush up to the helm, tear them apart, and beat Hanson senseless. Maybe I didn't love Tamara, but she was still mine and I wasn't going to let anyone stand between us. Reality set in instantly, though. As angry as I was, there was nothing I could do right now. I was too weak, too spent.

Instead, I called out, "Tamara! Tamara! There's been an accident!" putting panic and fear into my voice, mentally adding, *"And there'll be another before long."*

The next one would have to be on dry land, though. I knew when not to push my luck. And besides, I like to challenge myself. Never in the last two years did I use the same method twice. Variety and innovation - those are the keys to keeping a relationship alive, after all.

Lady Parabellum

DJ Tyrer

Death moves with a graceful ease
Softest rustle of layered skirts
Beauty and style combined
In a lethal singularity
All it takes is a single shot
Skull fragments, brain brutalised
Death almost instantaneous
Riding a vicious shockwave
Body topples in a clumsy arc
As she pirouettes away
Mission accomplished, perfect
No sense of shame, guilt
Collects her assassin's fee
The incomparable Lady Parabellum

An Invitation to Our Friend, Professor Moriarty, from the League of the Damned

Max Jason Peterson

Put Moriarty on the guest list:
Our evening for the damned
Revels in diabolical plots,
Infernal minds, schemes grand.

Make Moriarty feel welcome
In his best brimstone suit.
He who'd rule hell must take a risk
Or risk getting the boot.

We're on the brink of something big -
Or a colossal fall.
Our web of lies sniffed out by one
Marked "Nemesis" to all.

Tell Moriarty he's invited
To our next soiree.
The underworld could use two heads:
Bring Sherlock's, he can stay.

Val McDermid - Reinventing Originality

Hunter Liguore

"Is THERE ANYTHING NEW TO WRITE? A voice from the back of the classroom asks. It's a serious question. All heads turn, including mine to see who asked it. It's the quiet kid, the one who comes to every class, homework always done, who rarely interjects a comment or discussion point. So the fact they have spoken means a lot.

I would love to just assure my creative writing student - and the whole class - that in 2020 there are still plenty of new ideas to explore and that the best writing is yet to come, it just takes a keen imagination. But as we discuss 'original' books, we find ourselves rather quickly knee-deep into all the copycat stories, the marketing ploys reinventing classics, the endless reboots, the ripped from the headline tales, and even the resuscitation of *Hunger Games*, coming this year as a prequel. My students groan and sigh and feel a bit hopeless.

Enter Val McDermid.

If you didn't know, Val McDermid is the author of forty+ novels, several TV series, plays, and radio shows, as well as a couple of nonfiction books too. She's been hailed as the "Queen of Crime," a title originally given to such classic authors as Agatha Christie. Earning the title means she had to have gotten something right in a genre that is not only highly competitive, but at risk for being cliché and redundant. Her books are far from either. In fact, she has a track-record of creating the unthinkable, making her an author to sit up and pay attention to.

Val McDermid was born on June 4, 1966, in Kirkcaldy, a linoleum industry town on the eastern coast of Scotland. Her grandparents worked and lived nearby in the coalmine district, where McDermid spent the summers, many of which inspired an early interest in the outdoors and a carefree sense of freedom that stayed with her and later informed her writing. Her working-class parents notably taught her the value of reading, taking McDermid to the library, where she cultivated a deep interest in all types of books and grew absorbed in them. She cites as her earliest influences in crime fiction as Agatha Christie and Ruth Rendell; one non-mystery influence was *Treasure Island* by Robert Louis Stevenson.

Growing up, McDermid's biggest role model was her cousin Senga who guided her interest in pursuing college and a career, as well as to follow her dreams to write. During high school, McDermid was active on the hockey team and debate club, and in her spare time, she played guitar and even performed at folk clubs. After passing her entrance exams, she pursued an English Literature degree at St Hilda's College in Oxford. An all-girls' school, McDermid cites this as the period she gained her independence from her family, as well as a connection to the world-at-large that offered a place for her to fit in and feel equal, especially in light of her own feelings of alienation as a lesbian. Notably, towards graduation, McDermid read Kate Millett's feminist classic *Sexual Politics*, which gave her a deep interest in feminism and later socialism, both of which go on to become foundations in her books.

Although McDermid always had an interest in writing, she was raised during a time that pressured her to pursue a career as a journalist. Out of college, she trained for two years in Devon, where she earned the Trainee Journalist of the Year award (1977), and later, spent fourteen years writing for newspapers in Glasgow and Manchester. During this time, she learned to make connections and gain access to people and locations in and around the news stories that she covered.

At the age of twenty-three, McDermid tried her hand at a novel, but ended up turning the idea it into a play, one that gained the interest of an agent and was later produced. Unable to replicate her success, she eventually lost the agent. It wasn't until years later, while she was working as the Northern Bureau Chief of a national Sunday tabloid, *The People*, that she covered the Yorkshire Ripper case and the Moors murders, allowing her to acquire real-life experience in how murders were solved. Ultimately, she grew disenchanted with the business and began to write her first crime fiction novel, *Report for Murder*, published in 1987 by the Women's Press; her fourth went to HarperCollins.

Val McDermid brought two very distinct characteristics to the 'new wave' of crime novels appearing in the 1990s and on. First and foremost, she crafted stories that contained social justice themes, specifically feminism and socialism perspectives, which hadn't been done much prior. *Report for Murder* redefined the genre by introducing the world to the first lesbian detective, a major milestone and contribution to the field.

In *Report for Murder*, Lindsay Gordon, the lead detective, mockingly describes herself as a "cynical socialist lesbian feminist journalist." After being let go from the *Daily Nation*, and loathing "popular" journalism, she finds herself unable to gain employment, until she's asked to do a free-lance piece on an all-girls' boarding school that leads to solving murders. She wrote six novels in this series, including one in 2003.

Challenging herself to write another series, in 1992, McDermid followed with Kate Brannigan, a law-school-dropout turned accidental PI, who worked as a junior partner for Mortensen and Brannigan in Manchester, England until she eventually goes solo. She's known for being a kickboxer, with a grandmother she cares for and a rock-journalist boyfriend that is also her neighbor. One for wisecracks and having a social conscience, she never gives up when trying to solve a case. There were also six books in total.

A decade later, McDermid introduced the world to DCI Karen Pirie, a member of the Fife Police Department in Scotland, who's assigned to a cold case that eventually leads to her working for and running the Historic Cases Unit. She's known for her compassion and empathy in dealing with the sensitive nature and violence attributed to cold cases. At the same time, she gives off a 'best mate' vibe, since she's down-to-earth and uses simple language no matter whom she's speaking to; she also likes to wind down with a Bacardi Breezer after work.

McDermid's signature-style was established through her ability to create crime stories that also gave visibility to women's rights and LGBT equality, and doing so in a way that wasn't perceived as heavy-handed. At the time McDermid introduced her openly gay, female detective, the crime genre was dominated by heterosexual male PIs. Besides the obvious parallels to her own life - journalist, feminist, political leanings, lesbian, covering an all-girls' school, like the one she'd attended - Lindsey Gordon, Kate Brannigan, and Karen Pirie gave readers protagonists "with brains who didn't need to call the guys in every time something difficult happened," as McDermid herself explained.

After three decades of writing crime novels, you might ask, like my student, was there anything new to write? Aside from bringing the mystery novel to the shores of the United Kingdom, and specifically her home country Scotland, McDermid is also regarded as someone who greatly advanced the genre byway of stories that involved forensics and criminal profiling. She did this through her next series, the one she's most known for, featuring Tony Hill and Carol Jordan.

The Tony Hill and Carol Jordan series focuses on two investigators with a relationship that is both professional and personal. Tony Hill is an anti-social, clinical psychologist and criminal profiler, who suffers from occasional bouts of dyspraxia. His own troubled and emotional past, stemming from difficult and abusive parents, surfaces and at times interferes with his work. His specialty is seeing patterns, especially with repeat offenders. Despite his oddities and off-putting nature to most, Carol Jordan, a detective chief inspector (DCI), finds him endearing, making them an interesting crime-solving duo.

Always challenging the genre, McDermid wrote *The Mermaids Singing*, the first in the series, which as a whole, was a deviation from writing a main character that was similar to McDermid's own life in any way, something she credits with helping her grow as a writer. It also offered another gender switch not common in the field, whereby the victims weren't women, but men, and the killer, (spoiler) turned out to be transgender, another pioneering moment that in McDermid's hands provided visibility to the discrimination facing transgender experiences.

Mermaids Singing

The story behind *Mermaids Singing* revolves around a serial killer, Angelica, who it's later revealed is a transgender woman, one that begins murdering the men she attempts to have relationships with, who won't return her affections. As the body count increases, Tony Hill begins to see a pattern in the case that he believes is leading him closer to solving it. Meanwhile, Angelica is really luring Tony in as her next victim. Although on the surface, Angelica demonstrates extreme violence, she also displays vulnerability through her desire and want for love, often showed through the frequent calls to Tony Hill for phone sex. In the end, Tony Hill is kidnapped; he uses his expertise in profiling to turn Angelica's need for love against her, in order to get free, and bring her to justice.

McDermid's portrayal of Angelica is similar to those found in the subgenre of Scottish detective fiction popular in the 1990s called, *Tartan Noir*. Said to be rooted in the classic novel *Dr. Jekyll & Mr. Hyde* by Robert Louis Stevenson, the subgenre catered to the complexity of good and evil, often depicted as an internal battle or struggle experienced by the characters - in this case, it's McDermid's killer, Angelica, who battles between the choices of love and murder, and even Tony Hill, who struggles with his own personal demons while actively engaging the killer despite the obvious risks. At the same time, the novel broke new territory by bringing awareness and understanding to the transgender experience, while simultaneously challenging perceptions and social norms on the stereotypes of gender and violence.

The success of *The Mermaids Singing* brought McDermid's work to a new audience and earned her second Crime Writers Association Golden Dagger. The next book in the series, *Wire in the Blood*, received worldwide attention and was turned into an award-winning TV series staring, Robson Green as Tony Hill. Though her novels are gender-bending and debunk sexual norms, they also have a strength in taking on social issues, like violence and crime, and more so, how they can be linked to the psychological struggles that underlay a murderer's motivation and intent.

A Place of Execution

Flexing her ability to create a masterful plot, Val McDermid's *A Place of Execution*, also redefined original in the genre by spinning two time-periods together to make a stand-alone crime thriller. It begins in 1963, where a thirteen-year-old girl, Alison Carter, goes missing and is believed to be murdered. The story then flash-forwards to the present, and to Catherine Heathcote, a journalist, who is writing a book on the case. Having grown up in the same village (Scardale) and lived through Alison's disappearance, Catherine remembers it well, especially the fear she experienced as a result of her parents and neighbors being much alarmed and on high alert. To complete the book, Catherine seeks out the detective that had worked on the case, George Bennett, now retired. Although Bennett brought a convincing case against Alison's stepfather, Philip Hawkins, who was executed for the crime, there were loose ends, including the fact Alison's body was never found.

As Catherine's book is finalized and about to be published, Bennett contacts her and insists she stop it from happening, giving no explanation. It's enough for Catherine to dig further, and even resorts to extorting a close friend to gain the deeper truth of the story. The more she digs, the more the mystery evolves, moving in and out of two periods, and the story-within-a-story through Bennett's case file and Catherine's book. The reader eventually learns (spoiler) that Hawkins had repeatedly raped and impregnated Alison, and that to protect her, the village came together to hide her away, while making it look like she'd been murdered, so Hawkin's would take the fall.

In classic McDermid-style, the book serves to elicit a conversation about the social construct of a tight-knit community and the lengths it would go to cover up a crime. It is also about the weight and meaning of guilt, brought on by violence, as its own form of punishment over the decades. Equally, McDermid's novel serves as a platform to show how the truth can be manipulated not only by the media (here represented by Catherine) but also the police, lawyers, courts, and then the village, that essentially creates its own form of 'truth' to exact a distorted type of justice.

Reception for *A Place of Execution* was positive, and earned McDermid the Edgar Award, the Dilys Award, and the Los Angeles Times Book Prize. The novel was also shortlisted for the Gold Dagger Award and was consider a notable book of the year by *The New York Times*. In 2010, it was made into a TV mini-series for ITV staring Juliet Stevenson as Catherine Heathcote.

The "Queen of Crime," known for crafting diverse characters and for making forensics and technology accessible to the public, has won countless awards in the field, including: the Crime Writers' Association Macallan Gold Dagger for Fiction; she also won it in 1995, 1999, 2004; she won the Crime Writers' Association Dagger of Daggers Award, 2005; and the Crime Writers' Association Cartier Diamond Dagger Lifetime Achievement Award in 2010.

Other notable awards include the Stonewall Writer of the Year, 2007 and the Pioneer Award given at 23rd Annual Lambda Literary Awards, 2011. In 2006, McDermid received the Portico Prize for Fiction, which praised the quality of storytelling and prose style in her work. In 2013, she was given two Honorary Degrees awarded by Dundee University and Northumberland University. In 2017, she was elected to become a Fellow of the Royal Society of Edinburgh and in 2018 she was awarded an honorary doctorate from the University of Bath Spa.

Today, when it comes to crime and forensics, McDermid is a household name. With new work on the way, she'll be hard to miss: like *Imagine A Country: Ideas for a Better Future,* released March 2020; a play called, *And Midnight Never Come* (2020); and a brand new TV series, *Traces* (2020); a new novel, *Still Life* (2021); she's also a regular guest on BBC Radio Scotland.

Back in my classroom, the quiet kid is impressed with the impact McDermid has made, not only to the crime genre, but to writing and social commentary, as well. While there are plenty of wheels turning in publishing that recycle stories that lack originality, there are plenty of authentic authors, like McDermid, willing to assert a higher bar, one my students feel motivated to reach.

As a whole, the classroom has a new, vivid look of inspiration and is ready to get started with the day's first writing prompt. All hail the Queen of Crime!

The Magic Portal

(for Sir Arthur Conan Doyle)

Frank Coffman

I know a gateway gilded round its edges
(Although the realm it opens to has many
And plainer entrances, and really any
Will suffice). The paving stones are pages
On which we walk a century or so
Back to the England of a grand old day,
Of London nights where gas lamps light the way
Where two friends venture - both Now and Long Ago.
And soon we see their silhouettes through the haze,
Or home at Baker Street beside the fire,
Upon a train from Euston, daring the Grimpen Mire,
Through fogbound streets by hansom, solving the maze
Each separate tale unfolds before our ken.
Sometimes it seems that our world is less real
Than the living place those pageway paths reveal.
It calls us back again - and yet again -
(Beckoned by magic wanded with a pen)
Again to wend out through that wondrous door -
The portal passed, "the game's afoot" once more.

Fantasy

Being Section Three
of the JOURN-E

THE GENRE OF FANTASY, moreso even than "Adventure proper," may be seen as the extension of the oral types of Myth, Legend, and Folklore into the "Age of Print." It directly presents the magical and supernatural and miraculous as "Real." For the genre of Fantasy (and for it's supernatural counterpart "Dark Fantasy" [a name sometimes given to Supernatural Horror]) the laws of the world - as we know it - must be broken.

But, as both George MacDonald and J. R. R. Tolkien note - men who were both creators and theorists on the topic of Fantasy - an invented world with different physical and "natural" laws may be invented by the

Dragon
by Marge Simon

human mind. But this newly invented and decidedly "different" world - what Tolkien importantly calls a "Secondary World," made by an act of "Secondary Creation" - must hold to its own invented laws and maintain an "inner consistency of reality" (Tolkien, "On Fairy-stories") or it cannot hold for us as readers or hearers of the tale.

Among the sub-genres of Fantasy, we may list several, some of which have decided "overlaps" or which have been variously enough interpreted and defined as to blur clear distinctions:

First of all, let us define two major divisions of Fantasy literature. First, the type commonly known as **Mythopoeic Fantasy** [from the Greek: "myth creating" / *mythos* and *poeia*]. This type, invented as most critics believe by William Morris and carried forward by such writers as George Mac-Donald, Lord Dunsany, J. R. R. Tolkien, and many others, presents tales that are sprung from an individual teller's imagination and - while perhaps owing something to traditional mythic, legendary, and/or folkloric antecedents for inspiration - are decidedly "created"/"uniquely invented" Fantasies.

A second major division is what the present editor calls **Mythomorphic Fantasy**. Again from the Greek: *mythos* and the stem *morph-* / "myth reshaping/retelling." This type of fantasy reshapes and approches traditional myth, legend, and/or folktale with the intention of recasting or viewing the tale from a different emphasis or point of view. T. H White, Evangeline Walton, John Gardner, and many others have used this mode.

JOURN-E is seeking work in both of these major divisions. But getting to well established sub-genres within the Realm of Fantasy, we may list:

1) Heroic Fantasy - Morrisesque, MacDonaldesque, Tolkienesque might be best indicators of a definition

2) Sword & Sorcery - pioneered by Robert E. Howard, advanced by such writers as Fritz Leiber, etc. (this would, perhaps, subsume such off-shoots as "Sword & Planet," etc.

3) Invented Fairy Tale (and other folk types: fables, proverbs, riddles)

4) The Tall Tale - traditional: Pecos Bill, Paul Bunyan, etc. OR invented: Robert E. Howard's Breckenridge Elkins, etc.

5) Science Fantasy - a blend, such as *Star Wars*: damsel in distress, "knights," a Black Knight!, battles and quests.

6) Surrealism and "Magic Realism"

7) Newly invented Comic Superheroes - keeping in mind the 6x9 trade paperback format of *JOURN-E* for the creation of "cells."

8) Epic Fantasy - ruled out from *JOURN-E* due to its necessarily lengthy nature.

9) Let the Imagination Be Your Guide.

Skullduggery

Scott J. Couturier

"**N**EEDED SOME SKULLDUGGERY DONE. Thought of you."

Ravadar glanced up from contemplation of his cup. The wine swirled in concentric circles, according to his will; he'd been 'meditating' thus for a long while, and the stink of drink rolled off him. "Good to see you, old friend. Or rather hear you. How is it you always find a shadow to lurk in?"

His visitor chuckled. "Shadows are a tool to me, as blades and quills are tools to others. Like attracts like."

"I suppose. How'd you find me?"

Another chuckle. "Shadows, my dear boy. Let's not belabor. I have a job for you - are you available, or not?"

Spoken with a hint of disdain, those final words. Ravadar stirred and rose from his stool, swaying as he turned to confront his guest. The rental was an old loft, ribs of in-bowed kah wood curling up to vanish in pitched darkness. No windows, no skylight. A cheap room, an invisible room, a room to get lost in. Now, irritation and venom stirred in him at being found.

"I don't need any coin. Owe allegiance to none and nothing. Not interested in killing, for pay or pleasure. Can't be swayed by threats - the gods have had done with me, as have the Fates, so there's no point in trying to curry favors. I keep my own counsel, care for no other's code. Having said all this, do you still have a 'job' for me?"

His visitor's mirth deepened. "I'd hoped to still find you a creature of principal, if nothing else. The task is easy - a mild act of mental coercion. I said skullduggery, not murder or rapine. As to pay, I leave that for you to determine. Surely a man who claims to desire nothing should have the opportunity to name his own price."

Ravadar swayed where he stood. Dark of eye and beard, despite his too-long years; lean and hale with sinew, though for centuries he'd walked with a slight limp, courtesy of a Tygar spear-thrust. His hands - huge and weathered, twining with scars - clenched at his sides, then uncurled, fingers trembling. "I want what you cannot give," he said with bitterness.

"Oh? Now you've piqued my curiosity. I insist you name the price, that I may accordingly balk."

Ravadar's black eyes flickered. "Oblivion. Unmaking. Destruction beyond any reincarnation or afterworld. I only cling to this life because what comes after will be worse. Tell me, Panquin, can you give me that?"

From the shadows, two azure eyes sparkled with intrigue. "My dear Ravadar, I think we can make a deal."

***

He stepped into the ether-trail and floated silently into the sky.

Veins of radiant energy latticed the firmament, a webbing by which the City could be traversed. One need only step into the luminous rays to be borne skyward, flesh tingling as particles of airy light caressed and permeated. The ether-trails were maintained by the Sages, as was the City; beyond the Edge all shone starry black. Ravadar knew those slum-crowded borders well, had been over the Edge more than once.

The City, as always, shone beautifully. A million windows blazed amid perpetual nighttime, glowing a kaleidoscopic spectrum which put the stars to shame. Ravadar savored his slow, soothing trip through the sky, riding the ether-trails one of few pleasures left to him. His fingers toyed with a flask in his pocket, but he resisted drink, reluctantly willing himself to honed sobriety. He'd hidden away in that attic room for ages, paying his rent and taking wine through a slot in the door. With his mind he roamed the City, sending out tendrils of sensory perception that transmitted back myriad passions and terrors, debauches and euphorias. He knew her of old...had been born in the City, true of so few. Most came when it was their time to come, went when it was their time to go.

Panquin's offer intrigued him. All he need do...it was too simple. A young magician, recently arrived in the City, had developed delusions of grandeur and was nigh-set to summon One From The Void. She (barely more than an initiate) had built an altar, and sounded on certain rituals long-lost to even the Black Keepers of Aü-Tai. The Name of the god was unknown to Ravadar, was unknown presumably to Panquin; learning such Names risked flensing the mind. Doubtless only an advanced state of insanity compelled the mage to even attempt such a ritual.

Ravadar's part in the operation was simple. He must botch her summoning. But, it must be done discreetly, via subtle powers of the mind. The ritual being disrupted by outside forces could draw the ire of the One...no, she must stumble in her incantations, stoke her braziers to smothering, draw her circle with whore's blood instead of virgin's. It was Ravadar's task to penetrate her mind and sow suggestions of error and doubt. Then, he need only sit back and watch as the god came to claim its undisciplined disciple.

He alighted invisibly outside her window at the height of a tall tower near the western Edge. The source of his powers was a mystery to himself. Immortal and inhuman, though he resembled a man externally, he never knew his parents. They came from Outside, vanishing from the City soon after his birth. He possessed a knack for magic, could smell change or danger in the air, read auguries in water or the idlest dance of flame. Hence, long ago he took to meditating on cups of swirling wine stimulated by his own willpower, seeing only his distorted, ageless reflection. Nothing to interpret, nothing to dread.

Crouched outside the mullioned window, he felt shame. Before going into exile he'd sworn to never again bend his magic to sordid ends. His time as Marjoda of the Thieves' Guild was legendary - most thought him dead, though several privileged informants kept him updated on the few matters his craft was insufficient to scope. This poor wizard-girl wouldn't be expecting him. No one would be expecting him, should he re-enter the City.

Ravadar sat on her windowsill for an entire long, night-shrouded day, observing the magician as she prepared her ritual. Small and humped of stature, one eye a blear of cataract, her name was Alurial. Skin black as always-midnight, good eye bloodshot and fierce, she bore the scars of fire on her body, on her mind and soul, a witch from some forsaken land where magic-workers were persecuted instead of revered. Coming to the City already mad, her insanity attracted opportunistic powers. The tome she bore about her laboratory was almost too heavy for her stout little arms, bound in some unidentifiable flesh, the pages wriggling with anticipation as she flipped them. Ravadar admired her work ethic, even as he contemplated how best to undermine it; she was a natural. Witches, as a rule, were his allies. Beyond a certain energetic sympathy, it always paid to stay on their good side.

By degrees, he wormed his way into Alurial's mind. Oblivion! It beckoned to him. Seven opposing Demon Princes had sworn stakes on his soul. Beyond his merely incurring their wrath, there was something special about it, something unique. Not a jewel of a soul - but a diadem, the Archrecki once told him. There were godlike beings who lusted for him, entities encountered in his astral travels - he felt them flocking in the void beyond the City like cosmic carrion birds, slavering for his death. So much was uncertain, even to one who lived for centuries, yet his damnation was assured.

Ravadar snapped back to himself, apt to engage in morbid introspection by both habit and inclination. The winds gusting up from the City bore almost-forgotten scents. Spices and offal and cook fires, grease and sweat and incense and blood: so much blood. The people killed each other for amusement now, in a place called the Arena. Grotesque modern decadence. Ravader wondered idly how he would fare on the arena floor. I could butcher the whole City for its own lurid sport.

Again, Ravadar's focus drifted. Alurial stumbled as she went about her work, mind uneasy with suggestions of incompetence. She dropped a vial of powdered foxglove, scuffed a sigil with her robe's hem. Her words became garbled, and a thick miasma of flies manifested in her laboratory, signaling the Outer One's displeasure. Even lost in bleak reverie, it was excruciatingly easy for Ravadar to affect her.

Why did Panquin care about Alurial? The question grew on Ravadar's mind. The organization he represented - the Shadow Watchers, Those Of The Velvet Glove. Of course, keeping Outer Ones ignorant of the City was a priority, but to call on him to handle it, offering the ultimate, impossible reward…. He shivered as he crouched on the windowsill, peering in at Alurial's degeneration. Blood and feces now wept from the walls, signaling the Other's mounting rage. The sorceress cried and gnashed her teeth to bloody shards, but carried on with her ritual, the book snapping as it squirmed and bucked in her grip.

The poor witch. Why him? And was this petty mental assault really the price of his freedom? Where was the nobility in it? Where was the nobility in anything?

Ravadar frowned as Alurial knelt before the shrine to her deity, a black hunk of meteoric metal exuding an oily sheen. Flies sloughed from the stone in gobbets; a chill reached Ravadar, and he knew the moment was near. Almost he reached out and rapped on the window. Perhaps he could save her, learn her secrets, nurse her back to health? He'd done it for other witches. Panquin wanted her dead, and that meant the Sages wanted her dead. She was beautiful in her own way. How long since he'd lain with woman or man?

Stirrings of desire and sympathy coursed through Ravadar, unfelt for ages, yet he maintained his focus. He watched as Alurial completed her supplications, raised the dagger and made her sacrifice. She drove the blade into her heart. But, the point slid between chambers - missed the killing blow. Alurial gagged as her own offered life failed to leave her. The stone trembled, gushing fly-fraught oils. A void opened above her head, a gaping window into nothing. Nothing, merciful Nothing! Ravadar beheld oblivion like a far halcyon country. He flung himself at the window, but too late: Alurial hurled into the onyx maw, her jaws flapping in silent lamentation. The Outer One's breath filled the chamber, frost flash-freezing over the panes. All the torches and braziers extinguished. Ravadar listened as the swarm of rimed flies fell to the tiled floor, going clink clink clink, like a sounding of chimes.

***

"You did well, as always. Thank you for coming out of retirement at my whim. You've put minds at ease that are best kept at ease."

Ravadar glared at the cluster of shadows concealing Panquin. He was back in his own cramped attic rooms. The cup of wine was empty, dashed to the floor. "I remember nothing. A room full of frost and dead flies. Empty clothing crumpled on the floor, a magician's robes. Why is it I can't recall the object of this commission?"

Panquin smiled, a crescent of filed white teeth leering in the dark. A velvet-gloved hand extended forward, holding an exquisite rose. One-by-one the petals withered, quivered, and fell, until all that remained was the twist of a thorny stem. "My dear boy! I'd think one of your lineage would realize memories so expunged are best left unremembered. There are always sound reasons for such things." He flicked the stem towards Ravadar, thorns catching on his coal-black tunic. Ravadar brushed it aside furiously.

"Enough! I've done your dirty work, whatever it entailed. Now I want my reward." His voice was high, almost hysterical; every hair on his body stood at prickling attention. There was something he yearned to remember...to know.

Panquin's ever-present smile widened. Azure eyes sparkled as he stepped from the shadows, revealing his body - a withered stalk of starlight-pale flesh topped with a bulbous, bobbing head. "Indeed. As you know, the Shadow Watchers never renege." As he spoke his mouth gaped open, revealing three concentric rows of needle-sharp teeth. "But, before the plunge, could I have just one little taste? All these years I've wondered, hungered, and soon you will be gone forever." He smacked his lips, displacing coils of drool.

Ravadar drew away from the ghoul in disgust, feeling a profound shock. Always, in their centuries of warm acquaintance, the emissary kept himself veiled in both shadow and mystery. Ravadar knew he was inhuman, but subhuman! "My blood is not for you, or the seven Lords of Hell, nor even the great Queen Spider herself to suck. Away, Panquin! At last you reveal yourself, a mere tomb leech. Tell me how you plan to satisfy my price, or - I'll slay you where you stand." His voice quavered as he declared this last.

The creature receded into darkness with preternatural haste. "Fool," Panquin hissed, saliva spattering the floorboards. "You have immortality, but only mourn it. Very well. Come to the Sages' Temple at moonstrike tonight, and I will show you the path to nonbeing."

***

Ravadar gazed up at the Temple's towering graven mount. The opulence of the City centered here, the Old Dead Gods eternally venerated; Ravadar had little use for gods. Conversely, they had ample use for him. Like demons they coveted him, yearning for his veneration, his obediance. He knew his incarnation in this body as a blip in some extraordinary energetic transformation - whatever he became at death infinitely more powerful than he-as-Ravadar, a revelation that alone infuriated him. He knew his individual ego would dissolve, but his essence endure, to be wracked on the devices of demon kings for aeons until being transmuted into some higher, superior form. This blurry god-aspect haunted Ravadar, living always in the chill of its imminent shadow.

He would die. Be beaten, tortured, eaten, excreted, melted, smelted, refined. Used as a generator, fed on, torn apart, reassembled. Cast into new forms, consumed again, shit out, brought to a purifying boil, the endless cyclical alchemy of reincarnate predestination. All to some unfathomable end - just contemplating it exhausted him beyond mortal reckoning.

Better to rest at death, to just cease. Oblivion. Ravadar's hairs prickled as he approached the Temple at moonstrike, mournful gongs sounding from precipice and concealed grotto. Skeletons on staves of wood and iron protruded from a lake of translucent azure water, candles lit in skulls carved with arcane symbols. The priests gathered at the lake's edge and waded into the water, splashing their nude bodies. A dolorous chant could be heard emanating from deep in the mountain, where the Sages congregated. All joylessness was gathered in this place - the incipience of death, even for gods, memorialized in monuments of ghastly funeral paraphernalia. It left the rest of the City free to a wild hedonism of sensation, death banished like an unwelcome guest from every home, tavern, market, drug den, and brothel. The City was old, older than histories could tell: but always it was the same. Full of displaced dreamers lost in an orgy of maniac sensation, drifting through eternity on a crumbling disc of rock. Beer and wine flowed from taps that endlessly replenished, and it was forbidden for lute strings to break. The smell of hashish and opium wafted from refined parlors of opulence, where those already displaced in time and space sought ever-more dimensions of riotous disorientation. People appeared, and people disappeared; some died in the City, others went on. Many that died suffered some kind of reanimacy, as Panquin evinced - but then, could it be called 'suffering' when most of the Sages' Council were undead themselves? Though, of course, none of them were ghouls…the lowliest of the low. Ravadar shivered as he remembered Panquin stepping into the light. Lowering his veil of invisibility, he proclaimed himself at the Temple's gate, using an alias he'd cultivated to allow him covert movement abroad.

The octagonal bronze doors of the Temple groaned open to admit him. Looking over his shoulder, Ravadar caught a final mournful glimpse of the City. So many lights, gleaming in the blackness…a million transient lives. Stay or go, live or die. It was the same to most. But not to him. Those born in the City could never leave the City, save by death. Those born in the City rarely - if ever - reanimated. Often, Visitors vanished in puffs of blue flame, or shrank to inconsequential flecks of indigo light, bound for their next dimensional interstice. Others died in body, only to return as withered, decadent mockeries of themselves, animated by agglomerate bits of soul and demon. Ravadar long ago grew weary of friends and lovers - the knowledge of inevitable loss (or, worse, uncouth return) outweighed the benefits of temporary companionship. Those few who were born in the City shunned each other, since they alone could nurse no hopes of escape. Only death, and the endless night of revelry and madness, awaited.

The doors shut with a rumble of metallic thunder. Inside, the Temple was lit by sweet-smelling braziers, narcotic gums smoldering atop coals of fragrant cedar-wood. The pantheon of Dead Gods were worshiped here, revered by myriad obscure and secretive sects. Walking invisibly, Ravadar skirted priests and priestesses of a dozen different orders as he navigated to the shrine of the Shadowed One. Set deep in the Temple, her donation bowl was always empty, her bust a miniature scratched in chert and placed in a rude alcove. Beside this representation stood a stunted door: beyond this door lay the lair of Those Of The Velvet Glove.

Ravadar bent and rapped at the door. It opened at his touch, though no one stood beyond. He bowed and entered cautiously, back scraping against a lintel blackened by old blood. It was the Shadowed One's nature to always maintain the upper hand. Gazing from obfuscation, unseen by mortals, she could act with impunity. As such, her devotees often worked for the Sages in the capacity of spies and informants.

Ravadar straightened, finding himself in a featureless square room with no other means of egress. Looking back, he was unsurprised to see the tiny door had vanished.

"You came - and right on time. I must say I had my doubts. Many is the immortal stricken with ennui, boredom, frustration, but most balk at the brink of self-destruction." Panquin's voice, resonant from the shadows as always. The glint of his eyes shone pale and obscured.

Ravadar frowned and spat. "I'm no moping lich, to be pityingly laid at rest. My life keeps my soul from a terrifying transmigration. Only oblivion can preserve me, keep me from fates far worse than death."

Panquin smiled now, teeth glinting with salivation. "I thought you said the Fates had done with you," he mused as he emerged from the shadows, swishing a soiled white cloak of interwoven funereal sheets. "Or, was that all just a bit of melodrama?"

Ravadar stood in mute frustration as Panquin wove about him, humming a low ghoulish tune. "You could still choose to stay," he cooed, with a bow and swish. "Come back to the City, bring her to life! I can assure you, things haven't been the same since your hiatus. They tell tales, but that's all they do. The Black Stone doesn't make a peep...I think they've even stopped supplicating it yearly. The time is ideal for your recrudescence."

Ravadar snarled. He made a lunge for Panquin, and the ghoul drew a thin-bladed rapier from a sheath at his thigh. He mock-attacked Ravadar, who parried forcefully with his forearm. The blade shrieked and shattered as it struck against his skin.

Panquin fell back, aghast. "That sword cost me four thousand ginka. Forged by a master, who was only in-City for a few months. Iä! You are a humorless opponent. Though, I never need wonder if tales of your indestructibility are exaggerated."

Ravadar allowed himself the faintest quirk of a smile. "I mulled over whether to return while sitting like a gargoyle out on that windowsill. To live again among humanity! But, my reappearance would prove anticlimatic. A slumped and sighing exile, wanting nothing, needing less...I no longer serve or oppose the Black Stone, have no thief armies at my command. A sad dullard, plagued by obscure cosmic verities that pertain solely to himself. I imagine some lonely nights out drinking."

Panquin's ever-present smile wilted to a sad smirk. "Poor Ravadar. It can be dangerous to learn too much of oneself. Perhaps, if you let me drink from you and you drink from me in turn, I could make you of the undead? It's been known to work on a Born, once or twice.... Whatever it is they value in your soul would become distorted, demon-shot. It's not a bad life," he added, with a flash of mandibles, "so long as you don't mind the diet. 'A ghoul's larder never empties,' as they say."

Ravadar shook his head. "Thank you, old friend, for all your efforts, but they are in vain. My course is set."

"Well then. Follow me to the Gate."

***

Downward they went by tunnels of rune-inscribed stone, the temple mount honeycombed with secret passageways, tombs, and grottos, some abandoned, but most attended by living sects of the Old Dead Gods. Ravadar avoided the place for centuries, preferring to deal with emissaries of the Temple when necessary, far from the endless moil of oblique ritual. Now, he felt the mount's weight over him, the voices of dead deities projecting offers into his mind. Some were robust of intonation, big and booming with command, while others rasped like corpses yearning from the grave for fresh blood. Others caressed him with lustful intentions, while some worked to dazzle him with Beauty; still others offered favorable prophecy or promises of power. Ravadar endured these overtures with acute boredom, shuffling the menagerie of whispers and bellows and carnal hisses to the back of his brain. Only one god was absent, devoid of supplication: the Shadowed One, she whose temple-close he now trod. Ahead of him Panquin led the way, bearing a torch of pitch for his benefit. The ghoul needed no light to see; Ravadar frowned, wishing the fiend hadn't abandoned his age-long pretense of concealment.

"When I hired you for this job, I hoped it would renew your taste for life," Panquin jabbered as they came to a halt outside a high onyx door. The ghoul made a few perfunctory motions, and the portal grated open, sifting clouds of dust from the cavern ceiling. "The City has grown so... dull, these last hundred years. No more flesh parades or art installations - well, at least none worth attending. I don't feel the Powers bring in good stock like they used to, and the Sages agree. Now, the ale tap is teat, and people have reverted to worse than animals. They are stupid children, in need of a good culling!" He smacked his lips as he spoke.

Ravadar listened to Panquin's rant in silence. He felt cold air blast over him as the onyx door yawned wide on nothing. Panquin grinned, motioning him onwards with his torch.

"Here we are - at City's root. I fear you must endure at least one more terrible epiphany before your unmaking."

Ravadar's head jerked up as the chill intensified, frost gathering in his hair and beard. "What are you babbling about? Just show me the route to nonbeing. That is all you need do."

"Of course. Traverse this last mortal threshold, and the next you cross will snuff the very light from your atoms."

Ravadar growled faintly, having long come to despise shows of cryptic ostentation. With powerful stride he pushed past Panquin, stepping into the lightless gulf beyond. The ghoul followed him with a wet chuckle, azure eyes glittering like sapphires in the torchlight.

Ravadar looked to him disdainfully. "I preferred it when you stayed to the shadows," he muttered. "Seems unnatural to have you bearing a light."

"Indeed it does. I act in accord with my goddess's will; afterwards I will snuff this torch and perform due flagellation. Ghoul - Lightbringer - feh!" he snorted.

"Glad we see eye-to-eye. What is this place?"

In response, Panquin set his torch to a bowl filled with flammable oils. An inferno roared to life, pushing back the blackness and allowing Ravadar to see the mouths of many other tunnels, opening on a vast chasmic space. Panquin lit another bowl, and another, revealing upwards-curving walls pocked with the gaps of ten-thousand passages, all terminating in this chamber of nameless darkness. At cavern's center stood a tremendous black door, lintel veiled in shadows the fires failed to dissipate. It stood apart from the rock walls, and if opened would seemingly reveal nothing but the chamber's far side. Yet, cold flowed from behind its onyx panels, pushing air outwards with a radiant menace. Ravadar knew instinctively this door opened on Nothing.

Panquin made a sweeping gesture, set his torch on the cavern floor and smashed it to bits. Immediately a patch of shadow generated to conceal the ghoul, and he sighed in relief. "Welcome to the end of your journey. I will excuse myself before you take the final plunge." His voice wheedled with grief, a final unspoken plea for Ravadar to reconsider his course.

Ravadar stared at the door, suffused by a well-known feeling. His mind flashed back to the frost-blasted laboratory. There was an excision in his mind, a void in woman's form. She paced and fretted and cast foul spells as he watched, voyeuristic; then - she was devoured! Made nothing. Nothing. A moan escaped him, and he lurched towards the door before pausing to peer back at Panquin, swathed in his medium of shadow.

"Why do so many passages end here? I've never heard rumor of this place, despite all my connections. That feeling, I know it. My mission - the victim was unmade, deformed into nonexistence. That's why I have no memory of her! It wasn't the Sages tampering with my mind. She just ceased to be, and all memory of her followed."

Panquin's azure eyes sparkled with mischief. "You have the right of it, old friend."

"And this place, that door. It opens on…."

"Nothingness. Completion. The serpent devouring, but disgorging no tail. The void that makes mere space weep - the very thing you crave most, Ravadar. Ironic that your sole remaining desire should force this revelation upon you, but the Ones From The Void are the living pantheon of this City. They, whose eyes are unmaking, whose breath is bane to all life, these lords of entropy alone can erase from existence that which Is. Alurial - that was her name - sought to summon One inexpertly, to bring Above that which must be kept Below. The Ones desire anonymity and dread. They were entrusted with the City, and would unmake it in an instant were they not bound by certain edicts." Panquin chuckled nervously as he stared at the black door, eyes quivering with unease. "All our lives exist at the grudging whim of life's antithesis. As to why so many passages end here...all gods have annexes in oblivion. Especially the Old Dead Gods. The City is many things; I cannot claim to know more than the most recently manifested Visitor in some respects. However, I do know it is an afterlife for gods. They come here almost as we do, but as a result of death rather than sudden physical transposition. And here they reign, gloried in crypt and temple-close...we, the people of the City, are mere pawns of the ghosts of gods. And they all serve what is beyond that door, hoping to postpone their own inevitable dissolution."

Ravadar shook from foot to crown as he absorbed Panquin's monologue. He'd long suspected...but, how could it be? The simple hearth-gods, the fauns and sprites of the few forested glens - his stomach lurched as he understood how desperately the very tissue of life yearned to maintain itself against non-being. And he, what was his desire? To claim as prize the most dreadful finality. He restrained a gulp as he turned to Panquin's shadow.

"I wish you had just brought me here in the dark. Your goddess, she dictated the torch?"

The ghoul shrugged amid his miasma. "It seems you are to be spared nothing, not even the bitterness of your reward. But don't look at me; I'm just following orders. You could have gone ahead and opened it. Instead, you had to ask questions."

Ravadar nodded, advancing a step towards the door. "Then I will ask no more. Farewell, Panquin."

The ghoul's razor-sharp teeth ground together, the only betrayal of his anguish. "Farewell," he hissed as he receded from the cavern with a whisper of funereal gauze. "And never more to meet," he added, wistfully.

Ravadar approached the door without fear or hesitation. It groaned open at his approach, and he was assailed by a black, seething, dread-laced euphoria. The wrath of the Void radiated towards him, rippling the air with ice-feelers which scoured Ravadar's flesh even as they summoned him onward, nerves atrophying at each caress. Cold struck to his core as the doors yawned wide on Nothing, an emptiness devoid of matter's promise, the quietude of absolute uncreation. Ravadar wept frozen tears as he came to stand on the threshold. He bent his legs and prepared to leap.

A light sparked amid the utter dark. Ravadar watched as the illumination drew closer, awe-struck. It was a woman's outline, defined in silhouette of searing white flame. Her face, one-eyed - he felt that he knew it. Alurial. The name flared in his mind, defined by fires of matching brilliance. He looked on in silence as her effigy came to hover before him, her lips curled in a wicked, insouciant expression of contempt.

"We were lovers," she intoned, "in some lives. Enemies in others."

Ravadar gulped, saliva freezing to slush in his throat. "And in this life?"

The great flaming woman chuckled. Reaching down, she seized the lips of her labia and stretched them wide, an abyss yawning between her thighs. "I am the mother of your unmaking," she crooned, fiery fingers reaching to stroke the hued spark of her clitoris. "Crawl in, Ravadar. Find your release in me. Find a womb infinite and sterile."

A thrill shot through him. Not fear - not bliss. Something more primeval. He bent his knees, grit his teeth, and leaped into Alurial's nether-emptiness.

This is it, he thought as he fell. Finally, freedom. The freedom of nothing after.

Blackness encroached on his vision. Alurial's cackle died in his dissolving ears. His brain shot off meteoric synaptic bursts as its hemispheres went dark.

Then, a blaze of bright hot fire. Not like Alurial's compelling, feminine flame - this energy was masculine, commanding, cruel. Ravadar shrieked as he was swept from the abyss by a colossal hand of living flame, like a trout snatched from Lethe's current. He wriggled as he was drawn up toward the single white-burning eye of the thing, a god-like entity of incarnate inferno whose flesh spewed geysers of molten alloy.

Ravadar quailed into a fetal ball. The flames danced around him, licking at his flesh and hair and clothing, but they burned without heat. A voice came into his mind like thunder, a ripple of brain-rending dissonance from which he extracted few discernible words.

I AM.........YOU AN ELEMENT OF I.......CANNOT ALLOW YOU. Ravadar shrieked and clawed at his temples as blood wept from

his forehead. NOW.......GO BACK.......THE CITY......THE CITY...
.....I AM........YOU AN ELEMENT OF I.........!

Horribly, Ravadar recognized a hint of his own intonation in these final words. He wailed as he was expelled from the doorway, across the cavern. The portal swung shut with a hollow roaring.

***

Ravadar, bruised and sullen, found Panquin weeping in a nearby passageway, much to the ghoul's consternation. Nevertheless, at seeing his friend alive he leaped up with a half-feral hooting noise and wrapped long, gangrenous arms around Ravadar's shoulders.

"You changed your mind! I knew you would. Thank you, oh thank you!" he burbled, glee animating his eyes with a phosphorescent effect. He hopped and capered for a moment before disentangling himself from Ravadar, who stood stock-still, flesh giving off roils of steam as it warmed. He stared straight ahead, mouth and eyebrows beset with intermittent tics.

"I could not go," he managed at last, the statement barely more than a gasp. "Not allowed."

Panquin's joyful grin folded down at the edges. "What do you mean?"

"I saw myself. Or rather, what I will become a part of, in far-future incarnations. I...would not allow me to unmake myself." Ravadar's voice cracked as he spoke. A despair of impotence, unlike any he'd known in long eras of dejection, swept over him, and he staggered to one knee. Panquin was beside him in an instant, though he made no move to touch Ravadar, already abashed by his earlier familiarity.

At length, Ravadar felt strong enough to rise. He waved aside Panquin, who was peppering him with vexing questions.

"No more! I need to clear my head. I need a drink." Reaching for the flask in his pocket, he found it ruptured by the extreme cold. "Dammit," Ravadar muttered, tossing the broken thing aside. "Well Panquin, it seems you will have your wish. At the eternal expense of mine."

Panquin tried to conceal his jubilation, with some success. Still, a tremor of joy ran through his voice as he asked, "Does this mean you will return to the City? Even as a dullard, with no particular interests or passions, you will still surpass most of this last generation by sheer dint of your legend! Oh, tell me it's so, Ravadar."

Ravadar sighed and stood, brushing the last vestiges of melting frost from his tunic. "I need a drink," he repeated, "and there's only one place to get it."

"The Crooked Candle?" Panquin's voice held a blush of awe.

"Where once I held court. The minstrels will be singing a new tune come dawnstrike."

The ghoul scurried in a circle, practically manic with anticipation, his veiling shadow barely keeping pace. "I apologize," he said as he slowed his antics, having fallen onto all fours. "I know whatever happened in there... if you need to talk...."

"There's nothing to say. Go, spread the word if you will. Ravadar has returned, but this time as his own master. Go!"

Panquin blanched, his shadow deepening about him to a roiling purple. "I must go whisper in some choice ears. But first: if ever you want for occupation, Those Of The Velvet Glove would be most happy to oblige. We'd even waive the modest membership fee in your case."

Ravadar's lips twitched, ever-so-slightly. "Already on the recruitment path? Most would be shattered to madness by what I've just endured."

"Exactly why my Goddess wants you. It took years for our shades to track you down...I don't want to lose contact again." The ghoul slipped forward, a patch of mobile shadow, and tucked a scrap of mummy-wrap into Ravadar's breast pocket. "My card. And remember, you can join without swearing fealty. The Shadowed One respects those who dare to spurn her omniscience - though, she watches them closest of all."

Ravadar nodded uneasily, watching as Panquin gibbered off into the darkness, practically screeching like a tea-kettle. A deep sigh wracked him as he lit a torch and made his way toward the surface, feeling out the correct passages via his mentalism. He walked unseen, brooding over this horrid chain of events. Panquin claimed to have hired him hoping he would re-engage with the City. Yet, his assigned task involved thwarting the very forces of his salvation. Was the ghoul in league with the Outer Ones to the extent of orchestrating this all to their design and favor? Or was Panquin just a pawn, as he claimed all beings in the City were? Fate, or capricious plotting? An old quandary. Ravadar wondered most mortals weren't driven insane by it.

He strode invisible through bustling masses of clerics. He watched them acutely, wondering how many knew the secret of the black gateway at their Temple's root. The Old Dead Gods were jealous...doubly so, since they already knew the humiliations of forgetfulness. The City was their last refuge, and they clung to it with ghoul's tooth and talon. He found himself chuckling at the hideousness of it all as he revealed himself before the octagonal gates to request their opening. For the first time in a century, he announced his real name.

His throat itched. He strode through the gates at a feverish pace, bound toward the nearest ether-trail. He'd just re-drawn his weft of invisibility when a blue light flared to his left, accompanied by the thudding sound of a body striking stone at high velocity.

Ravadar stared as the light diminished to a dull cerulean sizzle. Before him lay a young woman, black of skin and eye, her limbs hale with muscle, left leg pierced by a wooden spear. She was naked, body cut all over with minor lacerations. She moaned and rolled onto her side, revealing damage done by her impact. Skin scraped off against the cobblestones as she shivered and gasped, looking around herself with an expression of extraordinary fear and amazement.

Ravadar blinked, and banished his new-drawn veil. The woman gasped anew as he materialized, scrabbling backwards up against a stone wall. To either side priests and worshipers looked on with interest; while it wasn't uncommon for new Visitors to materialize in the City, it was rare to witness these manifestations. Most took place somewhere discrete, out-of-sight, but this woman - Ravadar drew back. She flickered and vanished, replaced by a writhing mass of purple protoplasm. The thing lurched towards Ravadar, wriggling several suckered pseudopodia. Then, it disappeared in a blue flicker, replaced again by the woman, this time even more terrified and disoriented. And no wonder - she had transposed with that thing, likely experiencing for a moment its native sphere.

Such mix-ups were rare with the Powers. Non-anthropomorphic forms of sentient life were allowed to linger in the City only under extraordinary circumstances. People came and went as part of some ineffable cycle; it was understandable that wires occasionally got crossed. Ravadar suspected his own parents of having been accidents, inhuman creatures that resembled humans, brought to the City by mistake and whisked away to their proper destination after his birth. But he - born to the endless night - he must remain here, forever at her bosom. Until death finds me, in whatever guise.

Kneeling down beside the girl, he worked to calm her. He relied on certain mental tricks, and within minutes had her breathing more easily, the fires of madness and desperation dimming in her eyes. He moved her into the privacy of a prayer alcove, shrugging off offers of help - and ignoring the whispers as word spread among priest and pilgrim of his announcement at the gate. Ravadar! Ravadar! The flame was already caught. He'd barely needed to stoke it. He secured a generic pilgrim's shift and helped her dress, explaining in even tones that she could understand him not because he spoke her language, but because everyone understood everyone else in the City, regardless of tongue. He told her about the City, and asked her her name.

She winced as he worked the spear-tip from her leg, Ravadar deadening her pain with subtle mental probes. "Shara," she answered at last, just as the bloodied hunk of wood slid free. "Of the Mari people."

"And who did this to you?"

A look of dread returned to her face, overcoming all his calming suggestions. "My own kin."

"Why?"

"They say I am a witch."

Ravadar's eyebrows shot up, and he dared a seldom-used smile. "And - are you?"

Her eyes flared as she looked away. But something in his demeanor caused her to look back, incline her chin and say, "Yes."

His smile broadened. "My name is Ravadar. Once this was my City. Now, I am but a humble resident. Nevertheless, I bid you welcome, Shara of the Mari people. You will be safe here." He bound her wound, took her hand and helped her to unsteady feet.

She took a few awkward steps, stumbled and looked to him oddly. "Once this was your City, you said?"

He nodded. "Yes. I ruled poorly, if you wish to know."

"But you rule no longer?"

Ravadar waited a long moment before responding. "We shall see," he said at last. "Now, come. I'll hire a rickshaw to carry you to a healer. Afterwards, I figure we could both use a drink."

Papilio Deiphobus

Emma Louise Wells

I fly solo
with charred edges,
scorched wingtips
as Icarus,
but mine are authentic,
not fashioned by man
mimicking nature
falling short
plummeting far
like Icarus
with waxy feathers
that melt, drip, burn.

Yet I'm resplendent:
Black Beauty league.

No sun touches me
I lay in shadow
mutely merging
there's no exposure,
silhouette free
I fade in darkness,
swallowed whole
as salty oysters.

Likewise I'm rare
 - a delicacy.

Collectors roam
searching for glimpses
longing to pierce my heart
with a pointed pin
pining to possess,
display in glassy prisons
where faces merge
drinking gothic spectacle
as a dwarf at a fair:
ridiculed,
squashed
deeper into earth.

Moonlight dapples my wings,
lace-covered as brides
ebony veins flow
gothically bloodied
like vampiric bats.
I'm nocturnal,
lost to day.
I slumber in shade,
graveyard corners
fluttering wings
nightmare-fringed
opening portals
for captured souls.

Red Admirals fly
on uplifts
sun-ray basking
as bees with pollen
stoking orange fire
dazzling deep.
I watch, death-stamped
amidst ivy-topped graves
as circus crowds draw.

I mumble, mellow
as monotone Mondays.

I'm incandescent
hooded as villainy.
Catch me, cuff me
pin me, break me
but I'll delude you,
turning to powder

a
black
dust
in
your
hungered
hand.

Mage's Adept Apprentice

- thanks to Ursula Le Guin's Wizard of Earthsea

Gerard Sarnat

Listening look on foggy face,
Old Speech of forest leaves
enchants our tinkerer's
mysterious domain.

To hear rainclouds blunder
slowly from side to side
in that fresh new snowfall,
one must remain silent.

Toward Sunreturn, simple
words of bread, water, sleep
and weather were heard
from the goatherd's alcove.

The Ever Barbarian

(For Robert E. Howard and Richard L. Tierney)

Charles Danny Lovecraft

Barbarian galleys churn the waters deep
And sounding as they thrash against the sides,
While up on decks those dressed in leathern hides
With eagle eye a constant vigil keep.
You, Scribes, see these as clearly as the dawn
That skewers day in brightest arrows sent
From bows of Hours around the great skies bent,
And say these roistering souls are merely pawn.

Still raiders come and mewling cities fall
Like decks of sorcerous cards that fates foretold,
And menaces remain as grim, as bold.
Hybori kingdoms and their war horns call
To arms the thrill that rippling muscles bear,
The fire of great strengths, and the flame of dare.

Narrow's Glade

John Dukes

An earthen ribbon at best
A rivulet's course once carved
Now a path for a wayward hart or curious soul
Destined never to return
Among the fallen leaves and needles
The footpath ever climbing like an ominous stair
Weaving through courses of ash and oak, spruce and pine

Past the old coppice, beyond the sounds of the road
To the silent glades
Where shadows whisper and kestrels rest
Where grey muzzled bruin stand watch
And sunbeams cast memories born
Of warlock chant and Walpurgis revel

In the ring, in the shadow lair
Are found forest runes carved
Already ancient when Empusa was spawned
From Hecate's foul triadic womb
Its masters bore ashen wands
Away from Mona's wasting
To the Summer Country of Madoc's memory

Songs forgotten, songs of Rhenish caverns
Portals to otherworld realms
A refuge from the hounds of Gwyn
From Morrigan spell and banshee screams

Through icy seas came Brendan's quest
Seeking beauty's memory in glades distant
In glades forgotten
In old rings buried in forest gloom

Elementals
[chained hay(na)ku]

Colleen Anderson

Golem
kneads bread
seeking a companion

Vulcan
pukes lava
soothing earthy turmoil

Undine
burps bubbles
swallowing sailors whole

Zephyr
sneezes hurricanes
after inhaling ghosts

Elementals
dream large
beginnings of transformation

Wandering Albatross

Jay Sturner

Outside the concern of human minds
where starry skies are the hum of consciousness;
where Time itself shuts an eye
in aquatic regions
beyond lighthouse and cove.

Where squids leap playfully across the moon
and harlequin ducks gather to gossip;
where sirens sing across valleys of wave
in enchanted realms
beyond foghorn and vessel.

Where kelp-haired fairies ride leatherbacks
and dead pirates haunt the bones of ships;
where the days are mine, and mine alone
in placid domains
between whale song and sun.

Where auroras serve their ancient purpose
and pelagic winds traverse the globe;
where I chose to be after my death at sea -
here, in uncharted waters
on gliding, spectral wings.

The Gods Do Not Pity Us

Darrell Schweitzer

The gods do not pity us because we know suffering and death.
They're jealous,
because we are truly alive and they are not,
because we can feel both sorrow and joy and they cannot,
because we embrace the world and taste all its flavors,
and they, mere abstractions nourished on sacrificial smoke,
cannot.

That is why they torment us and toy with us,
in an attempt to arouse those feelings they can never share,
and it is how we, when we live our short lives heroically,
or even hedonistically, defy them.
Because we can and they cannot.

Rowena's Map

Colt Leasure

THE SORCERESS KNOCKED on my door. I was reading the *De' nugis crialium*, a Medieval Latin work on Hell and its mythical inhabitants, when the sound of her interrupted me. I dropped the hardback, stood, unsheathed a knife I kept on the night stand, and crept towards the front.

Hoary bracelets were on my wrists to keep evil at bay. My favored maroon trench coat with a multitude of weapons which adorned the inner lining of the jacket hung on the wall. Pouches of herbs and salts were in its pockets.

I cracked the door open. The sorceress wore a three-ruffled ruby-colored dress and gold rings with red glass centers and v-shaped signets.

It was evening and the sun had lowered. The plains of New Mexico which surrounded my dwelling had chilled and taken on a cobalt hue as the moon peeked out when she came into my life in 1866.

"Give me your name," I said. "Why are you here and what do you want?"

"I am Rowena Lynx. I need your help."

"I don't drink, so look for rye at a saloon along the trail."

"Something of otherworldly value was stolen from me. I will pay you for your assistance."

The sound of a cloth bag rustled. I opened the door wider and feigned a smile to show her my front metal tooth, but still kept the blade clutched tight. Rowena dug into her small purse, and presented a few greenbacks in her palm.

"Come in," I said as I peered over her shoulder to make sure there was no one lurking in the rolling landscape before I shut the access. "Have a seat and tell me how dangerous this displaced item is."

She grabbed a chair in front of my dusty, cobweb-strewn bookshelves. "Why do you reason it's unsafe?"

"You approached me instead of the Sheriff and claimed the object was not of this realm."

"It's a chart which leads to wealth of all varieties. It helps me in my profession. I'm a mapmaker, and I help the diggers find life-changing fortunes, with the presumption they will ration their loot with me. If they fail to, I use other means of shifting their fates into terrible ones. I didn't have to share it with anybody, but I like changing people's lives around."

"Where did it go missing?" I asked as I took out a leather notebook.

"I awoke in my chateau near Sumner Lake and it had been taken from its casement. There's no need to make a list of would-be thieves. I do not know who did it, but I know where it is located, because I consulted an Oracle. She is the one who led me to you."

"So you want me to find and return it, since the prophetess did not offer its repossession as a service. How did you know where I was?"

"Stories travel fast. I've heard tales about you going into crystal caves and stealing the boots of giants filled with diamonds, how you roamed the forests of Hamburg and read every bit about the arcane arts in the Ravenscroft library."

"Campfire folk legends with some truth in them," I said. "I was raised in a house full of books by a woman who couldn't face the outside world without being overwhelmed by crippling fear, before it was torched by a Texas Ranger whose love was scorned by her. As an adult, my time in Louisiana was comprised of helping grieving family members connect with deceased loved ones."

"It's been told you were hired by the Freemasons to grow their power by carrying out their missions on the east coast."

"Maybe so, but such a task is different from what you are asking of me."

"Whoever did this yearned to keep their anonymity and they will not. What I want you to worry about is how to get the chart back to me. I have been able to find unknown phenomena since I was six years old, as though there is an unseen guardian directing me to the uncanny, but I cannot retrieve this one without you, since too many know who I am, but none are aware of you."

"Does it have a name?"

"Thoth's Guide." It's what I call it, anyhow, and the well-being of my family from here on out rests on the map. The gold rush was built on false hope and lies. Humans need help from the beyond for change. We are incapable of doing it on our own."

I found her statements alarming. Who was she to proclaim herself to have such a complete ceremonial cabinet as to wield the lever of Archimedes? I had met many a magus, had been exposed to countless systems of magnetism, cosmic and scientific. I had dealt with dream magic and heard apocalyptic ideas by seers who preached doom. Yet this was a new type of case to me.

"Where is the place?" I asked.

* * *

I made my way near the thief's house on horseback. I did not expect it to be a palatial manor. The home had patios, tree lined acequias, traditional arched doorways, and kiva fireplaces which were visible from unglazed openings. The estate was enveloped in Taos desert country, and it had a view of mountains from its clay architecture.

As I circled the property from a greater distance, I saw tetragrammatons drawn in the soil, Occult symbols I had read about in esotericism-based tomes by the famed poet Eliphas Levi. They were so small a passing wanderer would not have observed them, or may have supposed the ciphers to be nothing more than natural indentations of the earth, but they caught my eye. I knew they were not merely for protection, but manipulation.

"Halt," a gruff voice said from the rear of the residence.

I turned to the noise of the unwelcome greeting. My fingers graced the handle of the Navy revolver strapped to my side. A man stood on a perch with a large blanket draped over a massive box in front of him. The individual stripped the covering off and revealed a .58 Ager machine gun pointed at me.

"You dare trespass on Congressman Tygart Steed's house, stranger? You're a dullard, ain't ya?"

"I was not aware this place was his."

"Landmines are everywhere out here, boy. Count yourself lucky you're not a pile of molten flesh. Today's a good one for you, because I don't suspect you're lying. Your spiffy outfit tells me you got lost. Best leave, though. Safest way is to follow the marigolds out yonder. I don't want to clean the mess of your blown apart corpse later."

* * *

I waited for nightfall behind a lacebark elm tree and sought an opportunity to enter the place. Even if there were multiple protectors of the estate, there were inevitable moments where they distracted themselves from their assigned errands and fell into complacency, as all guards are prone to do.

Some of the candles were extinguished, and the bulky silhouettes of the men crossed the corridors. A carriage rolled near the front. A woman with blonde hair stepped out and was greeted in the courtyard and allowed in. She did not look like etchings of Steed's wife I had seen, and I made sure to take note of the late rendezvous with a description on my pad.

I performed reconnaissance for another few hours, and the air grew cooler. All activity in the house died. A white-tailed rabbit bounded away as I inched along a mound to get a wider view of the house. I belly-crawled into the square and went through a window ledge.

The main foyer was decorated with plush red lounge fixtures and white, translucent chandeliers. The scent of wax, grilled meat, and dust greeted me.

My foot struck something which jutted from the ground, and when I looked at the flooring there was a metal latch. I opened it and walked into a cellar. The nethermost chamber had collections and massive shelves full of wine bottles and statues of Greek origin, Apollo and dried out fountains of Cupid. Numerous chests without locks were in a row against the barriers, and I stalked around in search of the chart.

In the space was a rusted and feminine figure with oil which leaked out of her neck. The bust was blanketed in the sort of residual powder I had seen discarded bits of dynamite covered in on the Siege of Petersburg years earlier, when I was in the Army of the Potomac. Her curves were shrapnel from chunks of what could have been elevator safety breaks in tall buildings, an assemblage of steel parts inventors and architects had no use for anymore. The strangeness of her physique intrigued me, so I got closer.

She came to life and pummeled me to the ground.

I struck her under the jaw, but all it did was send a searing pain through my hand. I kicked her with my boot, and pushed myself off of her far away enough to stand, though it did not make her budge.

She slammed two hands on my shoulders. I was flattened out on the ground again with a punch to the gut. I turned over and she dug her knees into my chest. I was suffocated and my heart was almost crushed as I choked.

I snapped out a small bag of green balsam and threw it in her face. Its intended purpose of scaring off whatever demon possessed her did not have the intended effect, but it blinded the black marbles of her eyes.

I scaled the stairway and dove through the window as bullet fire cascaded behind me. I whipped around and saw Tygart Steed in his britches with a shotgun in his hands. Steed fired again. The ceiling above me exploded in dust as the Congressman shouted numerous expletives in my direction.

I fled into the night after I touched a few thin cuts I had sustained, sprinted to my horse, cut the bindings from the animal, and trampled across miles of brush.

I met Rowena at her house. Her place was hand-carved from Ponderosa pine and had Spanish colonial construction.

We sat outside with ice teas between us on a cedar table as the junipers around our meeting-spot shook in the wind.

"He saw my face," I said between sips. "I'm on wanted posters. I have to keep cloaked and hide. A bullet grazed my shoulder. Ol' snakehead whiskey cleaned it. It would have been helpful if you told me the thief was a prestigious man in the community."

"I would have if I'd known, but if I did I wouldn't have to pay you to investigate, now would I?"

"I have something new for you. Steed is being unfaithful to his wife."

"How does your little bit of slangander help me get back what's mine?"

"I can do one of two things to get it in your hands. I can threaten his crew with Trimble's. They are hangmen who were let go of their job duties due to how they would bully the damned on their way to the gallows, with torture and some of the foulest insults this side of the equator. Spectators could not handle the vulgarities. They are wild, and they will do our bidding with the promise of good pay."

"What's the second?"

"I tell him how I will bring evidence of his infidelities to the press here and abroad. He would lose approval by his Pentecostal denominations."

"You believe he would care?"

"Yes. He cannot manipulate the entire township."

"What if he slits your throat?"

"I would insure him how even if he killed me on the spot, the message is held by a source who would spread the word about his cheating ways should something happen to me."

"Why can't you go in there fully armed and take it by force?"

"He has a creature guarding it. It may be a Cauchemar - or a Sarramauca. She's a pale demon who stops the breathing of her rivals, and is kept together by elements of earth and man. My research shows Steed learned to conjure when he joined Order 322 at Yale University, a secret-elite. The usual remedy to harm her was useless. I will have to lure him out of his element and warn him of widespread repudiation. He bets at an illegal parlor at a bungalow on the Gallinas River. I need you to do something for me. I can get him away from the degenerate gamblers there, but I need you to pose as a lady-of-the-night. Convince the yellow-bellied scum to escape for a kiss. We will kidnap him to tell him our commands. It's the map in exchange for the saving of his reputation. His ego won't let him say no."

* * *

I hid behind a mass of spruces and gazed at the low house situated next to the shimmering waters. I spied on Rowena as she exercised her charms through a wide veranda near the front. At first, the two smiled at one another and drank. Steed smacked her on the top of the head. The Congressman and his allies dragged her out with her hands fastened. I crept nearer until I could make out his voice.

"This is the sorceress who sells those fraudulent elixirs at cattle shows," Steed said. "Search her for stolen goods. We should bury her in the Magadalena Mountains near Socorro and see if she can't fly away from beneath tons of lead ore. Let's cut out her tongue for trying to seduce me. A lie, all she wanted was strands of my hair to put a curse on my kinfolk."

They built a large makeshift tower out of sewn-together sticks. They bound her to it, drank bourbon, and drew sigils around her body.

"We'll have to light myrrh over her in Greenwood cemetery," one said with a cackle.

One man lit a torch as another pulled out a fiddle and played a jig called "The Devil's Dream."

I ran to them with papers in hand and screamed out for them to let her go.

The group aimed their revolvers at me.

"If you don't," I said with my eyes on Steed, "I will have witnesses come to report your liaisons with the brunette around the area. You'll never be forgiven. Redemption in anyone's eyes, a lawman's or higher, is a myth and you know it. Your wife will be aware, along with the newspapers. I don't have to let anyone in the township in on it. All we ask in return is the map you stole from Miss Lynx."

"You're fabricating," he said as he spit out a wad of chew. "I have the purest of Christian hearts."

I showed a charcoal shaded sketch of the man's mistress, and repeated the three locations he was last at with her.

"Shoot the falsifier, boys."

I drew my cap & ball 44. Caliber and shot at the head of the politician. It narrowly missed Steed and pierced a white fir behind him. All of the guards pulled out their weapons and squeezed their triggers.

The lightning of burnt gunpowder cascaded through the ether. The sky seemed to crack in two as I crouched for concealment, though there was little cover in the stretch of acreage. One of the enemy's fell in front of me, and I grabbed him and used him as a shield while I shot back at my opponents.

Trimble's gang came out from the hills. Their coats flowed behind them as they squeezed their triggers.

Steed chanted a phrase I had heard before, a few words in an archaic language.

The Cauchemar arose from towering dunes nearby as dirt sprang upwards. She resembled a locomotive with feet, her size much greater than when I had encountered her in the basement. She advanced and her arms swiped men aside as though they were nothing more than cloves and their wails pierced the night as they landed in thorn bushes and shattered bones when they hit the earth. The rusted giantess did scream as bullets lodged in her. Her forward attack did not cease as sparks rained from her torso and limbs.

I looked over and saw Steed control her; every move he made she was forced to emulate. It occurred to me what I had to do. I spoke a rhymed incantation to cripple her, a slogan engineered to rid this place of familiars. Her monolithic body became brittle and disassembled with my invocation.

The mechanical contraption sprawled on the ground, and with each motion it sputtered and clanked.

I dove behind one of the masses of metal, and tried to keep my head down below the edge of the new shelter as the sound of ricocheting covered the space. I peeked out and fired some more as Steed's gang started to gain momentum for a brief while before more of them fell with the advent of Trimble's people gaining higher ground near the bungalow. I whipped back towards them and bounded across while I reloaded.

A man tried to refill the cylinder of his pistol as he gawked at me, his eyes focused on my chest, where he clearly intended to put some cartridge ammunition. I threw a left hook at his face and he crumpled.

I looked over and saw Steed make a sprint at me. A saber was raised in one hand and his gun in the other. His eyes had pure menace in them. Smoke came from the barrel of his weapon, and it missed my left leg by a mere half inch as I darted out of the way of his blade when it was swung at my chin.

I brought a knee to his stomach, and struck the bottom part of my foot at his ankle. He fell. I shot him dead center. Blood blossomed on his front as he gave me a rage-filled look in his last few moments of life.

The rest of his men either scattered or perished, and Trimble's men let out celebratory shouts as they initiated their scavenging of the bungalow and wrapped those in ropes who survived.

I pulled out my knife and cut the bindings on Rowena's wrists. I searched Steed's body and found a pentacle painted on his chest with mud to futilely ward off bad luck. The map was tucked in the man's back pocket.

* * *

We stood on the deck of a casino boat and looked out at the Rio Chama canyon. The mesa was blackening. We had spent sundown playing cards with currency she helped me find with the guide.

"How did you make the monster die?"

"The spirit-pets a warlock creates are only as durable as its owner. He was inexperienced."

Rowena handed me a knapsack.

"What's this?"

"Gems."

"Don't," I said as the boat docked. "You've given me more than enough."

"I appreciate everything you've done for me, Mr. Aurelius. I want to make you a rich man for your troubles."

"Make yourself wealthier."

"If you stay with me, we can bribe the officials around here to get rid of your wanted status. We can use the guide well."

I stared out and said, "I've won my hands here and shouldn't press my luck. I did more than break even. Those who get too comfortable in one place become defenseless. You take care, Miss Lynx."

I tipped my hat and made my way to the boardwalk.

Godmother-Plex

Claire Davon

THE PLUMP WINGED WOMAN might have been innocuous if she weren't hovering three feet off the ground - and pointing a wand. A girl stood in front of her by the lockers. Before them was a human sized frog dressed in a school uniform slumping to the vinyl floor.

"You do as I say from now on or that's what will happen to all of you." She pronounced that as "zat", speaking with a slight accent that sounded French.

The creature that used to be Robbie let out a ribbit, his protruding eyes flicking around the gathered teens. His tormentor gestured to the woman behind her. He transformed into his normal form, a final croak lingering in the air. Robbie turned his hands over before grabbing his backpack and dashing off. Derisive laughter trailed behind him. His brief time as a frog would not be forgotten. He would be the butt of jokes for a long time - maybe the entirety of his high school career.

"That's right, run," the girl said and glanced around at the teens who surrounded her. "I've got a fairy godmother. Things are going to be different around here."

Lillie stopped, clutching at her backpack. The girl was about her height, with the kind of brown hair that came from regular salon visits and a lot of expensive product. Or a helper who kept it that way.

The bell rang, reminding them they had only a few minutes to get to their destination.

"Hey. You there. What are you staring at?" The French accent left Lillie no doubt who was talking.

Lillie glanced around but the kids shifted their gazes, afraid that they'd be next on the reptile brigade. Or…no…frogs were amphibians.

The idea of retrieving her book abandoned, Lillie shrugged. "My locker. That lady is blocking it."

The students who gathered around the new girl snickered. Lillie recognized them as Roberta, a girl she'd associated with since fifth grade, as well as her best friend Doreen. Andi, the third girl, refused to meet her gaze.

"That 'lady' is Primrose Pixiedust. You shouldn't forget it. Don't let me stop you from your locker."

The girl swept aside, casting a meaningful look at her fairy godmother as she did so. The woman raised her wand.

Whatever might have happened next failed to materialize when a teacher stepped into the hallway. The other girl whistled in frustration as her protector turned into a normal woman, leaving behind a dusting of glitter.

Lillie wasted no time in hurrying toward her classroom, breathing out a sigh of relief at the timely interruption.

Lillie's new nemesis strode into the classroom as the bell rang. Their biology teacher, Mr. Kelley, gave the newcomer a disapproving glare.

"You're late."

The girl's demeanor changed. Her face went soft and she flipped that shining mass of chestnut hair over her shoulder. Many of the boys shifted in their chairs.

Lillie wondered if her fairy godmother had cast a spell on them as well.

"I'm sorry. I'm new and I got lost. It won't happen again."

Mr. Kelley harrumphed, but nodded to an empty desk two rows over and one seat up from Lillie.

"Everyone, this is Mallory Faure. She transferred from…where again, Mallory?"

"Fond du Lac." Mallory pronounced the words with a distinct lack of enthusiasm.

"That's a Frenchy name, ain't it?" Evan Rarnet, the resident high school quarterback, spoke. Mallory studied him with an impish grin, and then nodded.

"That's right. I'm French. Like…" she paused for emphasis. "…my relatives."

Like my fairy godmother.

When he turned to face the chalkboard, Mallory shot Lillie a malevolent glare. No question who Mallory had chosen as her next victim.

She had to talk to Berry.

***

Just ignore her. Bullies want attention. Do your schoolwork and don't engage her. It will be fine.

Berry's words sounded inadequate inside her mind. She had hoped for more.

Mallory got away with things, her fairy godmother doling out punishments when the teachers weren't around. Lillie could see her satisfaction in every smug smirk she gave the other kids. Berry suggested caution and patience despite that. Lillie knew better than to try and countermand her.

"Mallory, please. Why are you ignoring me?"

The quarterback's plaintive words filled the hallway. He trailed behind Mallory like a lost puppy, his handsome face crestfallen as she stormed ahead.

"Ugh. You're so annoying."

Lillie avoided her locker as much as possible these days, but sometimes there was no way around it. She tried to stay out of Mallory's path. She ruled the school now, and to the victor belonged the spoils. Spoils such as the popular quarterback.

"I thought you liked me. You said you did."

From the disgusted look on Mallory's face, she wasn't happy that Evan hung around. Roberta and Andi hovered near Mallory's fairy godmother.

Lillie walked toward the exit, expecting at any moment to be called out, but Mallory was focused solely on the abject boy who stood in front of her. When Lillie was near the door, she turned back to watch the drama.

Berry's words surfaced in her mind again. Bullies wanted attention, she'd said - and Mallory had all she could ask for.

"You're always around. Always calling. Always giving me gifts." Mallory flung a charm bracelet at Evan and he caught it in one hand. "Why can't you just back off?"

"But...Mallory..."

"No. Leave me alone." She rounded on him, motioning to her fairy godmother at the same time.

"Make him go away."

"Are you sure, cherie? He is very handsome and he loves you."

"I'm sick of him always being around. It's no fun. Send him to the next county."

Her fairy godmother sighed. "As you wish."

Evan's startled cry faded as he vanished from the hall. The few kids remaining stared at the spot but hurried on as though they had seen nothing amiss.

Mallory's posse gasped. She glared at them and they changed their gasps to nervous giggles.

"Oh my god." Roberta studied the spot where he had been. "Where did he go?"

Mallory waved a nonchalant hand in the air. "He'll be fine. Primrose sent him away so I wouldn't have to see his face." She glared at her group. "She didn't hurt him. What do you take me for?"

"He is not harmed," her fairy godmother affirmed. "It will take him some time to get home, but that is all."

"He'll miss practice. He'll get in trouble. We have a big game on Saturday."

Mallory caught Lillie staring at them and turned to her.

"Then he should have left me alone when I told him to, Locker girl. What are you eyeballing us for?"

Lillie shook her head and backed through the front doors. She almost told Berry then, but Berry's words echoed in her mind. Bullies want attention. She would keep this one to herself and see what happened next. She wouldn't tell Berry anything yet.

***

"Hey. You. Locker girl."

Lillie tried to ignore Mallory, but the rough tap on her shoulder could not be dismissed.

"Leave me alone." She mumbled the words, praying that a teacher would come by.

"I said hey you. Don't ignore me."

Lillie clutched her books to her. Those around them were backing away, creating a circle around the two girls. Then she turned around, staring up into Mallory's face. It would be a mistake to show fear. One look at the teens fleeing to the edges of the hall told her there would be no help from that quarter.

Her fairy godmother hovered just beyond Mallory; her wand aimed at Lillie.

"What can I do for you, Mallory?" Despite her best efforts, her voice wavered.

Mallory snickered and the girls followed suit. Several kids on the sidelines sniggered as well. Lillie's quick glance at the school front doors reminded her that there were dozens of yards between her and freedom. Even if Mallory and her squad weren't standing right there, her fairy godmother remained.

"What can I do for you, Mallory?" Mallory mimicked Lillie's word with a sneer. The gaggle of girls giggled. "I don't think you take me seriously. You act like I'm some kind of joke. You will respect me or pay the price."

"You didn't earn respect - it's because of her." Lillie pointed to Mallory's fairy godmother, who sighed and looked pained.

Mallory spun around, pinning Lillie with a glare. Then she turned to their rapt audience. "You see what I mean? She doesn't respect me. She thinks she's superior. Is that right, Lillie? You live in a shitbox of a house, with some random nanny who spends more time with you than your parents. You think you're better than us."

Lillie's hands started to sweat. "I don't…" Lillie began but Mallory stomped her foot to cut off Lillie's words.

"You're a witch, that's what you are. You're a witch and…you should look like one." Lillie's face expanded and something perched on her head. Instead of books she clutched a broom made of straw and bound together with a cord. Her face felt lumpy, her skin tight.

Mallory let out a belly laugh. "That's much better. Now you look like the witch you are. Isn't that right? Everyone?"

The crowd nodded as though their heads were on strings.

Mallory held out a hand mirror to the sputtering Lillie. "See for yourself."

Lillie's wrinkled face had large warts on her cheeks and forehead. Her nose was hooked and bent, with another wart on the end. A faint green tone shone through her skin and her grey and kinked hair stuck out under a pointy black hat.

"A witch!" The crowd pointed at her. "You're a witch, you're a witch." Mallory and her friends began chanting, with Mallory's fairy godmother waving her wand like a conductor's baton. Mallory beamed the entire time.

Lillie heard "headmaster" and "teachers" through her haze of rage and misery. An adult voice sounded in the corridor.

"Next time you disrespect me, don't forget I can turn you into a witch at any time."

Then the broom shifted back into books and her skin loosened. The kids around them cleared out, scattering like rats. Mallory gave her one more triumphant glare before dashing off.

Lillie touched her nose. Although it had been returned to its normal shape the feel of the giant hook Mallory had given her swam in her mind.

She went back to her locker just as the headmaster entered the hallway with another teacher. Lillie struggled to control her tears. She had to get home.

"Everything all right? What happened here?" His voice echoed through the empty corridor.

"Nothing," Lillie said, willing her mouth not to tremble. She slammed her locker shut and made for the exit.

She was crying in her room when Berry appeared. When she observed Lillie's red and blotchy complexion, Berry's face darkened.

"Something has happened. I can tell," she said, her voice steady with the sort of calm that preceded a thunderstorm. "What haven't you told me?"

Sniffling, Lillie relayed the recent events at the school. When she finished Berry rose to her full height and held out her hands.

"I am sorry this happened - I believed she would stop. It is not like fairy godmothers to behave this way. I cannot allow this to continue. Listen carefully. I have a plan."

***

Lillie's best running shoes were on her feet and her belongings were secure in her pack. She timed it so that she left the class last and then made her way into the hallway. Kids were dispersing for the day. Some were getting things from their lockers while others ran into the sunshine.

Robbie kept Mr. Kelley in the hallway, peppering him with questions. His Lillie-appointed task centered around keeping an adult at hand while Lillie made her move. That way Mallory's helper could not use her powers.

Lillie eyed the distance from the lockers to the front door. Then she powered through the crowd, and right into Mallory. Her tormentor shouted a curse word and grabbed for Lillie, but she was already out of Mallory's reach.

"Watch where you're going, locker girl."

Lillie flipped Mallory off, and then sprinted for the door.

She burst through the front doors and down the steps of her high school. Kids scattered in her wake, the shouts of rage as Mallory and her cohorts plunged after her audible.

Lillie shot down the street, hearing the pack behind her.

"You bitch! I'll mash your head into the ground." Mallory and her fairy godmother's furious tones left little doubt that Lillie would be in for it if she failed. It wouldn't just be a temporary face change this time.

She slid past people and ducked through seams in the crowds. She just had to get to the pre-arranged spot. Lillie forced more speed out of her tired legs.

Lillie ran around the corner and into the alley. Then she turned and faced the opening. She wheezed, her breath coming out in hard gasps.

The girls pounded in. Mallory's fairy godmother popped into view as soon as they left the street behind. Her gossamer wings buzzed and she sparkled like a glittery cloud.

Lillie bared her teeth in a feral grin.

They stopped dead when they saw what - or rather who - stood behind Lillie. Mallory gasped and her mouth fell open.

"Did you know that in French Mallory means 'unfortunate' or 'ill-fated?'" Lillie poked her finger at the surprised Mallory. "It's no surprise, considering what a bitch you are. Maybe I should call you 'Malaria.' It suits. Oh, I should tell you who this is. Meet Berengaria Nightdust - Berry for short. She's my fairy godmother."

Berry had on a flannel shirt, jeans and combat boots. Her close-cropped hair encompassed every color of the rainbow.

Primrose Pixiedust turned in a circle, her complexion ashen. At six foot two and two hundred-and-twenty-pounds Berry towered over all of them. Mallory's fairy godmother flapped her wings in an agitated rhythm. Her wand shot sparks into the air.

"You've got..." Mallory stuttered to a halt.

"You believed you were the only one with a fairy godmother. Most of us know to keep ours to ourselves. You had to use yours to torment the entire school. So foolish." Lillie pretended to examine Mallory, taking her time to check out every inch of the confused teenager.

Primrose chittered like a bird who had lost her chick.

"This is the one, Lillie my love?"

Berengaria's voice boomed, ringing through the fire escapes. Somewhere a cat yowled and fled. Andi and Roberta tensed, their attention going from Primrose to Berry. Doreen whimpered, scuffing her shoes in the dirt. Berry moved her hands and a shining veil fell over the alley. Lillie could see through it, but those passing by did not take note of the entryway any longer.

"This is Mallory - Malaria - and her backup. Have you two met? Mallory says she goes by Primrose Pixiedust."

Primrose's pasty facial color was matched by the dimming of the sparkles. Now she resembled a sagging and faded circus fairy, the glitter nothing more than cheap rhinestones.

"We haven't met, but I checked her records and she is on probation for failing to teach her charges correct manners." Berry waggled a finger at the second fairy. "You should have known better. We do not use our powers for ill."

Mallory stamped her foot. "Do something. Do it now."

"Mallory, cherie..." Primrose stuttered to a stop. Her face crumpled, and she appeared to be fighting tears.

"Primrose, didn't you teach Mallory our five basic guidelines? Lillie learned them when she was a child who couldn't pronounce my name."

Lillie turned her attention to Mallory. "First - protect your charges. Second - your responsibility is to teach. Third - Do not do harm. Fourth - no adult may see a fairy godmother. Fifth - Magic is for good and not ill."

Lillie's fairy godmother pointed toward Primrose, who shrank back, her body trembling. "You made a boy into a frog. Turned my Lillie into a witch. Embarrassed the quarterback when it was you who enchanted him to be in love with Mallory. You created a monster who tyrannized the school. You have allowed this girl to be a tormenter."

Berengaria stepped forward, her boots thudding in the alley. The area had an unpleasant odor of old food and dirt. Mallory's nose wrinkled at the stench.

"Oui. I'm her fairy godmother," Primrose said in a small voice. "What else could I do?"

Berengaria's wings hummed and she rose in the air. The girls squealed at the sight of the large woman rising. The debris littering the alley lifted by with movement, stirring the detritus of a dozen shopkeepers. A candy wrapper whirled around Berengaria and stuck to Mallory's face.

Andi backed away, and then turned and ran.

Berry raised her wand but lowered it when Lillie shook her head. The veil bulged as Andi plunged through it, and then she disappeared from view.

"You teach. That is why we are there."

"I am so glad that you're not who I got stuck with." Mallory waved a shaking hand toward Berry. "Some fairy godmother. You've got zero fashion sense."

"She appears how I thought she should, just like yours. I guess that's a combination of early 70 disco and a glitter factory explosion."

"You made her look like a dy…?"

"You foolish girl. You are a handful, aren't you?" Berry gave Mallory a measured gaze that conveyed disapproval.

Primrose smoothed her hand over Mallory's hair. Mallory shoved it away. Her baleful glance told Lillie how much she desired revenge.

"You are a bitch, you…" Primrose shushed Mallory and although she glared at her fairy godmother, she subsided.

Berry raised an eyebrow. "My word. And the French godmothers criticize the rest of us. They should not be so haughty if this is how they behave."

Mallory pushed at Primrose. "Do something!"

Primrose started to raise her wand but a bolt from Berengaria's turned its tip from bright red to dark. The plump woman shrieked and dropped it, shaking her hand. Sparks danced over her skin.

Doreen wheeled and fled. Berry once again looked to Lillie, who waved a hand in acceptance. Roberta inched away but appeared too terror struck to run. She held her pack in front of her, her eyes wide pools of fear.

"Let me go, please. I won't bother you ever again. I swear. I have to get home. Please. I'm not responsible - just Mallory."

Lillie pursed her lips, remembering the jeers and insults Roberta had flung at her.

"Lillie, remember what I taught you. Compassion…"

"Will serve you better in the long run," Lillie finished. She focused on Roberta. "You can go. But if you return to your bad old ways, Berengaria knows where you live."

Roberta gulped and nodded, her gaze skittering over the six-foot-two woman. "I won't forget. I'm sorry…for everything."

She scampered off, her feet sliding in the alley as she hurried toward the entrance.

Angry tears dotted Mallory's cheeks. "Help me. Fix this. You're all I've got."

"There are penalties for failing." Berry sniffed, her gaze taking in both Primrose and Mallory.

Primrose cast an imploring glance at Berengaria. "Berengaria Night-dust, s'il vous plait. I did not mean to offend. Perhaps…just a warning…?"

Berry shook her head. "Last time was your warning. This is not the first time you failed to properly instruct your student. I'm afraid I have no choice."

"No. Non. She is my petite fille."

Primrose clutched Mallory to her and flew into the air. Berengaria flicked her wand, stilling Primrose's flight. Berry's wand followed Primrose as she came down, stopping inches from the alley floor.

Mallory struggled free of her embrace when they landed. She turned on Berry with a snarl, although her lips were quivering. "I'm not scared of you. You look like those stupid old grunge bands - like Lillie. You must have dressed in a trash can and did your hair with a mixer. You're nothing but…"

"That's quite enough." Mallory's words cut off with a yelp.

"Give us a second chance. Please don't do this." Primrose bent her knees, apparently about to prostrate herself, but then glanced at the ground and stayed upright.

"This was your second chance. Once I informed Headquarters of the situation, they took it out of my hands." Berry gestured to Primrose. "You broke the rules that we hold most sacred. I'm afraid it's the laundry for you. After a suitable penance you can apply for reinstatement. There's nothing to be done for you and Mallory."

Primrose opened her mouth to protest but then bowed her head.

"Mais non. I am her fairy godmother and wanted to make her happy."

Berry waved Primrose forward. "Our jobs are to educate. We are not to allow those in our care to run wild."

"Don't be too hard on her," Primrose begged. "She's good at heart. The fault is mine."

"She has not behaved correctly. It was her choice to use you for ill, but you let her. Now you both pay the price." Berry's gaze rested on Lillie as she spoke, as though to remind her. "Do a good job and I may put in a word for you."

Primrose sniffled. "Will you visit?"

"We shall see. Stand straight. It has been a while since I've transported someone to Headquarters. Mallory, you will be on your own from now on. Primrose is going."

"Leaving?" Mallory stamped her foot. "No, you can't. I forbid it."

"I am sorry, cherie, but my hands are tied." Primrose held out her arms, but Mallory stood in place.

"Do something. I command you to." Mallory glared at her fairy god-mother; her arms crossed.

"You have no power anymore, child. Say your goodbyes." Berry's gaze was not unkind, but there was no softening in her expression.

"Turn them into chickens! Stop this." When Primrose didn't move, Mallory let out a wail. "What am I going to do? You can't leave. Then I will have nobody."

"I am désolé, cherie. Au revoir."

Berry waved her wand, and Primrose vanished with a popping sound. Glitter drifted down from the spot where Primrose had been.

Mallory lunged toward the now-empty spot. "No!" She glared at Berry, her hands balled into fists. Then her expression crumpled and she let out a wail akin to a trapped animal. "Please. She's all I've got. Bring her back."

"That is not possible. We are to instruct girls, not indulge them. She should have explained the rules to you long before now, as I did to Lillie here. Isn't that right, my sweet?"

Lillie nodded. "I didn't want to learn the lessons, but I did."

Mallory's face scrunched up. "Bring her back."

"What's done is done. Her time as your fairy godmother is over. Our guidelines are strict and she chose to ignore them."

"I didn't know," Mallory wailed, her lips trembling. Tears lurked in her eyes and her fists were clenched by her sides. "I'll be good. I'll change. I promise."

If this had been anyone but Mallory, Lillie might have felt sorry for her.

"Primrose failed and must be punished. Once her sentence has been served you will be too old for her to return. She will go to another girl. She is lost to you forever. You have proven you do not deserve a fairy godmother."

"It's not fair."

Berengaria motioned to Lillie. She stayed in place.

"It is the way of our kind. Power comes at a cost. It is better if you learn those lessons with our guidance but they still must be taught. Your life will be difficult in the months ahead. Lillie will help you."

Lillie stared at Berengaria, who met her puzzled, angry glare with a sanguine expression.

"I'll do what?"

"Mallory needs friends. Bullies are not so different from other children. She has forgotten humility. It is possible she can be redeemed. She will need support. We must always help those less fortunate than ourselves."

"Will anyone like me? Will Evan?" Mallory's words were plaintive.

Berengaria shrugged, and her wings fluttered. "It is impossible to say what will happen now that the spell has been removed. You have hurt many people and that is not always so easy to forgive, whether there is love in their heart for you or not."

Mallory wailed, fresh tears streaming down her face. "We move so much. Primrose was all I had."

Lillie sputtered, words forming and getting jumbled as her mind raced. "You can't mean…" She flung her arm toward the blubbering Mallory. "Her."

"I do. She is going to pay the price for her actions, of course. The school will see a different Mallory in the weeks ahead, as she is scrubbing the floors. Punishments are not forever, though, and a little charity is a kindness. Both of you had fairy godmothers for a reason. Being kind to one who has lost hers will not be out of place. Remember your lessons."

It took everything Lillie had to utter the next word. "Okay."

Mallory stopped wailing, her eyes going wide. "What?"

"You two will be friends, in time. Lillie will show the grace you did not. Isn't that right?"

Lillie nodded, although her mind still rebelled against the idea. She still had Berry. She could afford to be charitable. Berry engulfed Lillie in a one-arm embrace and then she gestured to Mallory. The girl eyed them uncertainly.

"Do not misunderstand me, Mallory. You must take this lesson to heart and not act out again. I will know if you disobey. You have an opportunity for redemption. It will be up to you to decide what to do with what you're given."

Mallory whimpered, fresh tears streaking down her face. She wiped them away with quick swipes of her hands but more fell.

"Can't you be my fairy godmother too?"

Berry shook her head. "I'm a one-child woman, my dear. I can be an auntie, but that is all."

"I'm sorry." Mallory's crestfallen expression was so heartbreaking that Lillie felt a pang of sympathy, despite everything.

"You should be. You did terrible things, Mallory, but you were young and should have been guided better. Allons-y, as the French say. I believe ice cream is in order. It cures all ills. Lillie?"

The alleyway opening lost its shimmer. A man nearby started, but then rushed ahead, intent on his day. The noise and bustle of the street resumed.

Lillie struggled against the idea of being altruistic. She wished she had a fairy godmother like Primrose, who would have done anything Lillie asked.

"Lillie." Berry's harsh voice reminded Lillie of past lectures - and the guidelines. She released that thought and nodded to Berry.

"Can I get a banana split sundae?" Mallory asked.

"Just this once. Let's go." She took both girl's hands and led them toward the street.

It wasn't the outcome she expected, but Lillie trusted she would understand, in time. Berry was her fairy godmother, and she always knew best.

The Fantastic Imagination

George MacDonald, LL.D.

(from *A Dish of Orts. Chiefly Papers on the Imagination,
and on Shakespere* (Enlarged Edition).
London: SAMPSON LOW Marston & Company, Ld.
St. Dunstan's House, Fetter Lane Fleet Street, E.C. MDCCCXCV PUBLISHERS)

[from the PREFACE.:
The paper on The Fantastic Imagination had its origin in the repeated request of
readers for an explanation of things in certain shorter stories I had written. It forms the
preface to an American edition of my so-called Fairy Tales.
- George Macdonald Edenbridge, Kent
August 5, 1893.]

THAT WE HAVE in English no word corresponding to the German *Märchen*, drives us to use the word *Fairytale*, regardless of the fact that the tale may have nothing to do with any sort of fairy. The old use of the word *Fairy*, by Spenser at least, might, however, well be adduced, were justification or excuse necessary where need must.

Were I asked, what is a fairytale? I should reply, Read Undine: that is a fairytale; then read this and that as well, and you will see what is a fairytale. Were I further begged to describe the fairytale, or define what it is, I would make answer, that I should as soon think of describing the abstract human face, or stating what must go to constitute a human being. A fairytale is just a fairytale, as a face is just a face; and of all fairytales I know, I think Undine the most beautiful.

Many a man, however, who would not attempt to define a man, might venture to say something as to what a man ought to be: even so much I will not in this place venture with regard to the fairytale, for my long past work in that kind might but poorly instance or illustrate my now more matured judgment. I will but say some things helpful to the reading, in right-minded fashion, of such fairytales as I would wish to write, or care to read. Some thinkers would feel sorely hampered if at liberty to use no forms but such as existed in nature, or to invent nothing save in accordance with the laws of the world of the senses; but it must not therefore be imagined that they desire escape from the region of law. Nothing lawless can show the least reason why it should exist, or could at best have more than an appearance of life.

The natural world has its laws, and no man must interfere with them in the way of presentment any more than in the way of use; but they themselves may suggest laws of other kinds, and man may, if he pleases, invent a little world of his own, with its own laws; for there is that in him which delights in calling up new forms which is the nearest, perhaps, he can come to creation. When such forms are new embodiments of old truths, we call them products of the Imagination; when they are mere inventions, however lovely, I should call them the work of the Fancy: in either case, Law has been diligently at work.

His world once invented, the highest law that comes next into play is, that there shall be harmony between the laws by which the new world has begun to exist; and in the process of his creation, the inventor must hold by those laws. The moment he forgets one of them, he makes the story, by its own postulates, incredible. To be able to live a moment in an imagined world, we must see the laws of its existence obeyed. Those broken, we fall out of it. The imagination in us, whose exercise is essential to themost temporary submission to the imagination of another, immediately, with the disappearance of Law, ceases to act.

Suppose the gracious creatures of some childlike region of Fairyland talking either cockney or Gascon! Would not the tale, however lovelily begun, sink at once to the level of the Burlesque - of all forms of literature the least worthy?

A man's inventions may be stupid or clever, but if he do not hold by the laws of them, or if he make one law jar with another, he contradicts himself as an inventor, he is no artist. He does not rightly consort his instruments, or he tunes them in different keys. The mind of man is the product of live Law; it thinks by law, it dwells in the midst of law, it gathers from law its growth; with law, therefore, can it alone work to any result. In harmonious, unconsorting ideas will come to a man, but if he try to use one of such, his work will grow dull, and he will drop it from mere lack of interest. Law is the soil in which alone beauty will grow; beauty is the only stuff in which Truth can be clothed; and you may, if you will, call Imagination the tailor that cuts her garments to fit her, and Fancy his journeyman that puts the pieces of them together, or perhaps at most embroiders their button-holes. Obeying law, the maker works like his creator; not obeying law, he is such a fool as heaps a pile of stones and calls it a church.

In the moral world it is different: there a man may clothe in new forms, and for this employ his imagination freely, but he must invent nothing. He may not, for any purpose, turn its laws upside down.

He must not meddle with the relations of live souls. The laws of the spirit of man must hold, alike in this world and in any world he may invent. It were no offence to suppose a world in which everything repelled instead of attracted the things around it; it would be wicked to write a tale representing a man it called good as always doing bad things, or a man it called bad as always doing good things: the notion itself is absolutely lawless. In physical things a man may invent; in moral things he must obey and take their laws with him into his invented world as well.

"You write as if a fairytale were a thing of importance: must it have a meaning?"

It cannot help having some meaning; if it have proportion and harmony it has vitality, and vitality is truth. The beauty may be plainer in it than the truth, but without the truth the beauty could not be, and the fairytale would give no delight. Everyone, however, who feels the story, will read its meaning after his own nature and development: one man will read one meaning in it, another will read another.

"If so, how am I to assure myself that I am not reading my own meaning into it, but yours out of it?"

Why should you be so assured? It may be better that you should read your meaning into it. That maybe a higher operation of your intellect than the mere reading of mine out of it: your meaning may besuperior to mine.

"Suppose my child ask me what the fairytale means, what am I to say?"

If you do not know what it means, what is easier than to say so? If you do see a meaning in it, there it is for you to give him. A genuine work of art must mean many things; the truer its art, the more things it will mean. If my drawing, on the other hand, is so far from being a work of art that it needs THIS IS A HORSE written under it, what can it matter that neither you nor your child should know what it means?

It is there not so much to convey a meaning as to wake a meaning. If it do not even wake an interest, throw it aside. A meaning may be there, but it is not for you. If, again, you do not know a horse when you see it, the name written under it will not serve you much. At all events, the business of the painter is not to teach zoology.

But indeed your children are not likely to trouble you about the meaning. They find what they are capable of finding, and more would be too much. For my part, I do not write for children, but for the childlike, whether of five, or fifty, or seventy-five.

A fairytale is not an allegory. There may be allegory in it, but it is not an allegory. He must be an artist indeed who can, in any mode, produce a strict allegory that is not a weariness to the spirit. An allegory must be Mastery or Moorditch.

A fairytale, like a butterfly or a bee, helps itself on all sides, sips at every wholesome flower, and spoils not one. The true fairytale is, to my mind, very like the sonata. We all know that a sonata means something; and where there is the faculty of talking with suitable vagueness, and choosing metaphor sufficiently loose, mind may approach mind, in the interpretation of a sonata, with the result of a more or less contenting consciousness of sympathy. But if two or three men sat down to write each what the sonata meant to him, what approximation to definite idea would be the result? Little enough - and that little more than needful. We should find it had roused related, if not identical, feelings, but probably not one common thought. Has the sonata therefore failed? Had it undertaken to convey, or ought it to be expected to impart anything defined, anything notionally recognizable?

"But words are not music; words at least are meant and fitted to carry a precise meaning!"

It is very seldom indeed that they carry the exact meaning of any user of them! And if they can be so used as to convey definite meaning, it does not follow that they ought never to carry anything else. Words are like things that may be variously employed to various ends. They can convey a scientific fact, or throw a shadow of her child's dream on the heart of a mother. They are things to put together like the pieces of a dissected map, or to arrange like the notes on a stave. Is the music in them to go for nothing? It can hardly help the definiteness of a meaning: is it therefore to be disregarded? They have length, and breadth, and outline: have they nothing to do with depth? Have they only to describe, never to impress? Has nothing any claim to their use but the definite? The cause of a child's tears may be altogether undefinable: has the mother therefore no antidote for his vague misery? That may be strong in colour which has no evident outline. A fairytale, a sonata, a gathering storm, a limitless night, seizes you and sweeps you away: do you begin at once to wrestle with it and ask whence its power over you, whither it is carrying you? The law of each is in the mind of its composer; that law makes one man feel this way, another man feel that way. To one the sonata is a world of odour and beauty, to another of soothing only and sweetness. To one, the cloudy rendezvous is a wild dance, with a terror at its heart; to another, a majestic march of heavenly hosts, with Truth in their centre pointing their course, but as yet restraining her voice. The greatest forces lie in the region of the uncomprehended.

I will go farther. The best thing you can do for your fellow, next to rousing his conscience, is not to give him things to think about, but to wake things up that are in him; or say, to make him think things for himself. The best Nature does for us is to work in us such moods in which thoughts of high import arise. Does any aspect of Nature wake but one thought? Does she ever suggest only one definite thing?

Does she make any two men in the same place at the same moment think the same thing? Is she thereforea failure, because she is not definite? Is it nothing that she rouses the something deeper than the understanding - the power that underlies thoughts? Does she not set feeling, and so thinking at work?

Would it be better that she did this after one fashion and not after many fashions? Nature is mood-engendering, thought-provoking: such ought the sonata, such ought the fairytale to be.

"But a man may then imagine in your work what he pleases, what you never meant!"

Not what he pleases, but what he can. If he be not a true man, he will draw evil out of the best; we need not mind how he treats any work of art! If he be a true man, he will imagine true things: what matter whether I meant them or not? They are there none the less that I cannot claim putting them there! One difference between God's work and man's is, that, while God's work cannot mean more than he meant, man's must mean more than he meant. For in everything that God has made, there is layer upon layer of ascending significance; also he expresses the same thought in higher and higher kinds of that thought: it is God's things, his embodied thoughts, which alone a man has to use, modified and adapted to his own purposes, for the expression of his thoughts; therefore he cannot help his words and figures falling into such combinations in the mind of another as he had himself not foreseen, so many are the thoughts allied to every other thought, so many are the relations involved in every figure, so many the facts hinted in every symbol. A man may well himself discover truth in what he wrote; for he was dealing all the time with things that came from thoughts beyond his own.

"But surely you would explain your idea to one who asked you?"

I say again, if I cannot draw a horse, I will not write THIS IS A HORSE under what I foolishly meant for one. Any key to a work of imagination would be nearly, if not quite, as absurd. The tale is there, not to hide, but to show: if it show nothing at your window, do not open your door to it; leave it out in the cold. To ask me to explain, is to say, "Roses! Boil them, or we won't have them!" My tales may not be roses, but I will not boil them.

So long as I think my dog can bark, I will not sit up to bark for him.

If a writer's aim be logical conviction, he must spare no logical pains, not merely to be understood, but to escape being misunderstood; where his object is to move by suggestion, to cause to imagine, then let him assail the soul of his reader as the wind assails an Êolian harp. If there be music in my reader, I would gladly wake it. Let fairytale of mine go for a firefly that now flashes, now is dark, but may flash again.

Caught in a hand which does not love its kind, it will turn to an insignificant, ugly thing, that can neither flash nor fly.

The best way with music, I imagine, is not to bring the forces of our intellect to bear upon it, but to be still and let it work on that part of us for whom it exists. We spoil countless precious things by intellectual greed. He who will be a man, and will not be a child, must - he cannot help himself - become a little man, that is, a dwarf. He will, however need no consolation, for he is sure to think himself a very large creature indeed.If any strain of my "broken music" make a child's eyes flash, or his mother's grow for a moment dim, my labour will not have been in vain. [italic emphases added]

Editor's Note: This essay had great influence upon Tolkien's seminal lecture and later long essay, "On Fairy-stories." Much of JRRT's commentary on Sub-Creation, Secondary Worlds, and the very nature of Fantasy echo MacDonald's earlier essay. Of course, for both men, their religion molded their respective visions of what "creative" literature was - and also what it should not or couldn't be - at least if successful.

Fantasy's Values

(an acrostic sonnet inspired by J.R.R. Tolkien's "On Fairy-stories")

Frank Coffman

"*Fantasy*" provides, as Tolkien rightly wrote,
"Arresting Strangeness" and - at its best - enthralls.
Not wishing to be universal, he added the note
That, if not consistent, the wonder world soon falls.
Another virtue stated is "*Recovery*,"
Such that we regain a sadly lost "Clear View";
Y'es, helped along to the blessed Discovery -
Seeing the Once-Lost Found, that Old is New.

Virtues include "*Escape*" - the positive kind -
About the "Prisoner" seeking to break free,
Leaving behind a dismal "Real" to find
Unrealized Ideals that yet could be.
"*Eucatastrophe*" is last, the story wending
Strongly to the Joy of the Happy Ending.

HORROR AND THE SUPERNATURAL

BEING SECTION 4 OF THE JOURN-E

CHULIE
BY GARY MCCLUSKEY

I N THE BRIEF INTRODUCTION TO HIS TREATISE ON
Supernatual Horror in Literature, H. P. Lovecraft makes the distinction
between "the Weird Tale" (which he confusingly also calls "Cosmic Fear"
and "Supernatural Horror) "Physical Fear."

> This type of fear-literature must not be confounded
> with a type externally similar but psychologically wide-
> ly different; the literature of mere physical fear and the
> mundanely gruesome.

This distinction is apt between the two major divisions of the tale meant
to arouse fear, horror, terror - what we might call "Supernatural Horror"
and "Natural Horror."

Poe, in his seminal review of "Hawthorne's *Twice-Told Tales*," (in
which, in the early paragraphs, he defines the "short tale" - establishing
him in the view of many critics as "The Father of the Modern Short Sto-
ry) notes that the author should strive to create a single, unified effect
upon the reader:

> A skilful literary artist has constructed a tale. If wise,
> he has not fashioned his thoughts to accommodate his
> incidents; but having conceived, with deliberate care,
> a certain unique or single effect to be wrought out, he
> then invents such incidents- he then combines such
> events as may best aid him in establishing this precon-
> ceived effect.

Of course, with the literature of Horror, this single effect is to evoke emo-
tional reactions from the reader - chief of which is Fear, causing at least
some shudders, perhaps the sudden urge to check to make sure the doors
and windows are secured, vicarious excitement of feelings of dread, dis-
comfort, uneasiness, shock - while likely not being felt strongly enough to
make one run screaming into the night (or day).

This, of course, rejects the ideas of both the "intentional fallacy" and
the "affective fallacy" promoted by the "New Critics" of the mid-20th c.
and also strongly says that the Horror Story is not intended to be fraught
with meaning or deep significance or message. While Fantasy and Sci-
ence Fiction often have moral or intellectual messages and meanings - ei-
ther directly stated or implied - the Horror story has a different purpose.

Thus, we may identify the sub-genres of Fear Fiction or Horrific Tale
into at least these severl types:

1) **Physical Fear** - brought about by things that we believe, or know
for certain, are possible in the real and "natural" world in which we believe
we live: serial killers, rabid dogs, psychopaths, etc. **The Serial Killer** sub-

sub-genre has become, perhaps, a type worthy of elevation to more major sub-genre status.

2) **The Monstrous Supernatural Entity/Monstrous Creature Story** - including the standard sub-species of vampire, werewolf, ghoul, djinn, creature of legend or folktale, etc.

3) **The Occult** - including any stories about the Forces of Evil, directly opposed to the Forces of Good (note that this requires the underpinning of some religion - not necessarily Judeo-Christian). So stories of witches, warlocks, demons, possession, the coming of an Anti-Christ, etc. fall into this catagory.

4) **The Ghost Story** - tales written in such quantity that they deserve a separate niche (although closely related to stories of The Occult). These come with all of their sub-sub-genres: various types of hauntings - residual, historical, vengeful, location with its own "spirit", the main character's discovery that he or she is actually dead and a ghost, the poltergeist, etc.

7) **Cosmic Horror/Cthuluvian/Lovecraftian/Chambersian** - anything in the established Mythos established by Bierce, Chambers, and Lovecraft and inclusive of many contemporaries such as Clark Ashton Smith and Robert E. Howard and many since.

6) **The Supernatural Occurrence Story** - a "catch-all-the-rest."

MASK OF DEATH

Jonel Abellanosa

LUIS WALKS OUT of the Office of Suicide Solutions, holding the one-page form the government requires to process his request for assisted suicide. He takes off his face mask and throws it to the sidewalk. On his way to his apartment room, he realizes he's walking through a ghostly field of face masks, of different sizes, fabrics and colors. Face maskers must have felt the same freedom he feels, buying themselves free seats on the decrepit bus ride, with strong smells of rust and crude oil, towards one of the thirteen hills hosting the City's last trees.

The government has designated acacias for the once-weekly mass suicides. Acacias have sturdier branches, gigantic boles, each able to hold two hundred nooses without bodies weighing it down. Six months ago, the Emperor signed a decree forbidding dead bodies to be removed from nooses. With crippling international sanctions against the country, traditional rituals of cleaning bodies and burials have become unaffordable. It takes around two weeks after death for the neck to rot significantly for the dead body to hit ground.

Critics have wondered why the Emperor wouldn't just let workers take down the dead and pile them on the ground to rot. The imperial spokesperson explained that in order to keep stray dogs and feral cats contained, preventing them from turning the entire city into a sanctuary of beasts, they shouldn't be allowed to feast in one go and leave. These wild animals should be held captive to their own excited anticipation as they wait for bodies to fall. The Minister of the Interior has imported hundreds of white-rumped vultures. He has been praised for his "insightful initiative," after the vultures have been observed to evolve a new behavior of feasting on hanging bodies, hastening their fall.

Years have passed since 2021, but it seems just two months ago when the country's medical and health care systems collapsed. Luis fights off tears remembering he had a good-paying job in the year when the pandemic tore through the planet. He was part of a company's motorcycle crew, delivering cash-on-delivery orders. It was a low middle class job, but the pay was good, enough for rent and basic expenses with leftover cash for his monthly savings. Since he entered the workforce seven years ago, he had been disciplining himself to increase his bank savings with any amount he could save. He remembers feeling proud to be counted among frontliners, with doctors and nurses and other essential workers keeping the economy afloat, some level of normalcy in the middle of the viral scourge. Overseas workers used to be treated as the country's heroes before the deadly disease disrupted every human being's life. The Emperor, who was the erstwhile president turned leader for life after the election was canceled, had declared frontliners the country's new heroes.

As Luis crosses the street towards his apartment building, he sees a brown doberman flee with a human femur in its maw. The pinkish meat and reddish stains on the bone are remarkable. A dog lover, he's saddened that the City's pets lost their comfortable homes, dogs and cats released and driven away because keeping them was impossible. The pandemic has brought out the worst from people - not because they wanted to, but because survival prevailed over cherished values. Luis grieves that domesticated dogs have had to turn into hunter-scavengers.

The rest of the world has shown that even a highly contagious and dangerous pandemic isn't powerful enough for the majority of mankind to lose cherished values. "Share" has become the operative word. Shared wealth, shared opportunities, shared responsibilities, shared power. No one else has successfully consolidated power as something never to be shared. The nation is paying the ultimate price for refusing to uproot the problem while salvation was still possible. Neighboring and first world countries have banned travel to and from the country, sending naval blockades for airtight control, because the country has become a breeding ground of deadlier viral variants. Multinational air sorties, with drones and fighter aircraft, have orders of shooting down any aerial vehicle that strays beyond the country's airspace.

* * *

The application form for assisted suicide is designed for simplicity. Luis pours his last glass of rationed drinkable water from the plastic pitcher. He wonders if his dread of dying from hunger and thirst is the underlying reason behind his decision to take the easy way out of life, like millions of his fellow citizens have done. The consent form stipulates that he has a week, after arriving in site, to spend for spiritual activities like prayers and reflections, after which he should hang himself or be bludgeoned to death. He'll be given his own room that used to be part of a huge quarantine facility. When the mass death program started, suicides had to hang themselves within the day of arrival; but fifteen months and counting since it all started have depleted the population, program participants turning fewer and fewer - it's now possible to allow a week of deep contemplation before an applicant should end their life through hanging.

Luis recalls the food industry collapsing next, the systemic problem taking only weeks to worsen beyond repair after the medical and health care systems caved. His delivery appointments significantly reduced, impacting his take-home pay, as his employer had to improvise to stay afloat - putting in place a per-delivery compensation system instead of a monthly salary.

As City dwellers scrambled in confusion and anxiety, sourcing basic needs like food through extreme creativity that bordered on or crossed into lawbreaking. Confined to the world's longest lockdown, cruel with the lack of official assistances, utility services broke down. Electricity and water supplies were the next to go, intermittently at first, till it became a source of socio-political unrest of catastrophic proportions that left tens of thousands of citizens dead. Viral outbreaks worsened when citizens had to forego social distancing to queue for hours, even days, for extremely scarce water supplies. When morgues, crematoriums, funeral parlors and burial services closed shop, cities all over the country smelled foul. Garbage collection and disposal systems collapsed. Criminality flew to stratospheric heights, especially snatching, robbery, murder and homicide, thievery, looting, property violations and destruction. Luis had to sell his motorcycle, after losing his job and savings. Like tens of millions of his countrymen, he felt hungry, not knowing when he'd sleep again with a full stomach, a pack of instant noodles like a feast. A kilo of rice and two cans of sardines from the City mayor made him cry. Checking boxes in the application form, Luis is sure he won't die of hunger or thirst.

Luis wonders what food they serve in the hills. He longs for barbecued pork or chicken, tinola with island mackerel, beef tenderloin or beef stew. He imagines hanging rice dipped in a mixture of soy sauce, ketchup, vinegar, calamansi juice, chopped onions and tomatoes. He plans to make his one-week stay a feast of the foods he hopes they give.

He signs the application form, giving the government permission, as if it needs one, to do whatever it pleases to his dead body. He doesn't know how the government does it, but he has heard rumors of human body fats and oils used to make soap. He thinks about being useful again after death, someone in an affluent country using soap from his body fat. The Emperor is desperate for hard cash, resorting to every imaginable depravity to profit and sustain his family's lavish and brow-raising lifestyles that go on after the imperial kakistocracy, the first of its kind in the region, has become virtually nonexistent in the international map, no longer considered a member of the international community.

Luis leaves his small rented room, walking towards the communal toilet at end of the dim and dank corridor. He folds the application form and, as he inserts it in his jeans pocket, realizes that ghostly apartment dwellers queue for their turns to use the toilet. Passing by the last working wall lamp with its yellowish light, he covers his nose with his shirt part covering his shoulder bursa, in a discreet manner to avoid offending his fellow apartment dwellers.

Feeling his stomach rumble, he rushes out, descending a couple flight of stairs towards the open. It's windy outside, the sky overcast. He turns towards the back of the apartment, which has been turned into a junkyard with rusting and flat-tired jeepneys and taxis. He's dying to defecate among grasses growing wildly, uncut for years.

Minutes later, walking back to the makeshift government office in an abandoned building, he's tempted to find a secluded corner or abandoned alleyway, which are everywhere in the ghostly City, to use the application form like a tissue paper to wipe his ass, because his wet underwear feels uncomfortably warm. The need to eat his first warm meal in a long time, which he expects to have at the suicide colony, makes him suffer and tolerate the indignity of being unable to wipe his behind clean after defecating, like human beings in other countries are presumably still able to do.

He should never use the application form for temporary relief. He presses his upper and lower teeth against each other, tears brimming, knowing that not so much a highly infectious pandemic but an unprecedentedly evil, greedy and corrupt leader could rob the whole citizenry of humanity, dignity and self-respect. He looks around, discomfort in his pants' seat unbearable. He wants to rub his butt against anything except turning the application form into a toilet paper. He picks up six face masks made of cloth from the roadside, and finds a discreet corner.

* * *

A homeless old man pushing a wooden cart with collected discards and throwaways appears on his pathway. The unshaven old-timer with a dirty red cap looks at Luis, his black-tooth smile remarkable for joie de vivre. The sudden eye contact dislodges Luis from his own despair into an ethereal kind of connection between two human beings that feels odd, as though he has never experienced connecting with another human being. The old man pulls his pushcart to a stop. He takes out a glass jar from among his things, uncapping it. Luis sees the old man's wrinkled hand stained with brown from the rusty cap.

"No," says Luis, gesturing with his hand, refusing to accept the piece of bread the old man hands to him.

"Take it," says the old man, his voice phlegmatic. "You're a young man. You need more energy to run and run fast and faster. Me, they could just shoot me and end my misery." The old man laughs.

Puzzled, Luis tightens his brows. "What do you mean I need more energy to run fast?"

"The rich hunters are here again with long rifles and noisy trucks. Tourists from other countries hunting people. It seems like yesterday when moneyed people hunt birds in the provinces. Now, rich people from other countries are hunting us down like animals. They up there in upper neighborhoods are forming a resistance group. They are going to fight these rich tourists who they say pay the Emperor millions to hunt our fellow citizens like deer or wolves. The young ones up there say they are going to be wolves armed with knives. You should go to them, run fast to them, before the pickup trucks with the rich hunters find you."

Luis looks around, alarmed. He hasn't heard about hunting trips to the City, but it's consistent with the Emperor's extreme greed and impunity to sell his own people to rich foreigners who pay big money for trophy hunting. He runs, to inspect left and right streets crisscrossing the highway, disregarding the old man yelling for him to take the bread. There are dozens of abandoned vehicles, some parked on sidewalks, others left topsy-turvy in the middle of the street, a few upturned. There are pockets of people, stray animals making streets look a normal; but there are no signs of distress, nor panic-stricken denizens fleeing from pickup trucks with death's rich army of trophy hunting tourists targeting humans.

Seeing a group of City-dwellers in chaotic jubilance, he takes a left turn towards a fire hydrant spewing joy into the heart of the street. Geysers shoot in several directions, children and adults plunging in water fountains, others filling plastic jugs, gallons and pitchers. Water containers are lined, giving a sense of order. Youngsters, more than ten of them who looked like gang members, wearing sleeveless shirts exposing heavily tattooed shoulders, remind older city dwellers to wait for their turns, keeping parts of the scene tidy. Some of them carry rattan sticks, others with chains wrapped round their palms. Luis espies two of them with guns tucked in their pants, several with long knife leather scabbards hanging from belts, others with wooden bolo scabbards.

"We must maintain order," says the bearded one with a loud voice. "We are still human beings. We must never lose our humanity, even if it makes the Emperor happy if we turn against each other like rabid dogs. Let us wait for our turns. This drinkable water is God-given. Enjoy while it lasts, but maintain civility. Drink, take a bath, but do it like you remember how to do it as human beings. We will get back the lives we lived before the pandemic. The greedy demon in the capital won't stop us upholding our shared values. We refuse to sink into despair and lawlessness. We will bring order to our lives. It is our defiance never to become animals ourselves, even if that's what gives corruption's Imperial Monster an erection. You, what's your name?"

"Luis."

"Where do you you from, Luis? Where are you going?"

"I live a few blocks down there, in an apartment. I'm on my way to the office for my application to be processed."

"Here, take this jug of water, Luis. Drink."

"Thanks."

"I encourage you to change your mind. Don't give the monster the spectacle of watching you and hundreds of others drop simultaneously to your deaths. This suicide program of the government must end. Come with us, Luis. You are welcome to live with us. We have built a shared community of human beings who hold on to hope, for a better and bright future for our land. Tyrants don't last forever. History has a way of dealing with them. It should still be very fresh to you what they did to Saddam Hussein, Muammar Gaddafi and their families. I used to teach history in the university. Let me tell you, no tyrants lasted."

After drinking his fill, Luis hands the clay jug to the bearded guy, who as Luis walks away goes around patting shoulders, consoling senior citizens who have been trying to survive.

Luis crosses the street, returning to the main thoroughfare. The fast wind sweeps discarded face masks, reminding Luis of spiraling leaves. But the face masks are too heavy to engage in a circular dance with the wind, he thinks. He wonders if it constitutes a dance with himself this sudden strong feeling to change his mind. The bearded guy has reacquainted him with his will to live out a meaningful life, years of faith in self-reliance carrying him through the most difficult trials. He remembers how, in the pandemic's early months, he trained himself to see and hear the communal even in incredible suffering. He's just been reminded he's not alone. Even if practically the rest of the world has returned to normalcy, lifestyles before the pandemic restored in other countries, the misery he endures isn't his alone. He's just been reminded that the sorrow of his countrymen, abjection of his City's dwellers, is one powerful motivation for living on - to make himself a cushion, an open space, a welcoming place of communal refuge, an example of hope. Together they shall overcome. He hears the voice of reason, pulling out his pocket the application form, ready to tear it.

He picks up his paces as he nears the office. As he nears the place where the end begins, he returns the application form he filled and signed to his pocket. Strange that the surrounding area is abandoned - no citizens lining to get inside the office for their applications for assisted mass suicide to be processed. There isn't a soul standing in front of the entrance.

Standing in front of the padlocked doors, Luis feels disconsolate reading the bond paper taped on glass — notice telling applicants to keep returning for updates to be posted on the glass doors, because mass suicides have been suspended in the City indefinitely. The text mentions that other cities continue hosting mass suicides, but for their own locals only — because travels by air and sea have been put on hold.

Panic grips Luis looking left and right, the ghostly street chilling his shins, his nape. The old man's words make sense. The City may have been hosting, after all, rich trophy hunters posing as international tourists. He runs to the main street's other artery, where the fire hydrant has been providing momentary reliefs.

But to his fear and debilitating anxiety, no one is around, as though everybody has fled the scene. Nor are there water containers left behind; they all just vanished, no geysers of water, the hydrant not broken, no sign of water on macadam and concrete. Luis looks around, not seeing any human being or animal, the street like a field of face masks whose owners are likelier dead than still alive.

He looks at the sky, feeling lost. Gray clouds have clumped and darkened, reminding him of cauliflowers and mushrooms. He feels the presence of pickup trucks and moneyed hunters, although he sees nothing of the sort, except a city that has become a humongous hollow skull, abandoned buildings and houses like designs and striations of the gigantic face mask of death.

A searing pain pierces into his neck, as though he were stabbed. He jerks violently as, shocked, he covers his face, counterattacking with his hands the raven assaulting him. He swings and swings his arms, as the black bird pushes him back with noisy attacks; taking in the thud of victory like a swig of beer as his fist hits the bird and sends it skyward. A gigantic dark shawl rises towards the sky, as thousands, from buildings all over the City, join the murder of crows and ravens in a mesmeric dance that disperses the clouds, or so Luis thinks. The last thing he sees, before he runs for his life, are windows like countless eyes of buildings, pallid faces the windows frame like dilating pupils.

INTERTEXTUALITY AND THE VIOLABILITY OF SELF IN *TWIN PEAKS*

Katherine Kerestman

*T*HE SECRET HISTORY OF TWIN PEAKS is a fictitious dossier which has been assembled under mysterious circumstances by a person or persons unknown and which has been recovered by the FBI amid equally ambiguous circumstances. A dossier is, by its nature, an intertextual manuscript, a collection of documents pertaining to a central subject, event, or person(s). The several discrete documents within a dossier are texts written by multiple authors, each of whom contributes a part of the story from his or her point of view and in his or her own voice; therefore, a dossier possesses the unique advantage of seeming to present a composite reality inhabited by individualized characters, which is told from a variety of perspectives, and which creates the illusion of being less biased than a novel told from a single narrator's traditional perspective.

The intertextuality of this dossier, however, serves a purpose of greater import than the creation of an illusion of realism and a more objective point of view: by obliging its reader to actively participate in the role of an investigator, and in the process of studying the letters, diaries, journals, newspaper clippings - and even the cave drawings and Masonic apron glyphs - contained within the dossier, in search of the key which will untangle the mysteries of *Twin Peaks, The Secret History of Twin Peaks* demonstrates that the intertextuality of this dossier is not the means to the answer but is the answer. Intertextuality in the world of Twin Peaks is not restricted to the written word - it is the nature of existence, and the only truth is the struggle between good and evil in a plastic world where self is a temporary and porous construct.

* * *

Before she opens the book, the reader already knows who killed Laura Palmer (her father, Leland) and that BOB played a role, but she does not know exactly what BOB is; she comes *The Secret History of Twin Peaks* hoping that it will elucidate all the tantalizing clues which have led her on thus far (from cliffhanger to cliffhanger, through three seasons of the show and a feature film) and that it will finally yield an explication of the hitherto mysterious workings of the realm of *Twin Peaks*.

Every component of *Twin Peaks* is designed to be mysterious, cryptic, and unsettling. Consider the dialogue, for instance: the characters in the show speak softly. . . slowly - with extraordinarily extended pauses and overlong images of silent-movie style expressions on the actors' faces - and these silent images are so protracted that every pause threatens to become an uncomfortable silence. Other visual elements generate dissonance, as well: the soft, red-tinted lighting, for example, blurs the focus. And then, things change before one's eyes: one minute Mrs. Palmer is looking at her living room, the next she sees BOB creeping over her sofa; and, again, as Dale Cooper is watching a chanteuse perform on a stage at The Roadhouse, the stage transforms into the Red Room. The multiple dimensions in *Twin Peaks* communicate by means of portals - dreams, visions, the pool of oil, the twelve sycamores of Glastonbury Grove, and the Red Room, where evil doppelgangers speak backward and move funny. Dreams, visions, and reality converge, begging the question of what is real - not what is real, as opposed to what is false - but what is the nature of Reality - because reality is not fixed. After a time, the viewer begins to doubt her own senses.

In good faith, she has participated in the mysteries of *Twin Peaks* in the expectation of reaping the customary reward for having persisted to the end, a revealing denouement; but at the end of the third (and final?) season of the television show, many problems remain unresolved. Numerous hints have been dropped of some plausible solutions for the manifold mysteries contained within the oeuvre - from the identity and motive of the murderer of Laura Palmer, to the significance of the Black and White Lodges - and several of these solutions, seemingly opposite, have seemed to be valid, simultaneously. A reader of speculative fiction and mystery is habituated to discovering, in the final pages, whether a supernatural phenomenon is really an encounter with the spirit world - or whether it is merely a delusion which can be explained away with common sense; her experience has taught her that magical encounters generally have either/ or resolutions. In *Twin Peaks*, though, the kaleidoscope of psychological, ontological, mystical, and scientific explanations which are suggested may all be true - even at the same time - for, in Twin Peaks, classifications are not mutually exclusive, and logic is not linear. In *Twin Peaks*, the answers dwell at the cruxes of its conjunctions and even within the contradictions of its sundry disparate and opposing elements. Thus, the viewer of *Twin Peaks* may experience frustration at the close of Season 3.

In which case, she will turn to the novels - *The Secret Diary of Laura Palmer; The Autobiography of F.B.I. Special Agent Dale Cooper: My Life, My Tapes; The Secret History of Twin Peaks; and Twin Peaks: The Final Dossier* - for an explanation. The earliest, *The Secret Diary of Laura Palmer*, reveals the multi-faceted and shifting "truth" behind the sexual and mental abuse to which Laura is subjected by her father and BOB, which culminate in her death; in her diary, Laura's narrative style becomes increasingly fragmented, as she herself dissociates into parts, the bad Laura emerging to defend the good Laura - with the result that the mystery is only deepened by reading this book. *The Autobiography of F.B.I. Special Agent Dale Cooper: My Life, My Tapes* is the coming of age story of a man of innate goodness who takes life in stride - first love, hippie chicks, and close encounters with the supernatural; through this novel, the enigma of *Twin Peaks* is only increased by Cooper's prolonged and unexplained disappearance as a young man. The last, *Twin Peaks: The Final Dossier* is a compendium of FBI files on the individual characters of *Twin Peaks*; while this book provides a continuation of their life stories, answering the questions of "whatever happened to so-and-so," it does not substantially contribute to an explication of the mystique. The focus of *The Secret History of Twin Peaks*, though, is the mystery itself - the unknown quantity in which the characters, so dear to the reader, live and move and have their being. Mayhap this is where the viewer/reader will find her answers.

* * *

The texts within *Twin Peaks*, the films, as well as the novels, are marked by the themes of contradiction and the coexistence of opposites in the same space; these themes are reinforced by the intertextual structure of films and the novels, wherein opposites mingle and vie. In the first moments of the television series, as Special Agent Dale Cooper approaches Twin Peaks, on assignment to investigate the death of Laura Palmer, the series enters the realm of intertextuality. When we first meet Cooper, he is speaking to Diane on his hand-held tape recorder, detailing the line items of his expense report, speculating upon professional considerations relative to the FBI's cooperative partnership with local law enforcement, and expressing an uninhibited delight in the wonders of nature, particularly the towering pines which he later learns are Douglas Firs. He inaugurates his investigation by reviewing the dossier on the homicide of Laura Palmer, which includes a videotape of Laura picnicking with Donna Hayward, and the video text writ on the pupil of Laura's eye is a reflection

of the motorcycle belonging to James Hurley, which will lead to his iden-
tification as the videographer. Other evidence in her file includes half of a
broken heart necklace, which speaks volumes of the circumstances at the
end of Laura's life, and her own diary.

The red morocco diary is a text with a life of its own. Although Laura
has hidden the book behind her dresser, BOB finds it, violating her pri-
vacy as he does her body and mind. Laura then secretes her journal with
Harold Smith, an agoraphobic botanist whom she befriends; later, seek-
ing information about the death of her friend Laura, Donna Hayward
seduces Harold in order to retrieve the diary, a scheme which ultimately
leads to Harold's suicide. Missing pages from the volume are later found
within the layers of a toilet stall door in the ladies' room at the Twin Peaks
Sheriff's Office. The diary bares Laura's soul, witnesses her degradation
and disintegration, and leaves a trail of the safe places in which she sought
haven in the throes of her struggle.

Among Laura's found texts are her tapes to Dr. Jacoby, her therapist,
whose help she has sought without her parents' knowledge. Through the
tapes, we hear the young woman crying in her own voice for someone to
help her - she is besieged, trying to save her own life - and her very self,
for BOB is trying to get inside her; regrettably, the psychiatrist's response
to Laura's plea is a mixed one, a professional desire to help her combined
with a personal attraction, which dilutes his therapeutic approach. In
Twin Peaks, people are not neatly divisible into good guys and bad guys,
nor right so clearly separated from wrong. Indeed, the autobiographical
texts and artifacts that are contained within her homicide file at the Twin
Peaks Sheriff's Department depict Laura as neither an innocent nor a
reprobate; rather, they paint a picture of a normal human being, possess-
ing innate goodness, vulnerability, and weaknesses. A fallen angel, still
she is an angel.

Angel imagery, beginning with the picture hanging on her bedroom
wall in *Twin Peaks*: "Fire Walk with Me," and continuing throughout
Season 3, becomes an attribute of Laura, transfiguring her life story into
a hagiography and her death into a martyrdom; yet, the clippings from
Flesh World magazine (the medium for the contact ads through which
Laura and Ronette had solicited men for sex) are the autobiographical
texts which provide some of the most valuable clues that aid Dale Cooper
in the apprehension of her killer. Laura's promiscuity and prostitution
are the reactions of a gutsy rebel - a colonized young woman who has
been branded a whore by demon BOB and her own abusive father - who
is asserting her right to define her own boundaries in a world that wants

to define her (alternately as cheerleader, homecoming queen, prostitute, drug addict). Once she realizes that she has made the wrong choice, a choice which will lead to her own death, she seeks the help of Dr. Jacoby; but, tragically, she is unable to outmaneuver Leland and BOB. The multiple texts of Laura's life present a woman full of contradiction, which is a qualifier applicable to almost every human being.

* * *

In addition to emphasizing this amalgam of good and evil which is the human being, the intertextuality of Twin Peaks also explores the interconnectedness of the individual with other people and with the cosmos. Contracts (both for business and for hit jobs), insurance policies, and double-entry account books are some of the texts which entwine the Hornes, the Martells, and the Packards, whose sordid double-crossing business deals and personal liaisons result in the deaths of their own associates in crime, as well as the burning of the lumber mill, the town's primary employer; these same texts position the first families of Twin Peaks within the Black Lodge. Because of BOB's intrusion into her life, Laura is joined to the demonic Black Lodge; the angels place her in the dimension of the angelic White Lodge.

Dale Cooper, too, is connected to both the Black Lodge (through his association with serial killer Windom Earle) and the White Lodge (through his admiration of the Dalai Lama). On January 28, 1979, FBI Special Agent Dale Cooper (not yet aware that he was set up by Windom Earle) records on his hand-held tape recorder:

> Diane, how I chose to isolate myself on an island at this moment in time I do not know. Caroline Earle has been kidnapped. According to my estimation, the abduction took place at the same time I found myself falling under the influence of the narcotic. How there could be a connectionbetween events 1,500 miles apart I do not know. But I am certain thereis. Perhaps it is the Tibetan notion that there is no such thing as unrelated events, that everything is connected. (Frost, Scott, 142)

A disciple of Tibetan mysticism aspiring to enlightenment, he is still a man who has loved deeply and recklessly the wife of the arch-villain Windom Earle, his sadistic ex-partner, who is now wreaking havoc in Twin Peaks. From the texts of his Tibetan map to the cryptic prehistoric glyphs in Owl Cave to the transcripts of his tapes, Cooper is shown to be a man of potent goodness, who has erred in the desire for the love of a woman, and whose error has resulted in both her death and horrific carnage in the small town of Twin Peaks, whose fate is somehow connected to an enigmatic cosmology.

Thus, the intertextuality of *Twin Peaks* posits a cosmic view in which every entity is a part of every other entity. Where one person ends and his doppelganger in another world (or the other Lodge) begins is unclear. For better or worse, boundaries are eroded and dissolve in the intertextuality of *Twin Peaks*.

* * *

Although an appreciation of intertextuality is vital to a full under-standing of the entire canon of *Twin Peaks*, intertextuality is the very heart of *The Secret History of Twin Peaks*. *The Secret History* opens before there was a town called Twin Peaks, with selections from the expedition journals of Lewis and Clark, in which it is revealed that Meriweather Lewis receives a jade ring with a peculiar mountain-like symbol (an enig-matic text which will later be worn by Dale Cooper and other charac-ters in the *Twin Peaks* saga) in the course of his interactions with Native Americans. Additional documents in the dossier include unbound, anon-ymous manuscripts - penned by an unknown author, who references a dispatch from another unnamed writer, regarding the Lewis and Clark expedition - which are found in an unpublished collection belonging to Thomas Jefferson. An invisible cord binding invisible authors, these texts hint of occult elements, while initiating the Masonic thread which runs throughout *The Secret History:*

> Lights from the sky, the silvery spheres…music, like some heavenly choir…fire that burns but does not con-sume. . .colors unseen or unimagined, flowing from all things…gold, all gold, bright and shining. (Frost, Mark, *The Secret History of Twin Peaks*, 16)

Lewis's mysterious death, the disappearance of the jade ring, and his "bloodied Masonic apron" (*Secret History*, 31) suggest murder and con-spiracies. Through the text of FBI Agent Tammy Preston (the margin-al notes of the dossier) we learn that Lewis and Clark were - not only mapping the western territories of the United States - but also secretly investigating mythical monsters and stories of a long-dead race of giants. From the journals of Lewis and Clark to newspaper articles telling of the recent discovery of gigantic human bones unearthed in Native American burial mounds, the recurrent refrains of Great Spirit, vision quests, and monsters yoke human interactions with the extraterrestrial.

At this point, the dossier narrows its focus to the particular history of Twin Peaks, beginning with the journal of a prospector who sketched the Owl Cave drawings (the archivist tells us that the journal was found in the Masonic Lodge in Spokane). Other newspaper clippings devolve the history of the lumber barons of Twin Peaks - the Packards, the Milfords, and the Martells - whose dynastic narratives are interspersed with reporting of logging fires and Andrew Packard's sighting of Big Foot.

Next, the dossier careens through a selection of FBI and Air Force files, texts which explain the role of Douglas Milford in the atomic testing at White Sands, the Roswell UFO phenomena, and Project Sign (the 1947 UFO investigation). These texts - the Top Secret documents, flight notes of flying saucer eyewitness Kenneth Arnold, even passages from the Book of Ezekiel (often construed as alien sightings) - DNA-like, interweave the life and death of Laura Palmer and ungodly, otherworldly forces, intertextuality giving emphasis to human connectedness with the unearthly and the inhuman. The generation with which the television series and film concern themselves most enters into the dossier through the medical records of Margaret Coulson, from Calhoun Memorial Hospital, where the children lost overnight in the wood were taken for treatment. Margaret is the Log Lady, whose primary text, when she is widowed, is the log which speaks to her, telling her of things beyond common human knowledge; the three-triangle symbol on her right leg is the sign that, during that period, she had been abducted by aliens. In all of the stories contained within the dossier - from Lewis and Clark, through Big Foot, atomic testing, and alien abduction - individuals constantly work against each other, even as they are being threatened by common enemies. And everyone's boundaries have been breached by extraterrestrial and alien forces, whether or not they are aware of having been invaded.

Forward to the recent past, and Dr. Lawrence Jacoby, Laura Palmer's psychiatrist, has written *The Eye of God: Sacred Psychology in the Aboriginal Mind*, a text about his research into shamanism and hallucinogenic flora. The dossier contains Interpol documents, too, which continue to trace the nefarious dealings of Josie and Andrew Packard and the current Martells and Hornes. A photograph of a bookshelf in the Bookhouse (the headquarters of the secret vigilante group of well-meaning citizens of Twin Peaks who are trying to counter the violence and drug trafficking of the aforementioned consortiums) is supplemented by the archivist's note, which informs the reader that The Warren Commission Report on the assassination of JFK is Dale Cooper's favorite; Sheriff Harry Truman loves *To Kill a Mockingbird*; and Lucy likes *The Stand*. Each of these books provides a window into the minds of the people who read them and a different insight into the nature of the human being; these texts also reverberate the *Twin Peaks* refrains of conspiracy, small-town evil, honor, aliens, demons, and Armageddon.

The documents of Douglas Milford, who, by this time, is mixed up in Watergate and *Star Wars* and still involved in Top-Secret extra-terrestrial investigations, are the textual link to Major Garland Briggs; Garland Briggs's involvement in Project Blue Book extra-terrestrial monitoring brings about his alliance with Dale Cooper. Major Briggs, it is revealed in the final pages of the dossier, is the heretofore anonymous archivist . Milford's documents disclose that - in order to maintain the secrecy of the extraterrestrial studies - the U.S. government suborns the silencing of witnesses through murder, the destruction of Project Sign documents containing the conclusions of their study, and the development of Project Grudge, whose raison d'etre is the debunking of existing extra-terrestrial theories. There are conspiracies within conspiracies, which touch the lives of the townspeople of Twin Peaks, and which link them to other worlds. The documentary evidence contained within the covers of *The Secret History* is a schematic for an Escherian universe, where space and time and progress coil into impossible spirals and geometry submits to no rules, and where self is a fluid concept.

* * *

As part of his ongoing undercover government UFO work, now-Colonel Douglas Milford investigates L. Ron Hubbard and Aleister Crowley, whose texts bear close reading for a greater understanding of the implications of intertextuality in *The Secret History of Twin Peaks*. L. Ron Hubbard is the founder of Dianetics, the theory underlying Scientology, which holds that the human, relieved of his engrams, is an enlightened, selfless, strong, healthy, and intelligent creature - i.e., a Special Agent Dale Cooper. The ills of Man can all be attributed to engrams, which are recordings of sense experiences (sight, sound, smell, touch) within the cells of the body (not the memory), while a person is unconscious. There are numerous mechanisms by which engrams can interfere with rational thought: a person can be "handled like a marionette by his engrams" (Hubbard, v) and "the entire physical pain and painful emotion of a lifetime - whether the individual 'knows' about it or not - is contained, recorded, in the engram bank." (Hubbard, vi) Engrams can be removed by Dianetic therapy. Hubbard emphasizes the fact that the most significant engrams are acquired prenatally, even as early as a zygote, when the fetus is rendered unconscious (i.e., by the mother's coughing or attempted abortions, or by coitus between man and wife, or the beating of the wife by her husband).

Hubbard calls engrams which effect the bypassing of certain electrical circuits of the mind "demons," which can cause false memories (i.e. schizophrenia). Hubbard's engrams sound suspiciously like the aliens which infest the narrative of *Twin Peaks*, especially in light of the emphasis on electricity - the electric "tree," which calls itself "The Arm" in Red Room; the aura from the lamp at the Great Northern, the frequent extended camera shots of electric lines, and Dougie's surreal experience resulting from his sticking a fork into an electrical outlet in Season 3. On March 8, 1968, a thirteen-year-old Dale Cooper logs his reflections on electricity by means of his reel-to-reel tape recorder:

I read in a science book that electricity is what keeps
us alive. I do not understand where it comes from and
where it goes when we are dead. (Frost, Scott, 13)

Engrams, aliens, and one's fellow earthlings erode the sovereignty of one's self.

* * *

Moonchild, a novel by Aleister Crowley, is cited on several occasions in *The Secret History of Twin Peaks*. Aleister Crowley, a member of the Hermetic Order of the Golden Dawn and Ordo Templis Oris, two Masonic-style occult organizations, founded Thelema when an angel inspired him to write "The Book of the Law," and *Moonchild* is his novel which allegorizes his occult philosophy. Set before and during the Great War, *Moonchild* is the story of two groups of occultists in England who battle for the child, conceived by magician Cyril Grey and Lisa la Giuffria, whose form, through nine months of the working of ceremonial magick, is entered by the entity known as the Moonchild. It is worth looking closely at *Moonchild*, for its many parallels with the mythology of the canon of *Twin Peaks* (the television series, the movie, and the books).

First, the White Lodge occultists of *Moonchild* strive to bend their wills to the "universal will," which is "Love giving itself to the beloved again and again, until its 'I' is continuous with existence itself." (Crowley, 99) As in the Tibetan mysticism with which Dale Cooper is enamored and which give him entrée into the White Lodge of Twin Peaks, enlightenment is achieved through negation of self.

Furthermore, for the White Lodge in Moonchild, opposites blend into Truth:

> All the serious words are jests, and all the jokes are earnest. . .You keep on reversing it; and it gets funnier and more serious every time, and it spins faster and faster until you cannot follow it, and your brain begins to whirl, and presently you become That Spiral Force which is the Quintessence of the Absolute. . .Wise, True Wisdom and Perfect Happiness. (Crowley, 139)

Twin Peaks, too, is a bubbling mass of contradictions, from opposing doppelgangers to alternate realities, to a twisted blending of horror and comedy.

Thirdly, Lisa, the madonna of Moonchild, is subject to visions and extra-corporeal experiences (for instance, seeing herself standing next to Artemis), while she abides in the Butterfly Net (the Italian villa where she prepares, through sex magick with Cyril Grey, to attract the Moonchild to her womb). In The Secret History of Twin Peaks, both Meriweather Lewis and Nez Perce Chief Joseph undergo vision quests of their own at the Twin Peaks double waterfall; and Dr. Jacoby takes part in a vision quest, too, as part of his research on hallucinogenic drugs and shamanism. Douglas Milford's report describes the Egyptian sex magick of the Thelema cult at the Parsonage (the mansion of Jack Parsons) and quotes Parson (speaking to Hubbard): Crowley "didn't need drugs. He was drugs" (Secret History, 247) and "Magick is just the name we've always given to things we don't yet understand." (Secret History, 250) L. Ron Hubbard, Milford tells us, is wearing the jade ring with the enigmatic mountain symbol, another text which works its way through Twin Peaks, inextricably entangling all the characters and their myriad adventures.

Fourthly, in Moonchild, as in Twin Peaks, there is also a Black Lodge, which, through rituals of black magic, engineers a train wreck in order to abduct Lisa and Cyril en route to the Butterfly Net, a scheme which backfires and causes the death of the black magician Akbar Pasha. The Black Lodge of Moonchild "rules by terror and torture; its first principle was to enslave its members" (Crowley, 76) and it is always "seething with hate," (Crowley, 78) descriptors which could just as well be applied to the Black Lodge of Twin Peaks. The villains of the Twin Peaks Black Lodge (the Martells, the Hornes, the Packards, and their henchmen) burn the lumber mill, swindle each other, engage in sex- and drug-trafficking, and kill in cold blood. In a race to the death with Cooper and the Bookhouse Boys - who are trying to halt the runaway train of gratuitous murder and suffering which have been deployed by Windom Earle - Earle is searching for the entrance to the Black Lodge. In Season 2, Windom Earle succeeds in opening the Gate of the Black Lodge during the conjunction of Jupiter and Saturn, at the portal in Glastonbury Grove, unleashing the powers of pure evil. And, in *The Secret History*, Milford's expose of Hubbard and Crowley narrates the decline and fall of Jack Parsons, subsequent to Hubbard's elopement with both Parsons's money and his girlfriend: Parsons, too, is hell-bent on finding a way into the Black Lodge. Now a beach bum (and head of the Pasadema Thelema cult) Parsons investigates "Hell's Gate" and the "seven gateways on the planet to hell" (*Secret History*, 258) and opens the gate via ritual magick, and a second "effort to open a second gate that they'd found in the desert, in order to bring across an entity he called 'the Moonchild.'" (*Secret History*, 261)

In both *Moonchild* and *Dianetics*, evil beings of all kinds are intent upon immersing and submerging themselves in the Black Lodge. And in both texts, enlightenment requires a similar renunciation of self, the subjugation of one's will into an altruistic "universal will" ("The Way of the Tao" in *Moonchild*, or becoming a "Clear" in *Dianetics*). There is danger in both white and black magick:

> An ordinary man would not have touched the Thing. It was on a different plane, and would no more have interfered with him than sound interferes with light. A young magician, one who had opened a gate on to that plane, but who had not yet become master of that plane, might have been overcome. The Thing might even have dispossessed his ego, and used his body as its own. That is the beginner's danger in magick. (Crowley, 44)

* * *

Suppose a person - like Laura Palmer - does not wish to relinquish her selfhood, either to the Thing, or to BOB, or to the universal will. Suppose she does not wish to repudiate herself to join either the White Lodge or the Black Lodge. In *Twin Peaks*, the borders of the self are repeatedly violated; they are blurred with the extra-human - recall the Red Room and the Other World of Season 3, in which all is one, where Dale Cooper chases his doppelganger (or, does the doppelganger chase Cooper?). In the story of Laura's exploitation and murder (as well as her father's possession by BOB) not only the lives of two people, but their selfhoods are at stake. The struggle of the individual - Laura, Dale Cooper, Garland Briggs, and the entire cast of characters - for a discrete selfhood in an enigmatic and unsympathetic universe is what makes *Twin Peaks* an epic in the most profound sense. Although it costs her her life, Laura refuses to allow BOB to "taste through" her.

Through the employment of intertextuality, a multiplicity of narratives can bring to novels a more composite vision that stretches the limitations of a traditional single, biased narrator; in *Twin Peaks*, the intertextuality of the dossiers, the films, and the novels yields a fragmented mosaic, not a cohesive whole, a puzzle with missing pieces in some places, and - in other places - two pieces vying to claim one spot. Boundaries are eroded. Opposites coexist in the same place and time, but not always peaceably. Doppelgangers, dimensions, angels, demons, and mortals merge and struggle. Self-definition and self-direction are questionable objectives. Objectivity does not exist. There is no framework. A mortal being moves in and through her own text and the texts of others - and they move within hers. This is the ultimate tragedy of our existence: the unavoidable fall of every individual human being, because we all have the hubris to believe in the existence of our own selves.

Laura, though, fights for her selfhood. "It's always been about Laura," the Log Lady says in her prologues on the DVD's. Yet, Laura is the golden orb sent to earth by the divine creatures, The Fireman and Lady Dido; and Laura is a doppelganger in the Red Room; and Laura is reincarnated as Carrie Page at the series' conclusion. What is Laura's selfhood? Has she saved it? Lost it? Or was it never more than a fantasy? This riddle is the dark and sublime tragedy of *Twin Peaks*.

Bibliography

Crowley, Aleister. *Moonchild*. Augusta, GA: Mockingbird Press, 1922, 2019.

Frost, Mark. *The Secret History of Twin Peaks*. New York: Flatiron Books, 2016.

Frost, Mark. *Twin Peaks: The Final Dossier*. New York: Flatiron Books, 2017.

Frost, Scott. *The Autobiography of F.B.I. Special Agent Dale Cooper: My Life, My Tapes*. New York: Pocket Books, 1991.

Hubbard, L. Ron. *Dianetics: the Modern Science of Mental Health*. Los Angeles: Bridge Publications, 1950, 2007.

Lynch, Jennifer. *The Secret Diary of Laura Palmer*. New York: Gallery Books, 1990.

Twin Peaks: A Limited Event Series. Created by Mark Frost and David Lynch, Showtime, 2017.

Twin Peaks. Created by Mark Frost and David Lynch, Lynch/Frost
    Productions, 1990-1991.
Twin Peaks: Fire Walk with Me. Written by David Lynch and
    Robert Engels, Twin Peaks Productions, 1992.

THE TEMPLE CATS OF BRIN-NA-BOOL

Scott J. Couturier

The Temple Cats of Brin-na-Bool
feed on midnight thieves as rule.
By day decadent on silken throws,
somnolent in sunlight: asleep in rows.
Pilgrims come to pay humble tithe
& stroke the guardians, lean & lithe.

Yet - when night-time's veil draws down
to drape that eld immemorial town,
they rise & stalk with gleaming eyes:
any intruder rent amid yowling cries.
The nave, full of Brin-na-Bool's jewels
serves as flytap for the tastiest of fools.

Come morning, the priests greet the day
& mop all excess of dried blood away.
Their god delights not in shows of gore:
nevertheless stained black is that floor
where his wardens lay in languid wreath,
strips of meat stuck in contented teeth.

So give always should you see a shrine
where sated felines sit with tails entwin'd.
Your gold will go to glut those coffers
of a god who takes (but never offers),
save - his sentinels are soft & sweet,
& rid us of robbers as rats among wheat.

HOW WITCHES AND WARLOCKS DO IT

Darrel Schweitzer

Witches and warlocks can uproot a mandrake
and hear its shrill scream
without going mad, because
they are mad already, though
their madness is not of this world.

Witches and warlocks can swim in the earth,
as in a dark pool, and grope
for the dead, then assemble their bones,
first to yield secrets,
and later to dance.

Witches and warlocks can cut out your heart
and put in a stone, so deftly, so subtly,
that you never suspect,
till one night they whisper,
the name of your death.

Witches and warlocks have to be mad,
to barter salvation for one moment's glimpse
of Satan's proud rage,
to embrace his despair
out of lust or revenge.

But that's how they do it.

MA DA

Ngo Binh Anh Khoa

In the silent veil of night
When dark clouds consume the light,
When the lesser whistling ducks
And the fretful coucals might
Cry their haunting mourning tune,
All the ma da, filled with spite,
Are about in streams and lakes,
Searching for a prey in sight.

Those foul remnants of the drowned,
By their woe and suffering bound,
Are condemned to stay on Earth
Till they pass their curse around
To the victims that they catch,
Who, when forcibly dragged down
To their murky watery graves,
Shall be lost and never found.

Many have become their prey -
Kids who would near water play
And poor folk who wandered close
To the riverbanks where they
Felt the frigid hands, which reeked
Of diseases and decay,
Grab their limbs and harshly pull;
Few would see the light of day.

Those abducted souls would see
Naught but pain and misery,
Trapped in rotting corpses while
Their own murderers walk free
Or move on and be reborn;
Soon corrupted they would be,
Thus repeating that accursed
Cycle of death endlessly.

In the shroud of darkness deep,
When creations are asleep,
Should the lesser whistling ducks
And the coucals wail and weep,
Stay away from streams and lakes,
And your feet on dry land keep,
Far from where the ma da lurk,
Waiting for a soul to reap.

WOMAN WALKING

Lori R. Lopez

Her steps brisk and light; shoulders bowed
A woman clad in dismal garb did tread
The most isolated course of fog and night

The image of fright, her spine hunched
Marla Bland would hasten full of dread
An eerie road with no house in sight

Drably frocked, intent upon her path
Bent to a journey the woman did speed
'Long a desolate lane so seldom walked

Hoot-Owls mocked; she stayed her route
In desperation, from the depth of need
Braving the dark as the hour tocked

When from the mist a companion rang
An echo of footfalls ahead of her tapped -
Another figure seen hurrying to a tryst

Such a curious twist, the pair so entwined
With matching pace and strides that adapt
Neither rushed nor slowed, they co-exist

She could not alone keep to this journey
Its lull disrupted, its quiet perturbed
Ruminations torn, into panic thrown

From dangers unknown, a stranger close by
Whether foe or friendly, kind or disturbed
The risks were many to a lady on her own

Joining the queue, a third party was heard
Following her tracks. Three spirits aligned
Maintaining a gait while traveling by shoe

Marla sought to subdue the sound of her trek
Concealed from each cadence before and behind
Ghostlike, she drifted toward her rendezvous

If only she recalled the precise destination!
Specters in a row graced a cheerless eve -
Caught in the middle Miss Bland, appalled

Together or enthralled, a trio promenaded
Grown anxious, the second began to grieve
For a fate that could not be forestalled

Unable to discern without peering in reverse
How near the last in this line had become
A threat or benign she must rapidly learn

With a quick headturn, she gaped at a wraith
Approaching her swiftly to harm or numb
And dashed to escape with feverish concern

No chance to appraise the phantom in the lead
To determine the worth and trust or revile -
Darting forth, heart cloaked by fear, malaise

She called in a daze, "Will you walk with me?"
Then faltered, astonished, and shook in denial
A woman stared back through a torpid haze

The form in bleak dress soon charged away
An echo trailed, the words from two lips
"Will you walk with me?" and nothing less

Born of macabre duress, the query hounded
A face in mirrors. A mad loop of trips
In pursuit of herself would Marla transgress

Dusk till Dawn. Trapped in the shadows
From Gloaming to Sunrise with hollow eyes
The lady marched for all women, a pawn

Whether colorful or wan; alluring, withdrawn -
Encountering her end in the guise of surprise
As she met a callous touch. Alive and gone.

IS *COLOR OUT OF SPACE* THE BEST CINEMATIC LOVECRAFT ADAPTATION?

Gary Hill

THERE HAVE BEEN a lot of films based on the works of H.P. Love-craft. It's often been said that his work is un-filmable. I don't think that's true at all, and plenty of the movies based on his writings prove that. However, I do think you have to walk a fine line between faithful inter-pretation and taking liberties with the material. Perhaps the story on which this film is based, "The Colour Out of Space" is one of the most problematic from a film-making point of view. How do you visually rep-resent a color that isn't like any other color humans have seen? I think Richard Stanley's movie does a great job of that and a lot of other things.

The movie, *Color Out of Space*, has a release date of 2019 some places and 2020 others. That's because it premiered at some film conventions in 2019, but had wider release, including home video debut, the following year. The movie was to be the first of a Lovecraft trilogy, but some recent events that I won't address in this review have thrown that into question, at least for the time being.

The story (and film) land somewhere in a shared land between science fiction and horror. That said, I would suggest that the movie, in partic-ular, lands more fully on the horror end of the equation. The premise of both is that a meteor crashes to Earth on a farm and begins infecting everything in the surrounding area. In order to talk about this movie in more depth, I'll need to bring up more details about the story, so it should be mentioned that there will be spoilers beyond this point.

Perhaps the first thing to discuss is Nicholas Cage. He plays the father of the family, one of the main characters in the film, Nathan Gardner. Cage is sort of a force of nature. In many ways you know what you are going to get with him. I know a lot of people dislike him. I personally like most movies I've seen with him, but neither because of or despite his performance. I have seen complaints about his over-the-top acting in this film, and I can see what they are talking about. The thing is, that mode really kicks in when he's in the process of losing his mind, so I think it makes sense.

Another factor that will determine the level of enjoyment for fans of Lovecraft is how you feel about usage of source material. Personally, I generally think that the beats and plots of a story are what makes it special, and that details can be changed without greatly altering the story. If you feel that movies need to be more faithful than that, you might have some issues with this film.

If you are a detail-based person, there are a lot of details changed from the text to the film. For one thing, the story takes place over a period of a couple years, but everything in the movie seems to happen over the course of a few days. Gardner's children are all boys in Lovecraft's tale, but he has two sons and a daughter in the movie. Tommy Chong plays a character who lives in a cabin on the property, and that character is an addition to the original story. That said, it almost feels as if that character takes the place of Ammi Pierce in Lovecraft's story. It's not a tight fit, though, as Pierce survives the tale, while Chong's Ezra does not. Beyond those things the other major change is that rather than creating a period piece, Stanley set the film in the modern age.

Lovecraft's story is told as a second-hand account by an unnamed surveyor, who is working toward the creation of a new reservoir. That character in the film gets a name "Ward Phillips" and he does (off camera) provide the opening narration (which is a direct quote from the story) and the closing one (partly on camera). Instead of a surveyor, he's a hydrologist, but his purpose is essentially the same. In the film he actually takes part in the happenings, and in the climax actually takes the place of Pierce's character. So, perhaps, in a way, the Pierce character has been split into two characters in the film.

One prevalent theme of the film is the sheer helplessness of mankind against cosmic forces. That theme, while perhaps not as blatant in "The Color Out of Space," is certainly one of the most common themes in Lovecraft's work in general. I think one of the most obvious examples in the film is that all the religious requests for help (of the Wiccan variety) made by Lavinia Gardner (Naham's daughter) make no difference. That includes a ritual performed with the *Necronomicon* (in a further knock against man-made religion the copy used is the *Simon Necronomicon*).

Another theme to the film, which is not present in the story really, is an environmental one. Certainly in the modern era, the symbolism of the water tainted by the cosmic entity infecting the farm is a metaphor for the damage being done by our poisoned environment. Also, a point brought up later in the film, that the mother of the family (who has been fused to her son by the light from the cosmic force) seems to be trying to absorb him. I think that might be symbolism of planet Earth seeking to pull us back into herself via climate disasters to come. Either way, this is an environmental statement that I don't think Lovecraft intended, but certainly fits the story.

Getting back to the idea of a color that can't be described, I think Stanley did a good job of it. That color seems to shift, but generally lands somewhere in the purple and pink range most of the time. The fact that you can never really pin it down, though, is a good way to simulate that indescribable attribute. I also love the way there are strange colors and changes that are almost background imagery throughout once the meteor hits. Some of them are subtle enough that you probably won't even notice them on the first viewing. They did some great post production work on the film.

The movie also makes great use of both practical effects and CGI. In the story, and the film, the meteor begins transforming everything around it. One of my favorite examples of that in the movie is a strange looking insect, almost part grass hopper, part mantis. It's at once beautiful and frightening. It's pure CGI, but it also looks very real.

In terms of the practical effects, there are a couple great examples of that. The family's alpacas (another small change from the story) become merged together and strangely distorted and grotesque. The use of effects and the look of the creature call to mind something from John Carpenter's *The Thing* to me.

The other example comes later in the movie when the hybrid beast made up of the mother and son moves around on four limbs. I should mention that the story has a reference to the mother moving around that way ("...By July she had ceased to speak and crawled on all fours...") When that is presented in the film, she has became a strange, almost spider-like, creature that reminds me of the Stuart Gordon Lovecraft film *From Beyond*.

In more general terms, this is a movie that starts as a slow burn. I often describe John Carpenter movies as a snowball going down a hill, gathering more speed and mass as it does. It's a trait I really like in films, and *Color Out of Space* has it for certain. There are some genuinely horrifying scenes here. The thing is, there is also an unusual dichotomy. Often the terror is beautiful and revolting at the same time, as some of the characters actually say. That is a really hard balance to pull off, and the fact that the filmmakers were able to do it so well is impressive.

Referencing my title for this piece, is it the greatest Lovecraft film ever made? That question is sort of a cheap trick I used to frame the piece.

I don't think you can really pick a movie as the best adaptation - many qualify for different reasons. If you want to get into faithful adaptations, certainly the two from the H.P. Lovecraft Historical Society would be at or near the top of the list. If you prefer crazed versions that take a lot of liberties with the material, you probably want some of the Stuart Gordon films. I think this one lands somewhere in between those two extremes.

From a totally personal point of view, this has become my all-time favorite horror film. John Carpenter's *Prince of Darkness* held that spot for many years until this movie. Certainly people who have trouble with Nicholas Cage, and those who want more literal representations of the textual source, will have problems with this. The movie is a piece of art that is also frightening, and it really does a great job of capturing the important points of Lovecraft's story. I've also found that it gets better on repeated viewings. That's a sign of a movie that is likely to hold up well over the years.

MATTHEW LANGTREE WENT HUNTING

Sarah Cannavo

THE WOODS HAD BEEN HIS SECOND HOME even before the war, so when the war came it was only natural Matthew Langtree became a scout in General Washington's army. So well he discharged his duties, helping the ragged Patriot troops avoid ambush and harrying the lobsterbacks as they marched across the colonies, that the British put a bounty on his head, which he remained unutterably proud of. It was said of Matthew Langtree that he was as good a tracker as any man had ever been, that a serpent in the grass was not as quick or quiet as he when he moved through the trees, nor as deadly as he when it struck.

He never fought for or sought glory, though, and if a man didn't recognize his name when it was said, that suited him fine. With the war several years over he lived contentedly in Connecticut with his cheerful wife, his bonny Annie, and a passel of incorrigible children, supporting his family hunting and trapping, as happy in the forest as at home.

The day that changed was a fine golden one late in summer. Recent evenings had held a hint of the autumn coming, crisp as the apple Matthew took a lusty bite into as he left his family's well-built house, wiping away with the back of his hand the juice that ran into his dark brown beard, but that morning was pleasantly warm, and green leaves nodded lazily in the sun-licked breeze.

Ahead of him Annie was hanging the wash on the lines and teasingly scolding the twins as they harried the hens in the yard, the laughing voices of the other children carrying from elsewhere around the property, Peggy and Peter and Ben. Their mother had two baskets at her feet, one full of damp linens and in the other their swaddled six-month daughter Mary squirming and cooing, and her back to Matthew, red hair blazing as it spilled down between her shoulder blades.

She didn't know he was there, and the children hadn't yet seen him. Matthew crept up behind Annie, caught her about the waist and lifted, burying his face in her neck and growling bearlike, playfully. She shrieked and kicked, long skirts rustling, and laughter bled through into her words even as she beat at his arms and demanded, "Put me down, Matthew Langtree! What kind of a man are you, scaring the shite out of your wife like that?"

He set her down and kissed her when she spun to face him, and when they broke apart she was grinning, face framed by a few loose curls and flushed to match them beneath her thick scattering of freckles. "I'm sorry," he offered, but he couldn't keep from grinning back at her, his brassy, buxom Annie, as she tossed her head. She was thirty-four, as he was, and neither her beauty nor her spirit had dulled a bit since the day he'd met her.

"You ought to be," Annie said, "but don't you make it worse by lying to me. Bad enough you decided to maul me - "

"As I remember, sweet Annie, there's been quite a few times you've enjoyed my maulings. And livin' proof's headin' this way as we speak."

The twins had seen Matthew and left off tormenting the hens, scattering them one last time as they charged towards their father, chubby, sturdy legs pumping. "Da! Da!" Jacob and Jeremiah cried happily, and Matthew stooped and scooped them up, letting out a mock-"oof" at the four-year-olds' weight and making them laugh with his bewhiskered kisses.

"You're gettin' to be pretty big now, aren'tcha, boys?" Matthew said, looking with pride at his youngest sons. "Aye, maybe not grown enough for me to take you hunting without losing my scalp to your lovely mother when we get back, but soon enough, I'd say." He tossed a wink at his wife. "Until then, listen to your mother. And leave off those poor hens!" he called as he set Jacob and Jeremiah down and they tore off again, straight back to the yard.

"You're in fine spirits today," Annie observed, catching Matthew's apple as he tossed it lightly to her and bent to tickle and make faces at baby Mary burbling in the basket, taking a large bite of the ripe red fruit herself.

"Why wouldn't I be? I've got a fine wife, fine children, the sun is shining - "

" - and you've got your boots on and your gun on your shoulder," Annie said as he stood. "As well as you know the woods, I know my man."

His grin was as broad as the brim of his hat. "And more than I love the woods, I love my woman."

She smiled back, but it was a small one, and when she spoke her manner was more subdued, a soft seriousness settling like a mist over her countenance. "Just make sure you come back to me, woodsman," she said, smoothing the lapels of his brown leather coat.

Surprised, Matthew caught her hands and held them close. "Of course I will, Annie," he said, his own tone softening as his brown eyes caught her green. "Always. No matter how far I roam, it'll never be enough to keep me from coming back to you again."

Annie nodded, smiling, and whatever cloud there had been cleared. "I know," she said, leaning into his touch as he cupped her face, and they had time enough for a kiss before the other children flooded over to wish their father goodbye.

Matthew waved to them as he went. He had bread and cheese to eat later, his hatchet on one hip and a whisky flask on the other, and his gun slung on his shoulder; he needed nothing more, and he was smiling as the trees swallowed him.

***

Dusk was falling when he first felt he was being followed.

Until then, things had been going well. The snares he'd set had worked and he now carried a brace of coneys on his back, a couple of quail rounding out the catch. The roar of his gun had shattered the stillness of the day and scattered the rest of the plump brown birds, but Matthew had made his shot and was smiling as he collected his fallen quarry from the sun-soaked clearing, leaves crunching beneath his boots as he leapt a fallen log and landed.

"They might not be Tories, Langtree, but they'll sure as shite be more welcome at the table," Matthew laughed, hefting the birds, the shots still ringing in his ears.

He'd dressed his catch beside a small running stream, washing the blood from his hands and his blade in the clear chill water, and rested there for a bit afterwards, chasing his simple meal with a few deep gulps from his flask. Warmed by the whisky's burn, and comfortably full, he'd drowsed there for a bit with his hat pulled low as the sun slanted in butter-colored bars through the trees, dreaming of Annie, and dinner. Matthew Langtree was a man of simple pleasures, and had never hidden nor attempted to change that, and those close to him knew no matter how rough his outer edges were, within was a soul as fierce and loyal as could be wanted, so most of those rough edges were forgiven him, and usually looked upon fondly.

After he'd woken he'd wandered more, tracking the trail of a buck half-hoping to find it and bring it down and half for the pure thrill of the hunt. But intent as he was on the trail Matthew had lost track of time, coming to only when he realized how low the light had gotten, how long his shadow stretched at his heels.

"Shit," he muttered, straightening from the hoof-prints he'd been studying and scanning instead the sky, the darkening bark of the trees around him. A violet stain had settled on the horizon and was seeping outward as the sun sank amid vivid scarlet streaks of cloud, and there was a bit more of a bite to the air now; Matthew drew his leather coat tighter and repeated, "Shit."

He had no worries about finding his way home, even in the dark; no, he had but one concern as he struck his lantern alight and lifted it aloft, and that was Annie. "Oh, she's gonna skin me alive," he said, setting off with lantern bobbing and rabbits thumping against his back into the deepening twilight.

He hadn't gone far before the back of his neck began to prickle, his skin crawling with the sense of eyes upon him, and he stopped short and looked around for the source, listened for footfalls that stopped an instant after his did. Aside from the shadows growing by the moment in the dusk Matthew saw nothing; apart from the rustling leaves and the rasp of his breath the woods were still and silent, but the feeling refused to abate, and he hadn't survived what he had by ignoring his instincts.

"Hello?" he called as the day's last light died and night settled, black and smooth, over the land, a crescent of bone-white moon shining faintly down through the dark. "Hey - is anyone out there?"

If there was, they didn't speak. *Maybe not a white man, then.* But a greeting in the local Indian dialect brought no response, either, save for the crickets' impassive chirping, and after scanning his surroundings a final time Matthew warily lowered his lantern and resumed walking, keeping his left hand closer to his weapon than before and his senses keen for the slightest disturbance.

He passed a winding mile in which his footfalls sounded much too loud on the detritus of the forest floor and the nearby cry of a whippoorwill pierced the chill hush like a knife. The trees loomed close around him; the lush green leaves had turned black, like drops of ink dripping from the boughs, and they shuddered at the touch of the low wind. The sense still crept up on him, that he was being followed, that there were eyes somewhere watching; at times it ebbed, but it never faded away completely, and it left him restless, on edge.

If somebody was following him - and it had to be another human, if it was anything at all; Matthew had hunted cunning animals before, but stealth and behavior such as this he'd never yet seen - why? he wondered as he walked, the brace of coneys he carried bumping against his back in time with his heartbeat. What purpose was it serving? An attempt to frighten him? The sense of being stalked was unnerving, to be sure, but at the moment Matthew was more angered than afraid, fuming as he moved further through the forest, the flame of his lantern flickering and shivering as he went.

And then came the snap of a branch somewhere behind him, the distinct sound of a footfall. He spun about, his heart giving a skip and a thump, and held the lantern high, light and shadow painting his face in wavering strokes.

"All right," he shouted, his blood a froth in his body. His gaze darted through the circling dark, but there was no shape weaving through the trees, nobody crouching amid the brush, and there came no more sounds to betray a presence. Still he shouted again, "All right, you've had your bloody fun; now come out and show yourself, if you've got the fuckin' stones, you bastard."

The wind moaned low in the trees. The crickets and night-birds had fallen silent. His blood thudded dully in his ears.

And then something blew out his lantern.

His heart started pounding then, as he felt something brush by behind him and the forest's unearthly dark swarmed him, black as a crow's wing. He spun, seeking a moving shadow among the still clustered rest, but his wild gaze found nothing as he fumbled one-handed, dry-mouthed, for his gun, still turning, always turning, unwilling to take his eyes from the trees.

No - the lantern. Light the lantern, Langtree, you halfwit.

But it was several moments before the message made it from his whirling brain to his shock-stiffened fingers, and as he groped in his coat for his matches his every nerve was already afire, each sense awake and alert. A laugh rasped from his throat as his hand closed on the matches, but there came a large rustle from the brush behind him as he went to light the lantern and it slipped from his grip, his stomach falling with it. He could tell from the sound as it struck the earth it had cracked, was worthless now, and a hissed "Shit" slipped through his gritted teeth.

But he didn't mourn the lantern long, couldn't; there was someone - something - out there in the woods with him, clever enough to blow out the light and somehow quick enough to keep behind him the whole time, allowing Matthew not even the briefest glimpse from the corner of his eyes. He pulled his gun from his shoulder, fingers flexing, eyes already adjusting to the dark, and kept a careful watch, and as the thunder of his blood settled a bit he found every other sound had died away - not just the insects and owls, but the breeze, the whispers of the leaves on the trees and the muffled crackles of those already fallen, as if in deference to or fear of whatever stalked him now.

He walked and watched, and watched and walked, and though each step brought him closer to home he wasn't nearly as close as he wished to be - inside, with the door bolted safely behind him. He'd challenge any man who called him a coward, but Matthew Langtree was no fool, either, and to not be unnerved by the unearthly precision with which this unseen foe was pursuing him would be, he was coldly certain, to gamble with his life.

He was still hurrying on when the noise crept out of the darkness, low at first and growing louder, standing the hair on the back of his neck on end and setting his teeth on edge. It was a strange sound, a rattling, almost, a chittering that came from the throat of no animal he knew, nor a swarm of insects, and as it came, and came again, the night around him seemed to hum with it; he felt like he'd swallowed lightning, his skin crawling and spine a line of fire.

"What the hell - " he managed, and then it came just a breath behind him, crawling over his sweat-soaked skin.

Matthew swung around with a shout, gun raised, and fired. The shot deafened him, blew the night to bits, and should have done the same to anyone behind him, but there was no spray of blood, no crumpling body, just a branch shattering on a tree several yards distant and falling to earth in a shower of bark.

How - ?

He stood there panting, disbelieving; he licked his lips and his tongue stung with salt. "How," he said aloud, hoarse as a crow's caw, "how?", and as the ringing in his ears died away the quiet crept back and lingered for a minute - and then, low, the noise came again.

He ran.

Branches reached down to snag, to snare him; roots protruded from the earth like half-buried bones and he swore as he stumbled over one, regained his footing and kept going. Matthew ran until he found better cover and once there dropped to his knee in the brush, reaching for his powder horn to reload his gun with sweat-slickened hand.

What the hell made a sound like that? What the hell was stalking him? The night itself felt alien, hostile; how could he be sure, cover or no, he wasn't still being watched this very moment?

"Get a hold a' yourself, Langtree, you bastard," he muttered, furiously reloading his gun, looking all around him as he did so. Moonlight shuddered and dripped on the brush, patches of white and black warring on the leaf-strewn ground. "You're actin' like you've never been in a fuckin' fight before."

But not one like this, he knew that now even if he couldn't figure the nature of it, no, never one like this, and if he made it home from this hunt Annie could be as angry at him as she liked for being late but she'd have to be grateful she still had a husband to howl at, though he had no idea how he'd explain any of this to her when he couldn't comprehend the cause of his fear himself.

Although as he cautiously peered from his cover, gun at the ready, he remembered unbidden a tale he'd heard a whey-faced private tell in camp during the war, after several soldiers on patrol had failed to return and all that'd been found were their guns and signs of a struggle, the tale of a creature Private Fitzpatrick had called "the hide-behind," some American beast he couldn't describe because, he'd said, it was always behind you, never seen.

"And it sucks its stomach in so it can hide behind any tree," he'd insisted, looking ready to shit himself then and there at the fireside, so much a boy Matthew had felt an old man beside him, young enough that he was himself. "And it hunts humans in the woods - my da's a trapper, he told me about it, it chased him once, and maybe it got those men tonight - !"

The other soldiers had laughed and passed the whisky around again. "Or it might've been those beasts called the British, lad," Leftenant Connors had said, clapping Fitzpatrick on the back. "No need to invent more enemies than we already have, eh?"

"If this hide-behind's such an American critter, you'd think it'd feast on a few lobsterbacks instead of our own," Matthew had added, swigging deep from the whisky.

Fitzpatrick had protested, persisted, but nobody had paid much more mind than they had at first, and the next day the company had moved out, and battle obliterated any thought of some forest spook.

But far from that fireside, being trailed by some unseen thing, Matthew Langtree found himself more willing to believe, and if tomorrow found him laughing at himself in the bright light of day - well, at least he was alive to laugh.

He thought back now - had Private Fitzpatrick mentioned some way to avoid or deter the hide-behind? Matthew thought he had, but he'd been half-listening, more concerned with where he'd be scraping up his next meal than some monster no one'd ever seen. What was it? *Think, damn it...*

The noise came again.

Behind him.

He spun and fired, and his gun jammed.

A wave of ice crashed down over Matthew, freezing his blood in his veins and his breath in his lungs. But by instinct his hand flew to his hatchet, and as his fingers curled tight around its notched handle some heat returned to him, his strength - a hatchet couldn't jam. It had seen years of use but he kept the edge keen, and he had it half-raised as he slung his jammed gun back over his shoulder and backed out of the brush, eyes on the area where the sound had last come from.

He was closer to home now; if he kept his pursuer at bay long enough, he thought, he could make it. But could he keep it at bay that long? His heartbeat was skipping, stuttering like a candle flame unprotected in a breeze. If he could just remember what Fitzpatrick had said deterred the thing, the day before a mortar had taken his life at Monmouth - what? There had to be something....

Each foot he traveled felt a mile; each mile seemed to take an eternity to traverse. And behind him, always behind him, the crack of a branch beneath another foot, the rustling of fallen leaves, that God-awful chittering creeping closer, ever closer, and did it come from the throat of his pursuer, that sound, Matthew wondered, or its stomach, some hideous sound of hunger from a starveling stomach shrunk beneath hollow ribs or bloated with the last unwary traveler to cross its path but still not sated, never to truly be - ?

"Stop it," Matthew hissed at himself, blinking sweat from his eyes. "You sound like Ben, scaring himself to death with spook stories before bed."

Crack.

Crunch.

Chitter.

So close, so close...

What did it look like? Tall? Thin? Covered in dark fur or cracked skin, with claw-tipped fingers to rend, to ravage, or paws, a mouth crammed with yellowed fangs or horribly toothless, soft and black, a moist black pit made for sucking? What did the beast stalking him down look like; with what eyes did it follow his progress toward home? Hot yellow ones, red embers, lightless pools of black boring into his back, marking him as prey, as game, just as he'd tracked the quail he carried now?

Chitter.

Crack.

Crunch.

So close.

And he was so close to home and safety, hurrying, hurrying on, just as his memories wheeled and whirled in his mind, as madly and muddled as the leaves he kicked up spun about his boots; the night wind was cool but his muscles burned and sweat ran in rivulets down his spine, his heart a hammer in his chest. His thoughts were less thoughts than animal screams for survival, his every moment an act of pure primal instinct.

CHITTER.

He whirled and hurled his hatchet; it sunk with a thunk into the trunk of a nearby tree, without a scrap of fur or flesh in sight. "Damn it." Matthew ran, yanked his weapon from the furrow it'd cleaved in the pine tree, fingers for a moment frighteningly slick on the handle.

For God's sake, Fitzy, what'd you say scared this fucking thing off - ?

But any hope of the hide-behind's fear was lost beneath a sudden rush of his own, each beat of his heart a plunge into cold, deep water as his circling steps slowed, then stopped, eyes still flicking wildly about as the thought struck him.

If this creature could hide behind anything - Matthew pictured a skeleton-like shadow-shape, looming and razor-limbed, sucking in its stomach to fit behind a tree - how would he know if it was there, pressed up against his own back?

And when the sound came this time, it didn't come loud but close, soft as a whisper - and right in Matthew's right ear.

He broke then, and bolted - not for cover, as he had before, but blindly ahead, as fast and far as his feet could carry him. He crashed through brush and branches whipped him, left bleeding scratches on his skin and leaves in his beard; mud sucked like starving mouths at his boots and his every step was a peril, his heart seizing every time he skidded or slid. His hat was knocked free and the wind raked fingers through his hair; his lungs burned and each breath was like swallowing fire. But still he ran, knowing he was chased and what would happen if he was caught.

A root caught his foot and he fell, sprawling hard on the forest floor. His mouth filled with earth and blood and he spit as he scrambled up and stumbled forward, forcing himself to find his feet and imagining as he did a swiping claw just missing his skin.

Fear had run screaming into every fight beside him, whether battle or ambush; fear had gripped his heart in a fist of iron and wrung it mercilessly as Annie screamed for hours in childbed with the twins, who were refusing to come. Fear was a hot snake in Matthew's gut now, stabbing through him and spurring him on, over fallen logs and through bracken, into surroundings more blessedly familiar; he was nearly home now, nearly there, and he couldn't die here, wouldn't let himself be dragged off and devoured, his bones gnawed upon, cracked open, in some dank hellish lair among the remains of how many other vanished travelers and left there to lie undiscovered forever, no, God damn it, no - !

Something lashed against his back, gripped him; he shouted and wrestle his way forward, felt his coat rip and a weight vanish from his back: the rabbits, torn away instead of his own flesh, and he kept running, and the chittering sounded angry now, he couldn't be imagining that, could he? The anger of a frustrated hunter -

- and then it burst to the surface of his mind, suddenly, finally, what Private Fitzpatrick had claimed would protect them from the hide-behind: alcohol. God only knew why, Fitzy certainly hadn't, but that was it, that was the answer (and how many times had he thought that in his life, and here he was for once proven right). His hand flew to his belt and he felt his flask was still there, and from its weight there was still some whisky left. Matthew let out a whoop and pulled it free as he ran, and with a prayer he tossed the flask's contents over his right shoulder, never looking back.

There came a sound then that made him glad he'd never seen the hide-behind, for he never wanted to set eyes upon the creature capable of making such a horrible sound as that. The whole woods rang with it, but no blow followed it, no swipes or tear or bite; Matthew ran on unmolested.

Then he was on his own land and his house was right ahead, and there was a light in the window - Annie up, waiting for him. She leapt from her seat at the fireside as Matthew crashed the door open, slammed it shut and bolted it behind him, leaning against it chest heaving and legs weak, ready to give.

"Matthew!" Annie hurried over. "What for the love a' - "

"Annie," he rasped, and swallowed hard. "D' you see - is there anything behind me?"

She stared at him for a moment, incredulous, but went to the lighted window and looked out into the darkness surrounding the house. "No," she said, "there's not," and Matthew rolled his eyes to Heaven and mouthed a fervent prayer, nearly collapsing where he stood. "What's all this about, Matthew?" Annie demanded, pale with concern as the sight of him sank in, the evidence of his panicked flight through the forest.

"There was something in the woods with me tonight, Annie," Matthew said hoarsely, peeling himself from the door and making his way to his chair by the hearth as Annie shooed the children, who had heard the commotion of their father's return and come out to investigate, back to their beds.

When they were gone Annie went to her husband. "Something in the woods?" she repeated, astonished. "What was it?"

Matthew looked up at her, and his gaze was haunted. "I don't know."

But it was a long time before he stopped shaking, and even longer before he ventured back into the woods.

***

As his children grew, Matthew Langtree taught them how to track, shoot, and trap as well as he ever had, but those old enough to remember saw the changes from the way he'd been before, as did their mother: how Matthew wandered the woods now with a warier eye rather than with a whistle on his lips, how he always made sure they were home well before darkness fell, how he always carried a flask of alcohol with him that he never drank from and urged them to do the same, for safety's sake.

"Above all else, always be aware of your surroundings, no matter where you are or where you're going," Matthew said as they moved among the autumn trees. "Even if you think you know the land well."

"Why, Da?" Peter asked, gun clutched in both hands, looking up at his father.

Matthew took a long look back over his left shoulder at the undisturbed landscape before he answered his son. "Because you never know what might be following behind you."

THE HIDEBEHIND
A LEGEND OF THE NORTH COUNTRY

(a poem in Split Couplets)

Frank Coffman

Our Forests teem with things to fear -
And some come near.

Of course the wolf and Grizzly Bear
Can be found there.

And cougars to West and angered moose
In East are loose.

But there are some, to most unknown -
From a different zone.

A thing that lives in Northern Wood,
Takes folk for food!

The legend warns all those who stray
Past light of day.

The tales all tell a ferocious beast
Will have a feast.

For human flesh - its favorite food!
It craves man's blood!

It is well known some lumbermen
Don't return again.

And yet no one can tell its shape.
For few escape.

The thing will hide behind a tree
So none can see.

Concealed by boulder it will lurk -
Then do its work!

Some say - who've lived - a sense of Fear
Grows when it's near.

But all insist it has a knack
To be in back!

Intestines are it's favorite part!
Sometimes the heart!

And all too oft remains are found
Upon cold ground.

So nights - though not logging - lumberjacks
Carry their axe.

But most, by the warm fire of the stove,
Refuse to rove.

Far better to be wary and not find
The Hidebehind.

(originally published in *Spectral Realms* # 13: 22-24,
Hippocampus Press, ed. S. T. Joshi,
Summer 2020)

Aril

by Toe Keen

Science Fiction

Being Section 5 of the JOURN-E

T HE GENRE OF SCIENCE FICTION has been considered by some critics to be a type of Fantasy. It certainly shares some characteristics - the unbelievable presented as true being the primary one. But the genre is clearly distinct in that its "unbelievable" is, as has been proven from the earliest days of "Skiffy," only *currently* or *at-the-time-of-writing* unbelievable. The "magic" of Fantasy has been replaced by that of technology and science. Things once thought "impossible" have often proven to be possible with the passage of time and the advance of science.

And certainly Sci-Fi has other distinguishing and defining characteristics that make it distinct from pure Fantasy (although the merger of the two in "Science Fantasy" [*Star Wars*, etc.] is a clear sub-genre. Usually, science fiction literature is set in the imagined Future - or a currently "not-widely-known" and usually "secret" Present. Clearly the elements of Science and/or Technology are present - hence the name of the type. But we also find the excitement of the underlying motivating question: "What if?"

From its inception with (some would include Poe, Hawthorne, and even earlier creators), Shelley, Verne, Wells; and through and into more modern times with Burroughs, Heinlein, Clark, Asamov, Le Guin, Bradbury, Dick, Sturgeon, Gibson, and many others (some whose names are not always associated with the type: London, Conan Doyle, Kipling, etc.) - Science Fiction has been an ever-burgeoning genre, hugely popular in both books and broadcast media.

There are several distinct "sub-sub-genres" of Sci Fi. Pioneered to some degree by Verne, with several being defined by Wells:

1) **Space Travel** - Verne, *From the Earth to the Moon*; Wells, *First Men in the Moon*, etc.

2) **Time Travel** - the epitome being Wells' *The Time Machine*, but many innovative others such as Finney's *Time and Again* or Twain's *A Connecticut Yankee in King Arthur's Court*.

3) **Alien Invasion** - again Wells with *The War of the Worlds*, etc.

4) **Colonization of Other Worlds** - Bradbury, *The Martian Chronicles*, etc.

5) **Biological Sci Fi** - Shelley's *Frankenstein*, Huxley's *Brave New World*, etc.

6) **The Science Fiction Monster Story** - *It, Alien* and sequels, *Invasion of the Body Snatchers, Godzilla*, etc.

7) **Other Dimensions and Parallel Worlds/Universes**

8) **The "Gadget" Story** - where an invention takes center stage. Some marvelous device like an anti-gravity machine, etc.

9) The Space "Opera"/Space "Western" - Think Buck Rogers, Flash Gordon and their ilk.

10) Robots and Automaton/Robotics/AI - Čapek's *R.U.R.*, Asimov's *I, Robot* and the "Three Laws," etc.

11) Cyberpunk - William Gibson gets the credit quite often for its invention, but the editor would place Phillip K. Dick and his *Do Androids Dream of Electric Sheep [Blade Runner]* at the forefront of this type.

And, of course, there are two major categories into which many of the abovementioned are sometimes subsumed:

Utopian Science Fiction - all the way from Moore's Utopia, to Butler's Erewhon to Clarke's predictions of progree; and

Dystopian Science Fiction - a world gone wrong. Too many examples to count. One of the major types and topics of contemporary Sci Fi. "What are we doing to our world?"

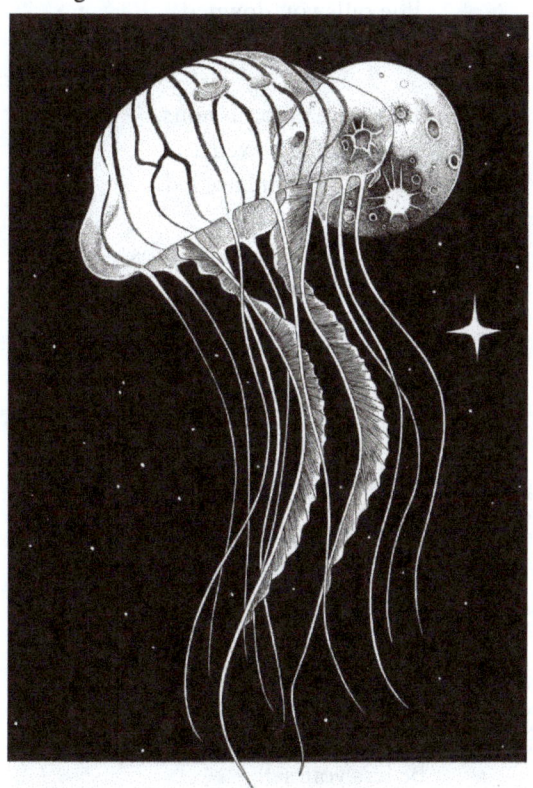

Leaving by
Shikhar Dixit

The AI Therapist

Bruce Boston

In the correction chamber
your mind is stripped bare
like a trout filleted and
splayed upon a plate.

The sensors attached
to your temples and body
adhere with a sticky,
blue, odorless fluid.
The pills you downed
begin to take effect

There are no omissions,
no denials, no excuses,
for the life you have led.

The AI Therapist plumbs
your heart and mind
to diagnose your faults
in thought and behavior,
balancing your meds to
theoretical perfection.

You know you are only
a single dot cast upon
a graph of millions.

Pick up your scrip
at the cashiers window.
You can be certain
that soon you will
be less yourself
than you ever were.

The Architect

Deborah L. Davitt

Near a star lost among
constellary Hydra's heads,
on a hothouse planet
with gravity so crushing,
the architect
must wear an exoskeleton,
strange habiliment -

machine limbs, spiderlike,
carrying his caged, sweating body
atop a palanquin,
thousands of drones
and spider-bots leaping at his commands
as he oversees building
the cathedral of his dreams -

(move that girder
lift that stone
watch the building rise
like a tangle
of broken fingers)

It's built, not to honor gods,
but to the grotesqueries
of the ancient human past,
as if by invoking them,
naming them,
they can be contained forever,
sucked down
into the gravitic well
of this hellhouse mirror Earth

See the monster in the corner
three times the height of a man,
naked and fearful,
wanting nothing more

than to be left alone
to wallow in his misery -
that grotesque's name
is Isolation:
it wears the architect's own face
carved,
with exquisite precision
by the spider-bots
at the architect's direction.

He knows his own sins;
he owns them
as he continues his work,
a slave to his vision,
master of his own hell,
and captive in it.

capt(ch)a

P. H. Low

scan initializing.
please hold still.
…

don't worry!
there's a 99.96% chance
you're clean -
that this cannon-shaped airlock
won't fire you
into space's punishing dark.
even if it does,
you'll be dead sooner
from nanite spores
slipped quick
beneath your eyelids,
or tendrils threading your neurons
like the gossamer smoke
of worlds
you bombed to dust.

choose the images of traffic lights.
choose the images of palm trees.
have you ever even
seen a tree?
have you ever tasted,
space-bred meat sack,
the scorch-storm velocity
of desert wind?

thank you for proving
your humanity.
please wait.
…

destruction sequence initializing.

yes, yes.
you thrust your fingers

every place
they were meant to go.
your precious gray matter
discerned life-forms
from bright pixels
clearly dead.

but did you really not notice
the weensy crack
in the side of your suit?
did it never occur to you
that we might not need code
to hack your systems?

why else did you think
none of your filthy
colonizing
predecessors
ever returned?

don't worry!

when your offspring
discover your remains
they'll read
in your fifty most-transmitted languages
the message we've etched
on your bones -

the same words
your people carved
on our mass graves
those nineteen generations ago:

go back
to where you came from.
...

you're welcome.
destruction sequence loaded.

please hold still.

The Sadness Will Last Forever

Eryn Hiscock

Have you ever wanted to meet iconic historical figures up close and personal and enjoy real conversations?

Transformative Genetics' Mechanical Innovations makes it possible!

Enjoy an authentic human-like experience with one of our UltraPremium models:
Break bread with Catherine de' Medici, Adolf Hitler*,
Mother Teresa and Martin Luther King
Book club with your favorite classic authors including
Shakespeare and Chaucer
Learn chiaroscuro techniques from Rembrandt,
da Vinci and Caravaggio
Discuss the theory of relativity with Einstein
Debate Oppenheimer, Curie and Hawking

Get up close and personal** with Marilyn Monroe, RuPaul,
Priyanka Chopra, Idris Elba and Ryan Reynolds
Witness curious deaths of the famous and infamous at your own
Macabre Endgame Event

Order one of the above combinations, a solo personality, or Mix-and-Match any** "Visitors From The Past" feature characters from our Catalogue of Characters for your own **personalized occasion

*Additional liability insurance may apply with some models.
**Exclusions and limitations may apply.

Full report for the Transformative Genetics Corporation -
Private and Confidential:

THANK YOU FOR YOUR RECENT DELIVERY of UltraPremium test models to our doorstep. Gord and I are delighted to contribute further personal feedback for your forthcoming campaign. We've received instructions for tonight's event and are prepared to follow through to the best of our ability. (See attached narrative.) - Jacques.

* * *

"Tonight, Gordon and I welcomed into our home three mechanical guests for our latest exploratory test session: an exceedingly blond and pale early middle age male model of moderate height who removed his fedora upon greeting as if programming compelled him to such ancient gallantry. He identified himself as F. Scott Fitzgerald in a pleasing, somewhat deep authentic-sounding and masculine voice, whose Cadence setting I'd place in the #175 Caucasian male origins Minnesotan-American speech range.

Our next mechanical guest was a bombshell type, probably of the vintage twentieth-century pinup variety who spoke with an affected, breathy and regressed baby-farce of a voice; she introduced herself as Marilyn Monroe.

A brooding, intense-faced very young man (John Doe) with a strong, definitive brow was our third guest. He shoved past all of us without introduction, strode over the threshold and moved quickly through our foyer and beyond before we could stop him; he finally stormed into our living room. Here, he paused and looked around frantically, somewhat wild-eyed, catching his breath, as if he'd just run a long, long way.

To reassure my safety, I patted my pocket to ensure my weapon's presence and nudged my partner, Gordon, indicating he do likewise. This angry young man stood there, demanding to see our garage. Our garage?

"What do you want to see our garage for?" Gordon asked.

We'd hosted similar models before and they'd asked to see many curious things, including their mothers, fathers, daughters, sons, husbands, wives, sisters, brothers; a favorite book, favorite pet, their first love, their firstborn, a favorite snack - (we only had gourmet recharging fuel packets to offer them) - however, I don't recall any one of them ever asking to see our garage as a first request.

Fitzgerald, wearing an apologetic look, stepped in. He placed a reassuring hand on frantic John Doe's shoulder. "Calm down, Old Sport. I tell you, it's not your turn tonight."

"How the hell would you know?"

"It's the 'Old Sport' thing. I can't stop saying it."

"I wish you would. I'm sick of it."

"They've got me playing Gatsby tonight. Time for the Gatsby bit, Old Sport. So, it's my turn."

John Doe looked frantically toward myself and Gordon, pointing toward us dramatically. "I won't believe it till I see their garage," he said.

* * *

Fitzgerald, in an attempt to explain John Doe's behavior, told us that firstly, this highly sensitive young model was an actor, and thus likely programmed to be overemotional as most members of his profession were; and that a four-wheeled automotive vehicle, a dinosaur once known as a Porsche Spyder back on old home planet Earth during his original lifetime was this young once-actor's greatly feared nemesis, 'Old Sport.'

Fitzgerald's explanation was accompanied by half-bows and compulsive utterances of 'Old Sport' and went like: "sorry...Old Sport...oh! He's afraid of a certain car, an ancient car he crashed once and it didn't end well for him ...oh, sorry...Old Sport...sorry...oh, godammit, stop with the Old Sport, Old Sport...."

"I once broke my neck...have broken my neck...they keep breaking my neck for sport, Old Sport..." John Doe muttered, continuing to pace, agitated.

"Gee," Marilyn tried to reassure John Doe in her breathy voice. "It's like if we visited a bunker and Hitler was around, we'd know it's his turn."

"Well, Hitler's not here tonight," John Doe said. "So rule that theory out."

Fitzgerald urged John Doe to cease pacing and sit down. John Doe did so reluctantly, sitting forward anxiously, white-knuckled hands kneading and clenching his knees, as if working off nervous energy.

"Gee, calm down. It happens to all of us," Marilyn said. "It's always anyone's turn at one time or another."

"Jesus Christ," John Doe said wiping his sweating hands over his dungaree-clad knees anxiously back and forth, back and forth in an agitated rhythm. "Let's get this over with."

Gordon finally agreed to take him to our garage for reassurance.

* * *

"At least I know it's not me tonight," Marilyn said after John Doe and Gord left the room to check the garage for his feared phantom death car.

She eased herself into one of our lounge chairs sighing, which sounded more like a child's coo coming from her. "I have my The Seven Year Itch dress on," she said. "If you had a wind machine to blow my skirt over my head, we'd be in business. Everyone just wants to see me with my skirt over my head, after all."

Marilyn's eyes teared up as she ran her hands over her white dress' satiny halter top, the pleats of its skirt, all the while bowing her gloriously designed head, seemingly lost in ancient reverie.

"Golly, this dress contributed to a divorce, you know? It makes me sad it's my costume now - my iconic, signature garment like Michael's sequined glove or Josephine's banana skirt and I'm condemned to wear it over and over and re-enact the same old scenes from my life that all ended so badly. Is this some eternal punishment? Is this hell?"

"Someone's version of it, Old Sport."

"Gee, you're a fiction writer, Scotty. Write us a happier ending."

"I'm a hopelessly romantic bootlegger who gets shot in a swimming pool tonight, not a fiction writer. Our makers keep blurring those lines between fact and fiction. You should see how many colored shirts I'm wearing over top of my bathing suit, Old Sport, if you need more clues."

Marilyn bit her lip. "Jimmy should relax, then. Sounds like it's your turn."

"Jimmy?" I asked.

"Your other guest's name is James Dean," Marilyn gestured in the direction where John Doe and Gordon had gone. "Jimmy's a famous actor. Gee, don't you recognize him?"

I shook my head. "I've never heard of any of you."

Marilyn looked surprised. "Well, if Amelia Earhart or Adolf Hitler or Josephine Baker or Vlad the Impaler showed up on your doorstep, would you recognize them?"

"Hitler yes; Earhart perhaps."

"Gee, Vlad's not my era, either, but we've done events together and they've all ended badly. Very, very badly."

"Vlad never fails to enthrall the morbid-minded, Old Sport."

"Golly, he'll disembowel you, eviscerate you, enucleate you, guillotine you and then impale your remains on a tall, sharp stake like a shish kebab."

"All these endgame traumas are buried in our hard drives, Old Sport. Collecting in our unemptied recycle bins - better known as the mechanical subconscious."

"Don't be nervous, Scotty. I really don't think it's you tonight." Marilyn made a pooh-pooh motion, waving her hand, straining to be cheerful. "Gee, you don't have a pool, do you?" Marilyn brushed cascading blond curls from her perpetually pained blue-grey OculoGlobe-EyeSpheres® as she turned my way.

"As a matter of fact, we do," I said.

Fitzgerald's DuraDermis® complexion paled even further with that news.

* * *

A breathless James Dean burst back into the room with Gordon trailing close behind. Even though the garage visit was intended to reassure him, Jimmy's agitation had seemingly not abated.

"Okay, so the car's not in the garage," Jimmy announced, pacing, running a hand repetitively through his hair. "But no car here now doesn't mean a thing. I mean, anyone can pull up in a silver Porsche Spyder at any time and it's adios muchachos."

* * *

Marilyn leaned in to stage-whisper to us, presumably so Fitzgerald wouldn't overhear, asking: "Is your name George Wilson?"

"No, I told you. My name's Jacques."

"How about Gordon?"

"He's Gordon. Or Gord."

"Okay, so neither of you are named George Wilson?"

"No. Who's George Wilson?"

"The man who shot Gatsby."

"I see."

"Gee, if neither of you is George Wilson, then I'll tell Scotty he's safe."

"I think you're all safe," I told them. Thus far, we hadn't received any wilful destruction or pillage instructions on our procedural riders for these particular models presently present and accounted for.

* * *

I offered our gourmet three-course fuel packets which they accepted, although Marilyn laid hers on the plate in front of her, leaving her envelope unopened, whispering she wasn't hungry; Fitzgerald harrumphed that this was his umpteenth Last Supper and scrutinized our living quarters slowly if taking in his last earthly visions again for the final time, while Jimmy complained that food sure wasn't what it used to be and continually shushed everyone throughout the meal, keeping his ears peeled for sounds of the dreaded Porsche Spyder approaching.

A distant clanging background sound did begin to form in the distance, and we all came to a consensus that this sound was real and definitive and not the product of Jimmy's compulsively ticking imagination or an aural mass transference among us a la folie à plusieurs.

"What's that?" Jimmy sprung from his seat, alarmed. "I'm pretty sure I heard a car door slamming."

We all listened again; Jimmy began moving around the room, quickly, stealthily, agile in his eternal youth, climbing on things, crawling under things, searching for the noise's source.

"It's the Grim Reaper sharpening his scythe, Old Sport." Fitzgerald stood and began doffing his layered colorful shirts: unbuttoning buttons, shedding the satiny, silky, vividly-colored materials matter-of-factly, tossing each discarded shirt in Marilyn's direction like some ritualistic and macabre burlesque.

"Say the line," Fitzgerald told Marilyn who watched him, never taking her eyes off him, eyes brimming with tears. "You know the one, Old Sport. About the shirts."

"I've never seen such fine shirts before," Marilyn flubbed the line purposely, gave no life to it, hoping to stall the inevitable, vivid silks piling higher atop her shoulder until she wiped her teary eyes with one shirt and pushed the rest aside so they cascaded to the floor in a vibrant heap.

"Say the line with feeling, Old Sport," Scott told Marilyn. "Take two! Put the old Method acting into it, the Method actors of what was once known as New York, in the once-country of the United States of America, on the once North American continent, on the once-planet known as planet Earth way back in the mid-twentieth century, no?"

Marilyn sighed resignedly and straightened up in her seat. She prepared to say the line, capturing a sob in her throat; she gasped and buried her nose in one of Scott's shirts which she held as a handkerchief, allowing its fabric to muffle her quavering voice as she uttered Daisy's line from Fitzgerald's book perfectly.

"Thank you, Old Sport," Fitzgerald peeled off the last of the shirts as Marilyn spoke. "Is George Wilson ready? Locked and loaded?"

"There's no George here tonight, Scott."

Scott seemed undeterred. Underneath all those silk shirts layered onto his TungstenTorso® before being powered up at the factory and revived from his 'sleep' phase by one of his dressers to attend our endgame soiree tonight, Scott wore an old-fashioned 1920s wool bathing suit with a horizontally-striped black-and-white top and a solid black, modest bottom.

He slid our glass doors leading to the patio open smoothly, perfectly, as if he'd done this many times before. He walked slowly toward the pool, where the Grim Reaper supposedly sharpened his scythe beneath the sapphire water's still baptismal surface. Scott took slow steps toward the pool's edge and we all walked a few paces behind, watching intently.

Soon, the clanging sounds from deep beneath the water ceased, replaced by bubbling sounds, splashing sounds and below the water's newly blossoming agitation, a figure swam steadily up from our deep end, the broken chains he'd busted through while anchored to the bottom threaded around his body.

This last John Doe, the final, surprise guest Gordon and I had been expecting dog paddled to the shallow end of our pool, gasping for air, like an almost-drowning human would. He grasped each side of the ladder leading from the pool and began climbing to the surrounding deck where we all stood.

As this machine emerged, we could see he was a compact, very athletic-looking male mechanical model with a seemingly powerful, sinewy body. In the deep end of our pool, I spotted the source of those mysterious clanging sounds: the discarded husk of the metal casing this model had been delivered in, a reinforced chamber that had been exploded underwater from the sheer power of this Lazarus-like machine's eternal desire to escape any known form of mortal bindings.

"Houdini?" Scott seemed to recognize the figure exiting the pool, shaking water off and catching his breath.

"Yes, it's me, Old Smoke and Mirrors, Old Sport. How are you?" Houdini spoke with an Hungarian accent as an inhabitant of once-Earth. He exhaled vapor into the air, just like a real human would.

"Did you wake up at the bottom of a pool again, Old Sport?"

Houdini nodded. "Never drowned me yet, so hard they try."

"We're still trying to figure out whose turn it is tonight, Old Sport. I thought it was mine."

"Hard to tell. For me, a sucker punch comes out of nowhere."

As Houdini and Scott conversed, Gordon, standing beside me, eyed Houdini's abdomen; he clenched his fist and readied for a good, solid punch to Houdini's unguarded belly. It was key Houdini be distracted according to the preparatory rider we'd received for tonight's particular test endgame session. If he tensed his abdomen and safely endured the blow, the desired result of mortal injury would not be achieved.

Marilyn and Jimmy saw Gordon wind for his punch a beat before it was delivered; they tried to warn Houdini; James reflexively put his arm out to block the blow a second too late.

Marilyn cried "Harry, watch out!" as Gordon's fist connected several times with Houdini's belly. Houdini bent over, grasping his abdomen, groaning. He complained through pained, gasping breaths that he was never given time to brace himself for the blows and that there was never any fair warning at any time before any of his coming deaths.

* * *

Gordon and I never really understood what these machines were so afraid of. They always come back, rebuilt, refurbished. New men, new women, better than ever. They're immortal now. There's no more dying, really - nothing left to fear - only an interruption of their power source, a reboot, possible refurbishment or replacement of damaged parts - maybe some shutdown time in the factory; time spent recharging in their power-up pods. Isn't immortality what every human wants, ultimately? Do these beings really care about how that's achieved?

* * *

Really, I think the basal ganglia and Pseudobellums® of this particular group tested tonight ultimately requires deep defrag and file clearing of all prior traumatic experiences to assuage their lingering fears going forward, much like the subconscious bypass performed on your latest model of Vincent Van Gogh who we witnessed reciting the lyrics to 'Tiptoe Through The Tulips' instead of repeating his usual last words, "the sadness will last forever," when we played out his endgame here on these very same premises just last weekend."

The Family Album

Elana Gomel

I **SAW A RED FLAG** snap in the breeze when I opened my eyes.

The flag was heavy, with a golden tassel at the end of the chrome pole that supported it. With a new gust of wind, the flag half-unfurled, the emblem in the upper left corner rippled, distorted into a strange shape like a reflection in the running water. Then the wind died down, and the flag sagged into dejected folds once again.

For some reason, I had ended up flat on my back when I entered the playspace. I extricated myself from the pile of white blossoms that swirled in the sunlit air as I stood up. They were boat-shaped, with a pink fluffy trim.

The tree was planted in a neat rectangle of freshly watered soil. The morning sunshine dappled the worn sidewalk and the brightly painted old buildings with wrought-iron balconies and intricate cornices. Some of them had red bunting stretched over their peeling facades.

A historical playworld? I was not crazy about those, but I would take anything to distract me from the memory of my mother's voice boring into my skull like a drill.

I had been hiking on the back trails of Martin's Woodside mansion, trying to walk off my anger. Exercise was not working the way my therapist assured me it would, so I was glad when I saw the familiar violet shimmer leaking through the curtain of leathery leaves between two manzanita bushes. I dove into it like an eager Alice into the rabbit hole.

I rubbed my head which was pounding with a hangover, even though the exclusive bottle of Viognier Martin and I had shared last night should not have produced such a plebeian headache. I looked down at myself and was shocked to see I was still wearing a Free People jeans and t-shirt I had had on my hike.

When you go through a portal, your clothes and appearance change to fit into the playworld you find yourself in. I had been in a Faery world where my clothes were spun of gossamer and rose petals - very decorative, though not particularly comfy. I had been in a Steampunk world where the whale-boned corset cut into my ribcage so badly that I had bruises afterwards. I had even blundered into some spaceship-and-aliens universe that I exited immediately as the clunky spacesuit induced a claustrophobic attack. But I had never been to a playworld that accepted me just as I was.

So, what kind of world was it? The red flag indicated it was fantasy-based but the street seemed more like history. There was something worn-out about it. I reminded me of the backstreets of Venice…or was it Bologna? Something I had seen on my European tour with Martin. Old buildings, unkempt; signs of water damage; litter on the scuffed asphalt. I remembered being bored with plaques in strange languages and churches filled with dim paintings. I had gone along to please Martin; it was his engagement gift to me. But the first time I saw a shimmering portal in some scruffy alleyway, I went through.

I decided to explore a little more. There are some worlds where the beginning phase is too long for my taste but once the game gets going, it gets interesting pretty quickly. I walked on.

And paused in front of a shop window. There was an iron grill on the inside, and through it, I could see the shelves packed with boxes and tins. An old-fashioned counter. All of it exuding the same patina of shabby aging as the buildings themselves. But what stopped me in my tracks was the language on the boxes. At first, I thought I could not read it. And then, with confusion and fury, realized I could.

I stepped away from the window and looked at the sign affixed to the concrete wall above the shuttered door. It said: "Gastronom".

I hated Russian. My parents had forced me to learn it, and I was surprisingly good. I read and spoke the language fluently. But it carried over the fusty smell of old things in our attic; of the misery that I wanted to know nothing about; of the history that was not mine.

How could I possibly have blundered into a Russian playworld? Game portals were geographically localized and tied to the language and culture of their physical embedding. There were ways to crossover into another locale's playworlds - when in Italy, I actually had to pass through a secondary portal to end up in my fave Fairy Romance world, in which everybody spoke American English. But I was absolutely sure I had not gone through another portal after my dive through the manzanitas.

Somebody walked softly behind me. I whirled around, my hands grasping the empty air where this playworld's standard weaponry should have been. I confronted a blond, blue-eyed boy of about ten. He flashed a gap-toothed smile.

"The shop opens at nine," he said.

Of course, this was not what he said. His exact words were: "Magazin otryvaetsya v devyat".

I licked my lips and answered - in Russian.

"Spasibo." Thank you.

He kept studying me with guileless curiosity. As an only child, I had not had much contact with kids below my age, but I thought I should get some practice - in case Martin and I decided to start a family soon.

"I am Lena," I said.

"Kolya," he solemnly shook my hand. I was trying to figure out whether he was an object, a character, or maybe even a secondary player.

More people were appearing in the street, exiting the buildings. Women, their morning-puffy faces blotched with engine-red lipstick, leading younger kids by the hand. Men in work clothes, slouching, their berets low on their brows. A gaggle of older kids, the age of Kolya, running by on their own. I studied the clothes, trying to figure out whether the play-world was supposed to be Historical Romance, Military, or Historical Fantasy. But I could not. The clothes were drab and utilitarian, but they would pass muster on any street in Fairfield or Vallejo.

The iron grill in the shop window was lifted and the door swung open. People poured in. The sweet smells of freshly baked bread and tobacco came pouring out.

"I have to get a loaf for my mother," Kolya explained, showing me some coins in his grubby hand. Maybe it was a sign for me to take them away? But while I was considering it, he slipped into the shop.

Still unsettled, I stepped away from the door and noticed a large red banner strung across the street. I read what was on it.

And decided to call it quits. This world was not for me.

Closing my eyes to avoid vertigo, I mouthed the string of characters that every child learns by heart before they are implanted with a play-world key. A failsafe exit button.

I opened my eyes to the bright sunlight on the horse chestnut trees in bloom, and the fresh breeze playing with the banner imprinted with the slogan in Russian: "All hail our honorable workers!"

That was impossible. Even if I had forgotten the key or somehow managed to mangle it, the software in my skull would deduce my intent and end this game. I would be back in California. Back in Woodside. Back in my life.

But I was not.

Kolya exited the shop holding a large loaf of rye bread, so fresh it dimpled under his fingers. The salesperson had not bothered to wrap it up. He stopped, seeing me.

"Are you OK?" he asked. "You look a little peaky."

The notion that this boy less than half my age was trying to take care of me was disconcerting, to put it mildly. But he was right. I was in shock.

"Come on," he declared. "Come with me. Mama is home now; she works the second shift today. She will make you tea."

He led me to the cabbage-smelling stairwell in one of the old buildings. The electric fixtures fizzled and sparked. Pictures were affixed to the walls and apartment doors: dour male faces with luxuriant face hair. I knew their names, rising like a bad smell from the cesspool of forgotten history.

Kolya pushed a ring bell. There were five different family names below it.

The woman, about my mother's age, who opened the door had frizzy dyed hair and the same harsh makeup as the rest of them: blue shadows like bruises and loud red lipstick. She hugged Kolya and stared at me quizzically. He launched into an explanation, but I was not listening. I had an epiphany.

Playworlds are constantly improving, designers striving for greater realism. I still remembered the worlds I had entered as a teenager where everything smelled like a bad air freshener. Now this would be unacceptable. This world, despite its weird theme, was stunningly well done. I could not spot the telltale haloes around distant objects or the glossy sheen on people's faces. Kolya looked - and smelled - like an active boy his age with poor hygiene. This world must be in production development, and I must have been shanghaied somehow to give it a test run. This would be highly illegal, of course, but I was not naïve. Martin was an investor, and some ontological software he was investing in would never be available on the open market.

Could he have done it? Arranged for me to be thrust into this...this kommunalka. The old word my mother used to spit out with profound disdain when we passed by the tiny "affordable" rentals being built all over California. Not that she had had any personal experience of communal living. She was born ten years after it had all collapsed in a pile of soured dreams and utopian disillusionment. Grandpa had remembered it, of course; but Grandpa had died when I was younger than Kolya.

The latter brought me back to the play-present when he tugged on my hand and led me into the dim hallway choked with coats of various sizes hanging on the hooks along the wall. There were lockers and boxes lined up under them. I banged my shin and grimly congratulated the designers on the realism of their playworld.

The two-room apartment where we ended up was relatively spacious, and the balcony outside was decorated with planters and the inevitable red bunting. I saw no sign of a kitchen or bathroom, but I knew better than to expect any. All the facilities would be located at the end of the hallway, shared by the tenants.

Kolya's mother, who introduced herself as Xenia, bustled out and came back with a large samovar and a plate of cookies. She proceeded to make tea, while Kolya prattled on about his aviation club. I understood every word. My mother's Russian lessons had taken root deeper than I thought.

Xenia poured the hot sweet tea into a saucer and slurped it. She made no snide remark when I tried to drink from the cup and burned my lips. The cookies were surprisingly good.

And suddenly I realized I liked being here, in this playworld where nothing, so far, was asked of me, no wizard appeared with a scroll of instructions, no aliens tried to take me prisoner, no labyrinth unfolded to lead me to the next level. I still did not understand the point of this game, but it felt relaxing. Homely, even. And it surprised me.

My parents would go back to Russia occasionally to visit distant relatives, but I never went with them. Why should I? I was Californian, born and bred. My future was laid out, bright and sunny, in front of me. So what if I dropped out of college? I did not need to make money. Martin had it in spades.

If you have no past, you have no right to a future.

One of my mother's enigmatic sayings. I had no idea what she actually meant.

I forced myself to listen to Xenia's chatter. I decided she was a character, not an object. And so was Kolya.

"...his father," Xenia was saying, pointing to a framed photograph on the dresser.

I looked obligingly. The photograph was black and white and showed a man in a complicated unform with a toothy grin and a cowlick. He looked too young to be Xenia's husband. Or a boyfriend.

"My father is a hero," Kolya piped in.

That was sweet but did not explain what function this picture played in the game. I decided to treat it as one of those old-fashioned sleuthing puzzles with trails of clues everywhere, and flapper characters with silly names. I still did not understand why I was trapped in it, but perhaps I could finish the first round, and whatever glitch was responsible would be fixed by then.

"Is he around?" I asked, figuring this was the moment for introducing a new character.

Xenia looked at me sharply.

"He fell fighting fascists," she said. "Kolya has never seen his father alive."

I swore to myself that when this was over, I was going to have the designer's balls. What right did they have to put me in this embarrassing position? Yes, it was a game, and these two were just bits and pieces of software but my feeling of mortification was as real as if I indeed had thoughtlessly insulted a widow and an orphan.

But at least now I knew what historical period this game was supposed to be set in. About a hundred years ago, after the end of WW2 that the Russians still call the Great Patriotic War.

I picked up the framed photo, trying to make myself look interested. It was ridiculous that I felt the need to apologize to game characters, but I did.

All the old photos I had seen looked the same to me, and this one was no exception. But as I studied the broad smile that looked like Kolya's but did not reach the intense eyes, I was beginning to see an individual.

"What's your Papa's name?" I asked Kolya. "Or wait, I see it!"

Indeed, there was an inscription typed in white letters on the lower part of the photograph: "Private First Class, Ivan Vernitzky".

I gingerly put the picture back, hoping my hand did not shake.

"So, you are Nikolai Ivanovich! Sounds good," I said to Kolya, addressing him by his full name including the patronymic.

"Nikolai Ivanovich Vernitzky," Xenia repeated proudly.

Surely, it was a coincidence - unless the game somehow had access to my personal data, which would be highly illegal.

My name was Elena Vern - but only because my father had Anglicized his family name after my parents immigrated to the US. Nikolai Ivanovich Vernitzky was the name of my great-grandfather, Grandpa's father.

I stole a glance at Kolya's beaming face. Was it the face of my great-grandfather?

Of course, not! It was some illegal ontological software messing with me, picking up bits of my family background and incorporating them into the playworld. It was all a game.

Except I still did not know what the game was.

"Don't you need to be at school?" I asked Kolya, trying to get the plot moving, but also finding myself strangely concerned about his playing hooky. From my parents' responses to my lackadaisical performance as a student, I knew school discipline had been pretty stringent in the USSR.

"School? It's Sunday!"

It was Wednesday, actually, in the real world. In the world where I did not need to worry about missing classes anymore, or being on time for my internship, or filling applications for a summer job. In the world where I could marry Martin and live happily ever after in a big house with private stables. In the world where I would spend my time...riding horses? Killing dragons? Changing diapers when the kids arrive? While my husband would be out there ... doing what? Taking care of me?

Making money.

"Kolya," Xenia said, "don't you have a meeting at eleven?"

He jumped up.

"Thanks, Mama! Am I late?"

She glanced at the loudly ticking clock on the sideboard with a funny cap on top. Its face was decorated with faded stencils of forget-me-nots.

"Not yet but you should get ready."

He disappeared into the second room, where I imagined he slept and did his homework. And where did Xenia sleep? I glanced at the sofa piled up with hand-embroidered cushions.

"Meeting?" I asked.

"Young Pioneers," she explained.

"Sorry, I should go. I am detaining you."

"Me?" Her inexpertly plucked brows rose in surprise. "I have nothing to do now. I work at the munition factory, but my shift starts in the evening. Please stay. It's so nice to meet somebody new!"

She meant it. Just as she meant it when she said she had nothing urgent to do. There was no need for her to take her ten-year-old son to the equivalent of a Boy Scouts meeting. He would walk down the streets alone, smiling at passers-by and greeting his friends. Or maybe he would hop on a streetcar, and chat with the conductor. And he would be safe.

As if to echo my thoughts, a clattering noise came from outside. I had never heard it in my life, but I knew what it was. A tram, slowly inching on its polished rails through the streets with no cars.

"Please stay," Xenia insisted. "Let me make more tea. And I have cherry dumplings. My neighbor made them. I can ask her for some crème fraiche to go with them."

I looked at her jarring eyeshadows, the deep creases framing her mouth, the fiery lipstick bleeding out. And I realized I liked her. She did not judge me. She took me as what I seemed to her to be: a young woman who had befriended her son. Nothing secret, nothing hidden, no social games to play. Nobody to impress, or to put down. It was incredibly restful.

The cherry dumplings were delicious. Kolya exited the inner room wearing khaki shorts, a white shirt, and a red neckerchief. He snatched one dumpling off the plate and ran away, avoiding his mother's playful slap at his bottom.

"He seems a good boy," I said.

"He is. It hasn't been easy, you know. The war, his father not coming back. I try to tell him about Ivan as much as I can but what do I have? A picture and a medal in a box. We had only been married for three months, you know, when he was drafted. And his parents starved to death, and mine were killed by the dogs, so Kolya does not have anybody but me. Are you married, Lena?"

I swallowed a cherry that went down a wrong way, making me cough. Xenia thumped me on the back while I tried to digest this information. There had been no self-pity in her voice when she delivered this litany of horrors: "starved to death", "killed by the dogs". The latter, I assumed, meant the Nazis; I knew "dogs" were a common insult in Russian. Or did she mean actual animals?

"I'm not married," I finally responded. My mother had told me I was too young to marry, especially a man fifteen years older than me with a contentious divorce behind him. A trophy wife! She had hissed. So, it was a sort of unintended compliment that Xenia believed me to be of a marriageable age. And despite my first impression, I realized she was closer in age to me than to my mother. The creases on her face were the tracks of hardships, not of years.

"And where do you work?"

Now, that was an interesting question. I tried to figure out a possible answer. A factory? No, I knew nothing about factory work. Retail? I had had a summer job at Macy's once. But did they even have retail here? Well, they had shops, but I had a vague idea that those were staffed by civil servants.

"I study," I said after a perceptible pause. "I study...in a Polytechnic. Chemical engineering."

And it was not even a complete lie. Before I dropped out, I had had plans to get an engineering degree.

Xenia's eyes lit up.

"This is wonderful!" she exclaimed. "Kolya wants to be an engineer when he grows up! Please, please, stay until he comes back, and tell him all about your studies! We would be so grateful!"

I almost groaned. So now I was supposed to influence my great-grandfather in his career choice? I vaguely remembered that Nikolai Vernitzky had indeed been a chemical engineer...or an EE? Was I going to generate a time paradox and plunge the universe into a black hole?

No, what was I thinking? It was a game. I had not traveled back in time. I was in a weird playworld that would surely fail on its first commercial run. And I needed to get out of it. Now!

I repeated the key, but I did not really expect it to work, and it did not.

Well, there was one way out. I had never used it before, but I knew players who did.

Xenia had set the rickety table with a white tablecloth and a complete set of utensils: forks, spoons - and knives. The knives were sharp, not the rounded butterknives I was used to, but all-purpose bladed instruments. I picked one up and stuck it into my leg.

Physical pain is the one absolute barrier no playworld will cross. Extreme emotional distress is supposed to be another one, but the regulators and the companies have been haggling over its definition for years. You can exit a game drenched in sweat and with your heart hammering after escaping a zombie horde. But you cannot exit bleeding from their bites. The first pain impulse delivered to your cortex will automatically yank you out and collapse the playworld.

"What happened, Lena?" Xenia exclaimed. "Did you hurt yourself? Wait, let me bring some bandages!"

She rushed out of the room, and I was left staring at the cut in my jeans, and the slowly growing maroon patch around it.

It was not bad, just a superficial laceration. But it smarted; and even more so after Xenia applied some weird green disinfectant, which stained my leg the color of pond slime. I told her the knife had slipped and sat in stupor as she bandaged my cut with actual gauze instead of slapping a Band Aid on it.

I was not in a playworld. I was not in a game.

So where was I?

I was back in the USSR: the country whose ruins my parents had escaped. The dead utopia. The poisoned paradise.

Suddenly something Martin had said floated into my mind. We were drinking Pinot Blanc on the open deck of his Woodside home, the gold of the sunset filtered through the black lace of fir branches. He was teasing me about my "game addiction", as he called it, and I was too drunk to object, passively accepting his jibes and trying to feel mellow and relaxed. I only pointed out that he made his money off people like me. Suddenly, he got serious.

"We have a new project," he said. "You are right; localized game portals were amazingly profitable, but the novelty is wearing off. The company needs to branch out."

"Branch out where?"

"Into the multiverse," he laughed and when I prodded him more, refused to say anything. We ended up in bed, but his secrecy had left an unpleasant taste in my mouth, adding to the accumulated weight of small fights and unexpected evasions. But suddenly it all clicked together.

The game portals transferred the gamer's body into a playspace where neural stimuli specific to the game created an authentic experience. But the playspace was not imaginary; it was an actual physical dimension whose unique properties allowed quick and cheap manipulation of sensory channels. When I dove through that portal, my physical body disappeared from the path in Woodside.

The playspace was part of the multiverse. But there were so many more branches of it - an infinite number. And one of them, was - that. The past. My family's past.

Xenia insisted I lie down, while she took the plates and the cutlery down the corridor into the communal kitchen. I could hear voices coming from there. How many people lived in what must have been a grand one-family apartment once upon a time? I remembered the five family names on the doorbell.

But was it really so bad? Yes, they were poor. Yes, Xenia and her son lived in two rooms and used communal facilities. Yes, her ugly makeup and poorly fitting dress indicated shortage of everyday commodities.

But the food was fresh and delicious. The rooms, though overstocked with old furniture, were clean and homely. And most importantly, they were happy, kind people. I remembered the guileless smile on Kolya's face, Xenia's capable fingers as she bandaged my cut. They took me in with no suspicions, no questions asked, no reservations. I had no doubt that if I told Xenia I wanted to stay with them, she would instantly organize a folding bed for me to sleep on.

What if I was stuck here forever? Surely, there were worse universes to find yourself in.

But how did I find myself in this one? Martin's secret project, whatever it was, could not have been anywhere near the production stage. The portal had been an ordinary one, a standard entrance into the playspace. I actually thought he had installed it for me what I saw it.

And maybe he had.

Martin knew about my gaming addiction. He knew that if I saw a portal on his property, I would likely go inside.

He also knew my background. I suddenly remembered, with a piercing clarity, how after a tense dinner with my parents, he whistled "Back to the USSR" through our miserable ride back to his place.

Martin had set me up.

The large engagement ring he had given me sparkled mockingly on my finger and I pulled it off furiously, shove it into my pocket.

Xenia returned with more tea, which she apparently believed to be the universal panacea, and I decided to come clean.

"Xenia," I said, "I wasn't totally honest with you."

"I figured," she said placidly. "You come from the countryside, don't you?"

I was not sure what this indicated - didn't people have to have to have some permit to move around? - but I decided to go with it.

"Yes," I said. "I need a place to stay. And if you let me stay with you…I don't have money, but I can give you this. It's real, a real diamond."

I took my engagement ring out of the pocket and gave it to her. She took it gingerly; her hands, I saw, were red and roughened by physical labor, the skin cracked. I suddenly doubted they even had money; after all, this was not the actual Soviet past but its equivalent in some branch of the multiverse. Would she be insulted by my offering her a payment? But I saw a slight smile of appreciation on her lips; communism or not, everybody loves bling. She shook her head.

"I can't take it. It must be very expensive. But you can stay with us, Lena, of course, you can."

"I want you to have it," I said firmly. "Please, Xenia, you must. The man who gave it to me…he wasn't worthy. Not like your late husband."

Her eyes lingered on the plain tarnished ring on her finger. It was not even gold, more like brass. But I knew she would never take it off as long as she lived.

So, it was decided; and Xenia, with the ease born of long practice of living in cramped spaces, set about carving a place for me in their apartment that was the size of Martin's master bedroom. A cloth screen painted with peacocks went up; a cot was unfolded; fresh linen distributed; and she started putting aside some cardigans and scarves for me to wear "when it gets cold in the evening." Fortunately, my jeans did not stand out; many women in the streets wore pants.

As she was rearranging shelves in the large antique wardrobe, a thick photo album poked out. Xenia took it out.

"Want to see?" she asked.

"Of course."

She opened it reverently, and I was reminded of Grandpa's arthritis-swollen fingers, as he slowly leafed through a similar album with thick cardboard pages and slotted-in family photos. What happened to it? I felt a fresh pang of guilt because I did not know.

The first photos, all faded to a sepia tone, showed a family in peasant clothing: embroidered shirts and bell skirts. The women's faces were dull with fatigue, the men worn-out, the kids undernourished.

"Ivan's family," Xenia said, pointing to a tow-headed boy squeezed between his older siblings.

"Kolya looks like him," I said. It was true. But now I was beginning to see a faint resemblance to Grandpa and to my own father in those wide-set eyes and unruly blond hair.

More pictures. Most were of the Vernitzky family; Xenia told me her own family were too poor to have their pictures taken.

"Any cousins?" I asked.

She shook her head.

"Killed by the dogs too," she said, her lips thinning. I squeezed her hand.

More pictures, still black-and-white but now the style and the content were changing. A couple of young men with their arms around each other's shoulders, smiles on their faces, antique guns holstered to their belts and bandoliers across their chests.

"Ivan's older brothers. During the Civil War."

And here was Ivan himself in a white shirt, marching in a group of youngsters with banners and signs held up high. It struck me how happy they all looked, how hopeful and enthusiastic.

A close-up of Ivan. The resemblance to his son, and to my grandfather, was unmistakable.

The opening ceremony of some factory, huge hammer-and-sickle banner above the entrance. The picture was blurry, the hammer-and-sickle a mere blotch.

Ivan and Xenia together, holding hands. Xenia had been lovely, with braided dark hair wound around her head and a radiant smile.

"Our wedding."

They were in ordinary street clothes, but I had never seen such a pure unadulterated happiness on the faces on the women I knew who got married in the Hamptons.

She turned the page.

"What is this?" I asked uncomprehendingly.

Ivan was posed with a rifle in his hand above a pile of what I first took to be dead dogs. That was shocking enough. But then I looked again.

These were not dogs or at least not entirely dogs. The creatures had snarling canine muzzles, now slack in death, and clawed paws, and long bare rat-like tails. But the paws protruded from the sleeves of military uniforms; the tails lay across the skinny legs shod in high boots; and the dogheads were crowned with helmets. They were thrown on top of each other in careless abandon, but I could see that in life, these things walked upright. The dark splotches on their white hairless skin were blood - or maybe patches of fur.

"What are these?" I repeated, my voice rising to a squeak.

"Fascist dogs," Xenia answered matter of fact. "The invaders. That was the first attack where the Red Army had to retreat but we gave as good as we got. The battle of Kyiv. Ivan sent it to me with his last letter. He fell a week later."

I stared at the horror on the page, and my brain felt as if it was being squeezed by an invisible hand. I turned the page.

A close-up of a dead doghead creature with a bullet hole through its bulging forehead. I could see it was not Photoshop - not that they would have it. The thing had once been alive, and as comfortable in its own chimera skin as I was in mine. There were tiny hairs above its thin black lips and one of its eyelids was slightly drooping. There was a badge on its uniform with a runic inscription that I could not read.

I turned the page.

The next photo was of…something. At first, I thought it was a close-up of a toadstool, pale and bloated, stippled with slimy spores. And then I saw human features squashed into the fungoid mass, tiny eyes and a mouth opened in a perpetual scream.

Xenia shook her head.

"I should not have it here," she said. "It's filthy. Polluting. But Ivan was so proud of it. Killing an Enemy, a traitor, with his bare hands!"

The creature was clearly dead, a rope cutting into its swollen flesh.

"Used to be our neighbor," Xenia whispered, lowering her voice. "A good man, we all thought. And then he turned. Can you believe it?"

I could.

This was not the past, not the dead ash heap of history. This was what might have been: a different timeline altogether, a path lost in the infinite forest of the multiverse. And in this history, what was ideology became reality; what were only words became flesh.

I remembered Grandpa telling me about the Great Terror, and how friends and neighbors would be "unmasked" as traitorous monsters, enemies of the state, and dispatched with a bullet through the head in the cellars of the security police. I remembered the hatred in his voice when he talked about the Nazi invasion that had happened decades before he was born, and his contempt for the "fascist dogs". I remembered that twenty million people were killed in the USSR.

There was a trill of bugle from the outside.

"It's Kolya's troop!" Xenia exclaimed, brightening. "They are back early! They must have caught one very quickly. Or he didn't tell you, did he? That was an Enemy hunt!"

On leaden legs, I walked to the window and looked down.

A group of boys and girls, sweaty and happy, marched in the middle of the street under the red banner. Passers-by clapped as they passed. And in the middle of the group, bound and tied, was a woman - or what once had been a woman. Her hair had been shaved or fallen out, and her pink skull gleamed greasily as an occipital crest pushed through. Her hands were like crow's claws, with long crooked talons. Her face was birdlike, the mouth and nose fused together into a fleshy beak. But her eyes, wild and despairing, were still human.

Kolya, prodding the creature with a sharpened stick, raised his head and saw us in the window. He waved at us, happy and proud.

The red banner unfurled, and finally I saw it clearly. The symbol in the corner was not a hammer and a sickle. It was a sword and a noose.

Mother Earth's Red Sister

Jay Sturner

SHE GLIDES to her favorite spot atop Olympus Mons. There she unfurls, dimension by dimension, at crater's rim. Her miles-long filaments caress the volcano like a sentient mass of ghostly seagrass. Photons coruscate beneath maroon skin. Life, the burden inside her, gnaws at its tether.

The sun dips beneath the blue horizon. She watches Earth come gently into view. In the course of a long sigh, moisture seeps from her thousand piercing eyes into a luminescent mist, sinks through floating red dust to solid ground. There, combined with the faint light of sun and star, a product of her being sparks into existence. This she quickly stomps out. Now is not the time.

Looking to Earth, she releases a pulsating stream of neutrinos. "Oh, dearest sister," she says. "I have watched you come so beautifully into your own: the landscapes, the seas, the magnificent flora and fauna. You're the envy of all the planets - an inspiration! But you suffer discord; you are trod upon by your own. And those who abuse you now set their wild eyes upon *me*. Well, let them come! I will be ready."

Science Fiction Cradlesong

C.S. Lewis

By and by Man will try
To get out into the sky,
Sailing far beyond the air
From Down and Here to Up and There.
Stars and sky, sky and stars
Make us feel the prison bars.

Suppose it done. Now we ride
Closed in steel, up there, outside
Through our port-holes see the vast
Heaven-scape go rushing past.
Shall we? All that meets the eye
Is sky and stars, stars and sky.

Points of light with black between
Hang like a painted scene
Motionless, no nearer there
Than on Earth, everywhere
Equidistant from our ship.
Heaven has given us the slip.

Hush, be still. Outer space
Is a concept, not a place.
Try no more. Where we are
Never can be sky or star.
From prison, in a prison, we fly;
There's no way into the sky.

Sonnet-To Science

Edgar Allan Poe

Science! true daughter of Old Time thou art!
Who alterest all things with thy peering eyes.
Why preyest thou thus upon the poet's heart,
Vulture, whose wings are dull realities?
How should he love thee? or how deem thee wise,
Who wouldst not leave him in his wandering
To seek for treasure in the jewelled skies,
Albeit he soared with an undaunted wing?
Hast thou not dragged Diana from her car?
And driven the Hamadryad from the wood
To seek a shelter in some happier star?
Hast thou not torn the Naiad from her flood,
The Elfin from the green grass, and from me
The summer dream beneath the tamarind tree?

"Pilots of the Purple Twilight"

from "Locksley Hall"
Alfred, Lord Tennyson

…For I dipt into the future,
far as human eye could see,
Saw the Vision of the world,
and all the wonder that would be;
Saw the heavens fill with commerce,
argosies of magic sails,
Pilots of the purple twilight,
dropping down with costly bales;
Heard the heavens fill with shouting,
and there rained a ghastly dew
From the nations' airy navies
grappling in the central blue;
Far along the world-wide whisper
of the south-wind rushing war,
With the standards of the peoples
plunging thro' the thunder storm;
Till the war-drum throbb'd no longer,
and the battle-flags were furl'd
In the Paliament of man,
the Federation of the world.…

SPECIAL TO *JOURN-E*

The Dark Muse of Karl Edward Wagner

John Mayer

> *"The Last Writer sits alone in his study. His eyes glow bright, and his gnarled fingers labour tirelessly to transform the pictures of his imagination into the symbolism of the page. His muscles feel cold, his bones are ice, and sometimes he thinks he can see through his hands to the page beneath. There will be a knock at his door.*
> *"Maybe it will be death.*
> *"Or a raven knelling 'Nevermore'.*
> *"Maybe it will be the last reader."*
>   - Karl Edward Wagner, "The Last Wolf"

"**WELL, WAGNER,** I hear your undeveloped twin is taking form on your back." Having had my long-distance service restored, my first call that summer evening in '94 was to Karl Wagner, my friend since our days as, it seemed, the only science fiction and fantasy fans at Old Central High. His ex-wife had told me of the ugly black mass growing on his left shoulder blade. He had stubbornly refused her entreaties to see a doctor, and I shared her concern.

"Yeah, Mayer, it's good to have a little company." Though he was dating a little, he remained disconsolate about the breakup of his marriage. Barbara had left him when, she told me, she had given up any hope of his overcoming an affliction common to writers: too much drink. Indeed, Wagner's friends often marveled at his capacity for alcohol; he seemed to regard drinking almost as an athletic event and was able to finish off a fifth without any apparent intoxication.

"Seriously, Karl, you need to see a doctor. I understand melanoma can be a real bitch once it gets going."

"Mayer, I am a doctor. That's why I'm not bothering. If it's melanoma it's too far gone to do anything about. I'd just as soon not know till I have to."

Wagner was, in fact a medical doctor, though he hadn't practiced in years having devoted himself to his writing. He was the only person in my circle of friends who had medicine to fall back on as a second career.

"But you don't understand, Wagner! If you let this thing go, I'll get it, too!" This was sort of a running gag between us. Whether it was because we'd hung out together so much since freshman high school, or due to our common German heritage, or because our childhood heroes were the baritone, manly stars of children's radio dramas such as *The Lone Ranger* and *Sergeant Preston* - neither of our homes held TV's, mine because my folks couldn't afford it, his because his father, TVA board chairman Aubrey "Red" Wagner, feared that it would stifle Karl's creativity - Wagner and I had almost identical speech patterns. This caused consternation among our friends who saw us together for the first time and would often remark to the effect that we were just alike. We'd respond along the lines of, "She says we're just alike! Ridiculous, Tweedledum!" "Preposterous, Tweedledee!" One Hallowe'en I found and sent him a card that seemed remarkably apropos. It said, "I wouldn't go out this Hallowe'en if I were you. But then, I'm not you... or am I? Hee hee hee hee!"

But now my jest concealed real worry. Wagner chuckled at the familiar gag. "I hope not, Mayer, but if you should get some sort of growth on your back, I'd appreciate it if you'd go ahead and get it removed. I 'xpect my neoplasm will fall off shortly thereafter." We shared a chuckle and I said good-bye quickly in an effort to keep my next long distance bill manageable. Imagine my astonishment when, a couple of weeks later, my visiting nephew remarked, as I worked shirtless in my garden, "Hey, John, what's that thing growing on your back?"

The possibility that Karl Wagner of Knoxville would one day be a world-famous writer of science fiction, horror and heroic fantasy, translated into six languages, winner of numerous awards for fiction and frequent guest of honor at fan conventions all over the U.S., Canada and London, seemed remote when I first met him in Mrs. Pace More Johnson's Latin class (we later styled her Post Mortem Johnson and speculated that Latin was her native language). I first realized we had interests in common one Hallowe'en.

Mrs. Johnson had softened her usually austere approach to pedantry to allow the talented among us to observe the day with musical performances and story-telling. The program had been at complete variance with my concept of how a black mass should be celebrated, and I was diverting myself with a book of ghost stories. Suddenly I realized that the story being delivered to the class by that great red-haired lout was drawn from the very library book I was reading. I had dismissed the fellow as a football player or some such ruffian on the basis of his hulking build and rather brutal features. Imagine my surprise to discover that behind those beetling brows was a brain as tasteful and perceptive as my own. Wagner was an intellectual…and big enough to get away with it!

We began to compare notes on our favorite brand of literature and our acquaintance grew into a fast friendship. This required a certain amount of courage on Karl's part, for I had already acquired an unsavory reputation that would have made Huckleberry Finn - or Jack the Ripper - reluctant to be seen chatting with me. Having come from the cloistered environment of a parochial school, free to members of First Lutheran Church, where my deadpan sense of humor was well known, I was not prepared for the literal interpretation the Central lads placed on my witticisms. It wasn't long before I was labeled insane by both students and faculty, a judgment I eventually began to accept myself, innocent though I was of the more eccentric behaviour rumour attributed to me. I did not, for example, sleep in a coffin, no matter how many of my classmates claimed to have peeked in at my window and seen it. The situation had at first seemed quite funny, but it got old fast. I developed a chip on my shoulder that led to fights with my classmates and detentions and suspensions from Principal Boring (he once remarked, referring to his extreme tolerance toward me, "John, if the school board ever saw your record they'd kick us both out on our ears!")

I was awed when I saw Karl's library, (a tiny fraction of the one he eventually acquired, but impressive even then). Karl ate, slept and breathed pulps, almost literally, for his monolithic bookshelves stood by his bedside and the odor of mouldering pulp paper filled the air like incense. And his lunch money went to purchase more.

We traded paperbacks and went on treasure hunts downtown (Knoxville actually had a downtown, then, with ten cent stores: Woolworth's and Kress's and Grant's, not one but two Miller's department stores, and four movie houses, including the Roxy where Bridgette Bardot movies were sometimes shown). We scrounged through (and under, and behind) the dusty shelves of Doc Black's New and Used Books and Costume Shop, or in the curio and junk shops in the area now called The Old City but then called Urban Blight, seeking the imaginative pulps and pre-code horror comics that had vanished in the drab and colorless fifties (Wagner would later sneer at fifties nostalgia; "It was like ten years in detention hall.")

Hard as it is to imagine now, science fiction was rare in the fifties and early sixties; pulps had ceased to exist and editors of paperbacks were convinced there was no market for sci-fi and less for fantasy. There was an upside to this situation; the few science-fiction volumes that did see print were those the editors found so compelling they were willing to set aside their commercial prejudices (a far cry from the nineties where any sort of dreck labeled science-fiction or fantasy seems to get published, and most of it in the form of trilogies).

Comics had experienced the birth of a true creative artistry evidenced, especially, in the horror, action and Mad comics of EC; this creativity had been smothered in its crib by the Comics Code Authority administered by John Goldwater of Archie infamy. The Code was the result of a national panic created when psychologist Frederick Wertham revealed that comic books were the cause of juvenile delinquency. He discovered in the shadows and details of the art subliminal obscenities not apparent to the layman (or layboy, either). It was the old joke: "So... all the inkblots look to you like genitalia. You certainly have a sexual obsession." "Me!? You're the one showing me all the dirty pictures!"

Except that Tennessee's own Senator Kefauver took the joke seriously and launched a congressional investigation resulting in the Comics Code Authority. The Authority boasted that it had "at its inception adopted as the cornerstone of its program the most stringent [censorship] code in existence for any communications media." In this sterile, conformist environment Karl and I hungered for the lurid prose and illustrations, the flights of fantasy, the rebellion we discovered in those forgotten and tattered publications. We had soon sniffed out every pulp and pre-code comic in Knoxville's shops, but Wagner had discovered mail order purveyors of these arcane opuscules. Regrettably, unlike the local shopkeepers, these merchants recognized something of the worth of their wares. I feared Wagner had gone off the deep end when he began paying as much as six dollars for copies of *Weird Tales*. At a time when you could live comfortably on a sawbuck a week, paying those sums for old magazines that had only cost two bits when they were in mint condition seemed extravagant folly. But Wagner had the collector's fever and was determined to own every issue.

If science-fiction was unpopular with publishers, it was abhorred by educators. More than once both Wagner and I had books confiscated in study hall for no reason other than that they were science-fiction and, ipso facto, trash. Of course, our teachers really didn't even know what science-fiction was. I once attempted to present a book report on a work by Poul Anderson based on Nordic myths. Mrs. Pierce, an especially malignant grimalkin, read the dust jacket, noted the references to Odin, trolls, elves and frost giants and said, gleefully, "I'm sorry, John, but I don't approve of science-fiction. I'll have to give you an F."

Mrs. Pierce seemed to take a special delight in tormenting both Wagner and me. It was she who caught us violating the Walk-Home, a special day when all public school students who customarily rode the school bus were to walk home and time their walk so that authorities could project how many of us would be incinerated in case of nuclear attack. Karl and I attempted to hitchhike and, naturally, the first car we thumbed was driven by Mrs. Pierce. We were two of only three people in Knox County required to seek absolution from the local head of Civil Defense. When I ventured that I welcomed nuclear war as a way of ending a repressive society and bringing about anarchy, the Civil Defense guy scoffed at my political naïveté'. "There could be no anarchy," he explained to me, "unless the key figures were already organized and prepared to set it up."

In an era when winning popularity was the principal reason for a teenager's existence, Karl was willing to burden himself with friends who could only be social liabilities. At the same time, he was not above subjecting his friends to the occasional cruel practical joke. Another of them was Dan Winter, the same Dan Winter whose family tragedy was the subject of a lengthy article in a Knoxville paper about a year ago. "Dan was a bright boy, but always, somehow... a little different," the writer told us smarmily. The only difference Wagner and I noticed, aside from his being perhaps a little overprotected, was that he was exceptionally intelligent. When he graduated from Central he would be offered a $5000 scholarship to Princeton, a $5000 scholarship to Yale, a $10,000 scholarship to Harvard and a $300 scholarship to UT. He had a football deficiency.

One night, after we got our drivers' licenses, we took Dan out and got him drunk, then brought him home, leaned him against the door with a pair of panties pilfered from one of our girlfriends hanging from his shirt pocket, rang the bell and fled. We laughed ourselves silly thinking of his mother's horrified expression. In the early sixties most guys, despite locker room epithets, had only the vaguest idea what a homosexual was. We had probably made his parents' day.

Dan had, apparently, been a disappointment to his parents. He moved to New York City and his parents met a young man who took his place in their affections and even moved into their home. A bit later his father, suffering from some form of dementia, got up one night, shot Dan's mother in the head, and went back to sleep beside her. The next morning he sought help from neighbors, saying that his wife wouldn't wake up. Dan Winter Senior died in October of 1990 and there followed some dispute between Dan Junior and his parents' surrogate straight son about the inheritance. I learned from the newspaper article that Dan Winter Junior had been found on the floor of the bathroom of his New York apartment, dead of complications from AIDS.

Another of our friends I'll call Max. He was from a broken home and was the subject of much persecution for the sin of a harelip. Our willingness to brave public opinion on such matters won us his devotion. He was especially interested in Karl's ambition to be a psychiatrist. He continually pestered Karl in study hall and the library to psychoanalyze him. At last Karl acquiesced. Over a period of days he subjected Max to a battery of tests, which he made up as he went along.

At last, one day in library, he revealed that Max's analysis was complete. "Well, let me see it!" Max demanded eagerly.

"No, I'm sorry, Max. The results of your tests have been... most unexpected. If the authorities were to become aware of this information - or even if you should see it - the results could be tragic! I urge you to avoid any sort of psychological testing in future. I've decided..." and he paused dramatically to look at the paper in his hand, "no eyes but my own must ever see these notes." And he stuck the paper in his notebook and got up to peruse the shelves.

Disregarding Karl's warning, Max sneaked a look at his psychological profile. It read something like this:

Max W. I have administered to this subject the Wechsler Personality Inventory, the Kent-Allard Survey of Abnormal and Sociopathic Indicators, the Bruce-Partingham Behavioral Profile and the Arkham-Miskatonic Instinctual/Adaptive Scale as well as standard verbal and performance tests. My interpretation of the results has led me to an astonishing conclusion: Max W. suffers from a condition described in some of the earliest psychological literature but not seen in a clinical setting since the days of Jung.

Max is a victim of lycanthropy, a condition believed to have been common in our ancestors but to have essentially vanished with Homo habilis. This was a psychosomatic adaptation of early man to the savage world in which he lived. In order to compete with and to defend himself against fierce predators, and in response to signals from the limbic brain, early man may have been able, judging from certain anthropological evidence, to alter the actual shape and metabolism of his body (hypnotic experiments on present day subjects suggest we still possess this ability in vestigial form). In his altered state lycanthropic man had the strength, speed and agility of the wolf (whose hunting strategies so closely resembled his own).

Furthermore, there are indications that his regenerative functions may have been accelerated in such a way that wounds healed almost instantly (due to its well-known caustic effects at the cellular level, silver would nullify this trait). These characteristics might seem to be advantageous, but with them comes the total suppression of any of the inhibitions associated with civilized man; society could not permit a lycanthrope to remain alive and free.

I have decided that this knowledge must be withheld from the subject; it is conceivable that being made aware of his unusual attributes might trigger a full-blown manifestation of his lycanthropic condition. Further, as an amateur in studies of the mind, I am under no obligation to call this remarkable case to the attention of psychological professionals; I fear that Max would become the victim of eager and callous researchers. Therefore, I have determined that all records relating to Max W. must be destroyed.

Max, as a recent convert to horror fiction, knew full well what lycanthropy was and was delighted to learn of his atavistic endowments. We directed his attention to Mrs. Pierce. Soon he was growling at her from deep in his throat when he passed her in the halls.

Wagner and I began considering the best way to transfer a pentagram to Mrs. Pierce's palm. We knew that Max had seen enough Lon Chaney, Jr. werewolf movies to know that he would see a pentagram on the palm of his next victim. Various methods were considered: a seemingly innocent handshake, some sort of stamp pad inlaid into the desk pad upon which she often leaned, and so on.

One day David, a fellow in one of my classes, expressed his concern about Max's sanity. "I was showin' him my knife collection and he dared me to hit him with my machete'. Said I couldn't hurt him 'cause he was a... a... a lycanther, or somethin'." The reality of our little experiment dawned on us and Karl was obliged to make it known to Max that modern manifestations of lycanthropy were usually very short-lived.

Karl was, in a more cerebral way, as unconventional as myself. One year Wagner got me out of the detention hall he had helped get me into by telling Assistant Principal Nicely that my help was needed in preparing the Science Club skit for the annual talent night. So I joined the Science Club. The skit they were burdened with was embarrassingly corny, so, at Wagner's urging, the club agreed to scrap it. Karl proposed that, since we had no chance of winning anyway, we could at least do something memorable. He told us of an art movement called Da-Da, something no other Central student, I'm sure, and probably few of the faculty, had ever heard of.

The curtain would open on a person reading aloud the want ads from a German newspaper. Another cast member would beat rhythmically on a 55-gallon steel drum. Another would simply sit in a folding chair, his back to the audience. A fourth person would ride a tricycle around the stage (mind, this was years before Laugh-In). This was to continue for our entire allotted ten minutes. Sadly, Mrs. Pierce was one of the Talent Night advisors and got word of our avant-garde concept. She vetoed it. When pressed for a reason she remarked that the fact that I was involved was reason enough.

In for a penny, in for a pound. Now that I was a Science Club member, in spite of my abysmal GPA, I joined the Knoxville Junior Academy of Science along with Karl. He became vice-president and I a member of the executive council. We published the Academy newsletter, The Cauldron, Wagner's first publishing venture. During the Cuban blockade we published a special Doomsday Issue. For our April Fool's Day Issue, we enclosed with each copy a demand for payment for the member's Cauldron subscription. This little gag prompted many angry complaints from members' parents. For the Hallowe'en issue Wagner wrote a detailed planning guide for throwing a black mass. This prompted cries of outrage from members' parents and a special meeting with Ben Sparks, the Science Club Advisor. There followed our special Serious Issue.

It was in The Knoxville Junior Academy of Science that we met Marjorie Mott, a meeting that was to prove fateful.

In spite of his freethinking, unconventional nature in a repressive milieu, and despite hanging out with losers like Max and me, Karl was affable enough to get along with most of the duck-tailed toughs of Old Central and big enough to intimidate the others. Even though he didn't actually involve himself in sports - he dropped off the wrestling team after a couple of weeks when he discovered, he said, that he wouldn't be allowed to wear a mask and a cape and rub soap in his opponents' eyes - he was one of the first Centralites to study a mysterious oriental art called ka-ra-te. When one especially aggressive tusk-hog challenged him in the locker room one day after gym, Karl agreed to fight him at Central's traditional dueling grounds, Fountain City Park behind the public library.

"I feel it's only fair to show you what I'll be forced to do to you, however," Karl warned him. He placed a two-by-four across two equipment trunks, had someone walk across it, and then split it with one blow of his hand. The hoodlum allowed as how maybe he'd been out of line. I often asked Karl how he'd done that stunt. "Just practice on a four-by-four till you can break it," he told me. "A two-by-four will be twice as easy."

Later he emphasized the point to a small crowd by striking the iron banister on the school's side steps. The dent, he told me privately, had, no doubt, already been there. But, even though Karl was never forced into physical combat, the sense of being at odds with his fellows showed up in his later work.

Science-fiction, fantasy and horror fiction was so unpopular that Wagner and I were compelled to try our hands at writing it. I liked the surprise endings of the vignettes and short-short stories of Frederick Brown and John Collier. Wagner was influenced by the weighty Gothic novels of the early 19th century such as *Melmoth the Wanderer*, *The Castle of Otranto* and *The Worm Ourobouros*. These were long, brooding, philosophical fantasies that bore no resemblance to the modern formula romances of the *Dark Shadows* stripe. He also was a great admirer of the cynical yet whimsical allegories of James Branch Cabell, popular in the 1920's. His first novel, *Bloodstone*, featuring Kane, the character for whom he was to become best known, had much of the tone of Cabell's mordant myths.

Then, in one of the South Central junk shops, I found an old pulp - *Unknown Worlds*, I think - that contained a story titled "The Black Stranger" by Robert E. Howard. The story was about a powerful barbarian pursued by adversaries and armed, initially, with only a knife who, through sheer will and stamina, ultimately triumphs against both human and supernatural foes. The character Conan was unknown to us, not having been seen on newstands since Howard blew his brains out in 1936 at the age of 30. Wagner liked Howard's bleak, two-fisted style - Howard was a better storyteller than might be apparent to readers who know his characters through the pastiches of lesser writers - and *Bloodstone* began to take on a less humorous, grimmer and more action-oriented tone. After several revisions *Bloodstone* was finally set aside for newer works.

We had been submitting our works to the only two outlets for fantasy, *Fantastic* and *Fantasy and Science Fiction*. Our efforts had garnered nothing more encouraging than a couple of complimentary, handwritten rejections. I began to lose enthusiasm for writing and Wagner offered to polish up my stories and submit them on my behalf. One of my last vignettes concerned a group of vampire hunters. Having found the monster's daylight resting place, the old priest briefs his assistants once more on thwarting the vampire's evil powers: his superhuman strength, his ability to change form, his hypnotic eyes. Thus prepared, they fling open the coffin and the vampire lifts his pistol and shoots them. After two rejections Wagner began to cast about for other outlets; Warren Publications was publishing *Famous Monsters*, which occasionally printed a short story. We got no response, nor was the manuscript returned. We forgot all about it until five years later when the manuscript appeared in Wagner's mailbox without explanation. Almost at that same time a story appeared in Warren's new publication, Creepy, which seemed a paraphrase of that tale. The vampire was now a werewolf and the pistol was now a bulletproof vest.

Long before then I had given up on writing and turned my efforts toward art. Wagner promised that he would call upon me to illustrate his first sale.

In '63 Wagner graduated without having broken into print and, with the aid of a National Merit award and a humble but reliable Falcon station wagon from his folks, Wagner headed off to Kenyon College in Gambier, Ohio. His premed major was history, a subject he felt would be helpful in his real career: writing.

I was left behind, a five-year man. Suddenly realizing that most of my few friends had gone on without me I took my classes a little more seriously and actually made the honor roll a couple of times (Mrs. Pierce was very proud). Even so, I graduated 334th in a class of 380.

Wagner sailed through undergraduate school but his writing efforts were less successful. *Tales of Conan*, though badly bowdlerized, were rediscovered by the public and Tolkien's trilogy was published in the states. The phrase "swords and sorcery" was coined to describe the work of hacks like Lin Carter and John Jakes. Still Wagner remained unpublished. Gradually, however, the rejection slips were replaced by encouraging personal notes. It was at this time that Wagner discovered, to his great disillusionment, that the quality of a story had little to do with its chances of being published, and that the function of an editor was not to separate the good from the bad but the marketable from the unmarketable. He received letters from several editors to this effect:

Dear Mr. Wagner:
We found your story to be exceptionally well written; your characters were vividly drawn and the fast-paced action and unexpected plot twists kept us up reading straight through the night. Unfortunately, our accountant informs us that the bottom has fallen out of the short-lived sword-and-sorcery market, the success of the Conan and *Lord of the Rings*

series having been, sadly, a fluke. Our *Blech the Barbarian* series isn't moving at all. We are sure if you will turn your obvious talents to a more popular genre, your efforts will be rewarded.

Yours, etc., etc.

But then, one evening, Wagner called me from Ohio. I was managing to go to the University of Tennessee with the help of a stipend from the Vocational Rehabilitation department based on my aptitude tests and my record of mental illness. I was living in a house that was becoming as notorious, under the name Toad Hall, as I myself had been at Central. "Mayer," he said, "are you able to accept a commission?" Powell Publications, a small outfit in California, had decided to diversify their catalogue from the porn that was their mainstay and was taking a chance on Wagner's latest novel, *Darkness Weaves*. Wagner had remembered his long-ago promise to let me illustrate his first published work. Neither of us realized how little say the writer actually had in these matters, but Wagner did, in fact, persuade his editor to let me do the interiors. In retrospect I realize that my work was crude, even amateurish, but Karl was especially fond of my frontispiece of Kane leering vindictively from beneath his brow; he was convinced it had been swiped by a much better known artist. In an interview in *Nightshade* years later he said that my depiction of Kane, among all the artists who had depicted him, was closest to his own conception of him. And why not? I was with Kane before the beginning.

Darkness Weaves was a bit too long for Powell's purposes, however, so they decided to abridge it by the simple expedient of yanking out blocks of pages at random, making for a rather disjointed read. Wagner was not consulted. Then the editor realized that the figure on the cover, painted by their staff artist, bore no resemblance to the red-bearded Kane. Wagner said it looked like an African-American with a cantaloupe stuck in his loincloth. The obvious solution: change Wagner's descriptions of his character to match the painting. So the editor dyed Kane's red hair black and stripped him of his beard, except in a few places, which she overlooked. Thus Kane's appearance alters throughout the book without explanation. The overall effect was rather surreal. Finally, the book was released through Powell's usual adult bookstore outlets. Still, *Darkness Weaves* appears to be the only Powell book to have sold out before the company folded. "It was an ill-favored, misshapen thing, sir," Wagner said, "but it was my firstborn and I loved it."

Wagner graduated summa cum laude (in the top ten) from Kenyon and was recruited by the University of North Carolina. They were looking for Renaissance men for their medical program and Wagner's history major was just the ticket. Wagner, for his part, chose UNC largely because Chapel Hill was the home of one of our favorite writers, Manly Wade Wellman, author of more than seventy books and countless short stories. In fantasy circles he was best known for his tales of John the Balladeer, a folk historian who wanders the Appalachians recording mountain songs and encountering the ha'nts and ghoulies of the backwoods.

Manly was in his seventies but still a big, robust man and a two-fisted drinker like Karl. They became fast friends, and over their glasses Manly regaled Karl with many tales of the early days of the pulps. Manly had also been a bouncer at a roadhouse during prohibition and a reporter in New York, where he often took to task smug Yankees who used the term hillbilly too carelessly. He claimed he had once challenged John Dillinger to step outside and fight.

Manly had also worked as a comic book writer in the early days of that medium. One of his publishers had made the mistake of killing off, irrevocably, their most popular villain The Green Claw, a sort of Martian Fu Manchu. They had blown him to bits, his death had been absolutely established, and thousands of kids were threatening to spend their dimes elsewhere. The staff was agonizing over ways to bring the Green Claw back, without success, when Manly came upon the scene and offered to save the day. In the splash panel of the next episode the myrmidons of The Green Claw were gathered about his bier lamenting his passing. Suddenly, in the next panel, The Green Claw sits up, casts off his shroud and cries, "Silence, fools! The Green Claw lives!" Manly saw no point in slowing the narrative drive with explanations.

Among the pulp writers Manly had known was L. Ron Hubbard, author of such classics as *Fear* and *Death Takes a Holiday*. One day he ran into him and remarked that he hadn't seen anything by him lately. "I don't have time for that stuff anymore," Hubbard told him brusquely. "I'm working on something that's going to make me a millionaire." That something was, of course, Scientology.

Of Manly's many anecdotes the favorite, among fantasy fans and bibliophiles alike, was one concerning the strange little shop Wellman came upon in New York surrounded by Confederate flags. It was a bookstore operated by an aged crone. "I was intrigued by the flags outside," Manly greeted her.

"It is the flag of my country," she answered.

"It is the flag of my country, too," Manly responded, acknowledging his great love for his native Southland. He looked over her books and was surprised to find many valuable occult volumes. Scarcely daring to hope he asked her, "Do you have *Malleus Mallifacarum?*"

"Yessss," she replied. Her bony finger traveled down a row of books and came to rest on an ancient leather volume. It was, indeed, that extremely rare book on witchcraft. It remained the prize of his collection until his death.

On a prankish impulse he asked, "Do you, perhaps, have a copy of the *Necronomicon?*" This was the apocryphal book H. P. Lovecraft referred to in his tales of Cthulhu and the Elder Gods. Many pulp fans refused to believe there had never been any such book.

"Yessss." Her finger again quested down a row of books and halted at an empty space. "Oh... I must have sold it."

College entrance exams revealed Karl to have the highest I.Q. ever recorded at UNC's med school. Yet, despite his recent honors, Wagner felt himself a failure. He had sold only one short story since *Darkness Weaves*, a ghost story set near Gatlinburg called "In the Pines", to *Fantasy and Science' Fiction*. He resigned himself to making the best of a medical career. But the rebellious streak he had held in check so much more successfully than I at Central, now began to get the better of him. In fairness, though, he now had more important things to rebel against. He had always regarded himself as a flint-hearted pragmatist with no time for sentiment, but medical school revealed a social conscience.

He told of a class where a helpless-looking, half-naked patient in a wheel chair was displayed before them like a lab specimen. "Class, we're very fortunate to have with us today," - the doctor turned the patient so they could observe the pattern of inflamed nerves on his back - "a case of North American Blastomycosis. The inflammation you see here makes the patient very sensitive to touch." A finger darted down and the patient, responding to this stimulus, said, "Aaaaiieeee!"

And of the similarly afflicted patient on a gurney who could not bear even the weight of the sheet. Inch by painful inch she would work it off her, only to have the next passing intern pull it back up for the sake of propriety.

Wagner said you could determine by ear when you were in the indigent ward: that's where the screams were loudest. Painkillers were expensive.

Wagner was also disgusted by most animal experiments, which he regarded as sadism in the guise of science. Most experiments were only the clumsy repetition by students of experiments described in textbooks.

Wagner was perfectly willing to accept the word of the authors as to the predicted outcome rather than subject inoffensive beasts to the tortures of the damned. At the start of vacations most experimental animals were summarily killed. It was cheaper to replace them to feed and care for them over the break.

When local pets began to disappear Wagner suspected UNC of dealing with Burke and Hare style animal-nappers. I happened to be visiting him in Chapel Hill one weekend when his huge cat Lucifer Sam went missing.

Karl and I broke into the animal labs and conducted a cage-to-cage search. I discovered science with an inhuman face. Some animals were bandaged, others had open wounds stitched with inept, Frankenstein stitches. Cats clawed at me as I came near, vowing not to be taken alive. I didn't enter the room with the "Danger - Radiation" sign, but peering through the window in the door I could see what had once been an Irish Setter feebly scratching at his scaly hide with a rubbery paw.

We didn't find Lucifer Sam, but when we returned to Wagner's home and told of our outing his housemate asked cryptically, "Oh, Wags! Did you set your people free again?" I was never able to elicit details from either of them about Karl's earlier excursion.

Wagner presented a dilemma to UNC. On the one hand his grasp of medical principals was phenomenal. More than once he was asked to take over the classes he was enrolled in while the instructor attended to other matters. His grades were excellent. On the other hand, he openly espoused socialized medicine. He lacked humility. Once he felt one of his instructors had insulted him and barred him from leaving the room until the doctor had apologized. And he rode a motorcycle and dressed like an outlaw biker with long red hair, full beard and denim "colors" (he referred to his home as The Valley Park Clinic and Cycle Shop).

Surgeons, in particular, hated Karl. He refused to accept the traditional hazing of students. If surgeons demanded, as they did, that med students walk up to the eighth floor while they rode the elevator, Wagner would simply shove in beside them. "They don't just want you to eat shit," Wagner told his wife, "they want you to say, 'My! This is really good shit! Might I have some more?'"

The last straw, for both Wagner and UNC, happened one day when he was on rotation with an instructor and another student. They were examining an elderly black man dying of tuberculosis and too far gone to be helped. But this was, after all, a teaching hospital. The other student was ordered to give some sort of injection. For several minutes he probed futilely with the needle in search of the patient's shriveled veins. The old black man endured the ordeal without complaint, saying only, and repeatedly, "Listen, I 'ppreciate what you boys are tryin' to do for me, but ain't no use. I jes' wanna go home and die amongst m' people." The instructor ignored him. Sweat began to bead on the old man's brow, and he began to hiss through clinched teeth in an effort to keep from crying out as the puncturing continued. At last it was obvious that no simple injection was going to be possible. A new learning experience was in order.

"Mr. Wagner, cut this man down and expose a vein, please."

"There's no point in subjecting him to more pain," Wagner whispered. "Nothing we do is going to change his prognosis."

"Mr. Wagner, I am the doctor here!" the instructor sputtered. "You are the student! Never! Never! contradict me in front of a patient. Cut down that man's arm!"

"I'm not going to be a party to this."

"Very well! Steve, please cut Mr. Anderson and give him his injection. Mr. Wagner, observe this procedure carefully. You will be here at two a.m. to give Mr. Anderson his next injection."

"No, I won't."

At about two-thirty the next morning Karl's phone began to ring. He placed his pillow over his head. After a long time, the phone quit ringing.

Wagner, of course, was called on the carpet. The deans confessed he presented a problem they had never before had to face. He had the highest rotation grades in the school. His other grades were likewise excellent. But his attitude... deplorable! How could such a dilemma be resolved? Not so difficult, it turned out. He would have to repeat third year.

Wagner was outraged. How could they flunk someone with an A average? He dropped out of medical school and contemplated a lawsuit against UNC. But, for now, he had plenty of time to devote to his writing. And it payed off. At last he sold a book, *Death Angel's Shadow*, to a real publishing house, Warner Paperback. Once again he persuaded his editor to let me do the interior illustrations. I was to share art credits on this book with Frank Frazetta, the best-known artist in the field then. It looked like, at last, we were both headed for the big time. "Getting kicked out of med school is the best thing that ever happened to me," Wagner reflected.

Karl Wagner's worst year was my best. I had met Barbara Mott in a campus coffee house run by her sister Marjorie Mott formerly of the Knoxville Junior Academy of Science. I had never met anyone so vivacious as Barbara, so full of enthusiasm. She seemed the very soul of youth while I had been born old. She sang along joyously with all the folksongs that I, until that very evening, had thought were tripe. She grabbed my hand and forced me to join in little impromptu dances. As Oscar Wilde observed, "A bad man admires innocence." And Jean Baudrillard said, "There is no aphrodisiac like innocence." She came with me that first night back to Toad Hall. She inspired in me an emotion I had never known: happiness. She had a special talent for making people feel good about themselves. She told her folks she was going to start staying with friends on campus and, essentially moved in with me. For one who had in high school literally provoked squeals of terror from the opposite sex, this was a season of epiphany.

She had not met Karl. During his undergraduate days he had managed to visit Toad Hall every couple of weeks, but medical school demanded more of him and he had barely found time even to visit his parents. We communicated mostly by post. But Barbara became fascinated with the illustrations I was working on for his book. I had done a small pen and ink portrait of him, and she said she'd like to meet the man who had such dreamy eyes. If only I had read "Face on the Barroom Floor."

After she and Karl were married he and I had a falling out that lasted quite a while, though I'm not sure he ever had much choice about the whole thing.

Gradually, I got over my grudge. Karl had, after all, given his freedom to save mine. Still, we were no longer so close. For one thing, we no longer shared the same concerns. He was a married man with a mortgage, car payments, insurance. He and Barbara seemed an unlikely pair to their Knoxville friends. He was the Apollonian, she the Dionysian. She was the pretty, bubbly, fresh-scrubbed Teen Board ingénue, he the brooding Byronic figure. With his long red-blond hair and beard, he had a definite leonine aspect. He very much resembled, in fact, Cocteau's Beast. Barbara and Karl, Beauty and the Beast.

Then, too, Wagner had less time for socializing. *Death Angel's Shadow* had, at last, established Wagner as an important writer of horror and epic fantasy (he hated the phrase "swords and sorcery"). It was nominated for the August Derleth Award in England for Year's Best Fantasy Novel in spite of the fact that it was not a novel. And he had steeled himself and returned to medical school where he did, indeed, repeat third year and graduated with honors.

Once out of school Wagner began to visit Knoxville more frequently. After calling on his parents he and Barbara would come around Toad Hall to drink and enjoy a toke or two. Once our appetites had been stimulated we'd head down to Brother Jack's for the food of the gods.

Brother Jack's was operated, with his wife Thelma, by Tip Jackson, the son of the original Brother Jack and the proprietor of the barbecue establishment that bore that name on University next to the ice plant. It was a black neighborhood and a rough one, though the only trouble we ever had there was with slumming rednecks. There was a great deal of drug use and violence in the neighborhood, a fact that added a special zest to the barbecued ribs when we made it back home alive with them. One night a young black man was at Brother Jack's showing around his X-ray as though it were a snapshot of his child. He had been shot in a drive-by (though that word was not yet hyphenated) while standing in front of the ice plant a few feet from Brother Jack's screen door. Wagner examined the X-ray and told him he was lucky to be alive. Wagner occasionally referred to Brother Jack's in his stories.

We often armed ourselves before venturing to Brother Jack's. Once we encountered two young white men who seemed to be toying with the idea of robbing the seemingly vulnerable little shop. "What would you do if somebody tried to rob you and your customers?" one of them asked Tip casually. Tip pulled out a .38 revolver.

"I'd shoot 'em with this gun," he responded blandly.

"Nice gun. How's about lemme take a look at it?" Tip slid it across the huge old stump that served as chopping block. One of the white men picked it up and pointed it at him. The other seemed to be groping in his pocket. "And what would you if somebody robbed you with your own gun," he asked grinning. There was a chorus of clicks and snicks and the two were ringed by a circle of pistols and knives in the hands of Tip's regulars. Tip himself produced a Magnum. "I'd shoot him with this other gun."

Another night four or five of us encountered a band of armed and obnoxious rednecks there. Most of us weren't heeled. Hotter heads prevailed, and we went back to the Toad Hall armory for more weapons. As we left the van headed for the showdown, Big Joe (whom we all regarded as slow-witted, though he later became a TVA engineer) elected to wait in the van with the shotgun. "You get 'em on the run' and I'll shoot the first one out the door," he called after us. When we entered, the rednecks had gone. It was then that Joe's parting comment registered on us.

"Did he say he was going to shoot the first one out the door?" Wagner asked.

"We better tell him everything's cool!"

"Right. Who's going to go tell him?"

Dr. Wagner began his psychiatric residency (he managed to skip internship) at a mental hospital near Chapel Hill, where he once again found himself at odds with the medical establishment. After a period of bad press, shock treatments were enjoying renewed currency and were a good revenue enhancer for hospitals. Wagner refused to prescribe a one, despite pressure from the board of directors. He said there was no more empirical evidence for electroconvulsive therapy's salubrious effects on brain structures than there was of chiropracty's nerve-impinging subluxations. ECT was the result he told me, of a psychiatrist exercising his God-like powers over one of his patients, pretty much on a whim. "Let's just plug 'er into the wall and see what happens!" Prevailing theories as to how ECT might work were of two camps. One maintained that shock treatments burned away the parts of the brain where all the bad memories were stored that had caused the mental problems in the first place. The other hypothesis was that shock treatments were so unpleasant that the patient felt that he had atoned for any wrong he might have done and was thus purged of the guilt that had tormented him.

Fortunately for Karl he was assigned to the men's ward. Shock treatments are used primarily to treat depression, and where women become depressed men become psychotic. But at the end of the first year he was reassigned to the women's ward. He saw the writing on the wall and resigned, never to practice medicine again.

Medicine had always been for him a fail-safe anyway, in case he didn't make it as a writer. But now he was making it. He sold several novels, most concerning his hero-villain Kane. Kane was essentially the Biblical Cain, but the tales told the other side of the story. Kane was the first rebel, cursed by an egomaniacal and repressive God to die by the violence Kane had introduced to the world. But, since Kane has been doing violence longer than anybody else, he was better at it than anybody else. So he lived on… and on.

Karl enjoyed demolishing "sword and sorcery" clichés: female warriors wear full armor instead of chain-mail bikinis, prophecies don't come true, characters' speech is translated into modern slang equivalents instead of the Elizabethan "thees" and "thous" of fantasy hacks, well-intentioned crusaders bring more grief than do amoral fortune hunters, and stories often don't have happy endings.

Kane himself is the most conspicuous departure from standard heroic fantasy. For one thing, he is not heroic. He is a hero-villain like Melmoth. Kane is insane, of course. The weight of aeons has done that to him, aeons of contending with the gods, ducking and weaving, thrusting and parrying, sidestepping through the centuries. Imagine knowing for a fact that God is out to get you.

This insanity, surfacing sporadically, prevents his always acting in his own best interests. Often his cold-blooded schemes are swept aside by berserker rage and he wades into battle, slaughtering the normal humans he hates and envies, and shortening their brief lives by a few inconsequential years. In so doing he risks the violent death he has been promised by an angry god, a death he fears and, perhaps, longs for. Fortunately for him he recognizes, along with his more esoteric studies, the survival value of keeping fit and battle ready.

His build is not that of the lithe, wasp-waisted swashbuckler; he is a power-lifter rather than a bodybuilder, more Sandow than Stallone. Some critics have protested that with 300 pounds of muscle on a six foot frame Kane would be so muscle-bound he would scarce be able to move. This is a groundless myth propagated by flabby, pasty-faced city dwellers with sinews like rotted cloth to excuse their own lethargy. Studies have shown weightlifters to have quicker than average reflexes. Paul Anderson, once touted as World's Strongest Man (not to be confused with Poul Anderson, the writer) once sprinted against the world champion in the 220 yard dash and gave a good account of himself.

A friend, Bob Simpson, originally of Knoxville, settled the matter as far as Karl and I were concerned. A power-lifter at five foot seven and 235 pounds, his proportions were similar to Kane's. In his prime he could lift well over 500 pounds overhead. He held black belts in both Isshynryu karate and Bando (a Burmese style). Karl and I once watched him perform weapons forms. His movements were a blur.

But, again, Kane differs from the typical barbarian hero in that he does not rely solely upon his strength. And he is no barbarian. One story, "The Dark Muse", begins with his discussing the nature of poetry with the poet Opyros (whose work is often quoted in stories set in later ages). Kane has a powerful and cunning mind and uses it to plot his grandiose schemes and to extricate himself from trouble. Other fantasy heroes muscle their way out of one sorcerous predicament after another. Kane knows a good thing when he sees it and studies sorcery himself. He has as much in common with Fu Manchu as with Conan, but he lacks Fu Manchu's noble motives. Yet there is something noble in Kane, in his refusal to surrender to cosmic forces beyond human comprehension.

Fans, naturally, came to identify Wagner strongly with Kane. One night he had a strange dream. He was back in the big, old house on Cedar Lane where he'd grown up. Upstairs in his boyhood bedroom he found a tall, raw-boned man staring out one of the dormer windows. "What the hell are you doing here?" he demanded. The figure turned to face him. He had coarse features and red hair. "I'm sure I never met you," Wagner said, "yet somehow you look very familiar."

"I should think you would know me," the red-haired stranger replied. "I'm Able."

After the first Conan movies Wagner's agent Kirby McCauley got a few nibbles from producers who were considering doing a Kane movie, but nothing came of it. Wagner was commissioned, however, to write the script for the third Conan movie for Di Laurentiis. Kirby said his friend Oliver Stone was very impressed with it, but it was never produced. Wagner also wrote one of the scripts for *Delta Force* and, his only movie to make the screen, a script for the Japanese animated film *Monkey*, an oriental myth. Even the unproduced scripts brought Wagner handsome sums.

He no longer sent out unsolicited manuscripts; editors were actually soliciting his work. But with success came a new problem: deadlines. And he no longer had the luxury of crafting a single story at a time. He must accept offers as they came in and juggle them as best he could. He began to relive the all-nighters of his college days. When he finally managed to grab some shut-eye, Jack Daniels helped him wind down.

With his stories more widely published Wagner became more famous. He was an honored guest at sci-fi/fantasy conventions all over the country. A few of his Knoxville friends and I attended some of the cons, basking in his reflected glory. He was the cynosure of our circle, the one who'd made good, and his friendship validated our own intellects. One of my fondest memories is of the first World Fantasy Convention, sitting with Manly Wellman on one side of me and Robert Bloch (author of *Psycho* as the blurbs on his 99 other books always read) on the other, talking past me about old times. Because I was a friend of Karl's I was accepted by the authors whose tales had frightened me as a child, people I'd thought of as Demiurges handing down stories from some dark Olympus.

Wagner would entertain fans, who often knew his work better than he did, all night long with discourse and drink. He was a splendid raconteur, but he could make everyone else in the room feel a bit superfluous. In the morning he would come around to my room and press still more alcohol upon me. "There's two ways to deal with a hangover, Mayer. You can treat it with aspirin, anti-nausea drugs and other nostrums... or you can postpone it indefinitely." And he'd pour himself another tumblerful. Straight. One time, while on a panel answering questions from the audience, he passed out clutching the microphone. The other panel members shuffled their chairs uncertainly for a while. Finally, Michael Moorcock pried the mike from his fingers and they went on with the program.

At one convention we encountered Frank Belknap Long, the last surviving member of the original circle of Cthulhu mythos authors and a personal friend of H. P. Lovecraft. He was in his eighties but still fairly spry. He was trying to locate a publishers' party in the hotel, and was quite angry at Kirby McCauley for not having seen that he got there. "Kirby's supposed to be my agent," he sputtered. "This party could be very important to my career!" The creative life is a hard life.

Once there was a wreck in front of the hotel where the convention was being held and Wagner, dressed in his usual regalia, hurried out to examine the victim and to keep the cops from moving him or elevating his feet. "He's suffered some head trauma," he told the EMT's when they arrived, "but he seems to be stabilized. I checked his vitals and for dilation and cyanosis; there doesn't seem to be any internal bleeding. Wouldn't hurt to use an oropharyngeal tube. If he comes to he'll be thirsty, but don't give him anything. You'll want to use oxygen, of course, but you won't need to hyperventilate."

As he returned to the hotel a female onlooker was heard to remark, "I never saw a biker doctor before."

The second World Fantasy Convention in New York was far less pleasant than the first. The wallpaper in the Hilton was peeling, the staff was unfriendly, and the food would have shamed the cooks at Old Central's cafeteria. And then, there was the city of New York. One night a few of us left the hotel and went a few blocks to a Chinese carry out. Sci-fi fans often dress in colorful costumes at conventions and one of the young ladies with was attired as, near as I could figure, a prostitute elf. Wagner was in his usual biker garb. I was probably wearing my Edwardian sharkskin suit (I chose it out of a catalog at John H. Daniels, probably not realizing it was out of style), with ascot and a bit of lace at collar and cuff. A couple of NYPD cops were scrutinizing us for offenses that might be illegal even in New York.

Now, as sophisticated as New Yorkers profess to be, you'd think they wouldn't give a prostitute elf a second glance. That's where you'd be wrong. I was the last to get my food and, as I headed back, I saw the young lady being detained by a big, young street tough. Ken Amos, the bookish and slightly built publisher of the magazine *Nightshade* had come to her defense, but the fellow outweighed the two of them together. As I caught up I stepped between them, punched the man in the belly, and the three of us continued across the street toward the Hilton. The native began to shout threats at me, and, stupidly, I turned to bandy words with him. As he started across the street toward me I realized, for the first time, that he was not alone. Other young men began to converge on us - I think some concert had just ended at Madison Square Garden - and I began to realize that these were not just onlookers. And their numbers kept growing. I thought of New York's Irish Ducky Boys gangs in the book The Wanderers. The cops seemed to have disappeared.

Though they were far ahead and could have abandoned me to my fate, pretending not to have noticed the hubbub, Wagner, Barbara and Ken returned to stand beside me and face down this throng. This confused our adversaries for a moment, but they resumed the offensive edging toward us, circling around, while we prepared to defend ourselves. Barbara, standing to one side, opened her purse and pulled a mother-huge pistol about halfway out and asked the punks nearest her, in the same voice with which she might invite them up for milk and cookies, "Do you want to eat some lead?" The ones who'd seen the piece began to drag their puzzled comrades away.

Finally, after all those years the very first novel he'd written, *Bloodstone*, was published. He brought me a copy and I began to read it. It was, of course, vastly changed from the version he'd scribbled on five-hole Blue Horse brand notebook paper when he was fourteen. I had flipped past the title pages, so it was some time before I realized the book was dedicated to me: "For John F. Mayer- Colleague and friend, Brother in infamy..." The phrase was a reference to one of my high school novel attempts, *Five for Infamy* in which Karl, Max and I starred with two other Centralites as a band of hired assassins. In the German edition the translator, unclear on English nuances, made it "Brüder in Schande" which translates as "brother in shame." Still, I was touched.

As many of the old pulp writers had done, Wagner often worked in hidden references to friends. In *Bloodstone* Kane remarks that he'd rather be lounging around Toad Hall partaking of yellow sunshine. Yellow sunshine was a 300 microgram variety of LSD. He also inserted little tributes to his favorite rock bands. On the first page of that same book is a reference to "Several Species of Small Furry Animals Grooving in a Cave with a Pict," a cut on Pink Floyd's *Umma Gumma* album. "Several species of small furry animals picked their way through caves and grooves in the moss-hung debris..."

Among the friends Karl made through his writing was Glenn Lord, the executor of the estate of Robert E. Howard. Lord was disgusted with the liberties editors (and posthumous collaborators) Lin Carter and L.

Sprague de Camp had taken with Howard's work. Back when Howard's work was little known L. Sprague de Camp had made arrangements to edit the Lancer Conan series. The series was so successful that de Camp, in order to keep up with demand, was obliged to print stories Howard himself had discarded or rewritten, to assemble and rewrite abandoned story fragments and stories Howard had written in other genres (a detective story, for example), old grocery lists, and finally, it seemed, to solicit passersby for new Conan stories. "Excuse me, sir, how'd you like to be the author of Conan?" The result was a Conan who would have been at home in Saturday morning cartoons. Those of us who knew Howard's work from the pulps were incensed at the indignities his literary corpus was suffering; we were prone to quote Baudelaire: "Is there, then, in America, no law to prevent dogs from entering cemeteries?" Lord knew that Wagner shared his sentiments and asked him to edit new collections of the original Conan tales as Howard had penned them. It seems there had been a clause in the Lancer series contract that reverted all rights to the estate in the event that the stories were out of print for such and such a period. Karl accepted with glee; not only was this a chance to pay homage to one of his formative influences, but, also, to right a wrong. The first volumes of the Berkley Conan series were printed, edited by Karl Wagner but without editorial "emendations". Alas, if only good Aquilonian steel could deal with lawyers as handily as with other monsters. There was a loophole. De Camp et al. brought legal action and Conan disappeared from newsstands for a time. Sadly, committees of evildoers worked a terrible transformation. *Conan the Conqueror* became Conan the Corporation.

Wagner began to move away from heroic fantasy in favor of modern horror tales. Many of these were set in Knoxville and environs. One day when he was in town I took him to meet my friend Mr. Brock who lived in a quaint little cottage he'd built himself from packing crates and scrap lumber in a large, otherwise vacant space between Broadway and the old foundry building (which latter was to become the Strohaus pub during the 1982 World's Fair), and beside a railroad yard. The lot was strewn with cinders left over from the days of steam locomotives and overgrown with weeds and scrub trees; there were no other houses in sight. He ran a little flea market in his front yard and Wagner collected old bottles; many of those on Mr. Brock's outdoor shelves had been dredged up from an old cistern on his property. Mr. Brock also managed to grow a sizeable vegetable garden in the coal dust along the tracks behind his house, though he waged a constant struggle against the kudzu that encroached upon it daily. He canned those vegetables and they helped see him through the winter. His struggle seemed to me to have a Hemingway quality. "Someday," I remarked to Wagner as we headed beneath the Asylum Avenue viaduct back to my place, "I'm going to write a story about Mr. Brock titled 'The Old Man and the Kudzu.'"

"You know, Mayer, if you're joking, I believe I can do something with that." I was joking - I hadn't done any writing since high school - and I gave him my blessings. The story became "Where the Summer Ends," a horror tale quite unlike the one I'd proposed. It concerned the creatures that lived in symbiosis with kudzu, and took place in Fort Sanders. I learned later from Barbara that Wagner had determined that the protagonist would survive or perish based on whether or not I got back together with Julie, my love at that time, called Linda in the story. Next to "Sticks," "Where the Summer Ends" is Wagner's most frequently reprinted story. Every person named in the story, including Old Morney, already dead when the story begins, is based on a real person.

Another local story is "Cedar Lane," set in his boyhood home on the street of that name in North Knoxville, back when there were still cedars on Cedar Lane, before they were cut down to make drive-throughs for Burger Doodles. It concerns the Walk-Home and paths his life might have taken. *Sign of the Salamander* is a serial written in pulp style about the adventures of John Chance, an occult investigator. It takes place in Vestal, Sequoyah Hills and the Smokies. "Spare Parts" was based on one of the Knoxville junkyards Wagner used to patronize, probably Red's or Bigfoot's.

Some of his stories were based on his medical experiences. One was rejected for its lack of realism. "You should spend some time around doctors, listen to how they talk," the editor advised him. His story "The Fourth Seal" about the way in which doctors insure their job security, was optioned for a movie.

With his writing finally paying off and Barbara doing office work, Karl was able to pay off the mortgage on the Valley Park Clinic and Cycle Shop and indulge some of his hobbies. He finally sold the faithful Falcon wagon and bought a new Thunderbird and a bootlegger's souped-up Cyclone Spoiler complete with welded-shut trunk. He and Barbara began taking trips to London just for pleasure; Karl had become fascinated with the city while there as convention guest. And, at long last, he was able to complete his collection of *Weird Tales*. He wouldn't divulge what he had paid for the earliest issues except to acknowledge that it was a pretty penny. Since the pulps had been generally considered as disposable as the daily paper, few people had saved them and most of those had fallen prey to tidy mothers and wives, silverfish, and wartime paper drives. The very earliest copies were so rare it seemed the only people who had kept them were those who actually had stories in them. Wagner's *Weird Tales volume'one*, *number two*, had belonged to H. P. Lovecraft. And it was missing the front cover.

His thousands of pulps were no longer just esoteric curiosities. They were now a working resource. At last he had the capitol to realize a childhood dream: to save some of the great pulp fiction tales - and their authors - from oblivion. With fellow Chapel Hill residents Jim Gross and writer David Drake. Wagner formed the publishing company Carcosa. Their first production, naturally enough, was a compilation of the previously uncollected work of Manly Wade Wellman. *Worse' Things Waiting* was about 400 pages long and bound in real cloth hard covers with special endpapers, on acid free paper and set with old-fashioned moveable type. It was a handsome volume. Ironically, considering Manly's association with the South (one of his best-known works is the Civil War fantasy "The Valley Was Still", adapted for *Twilight Zone*), it was printed by CSA. CSA stood, however, for Center for Spiritual Awareness. For the numerous illustrations Wagner recruited Lee Brown Coye, one of the last surviving *Weird Tales* artists, and possibly the artist who had produced that magazine's strangest and most disturbing pictures. His work had a primitive, almost tribal look, but the tribe would have been one whose ancestry was tainted by unholy liaisons with beings not entirely human. Coye's signature had once been a crescent moon subtly worked into his drawings, but in recent years the moon had been replaced by bizarre assemblages of sticks. Coye's explanation became the basis of Karl's most popular story, "Sticks".

When Wellman saw the finished book he told Karl, "I thought I was doing you a favor. Now I see that you were doing me one."

And, indeed, Carcosa was a labour of love. Though the first edition numbered only 2000 copies and sold for under $10.00 it took years to sell out. But profit was never the point. Even while Karl was working around cartons of unsold volumes of *Worse' Things Waiting*, he began assembling Carcosa's second collection, *Far Lands, Other Days*, stories by E. Hoffman Price, a prolific pulp writer who had once, in the thirties, stopped to scan a newsstand and seen ten different titles for which he'd written the cover story. He was a world traveler who had lived the fantasies he wrote about. A cavalryman, he could sabre dummies from horseback, jump hurdles and fire pistols accurately with either hand. He was also capable with the epee´ and had won at least one national trophy. He had been in the Philippines during the Moro campaign and had pursued Pancho Villa in Mexico. He, too, was a serious drinker and a connoisseur of exotic liquors. "I found demerara and half a dozen other kinds of rum, kao liang, Calvados, marc de Bourgogne, Armagnac, raki, slivovitz and many another." The illustrator for *Far Lands, Other Days* was George Evans who had drawn for EC and Classics comics and, appropriately, for Terry and the Pirates.

Far Lands sold even more slowly than *Worse Things Waiting* but Karl just stacked the cartons of the new book beside the older ones and began assembling *Murgunstrumm and Others*. This was an anthology of stories by another contributor to *Weird Tales* as well as *Strange Tales* and other shudder pulps, Hugh B. Cave. He had written nearly 800 short stories, but he'd lost every one of them in a fire. Happily, Wagner had his library. Coye was again called upon to illustrate. Wagner proudly presented me a copy of the new book. Across the top of the spine in large letters was the name Cave. "Cave," I muttered, pronouncing it CAH-vay.

"Ah, Mayer! Pace More Johnson would be proud of you."

Murgunstrumm, too, sold slowly, but Karl and Carcosa pressed ahead. Last came *Lonely Vigils*, a second volume of Wellman tales illustrated this time by Evans.

Wagner was becoming popular enough that he attracted the attention of copycats. The first installment of a serial starring a scheming and immortal mercenary named Cain appeared in a popular science-fiction magazine; it bore striking parallels to the long out-of-print *Darkness Weaves*, though it was set in the future instead of the past and science replaced magic (the fair young maiden's actual brain was switched with that of the evil old hag instead of just her persona). Copyrights are tricky things, but after Wagner and others complained the rest of the installments were dropped from publication. And one of Marvel's King Kull comics seemed to follow the story line of Wagner's short story "Reflections on the Winter of My Soul" more faithfully than was customary with Howard's actual Kull stories. In fact, the villain in that story, Thulsa Doom, who had appeared in only one of Howard's Kull stories, in his human form is depicted as looking very much like Kane. Somewhat ironically, this Kane-like Doom became a recurring villain in Marvel's heroic fantasies.

But success was beginning to take its toll on Karl. After all the lean years he could not bring himself to decline a commission, no matter how overworked he was. He would go days with little sleep trying to meet deadlines. And he continued to rely upon booze to ease the stress. Barbara, who had once enjoyed matching him drink for drink at con parties, became increasingly concerned. He refused to seek counseling with her. As a psychiatrist he regarded psychologists as witch doctors. At last they separated.

I mentioned that Barbara had a special talent for making a man feel good about himself. I well knew how painful it could be to have that intoxicating reinforcement withdrawn cold turkey. I don't think Wagner had ever before been troubled by self-doubt. He was still harboring hopes of winning back her affection when she remarried.

Wagner's mother had a series of strokes that left her unable to care for herself. Then his father Aubrey Wagner, whom Karl idolized, began to succumb to Parkinson's disease. At last Karl's siblings called on him to be the one, the "hired gun" as he said, to deliver his mother to Shannondale nursing home. As they wheeled her down the hall she had a moment of lucidity. She looked back at him and sobbed, "You're abandoning me here, aren't you?"

Shortly thereafter his father joined her there and, within a year, died. Barbara, whom Karl hadn't known was in Knoxville, showed up. He requested that I ask her to leave. Some old Key Clubbers from Central came to pay their respects. "You know," he told them, "I never liked you." Once they realized he wasn't joking they, too, left. Karl packed up his library of *Weird Tales* and other pulps and rare books, which had always been shelved at his parents' house, first on Cedar Lane, then in Suburban Hills, and carted them back to Chapel Hill.

He visited Knoxville only once or twice a year after that, to visit his mother, his old friend Tip Jackson and, sometimes, me. On nights when Brother Jack's was closed, we'd sometimes congregate at Tip's house on Boyd Street, drinking at a table in his front yard in warm weather. Tip held court for the neighborhood; a dozen people might stop by in the course of an evening to pay respects or to try to cadge a drink. One night one of the visitors, an attractive young black woman, was carrying a shotgun. Her brother had been kidnapped and was being held as a part of some dispute; she was on her way to free him. She had a drink, then continued on her mission. There seemed to be no thought in this neighborhood of applying to the police for protection

One night when Wagner left Brother Jack's, alone but for his German Shepherd Crystal, with a sizable package under his arm, the place was, evidently, under surveillance. It must have seemed suspicious to see a white boy with a package leaving a rough, black joint in a drug-infested neighborhood. Apparently, he was followed by an officer in an unmarked car. The suspicious behaviour of the pursuing car alarmed Karl and, finally, convinced he was about to be robbed and/or murdered, he ran the officer off the road and into a concrete abutment. Backup was called, but since these officers, too, were in unmarked cars, Karl led them a merry chase through the streets of West Knoxville. At last he was run to ground and pulled from his car with guns aimed at his head. His dog, naturally, growled at the men who were abusing her master. This seemed like a good reason to shoot her, but an older officer persuaded the younger ones to hold their fire till Crystal could be placated. Wagner called me that night, but I'd been getting crank calls so I had my ringers off and the volume all the way down on my answering machine. I still have the recording: "Mayer... I really need your help, Old Buddy. I'm in a world of shit."

At first Karl had trouble getting his car back: something about holding it for the DEA. When he did, his upholstery had been cut and the barbecue was missing. The officer who had been run off the road sued. "When he heard I was a famous, rich author he probably went right out and picked him out a brand new bass boat," Karl suggested. The officer arrived in court wearing a neck brace, but when Karl's lawyer pointed out that all the damage to Karl's car was in the rear while all the damage to the police car was in the front, the case was dismissed.

Karl pronounced Knoxville the Bad Vibes Capitol of the World and vowed never to return. And he never did. He began, instead, to make increasingly frequent trips to London where he had made a number of friends. The Brits liked Karl, liked his writing, and told him he was the only Yankee they'd ever met who could outdrink them. "I'm no Yankee," he told them.

Needless to say, these trips were not inexpensive and writing assignments were beginning to slow up for Karl. He was editing some anthologies (he almost got to edit the revived *Weird Tales*) and getting some calls for fiction from small specialty houses, but the big money guys were beginning to complain that he missed too many deadlines, that the quality of his work was declining. Maybe Karl could no longer shrug off the effects of a fifth of Jack Daniels a day, plus beer and wine. Or maybe a string of sorrows beginning with his divorce had taken the heart out of him. Big, powerful Manly Wellman broke his hip, went to the hospital and lost both legs to bedsores. He had always prided himself on his physical prowess; now, demoralized, he faded away. He died in Karl's arms.

Back in Knoxville Tip suffered several diabetic strokes, lost one leg, then the other. Barbara helped his brother Jeep care for him during the last two years of his life. When he finally died she called Wagner but before she could give him the bad news he interrupted her: "Tip's dead." He'd dreamed it the night before.

I, too, called, not knowing if he'd heard. I mentioned the growth on my shoulder blade. Didn't he think this was carrying a gag too far? Wagner seemed much more concerned about my neoplasm than his own. "You gotta get that looked at, Mayer. This is nothing to fool around with."

"That sounds familiar, Wagner. Isn't that what I've been trying to tell you?"

"A little late for me. But you're provided for in my will."

"Karl, I don't give a rat's ass about your will," I protested in a rare moment of seriousness.

"Well, then, I guess you're not interested in the collection of *Weird Tales* I was leaving you."

"Now, let's not be hasty!" I was kidding.

"By the way, Mayer, remember that story we wrote back at Central about the gun-toting vampire. I've rewritten it and it sold. I gave you credit on it."

"Hey, it pays to recycle."

"I'll send you a copy."

A week or so later it arrived. It was set in modern London and bore no resemblance to the original. With it was a note telling me where the story would appear and that he was off for London "one last time. Going with Lynn, my crazed punker. May not survive." The stamp showed a black locomotive. Underneath it he'd written "The Little Black Train," a reference to a Wellman story about the train that comes for the dying.

One morning I was preparing my coffee and playing back the messages on my answering machine that had been left while I slept. "John, this is Mike Elam." It was Karl's nephew. "I've got some bad news; Karl Wagner's dead." I've heard of being staggered by bad news; I actually missed a step and had to catch onto my sink, spilling the coffee grounds.

He had been found by a friend in Chapel Hill who became concerned when he didn't answer his phone. He was lying on his bathroom floor. It wasn't cancer that killed him; his liver had practically exploded.

No, it wasn't the airplanes. It was Beauty killed the Beast.

He'd died on Friday the 13th*, October 1994. You hear of statistical proof that people can postpone death till after special days; I'm surprised Karl didn't wait till Hallowe'en. It was his favorite holiday since childhood; mine too: there's a hint of adventure, a sense of potency for a kid at Hallowe'en that even Christmas lacks.

In settling his affairs it was discovered that most of his rare books, his autographed manuscripts, even his collection of *Weird Tales* had been sold to pay bills. His body was cremated and his remains were placed in a little cedar box. His mother was in her wheelchair at the graveside services in a pleasant, park-like cemetery in Knoxville. "I can't believe that's all that's left of Karl," she said. The little box was buried atop a hill from which the nearby Great Smoky Mountains can be seen.

And now it's after the end. I kept expecting to see something in the news, or Knoxville's daily paper, some sort of tribute to one of Knoxville's most successful writers, a native son who had produced enduring works of horror. But the man himself seems to have simply vanished, leaving only his stories, as though they had been handed down, without human intervention, from some Dark Olympus. It's as though Karl had never been. Horror indeed.

I did see a doctor about the place on my back. "It should come off," he told me. "If it's not cancer, it will be. It's as easy to take it off as to biopsy it." But I hesitate.

Though our voices were remarkably similar, I realize, of course, that the long-standing gag about Karl and I being the same person was no more than that: a joke. I'm sure we were as different as we were alike, and I know I never had a fraction of Karl's brilliance. I know, too, that the fact that Karl and I both had some sort of neoplasms forming on our backs at the same time was only a strange coincidence, and that the bit about the "unformed twin" was another gag, inspired by horror stories we had read as boys. Yet I feel, suddenly, so creative. This is the first real writing I've done in years. I'm not a superstitious person. None-the-less, I think I'll wait awhile on the surgery.

*The thirteenth of October 1994 is widely given as the date of Karl's death. Though he did die on the night of Friday the 13th, his sister, Audrey Elam, reports there is evidence that he did not die till after midnight. However, I think Karl would have preferred Friday the 13th for literary reasons, and the error is so widespread it will likely, as is so often the case, replace the truth, popular culture's version of artistic license.

Karl Edward Wagner
(1945-1994)

photo by John Mayer

THE JOURN-ALL

Being the Emails and Letters to the Editor Section of

JOURN-E: THE JOURNAL OF IMAGINATIVE LITERATURE

Send Emails to: mindseye@pobox.com
OR Write to:
Mind's Eye Publications
c/o Frank Coffman, Editor & Publisher
985 Deborah Avenue
Elgin, IL 60123-1918
USA

Your reactions to our inaugural issue are welcome. Anything regarding content, format, publication criteria, submissions, etc.

Comments on specific included items are also welcome. Constructive criticisms and positive (even rave) comments are welcome, but please use tact and decorum in phrasing your responses.

Looking forward to hearing from readers about the reception of JOURN-E.

Frank Coffman
Editor & Publisher

The Contributors
(The Company of Journ-E-ers)

Jonel Abellanosa lives in Cebu City, The Philippines. His poetry and fiction are forthcoming in *The Cape Rock* and *Poetry Salzburg Review*, and have appeared in hundreds of magazines including *Thin Air, Invisible City, Chiron Review, Mobius: Journal of Social Change, Star*Line, Liquid Imagination, The Lyric, Poetry Kanto* and *The Anglican Theological Review*, and nominated for the Pushcart, Best of the Net and Dwarf Stars prizes. His poetry collections include, *Songs from My Mind's Tree* and *Multiverse* (Clare Songbirds Publishing House, New York), *50 Acrostic Poems*, (Cyberwit, India), *In the Donald's Time* (Poetic Justice Books and *Art*, Florida), and *Pan's Saxophone* (Weasel Press, Texas). He is a nature lover, with three companion dogs, and three other beloved dogs who have passed on beyond the rainbow bridge. He loves all animals.

Colleen Anderson's poems have been published in such venues as *Mirror Dance, Polu Texni, The Future Fire, HWA Poetry Showcase* and others. She is a Canada Council and BC Arts Council grant recipient for writing and has performed her work before audiences in the US, UK and Canada. Colleen has also published fiction, including the collection *A Body of Work,* Black Shuck Books. Her poetry collection, *I Dreamed a World*, is forthcoming this May from LVP Publications. www.colleenanderson.wordpress.com

Brandon Barrows is the author of several novels, most recently *Stranger's Kingdom*. He has published over seventy stories, selected of which are collected in the books *The Altar in the Hills* and *The Castle-Town Tragedy*. He is an active member of Private Eye Writers of America and International Thriller Writers and was a 2021 Mustang Award finalist.

Bruce Boston is the author of sixty books and chapbooks, including the novels *The Guardener's Tale and Stained Glass Rain*. His poems have appeared in *Asimov's SF, Analog, Weird Tales, Amazing Stories, Daily Science Fiction, New Myths, Pedestal, Strange Horizons, Nebula Awards Showcase* and *Year's Best Fantasy and Horror*. His poetry has received the Bram Stoker Award, the *Asimov's* Readers Award, and the Rhysling and Grand Master Awards of the SFPA. His fiction has received a Pushcart Prize and twice been a finalist for the Bram Stoker Award (novel, short story).

Sarah Cannavo is a writer of prose and poetry haunting southern New Jersey. Her poems and short stories have appeared in anthologies and magazines such as *The Literary Hatchet, Liminality, Horror USA: California, Star*Line, The Cryptid Chronicles, Pulp Modern, Dates From Hell,* and DBND Publishing's *Halloween Horror Volume 3.* Her poems "Fallen But Not Down" and "Learning the Way" were nominated for a 2020 and 2021 Rhysling Award, respectively. Her story "Unreality" and novella *Wolf of the Pines* are available now on Amazon. She's occasionally been known to post on her site www.moodilymusing.blogspot.com, and she's been sighted tweeting @moodilymusing.

Frank Coffman is a retired professor of English, Creative Writing, and Journalism. He has published speculative poetry and fiction in a wide variety of journals, magazines, anthologies, and collections. His poetry collections include: *This Ae Nighte, Every Nighte and Alle* (chapbook, 2018); *The Coven's Hornbook & Other Poems* (2019); *Black Flames & Gleaming Shadows* (2020); and *Eclipse of the Moon* (2021). Individual poems have appeared in the journals/magazines *Spectral Realms, Abyss & Apex, Phantasmagoria, Gathering Storm, Cyaegha, View from Atlantis, Lovecraftiana, Jitter, Tales from the Moonlit Path,* and others. His verse has also appeared in the anthologies *Caravan's Awry, Quoth the Raven, 32 Horses on a Vermillion Hill, Time We Left, Bloodbond, The Phantasmagorical Promenade,* and others. His collection of short fiction, *Three Against the Dark: Collected Dr. Venn Occult Detective Mysteries* was recently published (March 2022). Another short story collection, *Maxime Miris: 12 Tales of Horror, the Weird, & the Supernatural* will be published in January 2023. In scholarly publications, he selected, edited, and did an introduction and commentary for his *Robert E. Howard: Selected Poems* (2006). In more traditional poetic work, his revised and enlarged edition of *Khayyám's Rubáiyát* will be published in later 2021. He created and monitors the Weird Poets Society Facebook site and is Editor and Publisher of Mind's Eye Publications™. A member of the Horror Writers Association and the Science Fiction & Fantasy Poetry Association, he lives in Elgin, Illinois, with his immensely understanding wife, Connie, and two cat people: Buffy (the vampire-slaying calico) and Binx (ghost chaser).

Scott J. Couturier is a poet & prose writer of the Weird, grotesque, liminal, & darkly fantastic. His work has appeared in numerous venues, including *The Audient Void, Spectral Realms, Eye To The Telescope, The Dark Corner Zine, Space and Time Magazine,* & *Weirdbook.* Currently he works as a copy & content editor for Mission Point Press, living an obscure reverie with his partner/live-in editor & two cats.

Deborah L. Davitt was raised in Nevada, but currently lives in Houston, Texas with her husband and son. Her prize-winning poetry has received Rhysling, Dwarf Star, and Pushcart nominations and has appeared in over fifty journals, including *F&SF* and *Asimov's*. Her short fiction has appeared in *Analog* and *Galaxy's Edge*. For more about her work, including her poetry collections, *The Gates of Never* and *Bounded by Eternity*, please see www.edda-earth.com.

Shikhar Dixit is a writer/illustrator whose two newest stories in print can be found in *Weird Horror #1* and *Space & Time #139*, both magazines available on Amazon. He has sold over thirty stories and one hundred illustrations to such venues as *Dark Regions*, *Strange Horizons*, *Not One of Us*, *The Darker Side* (anthology edited by John Pelan), *Songs From Dead Singers* (anthology edited by Michael Kelly) and two Barnes & Noble anthologies. He lives with his family in the deep, dark heart of New Jersey, where he is currently is at work on his first novel. To learn more, visit his website at SlipOfThePen.com

Claire Davon has written on and off for most of her life, starting with fan fiction when she was very young. She writes across a wide range of genres, and does not consider any of it off limits. Her novels can be found in the paranormal romance and contemporary romance sections, while her short stories run the gamut across all genres, as imagination dictates. If a story calls to her, she will write it. She currently lives in Los Angeles and spends her free time writing novels and short stories, as well as doing animal rescue and enjoying the sunshine.

John Dukes lives in rural Pennsylvania with his wife and children. In addition to writing, studying philosophy, history and theology he is filled with great affection for poetry. His greatest interest lies in reading translations of 18th and 19th century German poets such as Goethe and Hölderlin as well as 20th century figures like Borges, Pound, and Rilke. John has held a variety of jobs over the years and has been blessed to live in places as diverse as Alaska, California, South Carolina and Italy

Elana Gomel was born in a country that no longer exists and has lived in many others that may, or may not, be on the road to extinction. She currently resides in California. She is an academic with a long list of books and articles, specializing in science fiction, Victorian literature, and serial killers. She is also a fiction writer who has published more than ninety short stories, several novellas, and three novels. Her story "Where the Streets Have No Name" was the winner of the 2020 Gravity Award, and her story "Mine Seven" is included in The Best Horror of the Year 13 edited by Ellen Datlow. She is a member of HWA.

Gary Hill is the author several books including *The Strange Sound of Cthulhu: Music Inspired by the Writings of H.P. Lovecraft, Wizard Song* and *The Homestead*. He is the publisher of "Music Street Journal" and Tales of Wonder and Dread Publishing. Under Tales of Wonder and Dread he has published titles including *Horrifying Holidays: Holiday Spookfest, Lovecraftian Roots: Writers Who Influenced Howard Phillips Lovecraft, Lovecraftian Branches: Weird Tales Built on H.P. Lovecraft's Mythos, Spooky Berwyn, Spooky Rockford and Spooky Rockford Two*. He is also the curator of "Spooky Ventures." Hill has written for many other publications and organizations over the years including "Wormwood Chronicles," "All Music Guide" and G4TV. He is a music, science fiction and horror fanatic who lives in Northern Illinois.

Eryn Hiscock's writing has been published in literary journals, zines and anthologies internationally. Her online articles have earned millions of views. Her most recent publications appear in *It Calls From The Forest, Volume 2* (Eerie River Publishing, Canada) and *Inlandia: A Literary Journey*. She was most recently nominated for a Pushcart Prize for the short memoir piece published in *Inlandia*. Amazon author page: https://www.amazon.com/Eryn-Hiscock/e/B08J3QGW5J

Toe Keen

Katherine Kerestman is the author of *Creepy Cat's Macabre Travels: Prowling around Haunted Towers, Crumbling Castles, and Ghoulish Graveyards* (WordCrafts Press, 2020), a non-fiction travel memoir to destinations associated with macabre stories in history, literature, and film, as well as numerous short stories and horror non-fiction in anthologies and journals. She has a B.A. from John Carroll University, and an M.A. from Case Western Reserve University; and she is a member of the Jane Austen Society of North America, Mensa, the Horror Writers Association and the Dracula Society. She loves *Dark Shadows* and *Twin Peaks*, and is known to frolic in the graveyards of Salem on Halloween. You can keep up with her at www.creepycatlair.com

Colt Leasure is an American bouncer and writer who currently lives in the Sierra Nevada's. He is an SFWA (Science Fiction and Fantasy Writers of America) member. His story "Induction" was a pro-sale to Flame Tree Publishing's anthology *Agents and Spies*, the foreword of which was written by the renowned Martin Edwards. *Agents and Spies* is in Flame Tree's successful Gothic Fantasy series, and will be translated into Chinese. He has received three Honorable Mentions in the Writers of the Future Contest, and one Honorable Mention in a contest hosted by Italian horror publishing company Dark Regions. Other works of Colt's have appeared in printed and online magazines such as *Aphelion, Lovecraftiana, Blood Moon Rising,* and *Schlock!* among others. Bestselling author Christopher Moore told him "well, good luck, whatever you decide to do, but really, with that name if you're able to avoid becoming a professional card player, pool hustler, pimp or porn star, you'll be lucky." Moore was one hundred percent correct.

Hunter Liguore offers creative writing classes at several universities, nature centers, walking trails, online, and virtually anyplace where writers converge. An award-winning author, her work has been received internationally, including *Everylife,* a 16-time international winner in 2019/2020. She is writing for the next generation of readers who care about the world. hunterliguore.org

A weaver of tales, the wearer of many hats, **Lori R. Lopez** dips her pen in poetry, prose, song and art. Some of her poems have been nominated for Rhysling Awards. Books include *The Dark Mister Snark, Darkverse: The Shadow Hours* (nominated for a 2018 Elgin Award), *Leery Lane, Odds & Ends: A Dark Collection, The Witchhunt,* and *An Ill Wind Blows.* Lori co-owns Fairy Fly Entertainment with her two talented sons. They are Vegans, Activists, Filmmakers, and members of a Folk Band called The Fairyflies. Lori illustrates most of her books and believes that Quirky is her middle name, even though it doesn't begin with R. Verse and Prose have appeared in various Publications including *The Horror Zine, Weirdbook, The Sirens Call, Spectral Realms, Space & Time, Altered Realities, Illumen, Oddball Magazine, Bewildering Stories,* plus a number of anthologies including H.W.A. Poetry Showcases, *Dead Harvest, Fearful Fathoms,* and *California Screamin'* (the Foreword Poem).

Charles Danny Lovecraft

P. H. Low is Malaysian American writer with work published in *Strange Horizons,* Tor.com, *Fantasy Magazine,* and *Abyss & Apex,* among others. P. H. attended Viable Paradise in 2019; currently serves as a first reader for *khōréō,* a speculative fiction magazine featuring immigrant and diaspora writers and stories; and can be found on Twitter @_lowpH and at her website ph-low.com.

John C. Mannone has poems in speculative journals such as *Space & Time Magazine, Elixir, Nebo, Eye to the Telescope,* and speculative poems in literary journals *North Dakota Quarterly, Foreign Literary Review, Le Menteur, Poetry South, New England Journal of Medicine,* and others. He won the Dwarf Stars Award (2020) and the HWA Scholarship (2017). Some literary distinctions include: Impressions of Appalachia Creative Arts Contest poetry prize (2020), the Carol Oen Memorial Fiction Prize (2020), and the Joy Margrave Award in nonfiction (2015, 2017). He was awarded a Jean Ritchie Fellowship (2017) in Appalachian literature, Weymouth writing residencies (2016, 2017), and served as the celebrity judge for the National Federation of State Poetry Societies (2018). His two latest collections are forthcoming: *Flux Lines: The Intersection of Science, Love, and Poetry* (Linnet's Wings Press, 2021) and *Sacred Flute* (Iris Press, 2021/2022). He edits poetry for *Abyss & Apex, Silver Blade, Liquid Imagination,* and *American Diversity Report.* A retired physics professor, John lives in Knoxville, Tennessee. http://jcmannone.wordpress.com

John Mayer: said to say simply, "He knew Karl Edward Wagner."

Gary McCluskey has been a professional artist for more than 15 years. He's one book covers for every genre imaginable (such as the memoir of a coma survivor's trip through the afterlife) as well as artwork for comic books, children's books and RPG games. Recently he completed five ebook covers for Roger Zelazny's Amber series and several interor illustrations for a new harcover version of Edgar Rice Burroughs' "The Oakdale Affair." He's currently working on a comic book about a vampire-shark. You can see his work at https://www.behance.net/gmccluskey or look im up on Facebook.

Ngo Binh Anh Khoa is currently working at Ho Chi Minh City University of Technology (HUTECH) as a teacher of English, specializing in Translation and Literature. In his free time, he enjoys learning new languages, reading fiction, and writing speculative poetry for personal entertainment. His works have previously appeared in *Heroic Fantasy Quarterly, Liquid Imagination, ParABnormal Magazine, Star*Line, Weirdbook, The Audient Void, Spectral Realms,* and other venues. He also dabbles in the art of haiku composition, and some of his mainstream haiku have received awards as well as honorable mentions in different international contests in the USA, Japan, Canada, and elsewhere.

Max Jason Peterson (https://maxjasonpeterson.wordpress.com/, a member of www.gardnercastle.com) holds master's degrees in English literature and library science. With stories under the MJP byline published in *Mystery Weekly Magazine* and forthcoming in *Virginia Is for Mysteries,* Vol. 3, this award-winning author has over 450 stories, poems, art, and articles in *Analog* (forthcoming), *Strange Horizons, Flash Fiction Online, PodCastle, Seascape: The Best New England Crime Stories 2019,* and *A*

Study in Lavender: Queering Sherlock Holmes, among others. A gender-fluid night owl, Max loves samurai films, reading comics with cats, and working in the darkroom. Under byline Adele Gardner, their first Halloween poetry collection, *Halloween Hearts*, will be available from Jackanapes Press soon--possibly as early as October 2022.

Chris Preston is a writer of fiction and creative non-fiction from Ontario, Canada. Formal studies include University of Toronto's Creative Writing program, as well as various workshops. You can currently see work by Chris within *Mystery Weekly*, *Schlock! Webzine*, and *Asymmetry Fiction*. To find out more, feel free to visit www.seeprestonwrite.com. You may also follow Chris with the following twitter handle – @write_preston.

Gerard Sarnat won San Francisco Poetry's 2020 Contest, the Poetry in the Arts First Place Award plus the Dorfman Prize, and has been nominated for handfuls of 2021 and previous Pushcarts plus Best of the Net Awards. Gerry is widely published including in *Hong Kong Review*, *Tokyo Poetry Journal*, *Buddhist Poetry Review*, *Gargoyle*, *Main Street Rag*, *New Delta Review*, *Arkansas Review*, *Hamilton-Stone Review*, *Northampton Review*, *New Haven Poetry Institute*, *Texas Review*, *Vonnegut Journal*, *Brooklyn Review*, *San Francisco Magazine*, *Monterey Poetry Review*, *The Los Angeles Review*, *and The New York Times* as well as by Harvard, Stanford, Dartmouth, Penn, Columbia, North Dakota and University of Chicago presses. He's authored the collections *Homeless Chronicles*, *Disputes*, *17s*, *Melting the Ice King*. Gerry is a Harvard-trained physician who's built and staffed clinics for the marginalized as well as a Stanford professor and healthcare CEO. Currently he is devoting energy/ resources to deal with climate justice, and serves on Climate Action Now's board. Gerry's been married since 1969 with three kids plus six grandsons, and is looking forward to potential future granddaughters.

Darrell Schweitzer is the author of about 350 published stories and four novels, the most notable of which is *THE MASK OF THE SORCERER*. Recently PS Publishing brought out a two-volume retrospective of his short fiction, *THE MYSTERIES OF THE FACELESS KING* and *THE LAST HERETIC*. He is a former editor of *WEIRD TALES* (1988-2007) and four-time World Fantasy Award finalist (and one-time winner, for *WEIRD TALES*). If one makes a distinction between his humorous verse (which goes so far as to rhyme "Cthulhu" in a limerick) and serious poetry, he has two poetry collections in print from Wildside Press, *GROPING TOWARD THE LIGHT* and *GHOSTS OF PAST AND FUTURE*. A further volume, *DANCING BEFORE AZATHOTH* will appear from P'rea Press in 2022.

Jay Sturner is a writer, poet, and naturalist from the Chicago suburbs. He is the author of several books of poetry and a collection of short stories. His writing has appeared in such publications as *Space and Time Magazine*, *Spectral Realms*, *Tales of the Talisman*, *Star*Line*, and *Liquid Imagina-*

tion, among others. He has been nominated twice for the Rhysling Award, and in 2019 one of his poems was featured on a segment of NPR's *All Things Considered.* In addition to being a writer, Sturner is also a professional bird walk leader. He currently resides in Downers Grove, Illinois, a suburb of Chicago.

DJ Tyrer is the person behind *Atlantean Publishing,* editor of *View From Atlantis,* and has been published in *The Rhysling Anthology 2016,* and issues of *Cyaegha, Enchanted Conversation, The Horrorzine, Illumen, Scifaikuest, Sirens Call, Spectral Realms, Star*Line,* and *Tigershark,* as well as releasing several chapbooks, such as *The Tears of Lot-49.* The e-chapbook *One Vision* is available from Tigershark Publishing's website. *SuperTrump* and *A Wuhan Whodunnit* are available to download from the Atlantean Publishing website.
DJ Tyrer's website is at https://djtyrer.blogspot.co.uk/
DJ Tyrer's Facebook page is at https://www.facebook.com/DJTyrerwriter/
The Atlantean Publishing website is at https://atlanteanpublishing.wordpress.com/
The *View From Atlantis* website is at https://viewfromatlantis.wordpress.com/

Vicki Weisfeld's short stories have appeared in leading mystery magazines and various anthologies, winning awards from the Short Mystery Fiction Society and the Public Safety Writers Association. She's a reviewer for the UK website, crimefictionlover.com and blogs at www.vweisfeld.com. In April 2022, her first novel is expected from Black Opal Books.

Emma Wells has poetry published with and by: *The World's Greatest Anthology, The League of Poets, The Lake, The Beckindale Poetry Journal, Dreich Magazine, Drunken Pen Writing, Porridge Magazine, Visual Verse, Littoral Magazine, The Pangolin Review, Derailleur Press, Giving Room Magazine, Chronogram* and for the Ledbury Poetry Festival. She also has published a number of short stories and her first novel, *Shelley's Sisterhood,* is due to be published shortly.

Robb T. White has published several crime, noir, and horror stories as well as hardboiled novels in various anthologies and magazines such as *Down & Out, Mystery Tribune, Yellow Mama, Mystery Weekly, Hoosier Noir,* and *Close to the Bone.* White has been nominated for a Derringer. "Inside Man," a crime story, published in *Down and Out Magazine,* was selected for the *Best American Mystery Stories 2019.* "The Girl from the Sweater Factory," a horror tale, was a finalist in *The Dark Sire* Magazine's 2020 awards. He has two series private eyes.

COLOPHON

THE FANCY FONT
USED FOR THE TITLING
IS ORBE PRO

The body copy font is
Adobe Jenson Pro 11 on 13
in various weights and styles

Adventure Section Titles and Drop Caps
are in William Morris'
Golden Type Bold

DETECTION & MYSTERY TITLES AND DROP CAPS
ARE IN BOTANIST

Fantasy Titles and Drop Caps
are in Spirax

HORROR & THE SUPERNATURAL TITLES AND DROP CAPS
ARE IN NEVERMORE

Science Fiction Titles and Drop Caps
are in Orbitron

www.ingramcontent.com/pod-product-compliance
Lightning Source LLC
Chambersburg PA
CBHW050926030726
47503CB00007BB/2496